...or *USA*...

MARY DAHEIM

and her uproarious
BED-AND-BREAKFAST MYSTERIES

"The reigning queen of the cozies."
Portland Oregonian

"Daheim writes with wit, wisdom, and a big heart . . . Judith and Renie are sleuths to treasure."
Carolyn Hart

"Delightful mysteries."
Kansas City Star

"Like Joan Hess' Maggody series, Daheim's bed-and-breakfast mysteries show a funny and often stinging insight into people's relationships and behavior."
Houston Chronicle

"Mary Daheim is one of the brightest stars."
Seattle Times

"She is really good at what she does."
***Statesman Journal* (OR)**

Bed-and-Breakfast Mysteries by
Mary Daheim

THIS OLD SOUSE
HOCUS CROAKUS
SILVER SCREAM
SUTURE SELF
A STREETCAR NAMED EXPIRE
CREEPS SUZETTE
LEGS BENEDICT
SNOW PLACE TO DIE
WED AND BURIED
SEPTEMBER MOURN
NUTTY AS A FRUITCAKE
AUNTIE MAYHEM
MURDER, MY SUITE
MAJOR VICES
A FIT OF TEMPERA
BANTAM OF THE OPERA
DUNE TO DEATH
HOLY TERRORS
FOWL PREY
JUST DESSERTS

Available in hardcover

DEAD MAN DOCKING

MARY DAHEIM

This OLD SOUSE

A BED-AND-BREAKFAST MYSTERY

AVON BOOKS
An Imprint of HarperCollins*Publishers*

This is a work of fiction. Names, characters, places, and incidents are products of the author's imagination or are used fictitiously and are not to be construed as real. Any resemblance to actual events, locales, organizations, or persons, living or dead, is entirely coincidental.

AVON BOOKS
An Imprint of HarperCollins*Publishers*
10 East 53rd Street
New York, New York 10022-5299

ISBN: 0-380-81565-6
www.avonmystery.com

First Avon Books paperback printing: August 2005
First William Morrow hardcover printing: August 2004

Printed in the U.S.A.

10 9 8 7 6 5 4 3 2 1

This Old Souse

ONE

JUDITH MCMONIGLE FLYNN hurried to answer the front door, took one look at the hideous drooling green creature on the porch, and screamed. Panicking, she slammed the door and leaned against it. The thing was six feet tall, with gaping holes for eyes, viscous green scales, and sharp yellow fangs. Judith was so shaken that she couldn't move to call 911.

"Hey!" shouted a voice from outside. "Open up! It's me! Renie!"

Judith held a hand to her racing heart. Renie, along with other family members and friends, always used the back door. The front was reserved for guests at Hillside Manor. "Coz?" Judith croaked, and slowly turned to open the door just a crack. There, next to the gruesome green creature, stood Serena Jones, more familiarly known to her family as Renie.

"Did SuperGerm scare you?" Renie asked, brown eyes wide.

"Good grief." Judith wilted against the doorframe. "I thought I was going to have a heart attack. What is that awful thing?"

"I guess I shouldn't have stood behind it," Renie said, looking apologetic. "I would've gone to the back door, but this guy is kind of awkward to carry around." She gave the creature a pat on one of its long, scaly arms. "It's just a cutout. I created it for the county board of health's antigerm campaign. Garth Doyle made this model in his studio. The county will put posters of SuperGerm in all public restrooms to remind people to wash up."

"I'm about washed-up after that," Judith said, regaining some of her aplomb. "How about getting that thing off the front porch? It's not good advertising for a B&B."

"Hmm." Renie examined the cutout from stem to stern. "Probably not. But don't you think it's good advertising for hygiene?"

"Yes, fine, super," Judith retorted. "Now put it back in your car before you come inside."

Renie, who was on the small side, struggled a bit as she carted SuperGerm off to her car, which was parked in Hillside Manor's driveway. Waiting on the porch, Judith surveyed the cul-de-sac. Just three days away from the start of summer, the spring shrubs, trees, and bulbs had faded away. The grass was green, the leaves were glossy, and some of the roses were in full bloom. But the sky was overcast, the temperature lingered in the midfifties, and there was a 40 percent chance of rain. It was, Judith knew, a typical June day in the Pacific Northwest.

"All gone," Renie announced, bounding up the

steps. "I could use some strong drink. You got any Pepsi?"

Judith nodded. "I just got back from Falstaff's Grocery. I have a full house tonight, so I had to fill the larder. Now that school's out, the B&B reservations are pouring in. I'm pretty well booked up through early August."

"That's great," Renie said, sitting down at the kitchen table. "I'm not so busy. Summer's always a slow time in the graphic design business. Everybody goes on vacation. Good for you, bad for me."

Judith took a can of Pepsi and a diet 7UP out of the refrigerator. Even after more than a year, she was still delighted with the renovations—particularly in the kitchen—that had been made following a disastrous fire almost two years earlier.

"Say," Renie said as Judith joined her at the table, "have you got time to take a little ride with me?"

Judith frowned at her cousin. "And with SuperGerm?"

"Well . . ." Renie took a deep drink before finishing her reply. "Yes, actually. I have to drop him off at Garth's. He needs some fine-tuning. SuperGerm, I mean, not Garth."

Judith looked skeptical. "And why would I want to help chauffeur SuperGerm to Garth's studio?"

Renie reached into the sheep-shaped jar on the table and filched three oatmeal raisin cookies. "Booyoommerthathouthnmoofle?" she inquired with her mouth full.

Judith was accustomed to her cousin's voracious appetite; she had also grown adept at translating Renie's food-marred speech. "The house on Moonfleet Street? Sort of. Why?"

"Ahmobthethd."

"Oh." Judith nodded. "You've always been obsessed with that place, ever since you were a kid. What about it?"

Renie finally swallowed. "Garth lives in my old neighborhood, about four blocks from that house. As you may recall, it's Spanish-style architecture, very unusual for this part of the world."

"I recall." Judith turned as her cleaning woman, Phyliss Rackley, stomped into the kitchen carrying two black plastic bags. Upon seeing Renie, she stopped and glared.

"You," Phyliss breathed. "Don't start in on me with your Romish ways."

"Bite me," Renie snapped.

Phyliss kneaded the plastic bags with her skinny fingers. "False gods. Painted idols. Craven images."

"Funny," Renie remarked, about to pop another cookie into her mouth. "I thought they were *graven* images."

"You're a blasphemer," Phyliss declared, pronouncing the word as if it were "blass-FEMUR." She turned to Judith and shook the black bags. "I don't like giving these to the St. Vincent de Paul. What's wrong with the Salvation Army?"

"Nothing," Judith replied, ignoring the long-standing religious animosity between Renie and Phyliss. "I'm the one who's giving that stuff away, and it'll go to whichever charity calls first. For now, I want those bags out on the back porch. They're cluttering up the second-floor hall."

With one last dark look for Renie, Phyliss proceeded down the narrow hallway to the porch.

"The pope has spies everywhere," Renie called after the cleaning woman. "Better check the recycling bin, Phyliss."

Judith shook her head. "I never bait Phyliss the way you do," she admonished Renie. "I don't rile her. She's too good at her job."

"I didn't start it this time," Renie responded.

"You didn't need to," Judith said. "You've done it often enough in the past. Which," she went on as Phyliss returned from the porch and headed down the basement stairs, "brings us back to the house on Moonfleet."

"Yes." Renie finished the third cookie before she resumed speaking. "All the years my folks and I lived in that neighborhood, I wondered about that place. When I was in junior high and high school, I'd walk by it sometimes. It's basically a beautiful house, in a beautiful setting, with the original evergreens surrounding it. But nothing about it ever changed. I never saw anybody inside or outside. Oh, once in a great while I'd see a tricycle in the yard or a fresh load of wood in the shed, but otherwise, it seemed deserted."

Judith's memory stirred. She had grown up on Heraldsgate Hill, in the same house that she'd turned into Hillside Manor after the death of her first husband, Dan McMonigle. Renie and her parents had lived across the canal, in the neighborhood known as Langford. Judith recalled Renie talking about the house and even driving her past it a couple of times.

"So what's your point?" Judith asked her cousin.

"Working with Garth Doyle has taken me by the property several times in the last two months," Renie explained. "Going on fifty years later, it hasn't changed a bit. The trees are bigger, the house's exterior is shabbier, but otherwise it's the same. I asked Garth about it. He knows the place, of course, but hadn't given it much thought. Garth agreed he'd never noticed anybody outside, but it wasn't falling down, and it's never been for sale or for rent in the twenty-odd years he's lived in the neighborhood."

Judith toyed with her soda can. "Stop. It's beginning to sink in. You smell a mystery. How come? It's not like you, coz."

Renie grinned a bit sheepishly. "I know. It's more like you. Maybe I've got too much time on my hands. What with business slowing down for a couple of months and the kids finally married and living away, I suppose I could be bored. Bill's so self-sufficient. He seems almost as busy now as he was before he retired. He's like Joe—our husbands still keep occupied."

Judith allowed that was so. Bill Jones retained a few patients from his psychology practice and occasionally consulted at the University where he'd taught for over thirty years. Joe Flynn had his own detective agency, taking on as many—or as few—clients as he wished. Neither man was the type to follow their wives around, pleading to be entertained.

"You're at loose ends," Judith murmured.

"Not entirely," Renie replied. "I do have one big project, but the deadline isn't until late August. I'm doing the artwork on a brochure for your old buddy Bart Bendarik. He wants line drawings of every style of architecture in the city. The Moonfleet house is perfect. None of the wear and tear would show in my illustration. But if I have to get permission, I'd like to scope out the place first."

Judith sighed. Bendarik Builders had done the B&B renovations. Bart had extended deadline after deadline and seemed to prefer embracing problems rather than solving them. In some cases, Judith believed he'd actually invented difficulties, not merely to make more money, but for the sheer joy of passing the bad news on to the Flynns. He had also had the nerve to ask Judith if he could oversee her plans to build an inn and guesthouses on the former site of the family's summer cabins, but she'd turned him down. The river property could wait. She had, as Joe kept reminding her, enough on her plate as it was.

"Okay," Judith said. "I'll ride over to Garth's with you. None of the guests are due until late this afternoon. I'll make Mother's lunch and then we'll go. It shouldn't take us long, right?"

Renie brightened. "Less than an hour."

Judith stood up. "Just this once, though. You may not be busy, but I am. If I go with you today, at least I'll know what you're talking about when you jaw my ear off about your new obsession."

Renie finished her Pepsi while Judith prepared Gertrude Grover's lunch: egg salad on white, with butter, mayo, and lettuce; a half-dozen fresh strawberries, liberally doused with sugar; a few potato chips—the plain, old-fashioned kind. Gertrude didn't like any ruffles, riffles, or additional flavors.

"What's that?" Gertrude demanded when her daughter arrived with the tray.

"Your lunch," Judith replied, juggling the tray. There

wasn't a bare spot available. As usual, clutter was everywhere—decks of cards, magazines, newspapers, TV schedules, mail advertising that had been opened but never discarded, and a box of Granny Goodness chocolates. Judith was forced to place the tray on top of some typed papers her mother had apparently been reading.

"Stop!" Gertrude cried, holding up her gnarled hands. "Move that thing! It's on my movie script!"

"Oh!" Swiftly, Judith obeyed. "Can you move the script to make room?"

Gertrude placed her hands on the script, as if she expected Judith to whisk away the pages. "No! I'm making changes. They've got my life story all wrong. That writer fella in Hollywood keeps getting things mixed up. When did I ever fight in the Spanish Civil War?" Gertrude's wrinkled face was suddenly puzzled. "Or did I?"

"No, Mother," Judith replied. "It was Uncle Corky who wanted to fight in Spain, but Grandpa and Grandma Grover wouldn't let him. That happened around the time you and my father got married."

Gertrude brightened. "We eloped." She tracked the script with an unsteady finger. "This says we met in a rebel camp on some river. E-B-R-O. Ebro. Never heard of it. Your father and I met at a pinochle party at Doc and June Workman's houseboat on the ship canal."

"I warned you," Judith said. "So did your agent and the screenwriter. If your life story as a member of the Greatest Generation was to be made into a movie, they'd change things, even basic facts."

"I don't like it," Gertrude declared, stabbing at a

sugar-covered strawberry. "They describe your father as having wavy hair. Even when we first met, he'd already waved most of his hair bye-bye."

"Do you want to wave your money bye-bye?"

A year ago, Gertrude had received fifteen thousand dollars for the rights to her life story. She'd put every cent into her regular savings account and hadn't made a single withdrawal. "I'm saving it for a rainy day," she'd declared when Judith had hinted that her mother might want to spend some of the money to help pay for improvements to her apartment in what had once been the toolshed. Judith and Joe had benefited from their homeowners' insurance as well as from a generous sum given them by the film company that had been involved in the fire. But the Flynns had gone well over the original estimates. Still, Gertrude wouldn't budge. "If you hadn't married Lunkhead in the first place," the old lady had asserted, "I wouldn't have to live in the toolshed." It had done Judith no good to argue that if Gertrude hadn't been so stubborn about not living under the same roof as Joe Flynn, the old lady would still be occupying the third-floor family quarters. So she remained in her apartment, which—as Joe perversely put it—at his mother-in-law's advanced age, they might as well call the "drool shed." It was no wonder that the two couldn't coexist in the same house.

"I don't like it," Gertrude repeated. "I'm going to have my say."

"Go for it." Judith smiled. Gertrude always "had to have her say," no matter what the consequences.

As Judith went out the door, Sweetums came in. The

big orange-and-white cat sneered, sneezed, and made a beeline for the divan. To avoid hearing the cat's scratching and clawing at the floral fabric, Judith quickly closed the door behind her. She was halfway to the back porch when Phyliss, on the run and screaming, suddenly appeared from around the corner of the house.

"Beelzebub! Satan! The Archfiend!" She threw her apron over her head and collapsed on the bottom porch step.

Startled, Judith approached Phyliss. "What's wrong?"

But Phyliss could only shriek and moan. Her thin body shuddered. The cleaning woman was clearly on the verge of hysteria.

"Phyliss!" Judith cried sharply. "Stop it!" She grasped Phyliss's heaving shoulders and gave her a hard shake.

Slowly, Phyliss began to regain control. Judith didn't let go until the other woman removed the apron. Her face was drained of color; her gray eyes were huge.

"It's *him*!" she whispered in a terrified voice. "See for yourself—if you dare."

Judith was losing patience. "See where?"

Phyliss pointed in the direction of the driveway. "Your cousin's car. I told you she was in league with the devil! *She brought him with her!*"

Judith slumped in relief. She should have known. "Phyliss," she said, putting a hand on the cleaning woman's shoulder, "that's a cardboard cutout. It represents a germ. My cousin is working on a project for the county to promote hygiene."

"No." Phyliss's jaw jutted. "It's the Evil One. I always knew he'd look like that."

"That's odd," Renie said from the back door. "I always thought he'd look like the head of the IRS."

Phyliss jumped and screamed. "Help! I'm surrounded! The fires of Gehenna are at hand!"

Judith shook Phyliss again, but this time more gently. "You're being fanciful. Please stop. Renie and I have to go now. We'll take . . . the germ cutout with us."

Phyliss narrowed her eyes at Judith. "You will?" She sounded suspicious.

"Yes. I'll be back in an hour or so." She patted the cleaning woman's shoulder. "Come on, let's go back inside."

Still wary, and darting Renie distrustful glances, Phyliss complied. Five minutes later, the cousins were driving off in the Joneses' Toyota Camry.

"She's getting nuttier by the day," Renie remarked as they reached the top of Heraldsgate Hill and proceeded through the business district.

"Maybe," Judith allowed, "but she's still a wonderful worker. I gave her a raise the first of the month."

"You're too good," Renie declared.

"No," Judith responded. "She deserves it. During all the months that the workmen were repairing and renovating the B&B, Phyliss had to put up with a lot. We all did. And after everything was finished, upkeep had to be relearned by both of us. Different upholstery, different drapes, different appliances—it's an adjustment when everything comes at once."

"That's true," Renie agreed as they turned off Heraldsgate Avenue to head for the bridge across the ship canal. "I'm still figuring out all the features of my new washer and dryer. It's like flying a jet. The control panels have me baffled. By the way, we're dropping off SuperGerm first."

"That's fine," Judith said. "Should I stay in the car?"

Renie shook her head as they waited for a lull in traffic to get onto the city's major north-south thoroughfare. "It won't take long, and I'd like to have you meet Garth. He's a good guy. Creative, too, though he doesn't possess much curiosity about everyday things."

"Such as your mystery house?"

"Such as," Renie said, stepping on the gas as the Camry approached the bridge. "Bill isn't interested in it, either. Of course, being from Wisconsin, he didn't grow up in the neighborhood. But Madge Navarre did," Renie continued, referring to her friend from junior-high-school days, "and I think she thinks I'm crazy."

"I get it," Judith said with a smirk. "I'm supposed to prove you're not nuts."

Renie had taken the first right-hand turn at the end of the bridge. "Well . . . maybe. But you're even more intrigued by mysterious people and things than I am. In fact, I'm the one who usually tries to talk you out of your frequent flights of fancy."

"Which," Judith said, looking grim, "too often turn out not to be fanciful."

"All too true," Renie remarked. "So humor me, okay?"

Judith held up her index finger. "Just this once. I told you, coz, I'm getting into the busiest part of the year. I honestly don't have time to devote to your little mystery."

"You wouldn't say that if a corpse turned up in your freezer," Renie retorted.

Judith shuddered. "Don't say that! I've had more than my share of bad luck. It's been over a year since I've run into . . . any problems. Let's keep it that way."

"Of course," Renie said, slowing down on a street of relatively modest homes. "I'm not wishing for trouble. If I alter a couple of features in my artwork, I won't need to get the owners' consent. But I'd really like to find out why that house looks so vacant when it isn't. Or so I figure."

On-street parking was at a minimum. Judith and Renie had to walk almost half a block to reach Garth Doyle's residence. A trio of children in a neatly kept yard stared as Renie carried SuperGerm past them.

Garth's studio was in the basement of his Tudor-style brick home. The cousins entered through the attached garage and knocked on a wood-frame door with a brass plaque that read DOYLE DESIGNS.

Garth answered promptly. "If it isn't Serena and her cousin. Which is which?" He looked from SuperGerm to Judith and back again.

"Very funny," Renie shot back, then made the introductions. "Garth's quite the kidder," she added for Judith's benefit.

Judith observed that Garth was indeed a jovial man with a hearty laugh. He was of average height, but substantial girth; his hair and beard were turning gray; he wore rimless half-glasses and a shabby brown sweater over a denim shirt and blue jeans. Upon entering the studio, however, Judith noticed that everything appeared to be state-of-the-art. Or as far as Judith could tell from her limited experience. Renie was terrified of anything more complicated than a computer with basic design software. It had taken her several years to make that jump, and she remained entrenched in outmoded technology.

As Renie and Garth discussed how to tweak SuperGerm, Judith admired several works in progress. While Garth might rely on technology, he was also a hands-on kind of guy. There were several small clay models of all sorts of things—trees, animals, buildings, people. Judith was studying three-inch figures of Snow White and the Seven Dwarfs when Renie called to her.

"Garth and I have finished," she said to Judith. "Come join us."

Garth's expression grew curious as Renie launched into her explanation about the nearby Spanish-style house. "Have you asked anybody about that place since I last mentioned it?"

"I did," Garth replied, looking amused. "I saw a man come out of the house across the street—the south side. He told me that it was occupied, though when I pressed him for details, he admitted he hadn't seen anybody that he could recall. But he'd noticed the mailman deliver there a few times, so he assumed the owners might be elderly and not likely to go out much."

"They'd have to be elderly," Renie said, "if they've been there for fifty years. But that doesn't account for them not ever leaving the house."

Garth chuckled in his rich, deep manner. "Now, Serena, how many times have you actually been by that place over the years?"

Renie made a face. "Okay, until lately I probably haven't gone by it more than half a dozen times since I moved away. But in the old days, I suppose I'd walk by it once a month, coming from junior high and high school."

"Always at the same time?" Garth inquired.

"Well . . . yes, around three in the afternoon," Renie said. "I forget what time school let out. In fact, at my age, I've practically forgotten going to school. But," she added in a stubborn voice, "I certainly remember the house. It's as if it were in a time warp."

Garth rubbed his bearded chin. "Langford is such an ordinary part of town. Most of the houses are strictly middle-class, mainly built after 1910. Oh, there are a few big, expensive homes—including your villa, if it were better maintained—but by and large, this is what we used to call a lunch-bucket neighborhood."

"I know." Renie smiled. "Our house had four rooms until Dad expanded the attic."

Garth waved a hand. "This one was six rooms—until I finished off the basement and put in the studio."

Judith listened with half an ear as Renie and Garth discussed local demographics. Anxious to get going, she finally tapped her watch. "Coz, I hate to break up this—"

"Okay, okay," Renie snapped. "We're out of here. Thanks, Garth. Let me know when SuperGerm is ready for delivery."

"Will do," Garth replied.

Making hasty farewells, the cousins left the studio and walked back to the car. A few drops of rain were falling, but not enough to daunt native Pacific Northwesterners. Indeed, neither Judith nor Renie owned an umbrella. The rain was too unpredictable and rarely more than a drizzle. Umbrellas were only a nuisance, extra baggage that was often lost or mislaid by those who used them.

Parking was allowed on both sides of the street, creating a one-lane thoroughfare. Renie drove slowly, negotiating the traffic islands at each intersection. After two and a half blocks, she took a right-hand turn. At the next cross street, Judith spotted Renie's obsession.

The property took up the south end of the block facing Moonfleet Street. A rockery, now overgrown with large ferns, ivy, and Oregon grape, surrounded the lot on three sides. Tall firs and cedar trees obscured the house from view. Renie slowed the Camry to a crawl. Above the dense shrubbery, Judith could see beyond the peeling white stucco walls and the red-tiled roof, both of which sprouted large patches of moss. There was no lawn; there was no garden. A dirt track separated the property from its neighbors.

"I've never driven up that alley," Renie said as they pulled to a stop. "I don't know if Cammy would like it," she added, using the Joneses' nickname for their car. "It doesn't look as if it's ever used."

Judith put on her glasses for a better view of the house, which faced south on Moonfleet. The cousins were on the east side. The first thing Judith noticed was that the dwelling was a two-story structure with a one-story wing jutting from the main building. The wing had an arched passageway, a grilled window in the front, and one on the side. Ornamental tiles formed a pleasing pattern above the window that looked out onto the street. A tower almost in the center of the house rose slightly higher than the red-tiled roof. There was a balcony on the second floor of the main structure, and the only chimney was at the west end. Even though the stucco was peeling from the exterior and the roof was badly faded, the house was still impressive.

"The shades are drawn and the drapes are pulled," Renie noted. "It's always been that way."

Judith was still staring through the car window. "It's not a huge house—four bedrooms at most. And even though the land goes from corner to corner, it's a narrow block. Three legal lots at most. What do you figure the place would sell for, even without improvements?"

Renie considered. "Langford isn't as pricey as Heraldsgate Hill, but it's an up-and-coming area. I'd guess maybe seven, eight hundred thousand?"

Judith nodded. "That sounds about right."

Renie pointed to the yard. "The woodpile's down, but it's June. There aren't any toys that I can see, but if there were ever kids living in the house, they'd be grown up by now. There's a detached garage on the far side of the house that you can't see from here. In fact, you can't see it at all anymore because the trees and shrubs have grown so high since I was a teenager."

Movement nearby caught Judith's eye. She turned to look out the other window. Two women in their thirties were coming out of a modest Craftsman-style house across the street and heading for an SUV parked at the curb.

"Quick," Renie said as she rolled down Judith's window, "ask them who lives here."

"Hi," Judith called. "Could you tell us something?"

The taller of the two came into the street and stood by the SUV. "Are you lost?"

"No," Judith replied with her friendliest smile. "Do you know who lives in this wonderful old Spanish house?"

The woman frowned slightly. "Why do you want to know?"

Judith shifted into her small-fib-in-a-good-cause mode. "It's exactly the kind of house my husband and I've been looking for. That style is very hard to find in this city. I wondered if it might be for sale. It looks deserted."

"Heavens, no," the woman replied. "I doubt very much if the owners would want to sell. They've lived there for years."

"Then," Judith said, keeping her smile fixed in place, "they might be thinking of moving to a smaller place. I mean, if they're getting up in years."

"Doubtful," the woman said, opening the SUV's door.

The second woman was already in the passenger seat. She leaned over, calling to her friend. "Come on, Glenda, let's go. We're supposed to meet Maddy at one."

Judith waved a hand. "Please—wait. Do you know the owners' names?"

Glenda, who had started to get into the SUV, shot Judith an exasperated look. "Yes. They're Dick and

Jane Bland. Now will you please move your car so we can get out of here and go to lunch?" She sat down hard in the driver's seat and slammed the door.

"Twerp," Renie growled as she took her time starting the Camry.

"Well, now you know." Judith took off her glasses and slipped them back into their leather case. "An elderly couple named Bland live in your so-called mystery house. Are you satisfied?"

The question was met with an ominous silence. On the way back from Langford, Judith deliberately steered the conversation in directions other than the Spanish house. Renie's responses were terse, however, and her short chin was set at a pugnacious angle.

They had crossed the bridge over the ship canal when Judith realized that Renie wasn't in the right-hand lane to make the turn onto Heraldsgate Hill.

"Hey!" she cried. "Where are we going? I've got to get home."

"Open the glove compartment," Renie commanded. "Get out the phone book I use for my cell."

"Dammit," Judith began, but obeyed. "I really don't have time for this. Whatever *this* is," she added.

"It may only be a detour," Renie retorted. "Look up the Blands."

As fast as she could, Judith flipped through to the residential *B* section. There were a handful of Blands but no Richard, Rich, Rick, Dick, or any initials that might be the couple on Moonfleet Street. "Drat," said Judith, returning the directory to the glove compartment. "Now I *am* getting mad at you."

"Oh, be a sport, coz," Renie urged. "How many

times have you dragged me into all sorts of weird situations, not to mention occasionally risking my life and all my limbs?"

Judith grimaced. Renie had gone far beyond the call of kinship to help Judith solve her own mysteries, most of which had exposed them both to danger. It was not yet one o'clock. None of the guests were due until four at the earliest. Joe was over on the Eastside helping to sort out an insurance scam. Phyliss was used to working unsupervised. Gertrude wouldn't care if her daughter was tardy. The old girl was too wrapped up in her movie script.

"Okay," Judith said, leaning back in the seat. "Where are we going?"

"Downtown," Renie replied, sailing along at ten miles over the forty-mile-an-hour speed limit. "I want to check the rolls at the county courthouse."

It took ten minutes to get to the courthouse, another ten to park, and a quarter of an hour to find the right department and the proper records. Judith's artificial hip was beginning to ache, but she kept her mouth shut. Renie, who was carrying a large, worn binder, would retaliate with complaints about the shoulder that still bothered her even after extensive surgery.

Fortunately, the cousins found a place to sit down. "You do have the address," Judith said.

"No," Renie admitted. "I've never been able to see the house numbers. But since it's the only residence on that side of Moonfleet, I can't miss. The houses across the street are in the twenty-one–hundred range, odd numbers. Ah!" In triumph, she looked up from the big binder. "I got it! It's two-one-oh-eight."

Judith scooted her chair around for a closer look. The yellowed page showed the original plat, with a floor plan for the house and the garage. The date was April 11, 1925.

Renie moved on to the information about ownership. "The house was completed in March of 1926. The builder was somebody named L. R. Engstrom, and the first owners were Preston D. and Eleanor F. Conway, who paid thirty-five hundred dollars for it." She moved her finger down the page. "They sold the place in 1933 for five thousand dollars. Maybe they couldn't keep up the payments during the Depression. Anyway, the new owners were Ruben C. and Ellen M. Borbon. Ruben must have passed on by the time it was sold again for seventy-five hundred dollars in 1947 by Mrs. Borbon to . . ." She paused and took a deep breath. "To Richard L. and Jane C. Bland."

"You're right." Judith swiftly calculated the years. "They've lived there for well over a half century. Goodness, they must be old."

"Fairly old," Renie amended. "We aren't spring chickens, either. It's possible that they bought it as newlyweds. They might be in their early seventies."

"That's not old anymore," Judith said wistfully. "It used to be, though."

Renie stood up. "Let's go."

"Home?" Judith asked hopefully.

"No. Back to Moonfleet Street."

Judith did her best to catch up with Renie, who was sprinting toward the elevators. "Why?"

"That disagreeable neighbor is probably still out to lunch," Renie said, entering the elevator and poking the button for the street level. "I want a better look at the house."

"Coz—" Judith began in a pleading tone.

"It's only two o'clock," Renie interrupted. "I'll have you back at the B&B by three. I promise."

The elevator doors opened onto the lobby. "Okay," Judith said with a sigh. "I guess I owe you."

"You bet you do," Renie retorted as they waited for the light to walk across the street to the parking garage. "Besides, this is just a little harmless fun."

"True," Judith allowed.

Or maybe not.

TWO

On their return trip to Moonfleet, Renie found a parking place across the street from the front of the house. "We can't see much of anything from here except for that path that goes up from the side-walk," she said. "We'll have to get out and walk."

"Walk?" Judith responded. "How about carrying me? I'm getting gimpy from all this walking."

"Nonsense," Renie snapped. "We haven't walked any farther than you'd do at home, especially going up and down all those stairs. Furthermore, I can't carry you. My shoulder, remember?"

The drizzle had stopped, though the sky re-mained cloudy. As the cousins got out of the car, they saw a postal van pull up at the corner.

"Aha!" Renie exclaimed under her breath. "We can interrogate him."

"Why not?" Judith said in an indifferent voice. "Maybe I can spare my hip by riding around in his pouch."

Crossing the street, the cousins peered up through the narrow path that was flanked by towering camellia and lily-of-the-valley bushes. They could see the arched front entrance. The door was made of vertical mahogany planks with three ornamental hinges and a matching knocker. Faded multihued tiles surrounded the door. The large arched first-story window was made of tinted glass. There were two smaller rectangular windows in the tower, one on the first floor, the other on the second. There was no lawn—only dirt, rocks, and a few weeds. Despite the secluded setting and beauty of design, the overall impression was bleak. Judith sensed that this was not—perhaps never had been—a happy house.

"It's terribly sad," Judith declared. "It's not just the feeling of neglect. There's despair, too, and hopelessness."

Renie nodded. "I'm becoming depressed just looking at it. But doesn't it make you curious?"

The human element—or lack of it—moved Judith, who was always intrigued by other people. "Yes. Yes, I have to admit it does."

Renie turned to watch the mailman come across the street. "Good grief!" she exclaimed under her breath. "I don't believe it! That's Morty! I thought he would have retired by now."

"Morty?" The name rang a bell with Judith. "The one who always left a trail of mail behind him and read all the magazines before he delivered them?"

"The very same," Renie replied. "And here comes his awful dog, Zip Code."

"Son or grandson of Zip Code," Judith murmured.

Morty stopped at the curb, peering at Renie. "Do I know you?"

It had been going on forty years since Renie and Morty's last encounter. Both had been in their early twenties. Renie had bawled out Morty for delivering her copy of *Vogue* with mustard and ketchup smeared on its summer bathing-suit layout. Drool, too, she'd told him at the time.

"I don't think so," Renie lied. Then she smiled. It was a big mistake.

"Those teeth!" Morty shouted, recoiling so fast that he dropped several pieces of mail. "You! It's Fang!"

Zip Code, a shaggy golden retriever, hid behind his master and growled.

"Okay, okay," Renie said in an impatient voice. "Skip the past history. We're both older and hopefully wiser." Indeed, Morty's blond hair was almost white and his ramrod posture had deteriorated into a sorry slouch. "Have you always been on this part of the route?"

"Why do you care?" Morty shot back. "How many times did you report me to the Langford post office?"

"I only did that once," Renie said, "after I found my IRS refund in the hydrangea after the leaves fell off in the fall. It was my folks who called the post office about a dozen times. Dad hit the roof when you tore the fishing-hole maps out of his *Northwest Angler* magazine."

"So I had a hobby on my days off," Morty shot back. "What did you expect me to do? Play golf and walk eighteen holes? You should see my feet, they look like corncobs."

"Please." Renie put her hands over her eyes. "Why haven't you retired?"

"I will," Morty replied, "end of the month."

"Congratulations." Renie smirked. "To the people on your route, that is."

Judith tapped Renie's arm. "Coz . . ." None too gently, she pushed Renie out of the way. The ungroomed Zip Code came out from behind Morty and warily approached the cousins. "That's a"—there were times when Judith couldn't tell a fib even in a good cause—"a real doggie dog. How long have you had him?"

"This guy?" Morty leaned forward to pat the dog's scruffy rump. "Twelve years. Fourth generation. I've always taken a Zip Code with me. Keeps the other dogs at bay."

"So you've had this whole route all these years?" Judith inquired.

Morty glanced at Renie, then looked back at Judith. "Why are you two asking me these questions?"

"It's this place," Judith replied, gesturing at the house. "Doesn't it seem kind of spooky to you?"

Morty, who was now standing on the sidewalk, glanced up the path that led to the front door. "Spooky? Gosh, I've never noticed. It's just another house, another stop on the route, another slot to fill, twenty-five steps to three stairs, back down again, twenty-five to the street, fifty-seven steps to the corner, then—"

Judith interrupted, though quietly. "Have you ever seen anybody around the house?"

"Like people?" Morty shook his head. "I don't see many people. Most of 'em work. Like me. Besides, I've only been doing this end of the route for the past year.

My supervisor finally decided I'd had enough of that other part of Langford." He paused to glare at Renie. "What I put up with all those—"

"So," Judith said to prevent another monologue from Morty, "whoever lives here does get mail."

Zip Code was sniffing at Renie's shoes. Renie was doing a little dance to get away from the animal.

"Oh, they get mail," Morty replied with a shake of his head. "They all get mail, every day, except Sundays and holidays, rain, shine, snow, hail, heat, cold, earthquakes—"

"Lots of mail?" Judith interjected, ignoring Renie, who had stepped—not too hard—on Zip Code's paw.

Apparently, Morty didn't notice. "Well—no." The hint of a smile played at his thin lips. "I'll say that for them. Oh, they get the usual bills—utilities, mostly—and the flyers everybody else gets." He bent down to retrieve the pieces he'd dropped, but Zip Code had grabbed one of what looked like a personal letter and was chewing it to bits. "Never mind," Morty said, "that wasn't for these folks. It was for somebody in the next block." He stroked the dog's neck. "Yum-yum, huh, Zippy? What he really likes are those big manila envelopes that look so important but probably aren't."

Renie twirled around and wandered off down the street.

"At least," Morty went on, sorting through the rest of the mail he'd picked up, "these people here don't get all those horrible catalogs. Two years ago, I ended up in traction after I threw my back out. No more of that, I said to myself. I load those blasted things into the van, but I dump 'em off at the nearest recycling bin. Who needs all that junk? I figure I'm saving folks a lot of money. Besides, if they ordered the stuff, guess who'd have to deliver most of it?" He poked himself in the chest with his thumb.

"So they don't get actual letters here?" Judith asked, beginning to feel weary.

Morty scratched his chin, which looked as if it could use a shave. "Once a month, maybe. That's it."

"I assume everything's addressed to Mr. and Mrs. Bland," Judith remarked.

"Oh, yeah. Except for the stuff marked 'Resident' or 'Addressee' or—here's the one that really gets me. 'To Our Friends at . . .' Now, you know danged well, they aren't friends. They don't even know each other. It's just a—" This time, Morty interrupted himself. "Hold on. A while back, there was a letter addressed to somebody who wasn't named Bland. I noticed, 'cause I pay close attention to names and addresses. In fact, I think there've been some other letters to whoever it was."

Judith spoke loudly and quickly to drown out Renie's strangled cry of disbelief. "What was the name on the envelope?"

"I don't remember offhand," Morty replied, "but it was the right address."

"Maybe someone lives with them," Judith ventured.

Morty shrugged. "Could be." He glanced at his watch. "I'd better be on my way. Don't want to get behind." He scrutinized his watch more closely. "Gee, I'm already an hour or so off schedule. Guess I shouldn't have had that second cup of coffee."

Morty sauntered up the path, with Zip Code trailing behind him. Judith joined Renie at the corner.

"Did you hear that?" Judith asked. "There's a third party living in the house."

"I heard it," Renie replied grimly. "I heard all of it. I can't believe that after all these years, I had to run into Morty the Mailman."

"I wonder who else is living there," Judith mused, ignoring Renie's complaint. "A sister of Mrs. Bland? A child who's returned after a divorce? A friend?"

The cousins had turned the corner and reached the unpaved alley. "Any of the above," Renie said. "Are you coming with me?"

Judith studied the dirt track. "There are too many potholes and rough spots. I don't want to risk a fall. Go on without me. I'll wait here."

Renie paused several times during her mission. Upon reaching the garage, she went out of sight, apparently exploring from every angle. It seemed to Judith that the alley wasn't intended for communal purposes, but belonged to the Blands. There were tall trees and big shrubs on both sides. Through a thicket of blackberry vines, Judith could make out a wire fence that probably marked the property line.

All she could see of the garage was part of a red-tiled roof. She shifted her gaze to the house itself. From the side angle, the only windows she could see were two casements upstairs and the one with the grille in the arched wing. Heavy curtains drooped behind the small panes on the second floor; fusty drapes sagged behind the tinted glass at ground level. Judith swore she could almost smell the dust and mold inside the house.

And then, to her amazement, she saw movement behind the upstairs curtains. Ever so slowly, they parted. An inch, no more, not enough to allow her to see a person. But someone was there. Judith looked away, turned in every direction, and whistled shrilly.

"Renie!" she called loudly. "Come, Renie! Come, nice doggie!" Judith moved beyond the alley, toward the adjacent property with its one-story frame house.

A minute later, Renie came running down to the sidewalk. "What's up?" she asked, a bit breathless.

Before Judith could reply, Zip Code came bounding down the street, barking his head off. He leaped on Renie, almost knocking her down and licking her face. "Hey!" she yelled. "Cut it out! You've got letter breath!"

Judith firmly grasped Zip Code's collar and pulled the animal away from her cousin. "Zippy! Nice doggie! Go find Morty."

Panting, Zip Code eyed Judith for a brief moment before trotting away.

"You should have called for a cat," Renie said, taking a tissue out of her purse and wiping her face. "What's up?"

"Someone's peeking through the upstairs window," Judith replied, explaining how she'd seen the curtains move, but couldn't make out a face or a figure. "We'd better get out of here." She gazed up at the house on the other side of the wire fence. "Should we call on these neighbors?"

Renie pointed to the empty attached garage. "Their car's gone. It doesn't look as if they're home. We might have better luck with the guy on Moonfleet that Garth talked to."

"But he didn't know anything," Judith pointed out.

"True," Renie agreed. "I don't suppose canvassing the entire neighborhood would help, either."

It was starting to rain again. The cousins stood on the sidewalk, contemplating their next move.

"I really should get home," Judith finally said. "We can always come back."

Renie grinned. "You're hooked, aren't you?"

Judith winced. "Well . . . I guess. Now that we've put names to the owners and know that somebody's inside and the place feels so forlorn and sad—"

"Ha!" Renie rocked back and forth on her heels. "I knew it. You're a sucker for a sob story."

"Don't rub it in," Judith retorted. "We'd better go. I doubt that whoever was watching us is still at the window. They can't see us from there and won't know where we parked."

"Probably not," Renie agreed, "unless they've been on the lookout all along."

The cousins went back down the street and crossed over to the other side. Before getting into the Camry, they both looked back at the house.

"The mail's still in the mailbox," Judith noted. "There's a milk box on the porch, too."

"So I see," Renie said. "We could wait until somebody comes to get it."

"Like Joe on a stakeout?" Judith shook her head. "What do you bet they don't come out until after dark?"

"Could be." With a shrug, Renie got into the driver's seat.

"Tell me what the view from the alley was like," Judith said after they were under way.

"Not much," Renie answered with a scowl. "I could hardly see anything of the house. It's blocked off by the trees and shrubbery. They've got rhododendrons that must be ten feet tall. I could just barely make out a small storage shed and what might have been a greenhouse, but it's in a state of virtual collapse. Near the fence on that side was probably once a fishpond—you can see the rectangular concrete outline, but it's full of moss and weeds and scilla. There must be a back door, but I couldn't see it. As for the garage, it's locked up. There are two small windows, but they're covered with what looks like cardboard and chicken wire, not to mention cobwebs."

"Any sign of car tracks in the dirt alley?" Judith inquired.

Renie shook her head. "I don't get it. If these people are old, don't they ever go to a doctor? That's what old people do, right?"

Judith grimaced. "We ought to know."

"We're not *that* old," Renie retorted, flipping on the windshield wipers. "We've just had some weird medical problems."

"More than our share," Judith conceded. "But we started out as sickly kids."

Allergies and asthma had plagued the cousins from early childhood. Renie had suffered severe sinus problems as well. Judith had always been prone to hip troubles, exacerbated by using a pogo stick during a growth spurt. Judith had often thought that their mutual illnesses had helped cement their bond. They had been only children, growing up two blocks away from each other until Renie's family moved to Langford just before she started junior high. The cousins had always been close, even closer than some sisters. When they quarreled, both of them could retreat to their own homes instead of being forced to share the same roof.

"I'll drop you off and then stop in to see Mom," Renie said as they once again crossed the high bridge over the canal. "As usual, she insists I'm neglecting her."

"When were you there last?" Judith asked.

"Yesterday," Renie replied. "Twice. And I've talked to her on the phone three times since I stopped by. Today she needs ice cubes."

"Is Aunt Deb's refrigerator broken?" Judith inquired.

"No," Renie answered, turning onto Heraldsgate Hill. "But she complains that her arthritis is so bad that she can't get the ice-cube trays out of the freezer compartment. The trays are stuck."

"What does she need the ice cubes for?"

"Her water. You know Mom—she drinks about a gallon of water a day," Renie said. "And then she wonders why she has to go to the bathroom so often."

"Water's good for you," Judith declared. "I drink quite a bit myself."

"I don't," Renie said in a stubborn tone. "I drink Pepsi. Water tastes like . . . water."

Judith didn't argue. The cousins had had that discussion many times, and neither of them won—or lost. "It's a blessing that our mothers got those motorized wheelchairs. The walker was okay for my mother as long as she stayed in the toolshed. But when she'd go out, it was getting very hard on her. She almost gave up bridge club."

"Heaven help us if Aunt Gert and Mom had to stop playing bridge," Renie asserted. "Though I'll have to admit that Mom's work as a consultant for Wirehoser Timber helps keep her occupied."

"Ditto for Mother's movie script," Judith said. "I still can't believe those two old girls have managed to start new careers in their old age."

"More power to them," Renie responded as traffic slowed on Heraldsgate Avenue. "I'm still thanking my lucky stars for sending Mom to that graphic design conference to take my place. All her old-fashioned, commonsense ideas really struck a chord. She still can't believe she gets a twenty-five-hundred-dollar retainer every month even if she doesn't have to do anything. But being Mom, she feels she has to earn her keep. Thus Wirehoser gets their money's worth when she comes up with one of her quaint little ideas. The latest is Bucky Beaver. I think she named it after me." Renie bared her prominent front teeth.

"What does Bucky do?"

"He beaves," Renie replied, "as in 'behave.' 'Beave Like Bucky' is her slogan. It's to promote good manners for campers and hikers. Bucky will wear a napkin around his neck and spats."

"Cute," Judith remarked as they started down the steep counterbalance. "Frankly, I think it's wonderful that our mothers can still contribute. People live so long these days, and the younger generation has always tended to disregard the old folks' wisdom and ideas. It's not only a shame, but a waste."

"Speaking of the younger generation," Renie said as

she turned onto Judith's street, "isn't that your son's Range Rover pulling into the cul-de-sac?"

Judith leaned forward. "It looks like it. But there are plenty of Range Rovers and Land Rovers and every other kind of Rover on Heraldsgate Hill these days."

However, the beige-and-brown Range Rover had stopped in front of Hillside Manor. Sure enough, as the cousins pulled up behind it, Mike McMonigle got out.

Hurriedly, Judith removed her seat belt and all but lunged out of the car. "Mike!" she cried, hurrying to embrace her son. "How good to see you! Can you stay for dinner?"

Mike didn't answer right away. In fact, he clung to his mother much longer than usual.

"Hi, Mike," Renie called as she came toward the pair. "How are you?"

"Not good," Mike replied, finally stepping back from Judith. "Kristin and I've split up."

"*What?*" Judith cried, a hand at her breast.

"Mike!" Renie put her arms around her nephew. "What happened?"

"It's just not working." Mike hugged his aunt, then wiped at his eyes.

Judith was too stunned to speak and suddenly sick to her stomach. She stared at her son, realizing that he was pale and haggard. Even the red hair he'd inherited from Joe seemed to have lost its luster.

"Let's go inside," Renie said as the rain began to come down even harder. "Where are Kristin and the boys?" she asked.

"They're still up at our place at the ranger station," Mike replied in a heavy voice. "They're packing."

The trio entered through the front door. Judith felt dazed as she led the way into the living room. Mother and son sat down across from each other on the new matching navy blue sofas in front of the fireplace. Renie remained standing.

"I can make a discreet exit," she offered.

Mike shook his head. "No." He attempted a smile. "You're my favorite aunt."

"I'm your *only* aunt," Renie reminded him. "Can I get you two something to drink?"

Mike hesitated. "A beer, maybe?"

"Sure," Renie replied. "Coz?"

Judith was staring at the carpet. "What? No, I don't feel so good."

"I'll bring you a little brandy," Renie said. "Frankly, I could use a stiff bourbon." She hurried out of the room.

"Has this been coming on for some time?" Judith finally asked. "You all seemed so happy when you were here at Easter."

"I thought we were," Mike responded. "But that was the end of March. It was about a week later that Kristin told me she didn't think things were working out. She feels stifled up at the summit. She wants to have more of a life than chasing two little kids through the snow."

Kristin, like Mike, was a forest ranger. But she hadn't worked since their wedding six years earlier. It was difficult to post married couples to the same place. Little Mac was now five; Joe-Joe was going on three. Kristin was a big, hearty young woman with enough energy and endurance to run an entire wilderness area. Judith could understand that she'd feel frustrated, and said so.

"But," Judith continued, "she knew what she was getting into when you got married. Furthermore, she's only an hour from the city, and much less than that from the Eastside, with all its stores and restaurants and other things to do. What on earth does she plan on doing as a single mom? It's going to be harder than it is right now."

Mike looked bleak. "She wants me to keep the kids."

"Oh, dear." Feeling a headache coming on, Judith rubbed her temples. "Really, Kristin is going through a serious crisis."

Renie entered with the drinks. "I heard most of that." She looked at Judith. "You need some aspirin, right? I'll get it." She left the room again.

"Do you still love her?" Judith inquired softly.

Mike nodded emphatically. "Yes. Yes, I really do."

"Does she still love you?"

He grimaced. "She says she does. But she says she needs her space."

Judith frowned. "Does that mean this is only a trial separation?"

Mike sighed. "I guess. My head's so messed up I don't know what anybody means." He waited until Renie had delivered the aspirin and the glass of water to Judith. "I thought if it's okay I'd spend the night here and then go back tomorrow and get the kids."

Judith swallowed the pills and stared at her son. "And what?"

Mike looked upward. "There's room, isn't there? I mean, there's my old room on the third floor along with the guest room, right?"

"Wrong," Judith said, realizing she sounded harsh. "That is, we've rearranged things upstairs. Your old room is Joe's office. Granny's room is a sitting room. There's not much space for you and the boys."

"Don't look at me," Renie said as Mike turned toward his aunt. "Uncle Bill and I just spent thirty-odd years shoving our kids out of the nest. We're enjoying a little peace and quiet. Maybe that sounds selfish, but," she added wistfully, "there's always the chance that our children may come home to visit."

Judith looked at the grandfather clock across the room between the bookcases. It was almost three-thirty. Phyliss had left for the day, which was a good thing. Judith wouldn't want her cleaning woman to overhear this particular conversation. "I wish your father would come home," she said. "Maybe I should call him on his cell phone."

More than thirty years earlier, after Judith and Joe's engagement, she became pregnant. But Joe was a rookie cop at the time, and had become distraught after seeing his first teenage OD fatalities. To ease his pain, he'd gotten drunk in a cop watering hole and run off to Vegas with Vivian, the bar's hard-drinking chanteuse. Vivian—or Herself, as Judith had always called her—had somehow managed to get Joe to a justice of the peace.

The next day, Joe awakened in horror, not remembering exactly what had happened. He'd phoned Judith at once, but Gertrude refused to let him talk to her, informing him that her daughter never wanted to see or speak to him again. The old lady never mentioned his call. In desperation, Judith accepted a proposal from Dan McMonigle to provide a father for her unborn child. Dan had died at forty-nine, having eaten and drunk himself into a four-hundred-pound machine of self-destruction. When Judith and Joe finally met again, his marriage was on the rocks—bourbon-rocks, Vivian's favorite hobby. When she remembered to add the rocks.

Judith's memory of her nineteen miserable years with Dan made her angry. "You took a sacred vow," she asserted, snapping out of her dumbfounded state. "If your father—your stepfather, I mean—and I could stay married, so can you."

Mike sighed. "It takes two."

"No, it doesn't," Judith shot back. "Sometimes it only takes one."

"You don't understand, Mom," Mike began. "It's a—"

Judith cut him off. "I understand all too well. Don't you remember how it was before Dan died?"

"He was a good father," Mike asserted. "I loved him."

Judith's shoulders slumped. "I know. I give him credit for virtually raising you—since he wouldn't work and I had to have two jobs to support us. I went from being a librarian by day to a bartender by night. Sometimes I feel as if I missed out on much of your childhood. But yes, we had some good times—though I wouldn't call it a happy marriage."

"Gruesome," Renie noted.

Mike wore a surprised expression. "I always thought you two got along pretty well."

"We tried to, in front of you." Judith took a big swig of brandy. "Look—give yourselves some time apart. Think things over. Consider what's best for the boys.

Come up with ways that Kristin can have more of a life outside of the house."

"Like competing in tractor pulls," Renie murmured.

Mike turned toward his aunt, who was sitting on the arm of the opposite sofa. "What did you say, Aunt Renie?"

"Like meeting with actor girls," Renie said. "I mean, *actresses*. And actors. You know—amateur theatrics or something."

Mike shook his head. "She isn't interested in that kind of stuff."

The phone on the cherrywood table rang. Renie, who was closest to it, answered. "It's for you," she said to Judith. "A Mrs. Beecroft."

"Oh. She's one of our guests for tonight." Judith stood up and took the receiver from Renie.

Mrs. Beecroft had called to say that their car had broken down on the other side of the mountains. She and Mr. Beecroft would have to cancel. Could they stay tomorrow night instead? Judith informed her that wasn't possible, but she'd check with the state B&B association to find another nice inn for them. Would Mrs. Beecroft please call back in a couple of hours?

"Okay," Judith said to Mike as she resumed her place on the sofa. "You can stay in the empty room tonight."

Mike brightened slightly. "Gee, thanks, Mom. I really appreciate it. I'll get my gear."

When Mike was gone, Renie shook her head. "I suppose I can look forward to some of that, too. Damn, why does this generation have to be so egocentric? Kristin feels stifled, and her reaction is to bolt. Whatever became of holy matrimony? Whatever happened to remembering that 'we' isn't spelled with an 'I'?"

"I don't know," Judith replied. "It must be partly our fault. We were so intent on making sure they grew up with more than we had as kids that we spoiled them rotten. Maybe this bunch will figure it out before it's too late for their own children."

"Call me tonight," Renie said, picking up her purse. "Good luck."

Judith was certain she'd need it.

THREE

JUDITH DIDN'T SLEEP well that night, tossing and turning, fretting and fussing. She'd gotten up early, but in her muddled state had managed to drop two raw eggs on the floor, set fire to the bacon, and step on Sweetums's tail; the cat retaliated by shredding the new dish towel Judith had left on the counter. It was a rocky way to start a Wednesday.

Mike, as well as the guests, left by ten-thirty. Joe had stayed home, having another heart-to-heart talk with his son. The results hadn't pleased Joe any more than had the session the previous night.

"He's got an answer for everything," Joe grumbled, helping Judith clean up the kitchen. "Hell, I'm twice his age, and I still don't have the answers for anything."

"Yes, you do, Joe," Judith responded. "They're just not the answers Mike wants to hear."

Joe sighed. "I guess. God knows I mucked up my life when I was young."

"You were younger then than Mike is now," Judith pointed out. "I didn't do much better."

"That was different," Joe pointed out. "I did something very foolish, but it could've been mended if your mother hadn't interfered. Then you did something foolish, too. But the point is, once we'd married a pair of drunken sots, we tried to make a go of it. We wouldn't break our vows, even though we had damned good reasons to do it."

"You and Herself were drunk as skunks and got married by an Elvis look-alike, yet you managed to do your best to stay together," Judith declared. "Dan and I were married at SOTS," she went on, using the nickname for Our Lady, Star of the Sea. "To me, divorce wasn't really an option. Making marriage work, no matter what it took, was what most of my family believed in."

"Murder was considered, as I recall," Joe said with a bemused expression.

"I stabbed Dan in the rear end with a meat fork after he threw the Thanksgiving turkey, dressing and all, out onto the sidewalk," Judith replied, putting paper products in the recycling wastebasket. "He was so fat he didn't even feel it."

Joe shook his head. "We both had a hell of a lot to put up with."

"You finally got out, though," Judith noted.

"Leaving Vivian was my last attempt to get her to save herself," Joe declared, shutting the dishwasher with unnecessary force. "It didn't work. She kept right on drinking. And, of course, there was Caitlin," he added, referring to the daughter he'd had by his first wife.

"And there was Mike," Judith said. "He needed a father, especially since he was a boy."

The phone rang. Judith picked up the receiver from the counter by the sink.

"Hi, Mom," Mike said. "Guess what? Uncle Al says the kids and I can stay with him for the next few days while Kristin decides where she wants to go."

Uncle Al had never married, despite plenty of chances. By coincidence, he lived in a bungalow in the Langford district, about a mile from Renie's mystery house.

"That's very generous of Uncle Al," Judith said. "But what about your job?"

"I've taken the week off for family reasons," Mike replied. "If Kristin hasn't moved out by next Monday, I'll just have to commute for a while. It's less than an hour and we won't have snow on the pass this time of year. Say, can you do me a favor?"

"Sure," Judith said in a dull voice. "What is it?"

"I'm not going to get out of here with the boys until lunchtime. That means I'll have to stop along the way to feed them. By the time we get to Uncle Al's, Joe-Joe will have to take his nap. I left in such a hurry this morning that I forgot most of my stuff. Can you bring it over to Uncle Al's? He probably won't be home—he was going to the racetrack. Just leave it on the front porch."

"Sure," Judith said, sounding even less enthusiastic. "Have you thought any more about what Joe and I said to you?"

"I really haven't had time," Mike replied.

"Okay. Be careful. When will I see you again?"

"Dinner? Uncle Al will still be at the track," Mike explained. "He always stays for the last race."

"Fine." Recognizing the apathy in her voice, Judith

tried to make amends. "It'll be fun to have the boys here, too. What do they like to eat?"

"Fried chicken," Mike responded. "They love your fried chicken."

"Okay, that's what we'll have. See you later."

Joe was watching Judith. "Now what?" he inquired.

Judith related Mike's end of the conversation. "I'm going to Uncle Al's. Mike needs his gear."

Joe tucked his shirt into his pants. He still wore a size thirty-four belt, but it rode much lower on his torso than it had in years past. "Do you want me to go over there?"

"I thought you had to go back to the insurance company," Judith said.

"I told them I wouldn't be there until one," Joe replied.

"Well . . ." Judith paused. It would only be a few blocks out of her way to swing by Moonfleet Street. Focusing, however briefly, on something else would be good for her. "No, I'll do it. I need to get out of the house. The fresh air might wake me up. I still feel kind of out of it. But I could use your help loading the stuff into the car."

After collecting their son's belongings from the guest room and evading Phyliss's questions about why Mike had spent the night, Judith and Joe headed for the Subaru.

"We'd better put it in the trunk," Joe said. "Why did he have to bring a sleeping bag along with all this other stuff?"

"Maybe he thought he'd have to camp out," Judith replied.

Joe unlocked the trunk. "Since Uncle Al's out wheeling trifectas at the track, you be sure to carry each of the heavy items one at a time. Forget the stairs. Just dump it all on the lawn." He winced as he tried to open the trunk. "This damned thing's sticking. Why didn't you tell me? I'd have taken it in to be fixed."

"It's even harder to close," Judith pointed out as they loaded Mike's gear. "It just started doing that in the last couple of days."

"I'll make an appointment with Jim at Nabobs Auto Shop," Joe said. "You sure you can manage?"

"I'm sure." Judith gave Joe a quick kiss on the lips. "If I'm not back before you go to the insurance office, good luck. I've got errands."

Backing down the drive, Judith waved to her neighbors, Carl and Arlene Rankers, who were working in their impeccable garden. Impeccable, that is, except for the laurel hedge that seemed to grow a couple of feet every year. Judith wouldn't dream of complaining—Carl and Arlene were wonderful, kindhearted people. And Arlene, with her insatiable curiosity, had often proved an invaluable ally to Judith when it came to keeping track of any criminal doings on Heraldsgate Hill.

Reaching the avenue, Judith drove another five blocks before pulling over next to the Presbyterian church. She took out her cell phone and dialed Renie's number.

"Want to do a drive-by on Moonfleet Street?" she asked.

"Ohhh . . ." Renie sounded flustered. "I can't. Guess who gets to draw Bucky Beaver? Mom recommended me, probably figuring I could do a self-portrait. Wirehoser called this morning. They have a Monday deadline."

"You can use the money," Judith pointed out.

"That's very true," Renie replied. "How are you doing?"

"Upset. Sad. Tired." Judith gazed out at the church's playground, which was shared with Pooh Pals Preschool. The sun was out from behind the clouds, and the children were playing on the slides and swings and a small merry-go-round. They looked so happy. With a pang, Judith thought of Mac and Joe-Joe, who were the same ages as most of the preschool kids. She shook off the thought, and told Renie about Uncle Al's offer of hospitality. "I decided another visit to the Moonfleet house might distract me."

"Go for it," Renie said. "A good mystery always takes your mind off your own troubles. Keep me posted—on all fronts."

Judith went directly to Uncle Al's. Ignoring Joe's advice, she placed Mike's belongings behind a porch pillar that was shielded by a huge red geranium. But she made three trips to do it, not risking an overload on her artificial hip. The trunk stuck again, but she finally managed to get it closed. Or so she hoped. At least it didn't fly open when she started down the street. Backtracking for much of the way, Judith reached Moonfleet in less than five minutes.

To her surprise, there was activity in front of the house. A Dairyland milk truck was parked there, and the milkman was coming down the path carrying an empty delivery basket.

Judith parked behind the truck, hopefully out of sight from the house's prying eyes. "Hi," she called just as the milkman reached the sidewalk. "Can you spare me a moment or two?"

The milkman, who was middle-aged and slim as a reed, grimaced. "I'm already running late, ma'am. My truck broke down this morning. Can you make it quick?"

Judith noticed that his name, Vern Benson, was stitched on his blue jacket. "I'll try, Mr. Benson," she said, offering him her warmest smile. "Have you ever met the people who live in this house?"

"Call me Vern," the milkman said, looking somewhat surprised by the query. "No, I can't say that I have. I guess they aren't home much."

"I understood the Blands never left the place," Judith said.

"Then maybe that's why I never see them." Vern brushed a leaf off the front of his striped overalls before moving toward his truck. "All I know is they get the same order every week." He glanced at the checklist in his hand. "Half gallon of milk, pint of cream, pound of butter, dozen eggs. They pay the bill on time. The money's always in the milk box. That's all I need to know. Sorry, got to run."

Vern hopped into the truck and drove away. Briefly, Judith considered marching up to the door and knocking. But she had a feeling no one would respond. Maybe she'd try it another time when her spirits weren't so low. With one last look at the desolate house, she started back to her Subaru. Before she could open the car door, a UPS van pulled up where the Dairyland truck had been parked.

Judith retraced her steps. The driver was still inside, wrestling with a large parcel. As soon as he emerged, she greeted him with a friendly smile.

"Is that for the Blands?" she asked.

The driver, who was a good-looking black man of about thirty with close-cropped hair and a tidy mustache, nodded. "Excuse me, it's kind of heavy. I'll be right back with you."

With bated breath, Judith watched the brown-clad young man go up the path. She noticed he didn't use the knocker, but leaned the parcel up against the wall on the opposite side of the door from the milk box. A moment later, he was back on the sidewalk.

"How can I help you?" he asked.

"Ah . . . do you have any supplies on the truck?" Judith inquired.

"Sure," the young man replied. "What do you need?"

"Some forms—a half dozen will do," Judith replied. "And a half dozen of the standard overnight letter-size envelopes."

The deliveryman nipped back inside the truck, then reappeared with the forms and envelopes. "Here you go. Anything else?"

"Thanks. Actually, I do have a question. My name's Judith, and I'm a . . . neighbor. That is, my uncle is a neighbor," she amended for fear that the deliveryman might someday show up on the Heraldsgate Hill route. "Uncle Al is worried about the Blands. He heard they were very ill."

"I'm Kevin," the deliveryman replied with an attractive smile. "Gosh, I wouldn't know. I've been on this route almost four years, and I've never met them."

"Do you come by here often?" Judith queried.

Kevin chuckled. "No. As a matter of fact, they get one delivery a year, always around this time. They've waived the signature, so they never have to come to the door. Frankly, I worried a bit about them last year. While I was driving along Moonfleet, I noticed that it took three or four days before the parcel was removed from the porch. But before I got around to checking on them, the next time I came by, it was gone. Maybe they'd been out of town."

"That's kind of odd, though," Judith commented. "Are the parcels always so big?"

Kevin nodded. "Pretty much. They come from Austria."

"Really." Judith tapped at her chin. "Are they from a business or a person?"

Kevin made a face. "I can't tell you that, Mrs. . . . Judith." He winked. "You'd have to find out for yourself."

"Yes," she responded in a musing tone, "I suppose I would. Thank you, Kevin."

Judith waited for the UPS van to pull away before she went back to her car to slip the mailing supplies onto the floor on the passenger's side. Hesitating only briefly, she walked back down the street. Gazing up at the house, she waited to see if anyone was watching from the windows. There was no sign of movement. *No sign of life,* she thought. That seemed more apt. In fact, all of Moonfleet Street seemed deserted. But, as Morty the Mailman and the others had mentioned, most of the homeowners worked.

As a precaution, Judith decided to move her car. She drove it around the corner and backed up onto the dirt track just enough to keep the sidewalk clear. Then she walked around the corner and boldly approached the house. If she got caught, she'd have an excuse. Judith could invent a dozen pretexts on short notice.

She reached the porch. The parcel was at least a yard long, two feet wide, and four inches in depth. It was wrapped in plain, heavy brown paper with plenty of strapping tape. Judith bent down to read the return address on the UPS shipping label.

The sender's handwriting was hard to decipher. Judith surmised that the cramped, somewhat shaky printing had been done by an older person. The name was Bachman; the place of origin was Kopfstein, Austria; the air bill was for second-day delivery, dated Monday, June 17; the signature was illegible.

Judith was about to read the rest of the information when she was startled by a noise that seemed to come from inside the house. As fast as her hips would take her, she hurried down the path and moved out of sight behind the shrubbery next to the sidewalk.

Judith searched for an opening in a big rhododendron bush. With any luck, she might be able to spot someone removing the parcel from the porch. At last, she managed to part some of the glossy leaves, allowing a silver-dollar-size view of the front door.

The parcel was still there. A car went by on Moonfleet, but apparently the driver paid no attention to Judith. A second noise, very close by, gave her another start. A moment later, she saw a squirrel dart from under some blackberry vines and dash toward the house. The small gray animal climbed up a tall cedar tree and disappeared.

After at least five more minutes, there was no activity on the porch. A car, a pickup truck, and a gas-company van drove along the street. Judith shifted from one foot to the other. She was about to give up and go back to the Subaru when she heard what sounded like a door being closed. Hastily, she again looked through the shrubbery. The parcel hadn't budged. Could the sound have been made in the house? Maybe someone was coming to the porch. Another three minutes passed. Nothing happened.

Discouraged, she gave up. Moving quickly beyond the path, she walked to the end of the block and turned the corner. Telling herself she hadn't completely wasted her time, she got into her car and eased it down the dirt track and onto the street. At least she'd learned a few things about the residents of the Spanish house. And the yearly parcel from Austria was certainly intriguing.

But heading back to Heraldsgate Hill, her mood shifted back into gloom. She should stop at Falstaff's Grocery to shop for Mike and the boys. A cut-up fryer with extra drumsticks—Mac and Joe-Joe both loved drumsticks—along with fresh corn on the cob, an orange punch drink, and chocolate-chip ice cream were on her mental list. Those were all her grandsons' favorites. She had potatoes on hand, but decided to get some special Yukon golds. And, since it was on the way, Toys-O'-Joy might have some items the boys would like. They were probably tired of the stash of playthings their grandparents kept for them at Hillside Manor.

Judith had to drive around the block four times before a parking space opened up near the toy shop. Heraldsgate Hill had grown in population the past two decades, making for crowded streets and sidewalks in the commercial area. But twenty minutes and a hundred and fifteen dollars later, Judith was satisfied with her purchases of the primate zoo, the freight train, and the battery-run fire engine complete with siren and flashing red lights. With a small smile, she put the toys in the backseat and drove on to Falstaff's, two and a half blocks away.

It cost less but took almost as long to finish her shopping there. Kippi, the freckled courtesy clerk who had often helped Judith, carried the groceries to the car.

"It's going to rain again," Kippi said with a frown. "As soon as school gets out, it always rains. Darn."

"But never hard," Judith pointed out.

"Right." She smiled at Judith, revealing new braces on her teeth. "What do you think? Do I look too totally geekish?"

"Of course not, Kippi," Judith assured the girl. "And you'll look downright gorgeous when you get the braces off."

They'd reached the Subaru. "There's only three bags," Kippi said. "Do you want them in the car or the trunk?"

Judith considered. "I've got a bunch of toys for my grandsons in the car," she said. "We'd better put them in the trunk."

"Sure." Kippi waited for Judith to turn the key.

"This lid's a problem lately," Judith remarked. "We're getting it fixed. It's at an age where little things go wrong with it every now and then."

"But not nearly as old as Mr. Flynn's MG," Kippi noted. "He really loves that car, doesn't he?"

"Oh, he does indeed," Judith said, struggling a bit to open the back of the Subaru. "The problem is, it's hard to get replacement—"

The lid of the trunk sprang open with a labored creaking noise. Judith and Kippi both screamed.

Someone was lying inside the trunk, curled up in an awkward manner. Kippi screamed again and dropped the grocery bags.

Judith clapped a hand over her mouth and stared. There was blood by the man's head, not much, but just enough to scare the wits out of Judith. The man didn't move. As she kept staring, she was overcome with a feeling of horror. She knew the person who was stuffed into her trunk. She recognized the blue jacket and the striped overalls.

Vern Benson, the milkman, looked to Judith as if he were dead.

FOUR

JUDITH KNEW SHE shouldn't tamper with evidence, but she slammed the trunk shut anyway. Kippi was shaking like a leaf, her plump body huddled over.

"I'm calling 911," Judith said, taking out her cell phone and putting a hand on the girl's back. "You go back into the store and tell the front end manager what's happened. After that, you may want to lie down in the employee break room."

Kippi looked up, tears in her blue eyes. "Do you know who that is?"

"No. Yes." Judith motioned for Kippi to go as she heard the 911 operator's voice on the line. "I'd like to report an . . . accident. There's a milkman in the trunk of my car. I'm parked at Falstaff's—"

"Excuse me," the female voice interrupted. "Did you say there was a milkman in your trunk? What's he doing?"

"Nothing," Judith gulped. "I think he's dead."

There was a pause on the line. "Is this Mrs. Flynn?" the operator asked.

"Well . . . yes," Judith admitted. "And it's not a joke. I—"

"Of course it's not a joke," the operator broke in, sounding resigned. "You never joke about finding dead people. We'll have someone there right away."

Judith felt like an idiot. Customers were coming out of the store; a couple of cars pulled into the lot. Not wanting to attract attention, she picked up the Falstaff bags and managed to fit them onto the backseat floor. So far, no one had noticed anything out of order. She was about to get into the driver's seat to wait when Phil Erickson, one of the store managers, came striding out of the side entrance.

"What the hell's going on?" he asked, keeping his voice down. "Kippi said you've got a dead body in your trunk. Is it one of our customers?"

Judith grimaced. "Of course not. It's a milkman."

Phil's face had gone red. "You mean one of our delivery guys?"

"No," Judith answered, beginning to feel indignant. "Not unless your milk deliverers also do residential routes."

"They don't," Phil said, looking relieved. "You didn't run over this guy, did you?"

"Of course not!" Judith glared at Phil.

"Okay." Phil sighed and put a hand on Judith's arm. "I'm sorry. Like any business, we worry about all our people."

And your liability insurance, Judith thought. But her reaction was harsh. She could empathize with Phil after the death in her own kitchen sink. If the Flynns had been liable, they would have been sued into oblivion.

"Really," Judith said, "this has nothing to do with your store. I wish I could move my car out of your lot, but that's impossible."

"You ought to know," Phil retorted, then attempted a commiserating smile. "That is, with your husband being an ex-cop, and telling you all sorts of war stories."

"Yes." Judith knew that Phil was avoiding mention of her own involvement in several homicides on Heraldsgate Hill. The manager wasn't about to offend one of his best customers.

The cops, in fact, were driving into the parking lot. They hadn't turned on their siren or their lights. As Heraldsgate Hill grew in prestige and affluence, discretion had become a byword except for obvious emergencies or when drivers didn't move their brand-new Beamers out of the way.

The patrol officers were unknown to Judith. A husky dark-skinned male and a copper-haired female got out of the police car and walked tentatively toward Judith and Phil. So did two women who had just come out of the store and were staring with curious eyes.

"Do you need me?" Phil whispered.

"No," Judith murmured. "Only for customer control."

"Got it," Phil said, blocking the women's passage. "Hi, there, Ms. Farris, Ms. Ryan. Nothing to see here, nothing to see here. By the way, did you sample the local strawberries in the kiosk? They just came in this morning."

"Mrs. Flynn?" the female officer inquired. "You reported a corpse. Where is it?"

Fortunately, Phil had drawn the two women back toward the store. Judith noticed that there was an eager gleam in the young officer's hazel eyes. *Her first body. But not mine.* The broad-shouldered Samoan didn't look any older than his partner. He, too, seemed to be keeping a taut rein on his excitement.

"In there," Judith said, pointing to the trunk. "I know I shouldn't have closed the lid, but I didn't want to upset people coming through the parking lot. So many parents shop here with their children."

The Samoan officer, whose name tag read JASON PAOLUSOPO, looked curiously at Judith. "I see."

Judith wondered how much he saw. She caught a quick glimpse of the redhead's name tag: COLLEEN O'DONAHUE. She had her hands pressed to her sides, as if bracing herself. But she didn't speak.

"It may be hard to open," Judith warned Jason. "We've had a problem with the trunk lately."

"I guess," Jason said under his breath. But he was young and strong. The trunk opened on his first attempt.

"Oh!" Colleen cried, clapping her hands to her cheeks. "It *is* a body! Ohmigod!"

Seeing the young woman sway slightly, Judith put a steadying hand on her back. "It's all right. There's not much blood, at least as far as I can see. I didn't touch anything, of course."

"Gosh." Jason had removed his regulation cap and held a hand to his short black hair. "Shouldn't we have medics here? I mean, maybe he's not dead. Maybe he just passed out."

"Yes," Judith said, "medics as well as firefighters should have been sent. I imagine a homicide unit has been dispatched, or soon will be. In fact," she went on, hearing the rumble of a heavy vehicle coming along the avenue, "here come the firefighters now. If you have crime-scene tape, you'd better cordon the area off at once. We're already drawing a bit of a crowd."

At least a half-dozen people, including two young children, had stopped to see what was going on. Taking a deep breath, Colleen walked over to them and asked that they move back. Jason apparently had gone to the squad car to get the tape.

"Sorry," one of the firefighters apologized as he jumped off the truck. "We had a heart attack victim on the other side of the hill. The medics should be here any minute. What's going on?"

Once again, Judith offered an explanation. She recognized two of the firefighters. They recognized her. After checking the body, one of them shook his head. "Man, how do you do it, Mrs. Flynn? Do you find them or do they find you?"

Judith was spared an answer by the arrival of the medics. She also recognized one of them, a woman who had shown up at Hillside Manor when the movie producer had been killed two years earlier. It was no wonder that Jason and Colleen were staring at her. Judith figured that they must feel as if they were at some kind of macabre homicide reunion.

"You've done this before?" Colleen whispered in awe.

Judith nodded.

"We haven't," Jason said. "This is our first. No wonder you're so calm."

"I'm not, really," Judith protested. "If you could see my insides, they'd look like boiling pasta. But I do know the drill. My husband's a retired police detective."

"Wow," said Jason.

"Golly," said Colleen.

"Drat," said Judith.

As she'd predicted, an unmarked city car entered the parking lot, where minor chaos was erupting as customers tried to leave and newcomers were waved off. Phil reappeared, looking distressed.

"How long will this take?" he asked one of the firefighters.

"An hour, maybe two," the young man replied. He explained to Phil that the car would be towed after the detectives and the crime-scene experts checked it out. Photographs would have to be taken. Shoulders slumping, Phil went back inside.

"We can give you a ride home when they're finished here," Jason offered.

"Thanks," Judith said, "but I really have to leave before then. Maybe they'll let me go as soon as I answer some questions. By the way, I want to get my belongings out of the car. I hope that's not a problem."

If only, Judith thought, Woodrow Price, Joe's former partner, or one of the other detectives she knew would show up. But Woody and his wife, Sondra, were vacationing in Quebec. As the doors to the unmarked police car opened, she didn't recognize either of the men who got out. One was tall and slender, forty or so, neatly dressed and moving with precision. The other was a little older, but short, pudgy, and his shoes didn't match.

They brushed past Judith and went straight to the

Subaru. "What have we got here?" the taller man inquired in a brisk manner.

"Deceased male, forties, Dairyland logo on back of jacket," one of the medics replied. "I think he's been dead for less than an hour, Glenn."

"We'll let the ME decide that," Glenn snapped. He turned to his partner. "Camera ready?"

The other detective grunted a reply before producing the camera from under his rumpled raincoat. "Where the hell are the regular photographers?" he groused. "They get vacation—I don't, not until August."

Glenn beckoned the patrol officers. "Who found the body?" he inquired.

Jason pointed to Judith. "She did, sir."

Glenn's cold gray eyes rested on Judith. "What's your name?"

"Judith Flynn," she said.

"Address?" He turned to his partner, who was clicking off pictures at a rapid rate. "Get out your notebook, Trash."

"Hold your water," the man called Trash shot back. "I'm doing all the work. As usual." Clicking off a few more pictures, he unfolded the camera strap and slung it over his left shoulder. "Okay, okay, let's do it. What did you say your name was, lady?"

Judith had taken her wallet out of her purse. "Here," she said, pointing to her driver's license. "See for yourself."

Trash gave her a wary look. "You're a bundle of fun. Watch your mouth, Mrs."—he glanced at the license—"Flynn. Hey," he said to Glenn, "there used to be a

Flynn in the squad, but I heard he croaked. You remember the guy?"

"Only the name," Glenn replied. "It was before my time. Wasn't his wife a drunk? You're no relation, I assume, Mrs. Flynn?"

"Not to his drunken wife," Judith snapped. "I'm the second Mrs. Flynn, and I assure you, Joe is alive and well."

"Oh." Glenn seemed unfazed. "Where and when did you find the victim?"

"Here." Judith pointed to the Subaru, where the trunk was now closed. More than two dozen people, including Falstaff employees, were standing beyond the yellow tape. Out on the avenue, vehicles were slowing down to rubberneck. "Kippi, the courtesy clerk, and I found the body when we went to load my groceries."

"Where's this Kippi now?" Glenn asked, scanning the bystanders.

Phil spoke up. "She's resting in the employee lounge. She's barely sixteen, and she's had a terrible shock."

Glenn, as seemed to be his wont, was unmoved. "We still have to talk to her. Trash," he said over his shoulder, "go into the store and interrogate the Kippi witness."

"Stairs," Trash muttered. "Why don't you interview her?" He didn't wait for answer. "Right, right, you're the big shot, direct from L.A. I'll bet I'm going to have to climb stairs." With his raincoat flapping behind him, Trash lumbered toward the entrance.

Judith tapped Glenn's shoulder. "May I get my belongings out of the car now?"

Glenn shook his head. "We can't permit that. Your car is a crime scene."

"But there's fresh chicken and corn and . . ." Judith took a deep breath. "They're not in the trunk, for heaven's sake! They're inside the car and they were put there after Vern got killed."

"Vern?" For the first time, Glenn's expression altered slightly. "You know the victim?"

Judith looked pugnacious. "I'm not telling you another thing until I get my food and those toys. I refuse to disappoint my grandsons!"

"Disappointment's good for children," Glenn declared. "It builds character. Your car's off-limits. You ought to know that, being married to a cop."

Judith narrowed her dark eyes. She was almost as tall as Glenn and stood on her tiptoes to look at him head-on. "Okay. But may I leave for a few minutes to replace my purchases?"

"No." Glenn's lean jaw was set.

Judith squared her wide shoulders. "May I sue you for harassment?"

"If you like. Everybody else does," he added on a sour note.

"May I use the bathroom?"

Glenn considered. "Yes. But be back here in five minutes."

Judith returned in fifty-five minutes, huffing and puffing. She had gone into Falstaff's via the parking lot, acquired a shopping cart, and exited through the street entrance. Feeling like a bag lady, she walked the block and a half to Toys-O'-Joy. Fending off queries from the salespeople, she had bought duplicate presents for the grandchildren, returned to Falstaff's, and replicated the grocery purchases.

Additional patrol officers had been brought in for crowd control. After being thoroughly checked, customers were being allowed to leave, but no one was permitted to enter. Phil was at the parking-lot entrance, wringing his hands and making profuse apologies. Glenn and Trash were standing by the Subaru with a half-dozen men and women. Judith figured they were the crime-scene unit and perhaps backup from the homicide division. She stood off to one side of the entrance with her cart and fervently hoped Glenn wouldn't notice her. The store's overhang sheltered her from the drizzle, but she was growing more anxious by the minute.

Her hopes were in vain. Glenn saw her out of the corner of his eye and immediately marched in Judith's direction.

"Where have you been, Mrs. Flynn?" he demanded in a chilly tone.

"Here," Judith replied.

Glenn gestured at the cartful of purchases. "That's not true. Trash and I looked everywhere for you when you didn't show up after the first ten minutes."

"Men can never find anything," Judith said. "And why do you call your partner 'Trash'?"

"Because that's his name," Glenn replied. "Or rather, the short version. Jonathan Parker Trashman."

"What's yours, besides Glenn?" Judith demanded.

"Glenn Morris," the detective answered, exhibiting a hint of dignity.

Neither of the detectives' names rang any bells with

Judith. There had been so many changes and new hires at headquarters since Joe's retirement.

"Don't badger me," she said, shaking a finger. "I've had a terrible shock."

"You don't act like it, Mrs. Flynn," Glenn asserted.

"I tend to keep things bottled up," Judith retorted. *At least my reaction to things that happen to me far too often.* "When can I go home? Vern wasn't killed here, so I don't see any point in hanging out in Falstaff's parking lot. Besides, it's bad for business."

Glenn Morris didn't respond. Instead, he walked over to the patrol officers and exchanged words with them. Mostly *his* words, Judith noticed. Jason and Colleen seemed cowed by the detective's presence. But all three of them were distracted by the arrival of a beige Toyota Camry, horn honking and driver yelling. Judith didn't have to look twice to know it was Renie.

"Move it, scumbags!" Renie screamed. "I have to get Bill's snack!"

"Coz!" Judith cried, trying to hurry to the Camry before Renie drove right through the yellow tape. "Stop! You'll never guess what's happened!"

Renie stopped honking. She got out of the car and gaped at Judith. "You wrecked your car again?"

Renie was referring to the demise of Judith's previous vehicle, a Nissan with bad brakes. No brakes, actually, which had caused the car to crash into the concrete wall in Falstaff's parking lot.

"No," Judith replied. "Much worse. You'll never guess what I found."

"No!" Renie looked stunned. "Not again!"

Judith nodded. "I'm afraid so. It's a milkman. He's in my trunk."

"He's dead?" Renie asked in a bleak voice.

"I'm afraid so. It looks as if . . . Renie! Your car's still moving!"

Sure enough, the Camry was slowly but surely going forward through the tape and heading straight for the outdoor floral display.

"Yikes!" Renie cried, and jumped back into the car. "I forgot to set the emergency brake!" She stopped the Camry just short of dahlias and delphiniums. "Are you going home?" she asked when disaster had been averted.

"When they let me. Will you give me a lift? I'd rather not ride with the police," Judith said, then pointed to her cart. "I bought some things. Twice."

"Sure. I'll wait. Let's load your stuff now."

This time, Renie remembered to set the brake, though some of the yellow tape now decorated the Camry's hood. "Who's the stiff?" she whispered, glancing at Glenn. "I mean, the one who's still alive?"

"Glenn Morris," Judith murmured. "His partner's a guy named Trash. Never mind why. They thought Joe was still married to Herself and had died."

"Joe? Or Herself?" asked Renie.

"Joe. Or maybe both of them," Judith said, still keeping her voice down as they passed Glenn. "I didn't tell them that Herself was at her condo in Florida."

Vivian Flynn had had the gall to move into a house in the cul-de-sac several years earlier. But she also owned a condo on the Gulf, and her efforts to sell it had come to naught. Thus, to Judith's great relief, she was gone for much of the year. As Vivian put it, she preferred drinking on the beach instead of on the hill because she wouldn't roll when she fell in the sand.

Renie gathered up the toys; Judith took care of the groceries. Once again, Glenn was heading their way. This time, however, he advanced on Renie.

"Do you own this beige Camry?" he asked in a voice that barely concealed his fury.

"You bet. We paid cash for it. And no, it's not for sale. Excuse me, I'm busy." Renie elbowed Glenn out of the way and headed for the Camry's trunk.

"Hold it!" Glenn shouted. "Get that car out of here right now before I arrest you for impeding a homicide investigation!"

Renie turned to gaze at the detective. "That's what I'm doing. Leaving, I mean. I'll have to get Bill's snack later. But," she continued, folding her arms and looking mulish, "I'm not going to budge an inch unless my cousin comes with me."

Glenn glanced from Renie to Judith. "You're cousins?"

Renie nodded. "We have been, since we were born. Do we have a deal or not?"

Glenn shot Renie a menacing look. "You're impertinent," he snapped.

"I'm also impatient. Hurry up, time's a-wasting."

Glenn shifted his gaze to the Subaru. It appeared as if the law officers had concluded their examination.

"Very well," Glenn conceded in an irked tone. "Move along. Now." He turned to Judith. "We'll meet you at your house."

"Fine." Judith got into the car while Renie put the toys in the trunk and removed the yellow tape.

"Okay, tell me all," she said, reversing somewhat recklessly out into the street.

During the short drive to Hillside Manor, Judith was able to sum up what had happened from the time of her arrival on Moonfleet to the discovery of Vern Benson's body in the trunk of her car.

"Wow!" Renie exclaimed, stopping in the Flynn driveway. "Now I feel terrible. The Moonfleet house was my idea. You didn't want to get involved, but I insisted. It's my fault you're in another mess."

"No, it's not," Judith said with a weary sigh. "Joe's right. I'm a murder magnet. You know how it is—some people are lucky at cards, some keep making bad choices when it comes to mates, some have endless problems with everyday dealings, even though it's usually not their fault. A store clerk overcharges them, their mail goes awry, the bank makes a mistake and withdraws money from their account instead of the person who asked for it—it's like Job. One piece of trouble after another. I just happen to be the kind who finds dead bodies. Why couldn't it be stashes of diamonds and pearls?"

Renie opened the car door. "Some of it *is* your own doing. You're extremely curious, especially about people. That's bound to lead you into trouble."

Judith collected her groceries. "I suppose. Not to mention all the varieties of guests who come to the B&B. There's bound to be a clinker now and then."

"That's one way of putting it," Renie said from behind the pile of toys. "Tell me where I'm going. I can't see."

Judith led Renie down the driveway and to the back

porch. "Joe's gone," she said, unlocking the door. "He's going to have a fit when he finds out what's happened."

Renie stumbled slightly as she entered the house. "Don't tell him."

"That's impossible!" Judith cried, setting the grocery bags down on the kitchen floor. "It'll be in the newspapers and on TV."

Renie carefully placed the three toy boxes under the counter next to the computer. "They don't have to identify you."

"But they will, won't they?" Judith said, unloading the groceries.

Renie turned as the doorbell rang. "That must be the Grim Reaper and his sidekick, Trash. Let me handle this."

"Coz . . ." But Renie was already hurrying to the front door.

"Come in," Judith heard Renie say. "Take a seat. I'm the one you should be talking to. This is all my fault."

Despite her uneasiness at letting Renie take over, Judith stayed in the kitchen, finishing her tasks with the groceries.

"Here's how this all started," Renie was saying. She launched into her fifty-year obsession with the house on Moonfleet. "I coerced my cousin into going over there to have a look. She didn't want any part of it, but I insisted. Naturally, she became interested—who wouldn't? This morning, she had to go to Langford, where our Uncle Al lives. She wanted me to go with her, but I had to do a beaver. So on her way—"

"Excuse me," Glenn broke in. "*What* did you have to do with a beaver?"

"Draw him," Renie retorted. "Never mind. Anyway, she passed by the house just as the milkman was making his delivery. They got to chatting. My cousin is a very social being. Before she could leave, a UPS man arrived. She needed some supplies, which he gave her. After that, she left. End of story until Falstaff's parking lot."

Judith was slowly and silently approaching the living room. She'd reached the dining room archway that led to the entrance hall. Judging from the direction in which their voices were coming, Renie and the detectives must be sitting on the matching sofas.

"It seems as if you're leaving out some important facts," Glenn said stiffly. "For one thing, you weren't at the Moonfleet house this morning. Mrs. Flynn was. We still have to talk to her."

"That's not a good idea," Renie said. "She's not well. She suffers from anthurium sprue."

Renie didn't often tell lies, but when she did, it was usually a whopper. "Very sad," she murmured.

"I've never heard of it," Glenn replied, though given his controlled manner, Judith couldn't tell if he believed Renie or not.

"It's quite rare," Renie replied. "Judith contracted the disease when she was working as a missionary in Honduras. An attack—they're so severe—is usually caused by emotional distress. Anthurium sprue victims can be easily set off, especially when they're the center of attention. They tend to live very shy, withdrawn lives."

"Hey," Trash broke in, "I thought you told us your cousin was the social kind."

Glenn glared at his partner. "I'm asking the questions here. You're supposed to be taking notes."

Trash glanced down at the notebook in his lap. "I was, until I tried to spell 'anthurium.' You're so smart, you spell it for me, genius."

"Use shorthand," Glenn replied loftily. "Nobody can ever read your notes anyway. On our last case, they were covered in pizza sauce."

"I can spell it," Renie said, looking smug. "But I won't."

"Let's get back to Mrs. Flynn's problem," Glenn said. "Before I could speak, Trash asked how your cousin could possibly be outgoing when her condition is so delicate."

"That's part of the problem," Renie answered. "She has these relapses, when she thinks she's her former self. That," she added with a heavy sigh, "is when the trouble begins."

"Very strange," Glenn remarked. "Very."

"So," Renie continued, "I'd appreciate it if you'd be extremely gentle with her. And of course there must be absolutely no mention of her name in the media. That could easily finish her off." Renie choked on the last few words. "Excuse me, I must get a handkerchief out of my purse. I'm tearing up at the mere thought of what could happen to my poor cousin."

Some sniffing ensued, then a loud blowing of Renie's nose. "In fact," she finally went on, "it wouldn't be wise to tell Mr. Flynn what's happened. He worries about Judith so much. It's not good for him, especially in his present state of deteriorating health."

"I heard he was already dead," Glenn said.

"Not quite," Renie replied. "But it's just a matter of time." She blew her nose again.

A noise from the stairs made Judith jump. She turned quickly, seeing Phyliss Rackley on the landing. The cleaning woman had arrived late, having had one of her many medical appointments in the morning. Judith motioned for silence. Phyliss, who was carrying garbage from the guests' wastebaskets, looked puzzled.

Judith moved to the bottom of the stairs. "Police," she whispered. "They're talking to Renie."

"Ha!" Phyliss nodded approval, her gray sausage curls bobbing up and down. "About time, if you ask me!" she said in a low voice. "Have they arrested her?"

Judith shook her head. "Go on," she urged. "Keep working. But stay out of the living room."

With a snort, Phyliss went on her way. Judith picked up the conversation in Renie's midsentence:

". . . to be very patient with her. I'll bring her in here now."

Renie rounded the corner into the entrance hall and gave a little start when she saw Judith. "Oh, dear coz," she exclaimed, winking like mad, "did you hear me explain about your pitiful state?"

Judith shot Renie a disparaging look. "Yes. I'm feeling very feeble."

"Good," Renie said. "I mean, that's awful. You do get confused when you're having a spell. Come along, talk to the nice policemen."

Judith obeyed, but what she really wanted to do was kick Renie in the rear end. Fibs were fine, especially when no harm would come of them. Outright deception was wrong when Judith could foresee the tangled web into which Renie had plunged them both. On the other hand . . .

Docilely, Judith sat down on the sofa next to her cousin. "I feel better now," she said softly.

"You seemed fine in the parking lot," Glenn noted. "In fact, you acted quite unmoved."

"That's her defensive mechanism," Renie asserted. "She has to respond that way, to ward off the . . . attack and eventual collapse."

"I see." Again, Glenn's stiff manner made his words impossible to interpret. "So tell us about meeting this milkman."

"We talked," Judith said. "I asked if he knew anything about the people who lived in the Spanish-style house. He didn't, except for their weekly milk order. He left. I was about to drive off, too, when I saw the UPS van." Judith's voice had become more normal as she related her story. "I needed supplies." *Only a wee white lie, nothing to match Renie's monstrous fabrication.* "I decided to ask him about the people who lived in the house. He didn't know anything, either. He made his delivery and left. Then I walked around a bit before I got in my car and came back to Heraldsgate Hill." *Stretching the truth, maybe, that was all.*

"Was your car in view the whole time?" Trash inquired, bumping his knees against the new oak coffee table and ignoring his partner's baleful glance.

"Uh . . . no," Judith admitted. "I'd moved my car. Moonfleet seemed so busy. I pulled into the dirt alley in back of the house. I probably didn't see the car for maybe ten minutes or so."

Glenn cocked his head to one side. "Ten minutes? You were wandering around the property for ten minutes?"

"No," Judith responded. "I was just . . . mostly strolling along the sidewalk." *No need to mention going up to the door unless specifically asked.*

"Did you see anyone in or around the house?" Glenn queried as he smoothed his patterned silk tie.

"No," Judith repeated. "But I did hear a couple of noises—like a door being slammed. Oh!" She clapped her hands to her cheeks as she realized that what she'd heard wasn't a door in the house, but probably her trunk.

"What now?" Trash asked, hiking up his pants.

"The sound," Judith said with a little shudder. "It must have been when the body was put in my car. Whoever did it was closing the trunk."

Trash looked disbelieving. "You left your trunk open, lady? That's a bad habit." Again, he paid no attention to Glenn's look of disapproval.

"It's been acting up the last couple of days," Judith explained. She tried not to wince as she saw Phyliss lurking outside the French doors at the other end of the living room. "I probably didn't get it all the way shut when I left Uncle Al's."

"So," Trash said, leaning back on the sofa and again bumping the coffee table as he crossed one leg over the other, "whoever conked the milkman just happened to know you had a faulty trunk and decided to stash the body there. That's pretty far-fetched."

"Hey," Renie said loudly, "whatever happened to Good Cop–Bad Cop? Aren't you both being jerks? Don't make my cousin froth!"

Trash looked aghast. "Froth?"

"Froth," Renie said again. "Foam at the mouth. Take it easy, you two."

A cell phone rang. Judith knew it wasn't hers, which was in the kitchen inside her purse. But Renie and the detectives all reacted. The call was for Glenn. He listened for a few moments before saying, "Yes. We'll be there shortly."

Glenn disconnected and stood up. "The Langford Precinct has dispatched two patrol officers. They're at the Moonfleet house now. We're going to check the place out. Come on, Trash, let's move."

"Aw . . ." Trash, who looked as if he'd finally made himself comfortable, clumsily got to his feet. "Actually, I was kind of hoping to see her froth."

Glenn ignored the comment, addressing Judith, who, along with Renie, was accompanying the detectives to the door. "I trust you aren't planning on leaving the city," he said.

"No, I'm not," Judith replied.

"She can't," Renie put in. "She's far too frail."

"Good." Glenn waited for Trash to open the door for him. "Because as of now, we consider you a suspect in the murder of Vern Benson."

FIVE

GREAT!" JUDITH CRIED, slamming the door behind the departing detectives. "That's all I need! What the hell will Joe say about *this*?"

"Calm down, coz," Renie urged. "I repeat, why does he have to find out?"

"How can he not?" Judith fumed, going in the direction of the kitchen.

"Think about it," Renie said. "Being a suspect is the best thing that could happen to you. Even if my ruse didn't work, these days the cops rarely release names of suspects to the media unless they're holding someone in custody. If you don't tell Joe, who will?"

Judith considered. "That may be true about releasing names, but Joe still has ties to the department. Woody, for instance. He and Sandra are due back from Canada in a few days."

"I'll call him," Renie said. "Woody and I've always bonded because we both love opera. I'll tell him to keep mum."

"Woody's not the only one Joe knows at headquarters," Judith pointed out.

"But he doesn't keep in contact with most of the others except for the occasional reunion or holiday party," Renie replied. "Besides, the force has grown so in recent years, it sounds to me as if the cops don't know each other as well as they used to. Didn't Glenn say he thought Joe was dead?"

"Yes, he did," Judith admitted. "They thought Joe was still married to Herself. Maybe there's something in what you say. But it's risky."

"There's one other thing," Renie said with a sly smile.

"What's that?"

"You solve the case."

Judith leaned against the sink. "Oh, swell!"

"Well? Aren't you tempted?"

Judith took a deep breath. "Of course. But with Mike and Kristin splitting up and the B&B at its busiest, I don't know when or how I could do any sleuthing."

"But you will," Renie said.

Judith's shoulders slumped. "I don't know . . . but maybe I'll have to, if only to get myself off the hook."

"That's right." Renie slung her huge black purse over her shoulder. "Got to run. I still have to buy Bill's snack, remember?"

"Why doesn't Bill buy it himself?" Judith inquired. "I thought part of his snack ritual was the pleasure he gets from choosing which delicacy he's going to eat that night."

"It is. He does. But he's had a cold, and he coughed so hard this morning that he pulled a muscle in his side. I'm babying him." Renie headed down the narrow hallway to the back door. "I'll be in touch. I should be done with Bucky by tomorrow morning."

Renie went out as Phyliss came in. There was a brief hostile exchange, but Judith didn't hear the specifics. She was too absorbed in the task that lay before her.

"Police, huh?" Phyliss said as she entered the kitchen. "I just happened to—"

"How much did you hear, Phyliss?" Judith demanded.

"Well . . . not as much as I'd have liked," the cleaning woman admitted. "Those Dooley kids were playing out in their yard behind your place and they were making an awful racket. How many do they have now? About twenty?"

"Or more," Judith replied. "There are grandchildren and even a great-grandchild, I think."

"You wrecked your car, huh?" Phyliss remarked.

"What? Oh. Yes, in a way." Judith patted the other woman's thin shoulder. If the only thing Phyliss had heard pertained to the Subaru's trunk, Judith would leave it that way. "We won't tell Joe, will we?"

"How're you going to explain why it's not here?" Phyliss asked. "I saw that fiendish cousin bring you home. What did she do with Beelzebub?"

"She bested him, four out of seven," Judith murmured.

Phyliss cupped her ear. "What?"

"Never mind. He's gone." Judith was absorbed in thought. There was too much else bothering her: Vern Benson's murder, the Moonfleet house, being a suspect, dealing with Mike's dilemma, keeping secrets from Joe. She didn't know where to start. It seemed as if there were bells and buzzers going off in her head.

"Are you going to answer the phone or shall I?" Phyliss asked.

"Oh! Sorry!" With an apologetic look, Judith snatched up the receiver. Joe was on the other end of the line.

"I've got a problem," he said.

You've got a problem? Judith thought. "What is it?"

"I have to go to Omaha," he said. "The insurance company's home office wants me to come back there on this fraud situation. I'll have to leave tonight. I tried to get out of it, but I can't, not at this stage of the investigation. I'm really sorry, leaving you in such a mess."

You don't know the half of it. "Don't worry, I'll be fine. How long will you be gone?"

"Hopefully, we can wrap the whole thing up by the weekend," Joe said. "The insurance carrier wants to avert a trial, so they're trying to get plenty of evidence to either discourage the lawsuit or settle out of court. I'm thinking I could be home late Saturday or early Sunday, depending on the airline schedules. I'll swing by the house and stuff a few things in a suitcase. I have to be at the airport by seven."

Judith's reaction was mixed. She was relieved that Joe would be gone for a few days, but she'd still have to explain why the Subaru wasn't in the driveway. And of course she would miss him.

"Will you have time to eat dinner with Mike and the boys?" Judith asked.

"Maybe," Joe said. "It depends on traffic. You know what it's like getting across the floating bridge this time of day."

Judith, in fact, had lost track of time. She looked up

at the old schoolhouse clock, which informed her it was going on four. The commute between the city and the Eastside seemed to start earlier and earlier, even in midweek.

"I'll see you soon," she said, and rang off.

Staring through the kitchen window at the Rankerses' hedge, Judith put her thoughts in order. Logic was her byword. First things first. She had guests due soon, another full house. Phyliss would have to make up for lost time if she intended to finish cleaning before the first arrivals. Meanwhile, Judith would prepare the guests' appetizers and make a start on dinner. Murder must be put aside until she'd taken care of her family and her business. She also had to check on Gertrude, but that could wait. Wednesday was bridge club, and the old girl probably hadn't gotten back yet. Judith's mother had put a horn on her motorized wheelchair, and usually honked when she got dropped off. Sometimes she honked just for the hell of it.

Half an hour later, as Judith was husking corn, Phyliss announced she was finished. Putting on her long black raincoat and a plastic rain bonnet, she headed out into the June drizzle.

"I'll see you tomorrow if I don't get pneumonia," she called from the back door.

Ten minutes later, Gertrude honked. Judith put the corn on the counter and went outside.

"Did you win?" she asked, descending the steps to the backyard.

" 'Course I did," Gertrude replied, going pell-mell for the toolshed. "I got all the quarters, four dollars and twenty-five cents, despite having Deb as a partner. She goes to bridge club to visit, not to play cards. Talk, talk, talk. She drives me crazy."

"Mother," Judith said, opening the door, "there's something I have to tell you."

Gertrude twisted around in the wheelchair to look at her daughter. "You aren't expecting, are you?"

"No, Mother," Judith replied. "I'm a few years beyond that."

"You never know these days," Gertrude said, moving up to the card table. "I read about a goofy woman in *The Inquisitor* who had twins at your age. Their father was an alien. Like Lunkhead."

"I wish you'd stop calling Joe 'Lunkhead,' " Judith said.

"Fair enough," said Gertrude, allowing Judith to help her out of her coat. "I always called that first loser of yours that. How about 'Knucklehead' for this one?"

"Don't. Please." Judith sat down on the arm of the sofa. "I have some sad news."

"Knucklehead croaked?" Gertrude asked hopefully.

"No, Mother," Judith said through clenched teeth. "Mike and Kristin have separated."

Gertrude's wrinkled old face sagged. "Holy Mother!" she breathed. "That can't be! You don't mean a *divorce*?" The word came out sounding like a dread disease.

"Not a divorce," Judith said optimistically. "They need to be apart for a while, to straighten things out."

"I could straighten 'em out with a hammer," Gertrude asserted, but her chin trembled and her voice shook. "What's wrong with them?"

Judith reached out to take her mother's frail hand. "Frankly, to people like you and me, it sounds silly. Kristin wants more space."

"More space?" Gertrude scowled. "She's living up in the mountains, isn't she? How much more space could she want? Montana?"

"It's an expression," Judith explained. "I think she means she wants more opportunities for herself as a person. A career, maybe."

"She's got a career," Gertrude retorted. "A husband and two kids. That was enough of a career for most women in my day."

"You worked, at least part-time," Judith pointed out.

"It wasn't because I wanted a stupid career," Gertrude shot back. "We needed the money. That's why Deb worked, too. And your Aunt Ellen and your Auntie Vance and—"

"Yes," Judith interrupted, "I realize that most of the women in our family worked. But there are also two sides to any marital story."

"As Deb never tires of reminding me," Gertrude said. "She worked in a law office. She saw one divorce after another. I guess she ought to know," the old lady added grudgingly.

"That's true," Judith allowed. "Mike may be being unreasonable, too. Anyway, it's possible they can work things out. The problem is, the younger generation is self-absorbed and isn't very good at compromise. Or so it seems to me."

"You're right about that, kiddo," Gertrude said, still clutching at Judith's hand. "I'm too old for all this." She paused, shaking her head and looking off into the far corner. "You got married, you stayed married," she declared, her voice a bit stronger. "The only time I threatened to divorce your father was when he got that brand-new Chevy and drove like Barney Oldfield. A real speed demon he was in that car. It scared me. And then less than a year after he bought the car, he died of heart trouble. Maybe it'd been better if he'd run us both off a bridge. Then I wouldn't have had to be alone all these years."

Judith noticed tears in her mother's eyes. "But then I wouldn't have had you around to bully me," she said to Gertrude. "I wouldn't have missed it for the world." Judith bent down and kissed the top of her mother's white head.

Gertrude didn't say anything for a long time. The two women sat in silence, knowing their thoughts were the same, and finding quiet comfort in it.

Where's your car?" Joe asked as he breezed through the back door. "I thought you weren't home."

"The car?" Judith paused to wipe corn tassels from her hands. "It's gone," she said, kissing Joe.

"Gone where?"

"To . . . the shop. The trunk was driving me nuts. I had trouble loading the groceries." That was true enough. "I couldn't wait for the appointment you made with Nabobs. They'll work it in." Not true. But it sounded plausible.

"Oh." Joe started for the back stairs. "I'm going to pack. It's a good thing I called the shuttle to pick me up. You can drive the MG while I'm gone. Just treat it kindly." He disappeared around the hall corner.

The B&B guests seemed normal. So did Mac and Joe-Joe. But Judith, Joe, Mike, and Gertrude knew that their fried chicken dinner was anything but typical. The chair where Kristin usually sat had been pulled back from the oak dining-room table, but her absence hovered over the room like a phantom. The mood was so gloomy that even Gertrude kept her mouth shut.

Mike stayed on after dinner for a few games of cribbage with his grandmother. Joe skipped dessert. The airport shuttle arrived exactly at six-thirty. Judith's farewell kiss was fervent.

"Hey," he said, looking into her black eyes, "do you think I'm going to be taken hostage by terrorists?"

"You never know these days," Judith said somberly.

He kissed her high forehead. "I'll only be gone for a couple of days. What could go wrong in that short a time?"

Judith merely smiled. Weakly.

Upon leaving around eight o'clock, Mac and Joe-Joe were heartbroken when their great-grandmother informed them that their new toys couldn't go with them to Uncle Al's. The items Judith had purchased must stay with their other stash of playthings at Hillside Manor.

"Oh, go ahead," Judith said to Mike. She couldn't, of course, mention that the original purchases were at police headquarters. "We can always get them something else."

"Spoiled," Gertrude muttered, but for once, she didn't sound as if she meant it.

Two of the guests forgot their keys that evening and

had to be let in around midnight. Judith always handed out two keys—one for the room and one for the house. She locked up at ten. Late arrivals could let themselves in. Unless they left the keys in their room.

Another woman, one of four teachers on holiday, came down with a cold. Judith offered her aspirin, nasal spray, and cough drops. As always, when dispensing over-the-counter medications, she cautioned guests to read the labels carefully.

A Methodist minister lost his glasses and couldn't read his Bible before going to bed. He was sure he'd had them after he arrived at Hillside Manor. After a twenty-minute search, Judith found them between the window-seat cushions in the living room. The minister promised to pray for her. Judith said she could use all the prayers she could get.

She expected another restless night, especially since Joe wasn't lying beside her. But emotional and physical exhaustion had set in. Judith slept like a rock.

At nine o'clock Thursday morning when she was serving breakfast to her guests, Glenn Morris called. "Trash and I are coming by to ask you some more questions," he announced. "We'll be there in half an hour."

"Could you wait until eleven?" Judith asked. "I'd rather you come after my guests leave."

"Sorry," Glenn replied, sounding not the least apologetic. "We have a schedule to keep." He hung up.

All but the four teachers were checking out that morning. Hopefully, they'd leave early. When Phyliss arrived shortly after Glenn's call, Judith had to explain that the police were paying another visit.

"What for?" Phyliss demanded.

"It's a long story, Phyliss," Judith said. "I don't want to tire you with it. You look peaked." It wasn't true, but mentioning the cleaning woman's health always diverted her.

"I'm sure I do," Phyliss declared with a heavy sigh. "It's my chest. It feels as if an elephant sat on it." For emphasis, she pressed her hands to her flat bosom and gasped several times.

"Then take it easy," Judith cautioned. "I'll let you get started right away."

The Methodist minister and his wife left immediately after breakfast. A few minutes later, the couple who had forgotten their keys also departed. But the honeymooners from Oregon lingered upstairs and the grad students from UCLA decided to have coffee in the living room. As for the teachers, they were biding their time, waiting to see if their colleague with the cold felt like sightseeing.

At a quarter to ten, Glenn and Trash showed up at the front door. Judith ushered them into the parlor, making sure that both doors were shut tight.

Trash eyed the empty fireplace. "Damned near cold enough for a fire. Hell, October's warmer around here than June." With a grunt, he sat down on the settee and looked at his partner. "I suppose you're going to tell me how it's always seventy degrees and sunny in L.A."

Glenn ignored the other detective and assumed his place on the hearth, one elbow casually resting on the mantelpiece. "I have some questions about your car," he said to Judith, who had sat down in one of the two matching armchairs. "When did you last look in your trunk before arriving at the grocery store?"

Judith answered promptly. "Tuesday morning. I shopped for groceries to fill up the larder."

"Did you take the car out again that day?" Glenn inquired.

"Let me think—no, I didn't."

Glenn glanced at Trash. "Are you taking this down?"

"Down where?" Trash's expression was ingenuous—until he scowled at Glenn. "Yeah, sure, smart guy. Why do you think I have this notebook and pen? Or am I signing autographs?"

Glenn scowled right back before resuming his queries. "Why did you go to the Bland house yesterday?" he asked Judith.

"My cousin told you why," she retorted. "Mrs. Jones has been obsessed with the house for years. She used to live in the neighborhood. I went along with her Tuesday to humor her. But I'll admit, the place made me curious, too."

"Hey," Trash interrupted, "you got any coffee around here?"

"Yes," Judith said. But she'd be darned if she'd offer it to the detectives.

"How well do you know Mr. and Mrs. Bland?" Glenn inquired.

"I don't know them at all," Judith replied. "I didn't even know their names until day before yesterday when my cousin and I asked one of the neighbors who lived across the street."

"But you went back by yourself yesterday," Glenn remarked.

"Yes. I told you, I had to go to Langford to my uncle's. While I was in the area, I decided to have another look at the house. My cousin and I've already told you this."

Glenn gazed up at the ceiling. "Let's see. Mrs. Jones claims she's been fascinated by the Bland house since her early teens. Fifty years go by, but despite her alleged all-absorbing interest, she does nothing. Suddenly she convinces you to join her in surveying the premises. A day later, you go back—and end up with a dead man in your trunk. Tell me," he continued, his tone now deceptively benign, "does this make sense?"

"Of course not," Judith snapped. "I mean, it wouldn't make sense to most people. But it's simple curiosity. My cousin and I are both interested in people. And you have to admit, just looking at the house and its condition, it's certainly unusual."

"Unusual, perhaps," Glenn conceded. "But hardly a subject of repeated visits and querying of deliverymen. We understand you and Mrs. Jones also accosted the postman on Tuesday. He claims you're both very peculiar, particularly Mrs. Jones."

"Renie and Morty have a history," Judith said, exasperated. "They go way back. How did you happen to run into him so late in the day? You must not have gotten to Moonfleet Street until four o'clock."

"Mr. Mortimer told us he was running a little behind," Glenn replied.

"I like the guy," Trash put in. "He seems like good people."

You would, Judith thought.

"Let's go over yesterday's visit one more time," Glenn said.

"What's wrong?" Judith retorted. "Did Detective Trashman spill beer on his notes?"

"Hey!" Trash cried, looking offended. "It wasn't beer, it was a pork chop!"

Judith sighed. "Okay, but I'm going to tell you exactly what I told you yesterday." And she did, though again omitting a couple of details.

"I don't think you're telling us everything," Glenn said when she'd finished. "The crime scene people found damp earth in your tires, the same kind of dirt that's in the alley at the Blands' house."

"I told you—I backed up into the alley," Judith admitted. "With all those delivery people, I didn't want to take up a parking place on the street."

"Why did you get out of the car?" Glenn asked.

"I'm a gardener," Judith asserted. That much was true. "There's some very interesting vegetation on the property, including a camellia bush that's gone wild." Also true. "I was wondering what it looked like when it bloomed earlier in the year." Still true. Judith had noticed the tall, gangly bush, along with a couple of trees she couldn't identify.

Glenn's face was impassive. "What size shoe do you wear?"

"A ten." Judith knew what was coming next. "I was wearing these shoes yesterday." She pointed to her black loafers. "Do you want them?"

"Yes," Glenn said. "We'd like to make a cast."

Judith started to refuse, then reconsidered. The cast would prove that she'd gone to the front door. But she hadn't walked behind her car while it was parked in the alley.

"Go ahead," she said, slipping the shoes off and handing them over. "But I want these back as soon as possible. I have an artificial hip, and there are only certain kinds I can wear because I can't bend down too far."

"Pity," Glenn commented in an indifferent tone. He turned to Trash. "Bag them."

"Do you want me to shine 'em, too?" Trash grumbled.

"See here," Judith said, "the least you can do is tell me about the Blands. Are they elderly? Are they ill? Why have they let that house go to pot in the last half century? They had to be young when they moved in."

A gleam of amusement shined in Glenn's gray eyes. "My, my, Mrs. Flynn, you seem to be holding up remarkably well for a woman with a dread disease. Are you sure you don't want to rest now?"

"I'm having one of my good days," Judith asserted. "Come on, please tell me what they're like. And," she added a bit slyly, "who lives with them."

"They're quite old," Glenn replied.

"Older than dirt," Trash muttered, stuffing Judith's shoes into an evidence bag.

"But," Glenn went on, "they seem in relatively good health."

"For a couple of drunks," Trash put in.

Glenn gave his partner a warning look. "I believe Mrs. Bland may have a drinking problem. Or perhaps it's her inner ear. She doesn't have very good balance."

"And what about the third party?" Judith pressed.

"That would be Mrs. Bland's sister," Glenn replied. "She's elderly, too, though in rather good shape. Sprightly, you might say."

"Does she have a name?" Judith asked.

"Yes." Glenn gave Judith a nasty smile. "We'll be going now, Mrs. Flynn. Thank you for your time." He started for the parlor door that led into the entry hall. "And remember, stay within reach. Easy reach, that is."

"I have to," Judith said. "You've got my shoes."

SIX

As soon as Glenn and Trash had left, Judith called Renie. "How's Bucky?"

"He went away," Renie replied. "He said he didn't give a dam. Ha-ha."

"So you've finished the Wirehoser project?" Judith inquired.

"For now. They may require some changes. Most executives do, if only because they want to think they've made a contribution, other than cheating at golf or cooking the books."

"Can you come with me to Moonfleet Street? I want to meet the Blands."

"Jeez." Renie paused for almost a full minute. Stentorian moans and groans could be heard in the background. Bill uttered a few feeble monosyllables. "Which pills?" Renie inquired, away from the phone. "The mauve, the baby blue, the orange, or the yellow one shaped like a PEZ?"

Bill's voice grew stronger. "That *was* a PEZ you gave me," he shot back.

"Did it help?" Renie asked.

Some obscenities emanated from Renie's husband; Judith filtered them out to hear that Bill wanted the orange pill. Two, in fact.

"I'm not sure I can get away right now," Renie finally said to Judith. "Bill is near death. Can you hear him?"

"I could probably hear him without the phone," Judith remarked. "Dare I ask how he's feeling?"

"No," said Renie. "What's worse, he didn't like the snack I bought for him. He fed it to Oscar."

Oscar was the Joneses' stuffed ape, who had sat in splendor on the arm of their sofa for going on thirty years. Bill and Oscar shared a special bond, including Victoria's Secret catalogs and X-rated movies on premium cable. Renie humored both husband and ape. Her own in-house obsession was Clarence, a dwarf lop bunny that roamed free in the basement. The bunny had a varied wardrobe, including an angel costume with wings, a tutu, a smoking jacket, and bathing trunks. The only problem was that Clarence preferred eating his clothes instead of wearing them.

"Can you drive us?" Judith inquired.

"No," Renie replied as Bill bellowed from the living room. "I'm getting the damned pills," she informed her husband. "I'm on my way upstairs. Can't you see me? The moving feet on the steps are attached to the rest of my body." She spoke again into the phone. "Bill has a doctor's appointment at one. Why can't you drive Joe's MG and pick me up?"

"It scares me to drive that car," Judith admitted. "He's had it a lot longer than he's had me. He's so fussy that I don't think I've driven it more than twice since we got married. Besides, it's got a stick shift."

"Don't be silly," Renie said. "Driving a stick is like riding a bicycle. You never forget how to do it. We're only going a couple of miles to Langford. But what makes you think you'll be able to meet Dick and Jane Bland?"

Judith told Renie about the visit from Glenn Morris and Jonathan Trashman. "It's not fair," Judith griped. "They didn't even know about the Blands until yesterday, and now they can see them anytime they want. I'd be surprised if either of those two jerks has any idea of the house's history."

"Or its atmosphere," Renie noted. "Okay, I'm more or less conscious since it's well after ten. You know the old song—'Waking Up Is Hard to Do.' What time do we go?"

"An hour? I still have guests. By the way, did you see the brief article in the paper this morning?"

"Yes," Renie replied. "It didn't say much, just that a deliveryman from the Langford neighborhood had been found dead in the trunk of a car on Heraldsgate Hill. No names, including yours."

"They didn't even say he was murdered," Judith said. "I suppose they hadn't finished the autopsy before the newspaper deadline. All they mentioned was that foul play hadn't been ruled out."

"Now that we have two morning papers instead of only one and no evening edition, we get shortchanged," Renie complained. "The deadlines must be for around six in the evening. Maybe I should start watching the news on TV. Of course, I'm not up early enough to see it."

"But you're definitely awake now?" Judith queried.

"We're going to have to be on our toes when we try to see the Blands."

"Oh, yeah," Renie answered. "I have been, for about the last fifteen minutes. It took a while, though. I poured milk on Bill's grapefruit. Unfortunately, he was eating it at the time."

The cousins agreed on leaving at eleven-thirty. When Renie got into the MG, she broached the obvious question.

"How are we going to meet Dick and Jane? By claiming that Spot and Puff are running amok in their yard?"

"I'm working on it," Judith said, struggling with the MG's gearshift. "Just follow my lead."

The sun, which had sneaked a peek at the city earlier in the morning, had now gone behind dark clouds. Renie, however, kept her sunglasses on. Not only did she have a chronic eye problem, she was a typical Pacific Northwest resident who insisted she was so unused to the sun that its irregular appearances bothered her eyes. Judith never argued. They lived in a city that bought more sunglasses per capita than any other place in the United States. Renie referred to the locals—especially the natives—as Mole People.

As the cousins crossed the bridge over the ship canal, they could barely see the foothills, let alone the two mountain ranges that flanked the metropolitan area. Summer was only a day away, but it felt more like January.

Judith drove slowly and carefully along the narrow residential streets. To her surprise, orange cones and wooden sawhorses barricaded both ends of Moonfleet

Street, blocking off the property from east to west. There was yellow tape starting at the wire fence and apparently encircling the entire grounds.

"This isn't going to be easy," she said with a grim expression. "I'm trying to think of a plausible excuse to get us inside the house."

"Termite inspectors?" Renie suggested. "Jehovah's Witnesses? Campfire Girls?"

Judith found a parking place around the corner of the block where the brusque neighbor lived. "I don't see any police cars," she said, "not even the unmarked kind. I can't quite figure this. If Glenn and Trash believe me—*big if*—then they're assuming that Vern Benson was killed on the Blands' property. Or if he wasn't murdered on the site, his body was put in my trunk while I was parked at the end of the alley. The Blands—as well as Mrs. Bland's sister—could be suspects, too. It looks like the police are considering this a crime scene. But it doesn't appear that any cops are on duty. They probably patrol frequently, though." Judith chewed on her thumbnail, a childhood habit she'd never overcome. "Thus we become the police."

Renie shook her head. "That's a crime. It's called 'impersonating a police officer.' "

"I didn't say what kind of police, did I?" Judith responded.

"Swell." Renie brightened. "Why police? Why not investigative reporters? You're FATSO, aren't you?"

The nickname was a corruption of FASTO, Female Amateur Sleuth Tracking Offenders. Some locals who had admired Judith's publicized skills in uncovering a murder on Heraldsgate Hill had created a Web site featuring her abilities as an amateur sleuth. Somehow, FASTO had turned into FATSO. It rankled Judith, who had fought a weight problem for years. The entire notion of the Web site also annoyed her to the point that she never ever looked at it. It was tempting, however, in that she had managed to lose twenty pounds in the past two years—not by dieting, but by wearing herself out while trying to recover from hip surgery and keep the B&B running.

"Maybe you're right," she conceded. "Have you got a notepad?"

"I think so," Renie replied, digging and delving into her huge purse. "Yes. It's kind of beat-up, but it'll do."

"It'd help if we had their phone number," Judith said as she got out of the MG.

"We don't," Renie said. "It's unlisted, remember?"

"Of course." Judith examined the car from every angle, making sure that there was sufficient space in front and in back of Joe's precious classic automobile. "Does it look safe?"

"You're no more than an inch from the curb," Renie noted.

"Okay." The cousins crossed the street. "Have you noticed," Judith said as they started down the sidewalk, "how Glenn hardly lets Trash speak?"

"Yes," Renie said. "If Trash wasn't such a bigmouth, you wouldn't know Glenn had a partner. The man's all ego."

"Plus, Trash seems like a screwup," Judith pointed out. "I have a feeling he's been passed around from partner to partner. I suppose you can't blame Glenn in a way. The police have to be so careful these days about how they interrogate witnesses. And suspects, of course."

Approaching the yellow tape, Judith paused. "This may be a wasted effort. I have a feeling they won't answer the door."

"Let's hope they do," Renie said, looking up at the low gray clouds. "It's starting to rain."

Judith lifted the tape just enough so that the cousins could duck under it. By the time they went up the path and reached the porch, the rain was coming down much harder than usual.

"This is a downpour," Judith declared. "We certainly get some weird weather in June."

"It's turning into hail," Renie declared as frozen drops bounced off the porch steps and the barren ground. "It shouldn't last long."

Judith banged the knocker three times. Nothing happened. She banged again. No response.

"You're not loud enough," Renie asserted. Disregarding her bad shoulder, she whacked the knocker so hard that Judith's ears rang.

The cousins waited as the hail pelted down and the temperature seemed to drop twenty degrees.

"They won't answer," Judith said with a shake of her head.

But she'd barely finished speaking when the door opened a scant two inches.

"What it is?" a high-pitched female voice demanded.

Before Judith could speak, Renie leaned closer to the door. "We want to offer you money," she said.

The door opened another inch. "For what?" the woman inquired, sounding suspicious.

"For your story," Renie replied. "We're freelance journalists. We have an opportunity to sell an article about what happened here. Do you mind discussing our proposal?"

"Yes. I mind very much." But the door opened another three inches.

To Judith's surprise, the woman was in her forties, blond, trim, with small, precise features, and wearing a tailored linen suit.

"It won't take long," Renie said. "We'll focus on what it's like to be innocent bystanders in what appears to be a murder case."

"I'm not a bystander," the woman said. "I don't live here."

Thinking quickly, Judith relied on her patented logic. "You're the daughter-in-law, right?"

The other woman looked surprised. "Yes. I'm Lynette Bland. How did you know?"

Judith shrugged. "Who else could you be? You're on your lunch hour, I assume. As my . . . colleague mentioned, we won't take long. I'm sure your in-laws would want you to hear about this opportunity."

Lynette Bland tapped her foot on the tile floor. "Possibly." She hesitated, assessing the weather. The hail was turning back into rain, leaving the front yard dusted with melting pellets. "Okay, come inside. But all I can give you is five minutes."

Judith felt as if she were entering the Holy of Holies. But Lynette stopped just inside the gloomy entry hall.

"Let's hear it," Lynette said, folding her arms across her chest and leaning up against the stucco wall. As far as Judith could tell, the entrance area was bare except for a quartet of wrought-iron wall sconces with unlighted flame-shaped bulbs.

"How are Mr. and Mrs. Bland doing?" Renie inquired. "This situation must be hard on them at their age."

"Frankly," Lynette replied, "they aren't paying much attention to it. Why should they? It has nothing to do with them."

"Does Mrs. Bland's sister feel the same way?" Judith asked.

An ironic expression flitted across Lynette's face. "She ignores intrusions from the outside world. It's her way of coping."

Judith was about to ask why she needed isolation in order to cope, but Lynette wasn't finished. "So what's your proposal? You have four minutes left."

Renie took a deep breath. "Okay. Here it is. We interview Mr. and Mrs. Bland and Mrs. Bland's sister—" Renie stopped. "I'm sorry, I don't know her name."

"Sally Steiner," Lynette said. "Go on."

"Mrs.?" Renie queried.

"Yes. She's a widow."

"We'll ask them what it's like to have this invasion of their routine," Renie continued. "I gather they're up in years, and probably lead a quiet life. Suddenly this random act occurs, apparently on their property. Do they feel threatened? Fearful? Indifferent? Excited? Intrigued?"

Lynette glanced at her watch, which looked expensive. "You have three minutes."

Judith had the impression that Renie's approach

was a flop. "We're aiming the article for the senior citizen market," Judith broke in. "Like AARP or URP."

Lynette frowned. "URP? I never heard of it."

"United Retired Persons," Judith replied. "There are many organizations that are lesser known than AARP, but their publications still pay decently."

Lynette's hazel eyes narrowed. "How much?"

"We can't say," Renie replied. "It depends on the buyer. Of course, if we get into a bidding war . . ." She raised her hand and wiggled it in an upward motion.

"I'll have to talk to them," Lynette said without enthusiasm. "They're very private people. They had to be coaxed into speaking to the police."

"All three of them?" Judith said. "Goodness, you'd think at least one of your relatives would be more . . . social."

"They aren't," Lynette declared, with another look at her watch. "Time's up. Don't call me, I'll call you."

Renie scribbled both of the cousins' names and phone numbers on a sheet of her mangled notebook. "Here. My home phone is also my work phone. I'm listed under CaJones Designs."

"I thought you were a writer," Lynette said, still suspicious.

"I'm the artist." Renie pointed to Judith. "Mrs. Flynn's the writer. She's very good at fiction."

"Hunh." Lynette studied the phone numbers. "I'll let you know if they're interested. Good-bye."

"Maybe we should have been the cops," Renie muttered as they walked through the heavy rain. "My idea sucked scissors."

"Not completely," Judith said. "At least we got inside the house and we met a family member. We also learned the name of Mrs. Bland's sister, the alleged drinker. That's a start."

"Now what?" Renie inquired as they crossed the street.

"As long as we're this close," Judith replied, "maybe we should swing by Uncle Al's and see how Mike and the boys are doing."

"Uncle Al's probably teaching Mac and Joe-Joe how to handicap the horse races," Renie said as they got into the car. "It's your call."

Judith inspected the MG before getting in. Heaven help her if another vehicle had sideswiped Joe's car. But its red exterior looked as pristine as ever. "Okay," she said. "Let's go."

They'd driven five blocks when Judith spotted a Dairyland truck parked in the middle of the block. The milkman was going up the front steps of a house with a rose-covered trellis.

"Let's have a little talk with him," Judith said, carefully pulling into the house's driveway. "He must have known Vern Benson."

Renie, who seemed to be in one of her more affable moods, shrugged. "Go ahead. I'll stay in the car. It's still raining, and I might shrink. I'm already small enough."

The rain, however, was dwindling into a mere drizzle. Indeed, there were patches of sun in the western sky. Judith almost expected to see a rainbow.

"Hi," she called out as the milkman made his return journey to the truck. "I'm Judith Flynn. My uncle lives about six blocks from here. He saw the brief article in the paper this morning about one of Dairyland's employees getting killed on this route."

The milkman, who didn't have his name stitched on his blue jacket, grimaced. "I'm not supposed to talk about it. All of the Dairyland employees have been warned to keep quiet while the investigation's under way."

"Oh, of course," Judith said, looking sympathetic. "I should have realized that." She tried to think of some way to get the young man to open up, but nothing clever came to mind. He seemed like the earnest type, with his clear blue eyes, square jaw, and sandy crew cut. "Well. Please convey my condolences to Vern Benson's family."

The milkman winced slightly. "Thanks, but there's no need." The hint of a smile played at his mouth. "You see, *I'm* Vern Benson."

SEVEN

JUDITH WAS SPEECHLESS. "I d-d-don't understand," she stammered at last. "I th-th-thought . . ." Raking a hand through her salt-and-pepper hair, she stared at the young man in confusion.

"I'm sorry, ma'am," the milkman said. "Honest, I can't talk about it."

Judith decided to go on offense. "How do I know you're Vern Benson?" she demanded, and pointed to his jacket. "You don't have your name sewn on. You could be an impostor. How do I even know you're a milkman?"

Renie, aware that something extraordinary was happening, had gotten out of the MG.

"Somebody peddling phony buttermilk around here?" she inquired.

Judith turned to her cousin. "This person claims he's the late Vern Benson."

Renie looked startled. "That's impossible. Vern Benson is dead as a dodo."

"So if you insist you're Vern Benson, prove it," Judith challenged.

The young man looked miserable. "I can't. All my—" He cut himself off. "I just can't."

A light went on in Judith's brain. "Is that because someone stole your wallet, your driver's license, your jacket, and maybe even your truck?"

Several emotions seemed to cross the self-proclaimed Vern Benson's face. Finally, he spoke. "I can't talk about any of this."

Renie pointed to the truck. "If I were to hop inside and check the registration, would it be made out to somebody other than Vern Benson?"

The young man sighed. "Yes. I can't drive my own truck today." Suddenly he brightened. "Hey—I *can* prove I'm Vern Benson. Hold on." He fairly galloped down the street and zipped up the stairs to a small brown house with beige trim. The cousins trailed behind him. A few moments later, the front door was opened by a stout, white-haired woman.

"I was just coming out to get my milk," the woman said. "Did you forget something, Vern?"

"No, Mrs. Harmon," he said with a big grin. "Just tell these ladies who I am."

Mrs. Harmon stared at Judith and Renie. "Why do they want to know? Are they on your route?"

"I can't explain exactly," Vern replied. "Just tell them."

Mrs. Harmon eyed the cousins with suspicion. "This is Vern Benson. He's been my milkman for the past two years. He and his wife, Cindy, had a darling baby boy last month. Vern showed me pictures."

Judith gave both Vern and Mrs. Harmon a sheepish smile. "Thank you. I'm sorry for the trouble. It's just that Vern looked so much like—"

"He looks like Vern to me," Mrs. Harmon snapped. "What's going on in this neighborhood lately? First, the police going by, not just one car, but two or three. Then I walk my little dog, Doodle, this morning, and there's that yellow tape around that wreck of a house where the Blands live. Now you two, acting as if Vern were some kind of impostor. I've lived here for over fifty years, and I've never seen the like."

As Vern returned to the sidewalk, Judith held out her hand. "I feel terrible," she declared. "Please forgive me. I'm going to send you a baby present care of Dairyland to make up for being such a nuisance."

"Oh," Vern said with an awkward little laugh, "that's not necessary. But we could use another fitted crib sheet."

"Done," Judith said. "I'll send two." She shook Vern's hand before he hurried back to the truck.

"I'll pay for one of them," Renie said. "We can order them online and save a trip to Babies Be Wee."

"Fine." But Judith wasn't thinking about baby gifts. Rather, she was looking up at the brown-and-beige house. Mrs. Harmon had gone inside, but Judith had a feeling she was still watching the cousins. "Maybe we've just been given an opportunity."

"Mrs. Harmon?" Renie glanced at the house. "Hold it. I didn't catch everything that went on with you and the real Vern. What do you figure? The dead guy stole his truck and uniform and delivered something other than milk to the Blands?"

"Possibly," Judith allowed. "Or he went to collect. But what and why?"

"Did you see him deliver the milk?" Renie asked.

Judith shook her head. "No. He was coming back with an empty carrier. But he reeled off a list of items the Blands had ordered. Or that he claimed they ordered." She looked again at Mrs. Harmon's house, with its colorful splash of snapdragons and marigolds. The rain had stopped and the sun was peeking out from behind drifting clouds. "Come on, let's apologize."

"I thought you wanted to see how Mike and the kids were getting along," Renie said.

"I do. I will. But," she went on, "I can't dwell on them. It breaks my heart. Mike and Kristin have to solve their problems themselves. They know that Joe and I love them, but we can't interfere, especially these first few days."

Judith had already started for Mrs. Harmon's front door. Renie trotted along behind her. "Not to mention that you're a suspect," Renie noted. "Okay, I suppose you'll be more help to Mike and Kristin if you're not behind bars."

"You got that right," Judith said, ringing the doorbell.

Mrs. Harmon answered almost immediately, indicating that she had kept her eye on Judith and Renie all along.

"This is awkward," Judith said with an apologetic expression. "May we come in and explain ourselves?"

Mrs. Harmon surveyed her uninvited guests from head to toe. "You look harmless enough," she murmured as a black-and-white Pekingese with floppy ears came running to the door and began to bark. "Who are you?"

Judith introduced herself and Renie. "We grew up in this neighborhood," she said. "Our uncle still lives here. Al Grover. Do you know him?"

A twinkle came into Mrs. Harmon's blue eyes. "Al? That scamp! I've known Al Grover forever. Does he still ride in the sheriff's posse parades?"

"Not lately," Judith replied, relieved at making a connection. "But he keeps busy."

"Playing the ponies, no doubt," Mrs. Harmon replied, ushering the cousins inside and shushing the dog. "My late husband and I owned the little grocery store three blocks from here on the corner. It's a dry cleaners now, but Al used to buy his racing forms from us. He always made Jess and me laugh. Such a kidder!"

"I remember your store," Renie put in. "When I was a kid, I bought comic books there."

For the next five minutes, the cousins and Mrs. Harmon reminisced about the old days and how much the neighborhood had changed. Mrs. Harmon recalled Cliff and Deborah Grover.

"You were a skinny little thing with such big teeth," Mrs. Harmon said to Renie. "Looks like you've still got them."

Judith was growing impatient to steer the conversation around to the Blands. "Tell Mrs. Harmon about your fascination for the Bland house, coz," Judith said, nudging Renie, who was sitting next to her on a chintz-covered couch in the small but tidy living room.

Renie took the suggestion and ran with it. "Then," she said, "I managed to get Judith interested, too."

She paused. Judith understood why. Renie wasn't sure if she should reveal what a strange twist Judith's interest had taken.

Judith, however, felt there was no point in withholding the truth. She told Mrs. Harmon the entire story, bringing it up to the point where she'd accosted Vern Benson on the sidewalk.

Mrs. Harmon listened with only minor interruptions, including a couple of admonishments for Doodle, who seemed fascinated with Renie's purse. Instead of shock or even surprise, the old lady absorbed the information as if she'd heard far more outlandish tales in her time. Which, Judith realized, she probably had.

"My, my," Mrs. Harmon said with a sigh. "There was a mention of a body in a car trunk on TV last night, but it was very brief, and I didn't pay much attention. It didn't happen in our neighborhood, after all. I'm afraid that as I get older, I become more isolated from the rest of the city." She offered the cousins an apologetic look. "There's so much evil these days, you become hardened to it. Crime. Violence. Murder. Robbery." She sighed heavily. "Jess and I were held up three times in four years." She glanced at Renie. "Not while you lived here, but later. That's why we finally decided to give up the store almost twenty years ago. The new owners couldn't keep it going. So the dry cleaners moved in. Anyway, I can see why you'd be fascinated by the Bland house. We were, too. We'd take walks—Jess and I were always great walkers—and we'd often go by it. They moved in before we did. The first few times we went by, the house was very nice—beautiful, really, and so unusual for this neighborhood. There was a greenhouse and a pond and such lovely plantings. But after a time, it all began to go downhill."

"When would that have been?" Judith inquired.

Mrs. Harmon smoothed one of the crocheted antimacassars on the arm of her chair. "We moved here in '51. I heard the Blands had bought their house in '47, '48, not long after the war. As I recall, it was only a year or two after we moved to Langford that the place began to deteriorate."

"Did you know Mr. and Mrs. Bland?" Renie asked.

Mrs. Harmon chuckled softly. "I never met them. But they had two children—a boy and a girl—who went to school with our twins. I think one of them was adopted. That's the reason I know the name. Nice children, but quiet. They never played with our kids. But then we were a few blocks away, and ours were in between the Blands'."

"I mentioned," Judith put in, "that we met Lynette. She must be married to the son."

"Yes," Mrs. Harmon replied. "Yes. Now what was his name? Something biblical . . . Matthew, Mark . . . No, Luke. That's right, Luke Bland." She laughed, a merry sound. "It's coming back to me now. Luke was adopted. Now this is all hearsay, of course, from the other parents in PTA. I believe Mr. Bland served in World War Two. Mrs. Hermanson—or was it Mrs. Bruce? Anyway, whoever it was told me that Mr. Bland had been wounded in the war and couldn't have children. That's why they adopted. Then, when our twins were in second grade, the Blands had a baby girl. Unless there was some monkeyshines on Mrs. Bland's part, I guess it was just neighborhood gossip about Mr. Bland. He was wounded, though." She paused, holding up one finger. "Ah. I remember now. Anna, that was the daughter's name. I've no idea what became of her. Our Sharon and Roy were out of grade school before she entered kindergarten." Mrs. Harmon scooted forward in the armchair. "Could I make you some tea? Or coffee?"

"No thank you," Judith replied. "We should be heading for Uncle Al's shortly. Tell me, do you know if Mr. Bland had a job?"

"No, I don't." Mrs. Harmon settled back in the chair. "He may not have. It's possible that he had a disability pension from the army."

"Weird," Renie remarked, shaking her head. "Surely the neighbors must have speculated about why the Blands were such recluses. Not to mention why they let such a lovely house deteriorate."

"Of course the neighbors talked," Mrs. Harmon agreed. "At least, at first. Everybody had a theory. But that's what they were—theories. Like the army pension. If that's all they had in the way of income, they couldn't keep up such a grand house. Some thought they took in boarders. I understand someone else has been living there for quite a while. A few gossiped about a drinking problem. My husband figured there was money in the family, but either it wasn't enough to maintain the house or else they were just plain lazy."

"They had to shop for groceries," Judith pointed out. "Didn't anyone ever see them coming in or out?"

Mrs. Harmon smiled sadly. "Maybe the old-timers did. But most of them are gone now, in retirement or nursing homes—or passed away. The neighborhood has changed a great deal in fifty years."

"Except for the Blands," Renie said.

"Isn't that the truth?" Mrs. Harmon sighed. "I didn't

hear all of the gossip, of course. You must remember, I'm several blocks away. And if I'd seen them at the grocery store, I wouldn't have recognized them."

Judith started to rise from the sofa. It was very deep and very comfortable, but not easy to get out of with hip problems. "Do you know anyone near the Bland house who has been around for the past fifty years?"

"Oh, dear—let me see." Mrs. Harmon also rose as Renie gave Judith a shove. "Yes, Mrs. Bruce. Elsie Bruce. She must be almost ninety and is very crippled with arthritis. She has help, or she couldn't stay in her own home. And believe me, Elsie isn't going anywhere else until they take her to the mortuary."

"Do you know her address?" Judith inquired.

"I can look it up." Mrs. Harmon bent down to reach into a shelf on the end table. "Let me think—Elsie's husband has been dead for years, but his name was Elmer," she said, flipping through the White Pages. "I imagine she's kept the listing that way. Elsie's not one for change. Yes, here it is—Elmer Bruce, twenty-oh-nine. Do you want the number?"

Renie got out her notebook. "That'd be great."

Mrs. Harmon recited the phone number, but added a caution. "She's very deaf. We both attended the Presbyterian church, but she can't go to services anymore. She hasn't, for close to ten years, but she was deaf even then."

Offering their profuse thanks, the cousins made their exit. Behind the wheel of the MG, Judith cogitated. "Uncle Al or Mrs. Bruce?" She grimaced. "Uncle Al, for now. But we won't stay long."

Their visit was shorter than they'd expected. No one

was home at Uncle Al's, and Mike's Range Rover was nowhere in sight.

"I'll bet they went out for lunch," Judith said.

Renie suddenly looked wistful. "Speaking of which, I'm kind of hungry."

Judith frowned at her cousin. "Since when are you not?" Renie was one of those annoying people whose metabolism allowed her to eat like a pig and never gain weight. "We'll pick up burgers and fries at Doc's Drive-in. I'd like to call on Mrs. Bruce before I head home to get ready for tonight's guests."

"I want a vanilla shake, too," Renie said, pouting just a bit. "Maybe two hamburgers."

"Fine, but don't you dare trash Joe's car," Judith warned.

It was still the lunch hour when the cousins pulled into the drive-in that had been a landmark for almost fifty years in Langford. The lines were long.

"Let me do this," Renie said. "What do you want?"

"A plain burger and fries," Judith replied.

"Okay. Keep the motor running and watch this."

Renie got out of the car, walked toward the busy windows, and held up both hands. "Free Megabucks tickets across the street! Five minutes only! Don't miss out!"

All but three people turned to look at the convenience store across Langford's busy main artery. Sure enough, there was a partly visible banner over the store's entrance that read Free Mega . . . The mob took off like a shot, practically falling all over themselves to get to the crosswalk at the corner. Renie scooted up to the nearest vacant window and put in her order.

"Are they really handing out free Megabucks lottery tickets at the convenience store?" the teenage boy with purple hair asked Renie after he'd called out her request.

Renie turned around. The customers who had raced off were all standing at the corner, frantically pushing the "Walk" button on the traffic control post.

"Hunh," she said to the young man. "I guess I made a mistake. It says 'Free Megaphones.' I think I heard about that. It's a promotion for the baseball team."

Doc's fast food was really fast, one of the reasons the drive-in had prospered for almost half a century. Renie's order was up just as the light finally changed and the crowd started racing across the street.

"Thanks," she said, and ran back to the car. "Hit it," she ordered Judith.

After a brief glitch trying to shift into reverse, Judith sped out of the parking lot and down the side street. In the rearview mirror, she could see the now-irate customers storming around in front of the convenience store.

"Ah," Renie said complacently. "Food. Pull over when we get around the corner. We want to eat this while it's hot. Otherwise, the fries go limp."

"What," Judith asked as she found a parking place under a big maple tree, "would you have done if they hadn't fallen for your ruse?"

Renie paid no heed to the lettuce that had dropped onto her faded tee. "I suppose I'd have had to stand in line with the rest of the suckers. By the way, did you notice one of the three people who didn't rush off?"

Judith shook her head. "I was too busy watching the ones who did—and you."

Renie giggled, causing her to spew out a couple of diced onions. "Morty the Mailman. He was reading somebody's *Sports Illustrated* while he was in line."

"Morty," Judith murmured, tapping her fingers on the steering wheel. "I wish he'd been more helpful."

"I wish he'd retired," Renie said, sprinkling salt on her fries. "Like forty years ago."

"Still . . ." Judith let the sentence trail off. Morty hadn't been on the Moonfleet route for all that long. Maybe he honestly didn't have any information. He certainly wasn't the curious type.

"I'm done," Judith declared, wiping off her hands with a paper napkin. "You can finish my fries, along with the rest of your large quantity of food. We have to get going."

The cousins were only about six blocks from Mrs. Bruce's house, but they took a longer route to ensure that nobody coming from the drive-in would see them. Joe's MG was too easily identifiable. Judith had visions of a wild-eyed mob descending upon them and wreaking havoc with the car. And with the cousins.

Twenty-oh-nine Moonfleet was on the southwest corner, across the street from the Bland house. Elsie Bruce's home was a modest brick Tudor, showing signs of genteel neglect.

A plump, pretty Hispanic woman with a dish towel over her arm came to the door. *"Hola, señoras."*

"Is Mrs. Bruce at home?" Judith asked.

"Sí," the woman replied but didn't budge.

"May we talk to her?" Judith inquired. "I'm Mrs. Flynn and this is Mrs. Jones."

"Sí," the woman repeated, and still made no move.

Renie cranked up her rusty Spanish. *"Donde está Señora Bruce?"*

"Aquí," the woman said, stepping aside and pointing to a sitting room just off the hall.

"Gracias," Renie responded as the cousins entered the small, cluttered room where a TV was tuned into one of the shopping channels.

"Hello," Judith said in her friendliest voice.

Mrs. Bruce, who was small and wizened, didn't move. There was no sound coming from the TV set. Noticing the old lady's hearing aids and remembering that Mrs. Harmon had said Elsie was deaf, Judith raised her voice several notches.

"Hallooo!"

Elsie turned slowly. She straightened her glasses and adjusted the afghan on her lap. "What?"

Judith moved to stand in front of Elsie and leaned down so that their faces were practically touching. "I'm Judith." She pointed to Renie. "This is my cousin, Serena."

Elsie made a shooing gesture with one of her hands. "I can't see the TV," she declared in an irritable voice. "I want that ruby ring. Teresa, write that down." Elsie tried to peer around the cousins. "Where's Teresa? I want that ruby!"

"Aquí, señora," Teresa said, moving into Elsie's range of vision.

"The ring, Teresa! Call them! Act now!" The old lady pointed to an 800 number at the bottom of the screen. "Hurry up! They may sell out."

"Sí, señora," Teresa replied, and hurried out of the room.

"Stupid girl," Elsie muttered. "She'll get it all mixed up, as usual. She can hardly speak a word of English. Ah!" She pointed again at the screen. "Pearls! I adore pearls! Take down that number."

"It's the same one," Renie pointed out, all but shouting. "Shall I tell Teresa to order the pearls, too?"

"Yes, be quick." She dismissed Renie with a wave of her hand.

Fortuitously, the channel went to a commercial break. "I'd like to ask you some questions about your neighbors the Blands," Judith said, pulling up an ancient armless rocker next to Elsie's chair.

"Bands? What bands?" Elsie looked mystified.

"Blands," Judith said loudly.

Elsie merely stared at Judith. "You're mumbling," she finally said.

"I can't keep screaming at you," Judith asserted. She pointed to Elsie's hearing aids. "Are they turned on?"

"What?" Elsie scowled at Judith. She fiddled with the devices. "Hunh. I guess I turned them off. I don't need to hear when I watch TV. And I don't need to hear Teresa, either. She won't speak English. Imagine!" She stared at Judith with filmy blue eyes. "Who are you? An undertaker selling plots? A social worker? A burglar?"

Renie had come back into the room. There were no other chairs, so she leaned against the wall.

"My cousin and I are interested in the Spanish-style house across the street," Judith said. "Do you know the owners?"

"Those snobs?" Elsie sneered. "No, and I don't want to. They keep to themselves and that's fine with me.

They drink. The Lord abhors drunkenness. I see the police were there yesterday. I hope they arrested the lot of them. It's a good thing Arthur's dead. He was the only decent one in the family."

"Arthur?" Judith echoed.

"Yes, Arthur, Arthur Craig." Elsie scowled at Judith. "Are you deaf? Arthur was married to Anna. Died young about fifteen years ago. He couldn't have been more than thirty."

"Was it an accident?" Judith inquired.

"So they said," Elsie replied, her gaze again fixed on the TV screen. "Diamonds! Five carats! Teresa!"

"I'll tell her," Renie volunteered with a wink for Judith.

"What kind of accident?" Judith asked after Renie left the room.

"Arthur drowned." Elsie paused, admiring the twinkling stone on TV.

"A boating mishap?" Judith suggested.

"Ha! Where would Arthur get a boat? He drowned in the fishpond by the house." Elsie removed her glasses, exhaled on the lenses, and wiped them clean with a handkerchief. "The fishpond's gone now. The Blands never tended to it, or to much of anything else. That's why their place is such a wreck. Dirty, too. I've seen the exterminator there twice in the past year or so. Rats, if you ask me. And why not? The place is so overgrown, they could have a zoo living behind those big fences. Oh, I know my house is a little run-down, but I do what I can to keep it from falling apart. Those Blands—they never cared."

"Do you know Arthur's wife, Anna?" Judith asked.

Elsie wrinkled her nose. "Anna was always a spoiled brat. Fancies herself a fashion plate. She's some kind of buyer for Nordquist's. The second time around, she married a man named Philip French. Sinister fellow, if you ask me."

"What about Lynette?"

"Cold. Distant. Selfish." Elsie cocked her head to one side. "You're not asking me about the house. You're asking about the family. Come clean." With effort, she moved around in the chair and eyed Renie, who had just returned from her latest errand. "And clean up. You've got garbage all over your bosom."

Renie offered the old lady a strained smile as she haphazardly brushed off her tee. "People *are* houses," Renie said. "If somebody other than the Blands lived across the street, it could be a showplace."

Elsie considered Renie's words. "Yes, that's so. But I still don't—" She halted for a moment. "Go on, I'm not trying to get rid of you."

Judith assumed that the old lady was happy to have company, especially guests who seemed interested in her opinions. In fact, before Judith could speak again, Elsie said as much.

"I don't get many callers. Both my sons live out in the suburbs. Do you think they ever come into town? Too much traffic, they say. And the grandkids—they're all over the place, some with children of their own. What's all this soccer and swimming and gymnastics about? They want to be in the Olympics? Everybody's running around in circles. No time for old folks. Why can't children just *play* like we used to do? Or read. The Bookmobile still comes here, but it's getting so I can only read the large-print books. Maddy—the library lady—says I should try those Books on Tape things. I don't know—I've heard too much in my life already. A book, you can put it down. I don't want to fiddle with some crazy machine. I probably couldn't hear it anyway."

Judith was afraid the conversation was going too far afield. "I suppose," she said in an effort to steer Elsie back on track, "the Bland children aren't any better than most about calling on their parents."

"Oh . . ." Elsie again cocked her head to one side, eyes darting to the window that looked out onto Moonfleet Street. "They come by now and then. They never stay long, though. Who would want to in such a gloomy old house? I don't think those upstairs drapes have been opened in twenty years. They must be rotting to pieces. The downstairs isn't much better. If the sunlight ever got inside that place, it'd probably blind the whole bunch of them."

"But," Judith said, "you actually know the younger generation. Lynette, Anna, Philip, and . . . Did you mention Luke?"

"The son?" Elsie shook her head. "He's a bit touched, if you ask me. Always wears sunglasses, even when it's raining. Must think he looks like a movie star. Luke invents things."

"Such as what?" Renie inquired.

"I couldn't say. But that's what I've heard he does. Or does he develop things? I forget, something you can't put your finger on. Rube Goldberg contraptions, probably." Elsie sniffed with disdain. She pointed to the window that provided a sidelong view of the path to the front porch. "I see the young'uns coming and going once in a while. Alan—that's Lynette and Luke's son—he was here a week or so ago. I suppose he's close to thirty by now. When I could still work in the yard, I'd speak to them. I didn't care if they didn't want to speak to me. I call that bad manners, and I've no time for it." She looked at the back of her hands, which were covered with liver spots. "Luke was always polite, though. So was his son, Alan, even though he tended to be tongue-tied in his teens. Typical of adolescents."

"What about the older folks?" Renie asked. "Do you ever see them?"

"About once every five years," Elsie retorted. "Look! Sapphires! I've always wanted earrings like that! Go tell Teresa!"

Renie whisked around the corner, though there was no sound of her walking away. For the first time, Judith realized that Elsie Bruce wasn't wearing any jewelry, not even a wedding ring. Her joints were too swollen from arthritis, and the hearing aids would make it difficult to wear earrings. It was a game, harmless, and sad.

"What was I saying?" Elsie mused, her gaze still glued to the sapphires. "Oh—Dick and Jane Bland. Years would go by when I never saw them. Jane went from a willowy brunette to an overweight white-haired old lady. Dick was always nondescript, but when I did see him, little by little, he lost his hair. For a while, he had one of those terrible comb-overs. The next thing you know, he bought a toupee! Imagine! He looked like he was wearing a dead chipmunk on his head. Of course," she added on a gentler note, "I heard he had a terrible scar from the war. Shot by the Germans, just missing his brain. No doubt that's why he couldn't hold down a job. Sad, I suppose, but at least he got to come home, unlike so many of our other brave boys."

"What about Mrs. Bland's sister, Sally?" Renie asked as she reentered the sitting room.

Elsie bristled. "She moved in with them years ago, when the children were still small. A moocher, no doubt, though the few times I've seen her, she was all gussied up. I could see her jewelry from here. Why should she have all those emeralds and diamonds and such instead of me? I figure she married a rich man and was left a wealthy widow." Elsie leaned closer and lowered her voice. "Or a merry widow, maybe. Two, three times a long time ago I saw her sneak out at night and get picked up in fancy cars. Once, I saw her being dropped off in the wee small hours. What was I to think but that she was up to no good?"

"How recent was that?" Judith inquired.

Elsie made a feeble wave with her crippled right hand. "Five years ago? Ten? I lose track of time. I haven't seen any of the older bunch in maybe a year."

"What do you think they do inside all the time?" asked Renie.

Elsie sighed. "Who knows? I hardly ever see more than one light on at a time. Maybe they have séances. Maybe they really are all blind. Maybe they've turned into moles." She leaned forward in her chair. "Topaz! I love that color! It looks good enough to eat! Get Teresa."

The cousins decided they should also get going. Thanking Elsie Bruce, they headed for the front door, meeting Teresa on their way.

"Topaz this time," Renie said.

"Gotcha," Teresa replied.

Judith stared. "You speak English?"

"Sure," Teresa said with a puckish little smile. "I was born in Medford, Oregon."

"But," Judith began, "why do you pretend not to understand?"

"Because," Teresa said, still with the quirky smile, "it makes life easier."

Judith understood. "Does Mrs. Bruce ever ask what's happened to her jewelry orders?"

"Never." Teresa opened the door for the cousins. "She understands, too. And by the way," she went on, speaking to Judith, "I saw you at the Bland house yesterday. You had a different car, but I recognized you anyway. I don't know what you're really up to, but if I were you, I'd keep away from that Bland house."

"Why is that?" Judith asked.

Teresa's face grew solemn. "Don't ask. It's a scary place."

"Emeralds!" cried Elsie from inside the house.

"Sí, señora," Teresa called back. She lowered her voice and spoke to the cousins. "I'm not joking. Something strange is going on across the street. It's best that you forget all about it."

For Judith, the advice was worthless.

EIGHT

DOES TERESA KNOW more than she told us?" Renie asked as they headed back to Heraldsgate Hill.

"Yes," Judith said. "If she didn't, she wouldn't have warned us. We're going to have to get back to her. Meanwhile, our original mission has been thwarted. We may have learned a few things about the Blands, but except for Lynette, we still haven't met any of them."

"I have a feeling," Renie said, "that we never will. If it weren't for what those detectives told you about interviewing them, the Blands might not exist."

Judith, who had just turned onto the main thoroughfare that led across the bridge, darted a glance at Renie. "That's an interesting idea."

"Interesting, but unlikely," Renie said. "The cops wouldn't lie about it, and Mrs. Bruce sees them every now and then."

"She sees *somebody,*" Judith allowed. "Damn!" she burst out halfway across the bridge.

"Watch it, coz," Renie said in alarm. "You're almost in the other lane. What's wrong?"

Judith focused on her driving until they reached the turnoff to Heraldsgate Hill. "I'm an idiot," she declared as they reached the six-way stop. "Why didn't I look at the customs declaration slip on that UPS box? All I checked was the postmark, from Kopfstein in Austria. The form would have told me what was in the box."

"Which," Renie said dryly, "would have solved the entire mystery."

"Okay, maybe it wouldn't have," Judith said as they crossed the little bridge above the gully, "but it might have been a clue. Isn't it odd that UPS delivers to the Blands only once a year and always at the same time?"

"Odd?" Renie looked aghast. "It's unthinkable. If I didn't get a delivery from one of the stores or catalogs every week, life would have no meaning."

Judith had turned down Renie's street. "Oh? And who delivered that outfit you're wearing now? The Pony Express? It looks like it's been on the road a long time."

"You know I don't wear my good clothes except for business and social purposes," Renie countered. "I bought this tee for eight bucks ten years ago. As for the pants, somebody gave them to me."

"Who? Noah?"

"Funny coz," Renie murmured as Judith pulled up in front of the Joneses' Dutch Colonial. "I'm going inside and tend to my sickly spouse."

As she headed back to Hillside Manor, Judith's spirits plummeted. It wasn't likely that a doddering trio of senior citizens would kill a milkman. Or someone pretending to be a milkman. The real Vern Benson was a pleasant young man with a wife and baby. So why did the murder victim dress up like a Dairyland employee and make a stop at the Blands' house?

It made no sense. Had the Blands been younger, Judith would have considered that they could be involved in drug dealing.

But the Blands *had* been younger fifty years ago. Maybe they'd bought the Spanish-style house for that purpose. The city was a Pacific Rim seaport; drugs had been a problem for much longer than in other metropolitan areas. Renie recalled seeing a deal go down when she was barely in her teens.

Austria, however, seemed like an unlikely source. And what did the Blands do with the money they'd made? Not much, judging from the house and their reclusive lifestyle.

Judith was still mulling after she got home to find Gertrude in the kitchen, ransacking the refrigerator.

"Why did you get this great big stainless-steel piece of junk?" the old lady rasped. "It looks like a spaceship, and I can't find anything! Where's the dill pickles?"

"There's a big jar inside the door," Judith informed her mother.

"Where?" Gertrude leaned forward in her wheelchair. "Oh. Now, why would you put dill pickles *there*?"

"All the condiments are in the door," Judith pointed out. "Mustard, mayonnaise, olives, capers—"

"Capers!" Gertrude snarled. "Who wants to eat something that looks like dried-up dingleberries? Ugh!"

"I use them with lox and cream cheese," Judith explained. "They're really delicious."

"They can't be." Having taken two dill pickles out of the jar, Gertrude resumed rummaging in the fridge. "Where've you been? You forgot my lunch."

"Oh, Mother, I am sorry!" Judith apologized. "I've got too much on my mind."

"And not enough room for most of it," Gertrude snapped. "Somebody brought my lunch. Somebody didn't forget a poor old crippled woman. Somebody *cares.*"

"Who?" Judith inquired.

"Al and Mike and the grandkids, that's who," Gertrude replied, adding a couple of cheese slices to the plate in her lap. "They showed up about one with fish and chips. They'd been to the lake to feed the ducks."

"So that's where they were," Judith murmured. "Why are you eating now? It's only a little after two."

"Because I'm still hungry. Aha! Cantaloupe. Can you slice this for me?"

Judith complied. To her daughter's dismay, Gertrude shook at least two tablespoons of chocolate sprinkles on the cantaloupe. She was wheeling herself out the back way when the doorbell chimed. She stopped in the hall while her daughter answered the front door.

"We'd like you to come downtown," Glenn Morris announced without preamble.

"I can't," Judith protested. "I have guests coming in a couple of hours. In case you haven't noticed, this is a B&B."

"What's that stand for?" Trash put in. "At our house, it'd be Bed and Boredom."

"I'll bet it would," Judith retorted. "Really, if you

don't mind, I'd prefer answering your questions here. I honestly don't know what else I can tell you."

"Don't cause a problem," Glenn said without inflection. "You should know this is police procedure."

"Police?" Gertrude rolled into the entry hall. "What now, terrorists blowing up Rankerses' hedge?"

Judith put an arm around her mother's shoulders. "No. These two detectives think I killed a bogus milkman."

"Ridiculous!" Gertrude scoffed. "We don't have a milkman here. And what do you mean, 'bogus'?"

"The victim was posing as a milkman," Judith explained.

"Why would anybody do that?" Gertrude demanded. "That's hard work. Why not pose as a lawyer—or a policeman?"

Glenn was trying to ignore Gertrude. "Come along, Mrs. Flynn. We can't waste time arguing about this."

"Come along?" Gertrude snapped. "She's not coming along with you. She has to get my supper. If she goes, I go with her. She's my daughter. She does what I tell her to. You want two for the price of one?"

Clearly, the ultimatum gave Glenn pause. "It's not up to you to decide, Mrs. . . . ?"

"Grover. Gertrude Grover. I'm part of the Greatest Generation. You'd better not tangle with me, buster. We beat the pants off of Hitler." She turned in Trash's direction. "And stop looking at my pickles."

Glenn glanced at Trash, who seemed to be enjoying the confrontation immensely. "All right," Glenn said with a sigh. "But I don't like making exceptions. The living room or the parlor?"

"The parlor," Judith said. "But let me help Mother back into her apartment."

"Oh, no you don't!" Gertrude exclaimed. "I'm staying right here. I know about police brutality. I wouldn't abandon my little girl for anything."

Glenn didn't argue. Judith led the way into the parlor. Glenn positioned himself as before, in front of the fireplace.

"Now," he began, "I want you to go over everything that happened yesterday from the time you left this house until you finished your shopping at Falstaff's Grocery."

"I'd kind of like to hear this myself," Gertrude put in, casting a reproachful eye at Judith. "Sometimes my daughter keeps things from her mother. 'Course she couldn't stop me from seeing the dead gangster lying outside my door."

"Is that so?" Glenn remarked with indifference.

"Or the fortune-teller who dropped dead at the dining-room table," Gertrude went on.

"Really." Glenn didn't bother to look at Gertrude.

"Having that movie big shot drown in the kitchen sink was a blessing in disguise," Gertrude declared. "Some of the people who worked for him are making a moving picture about me."

Glenn's facial muscles had tightened. "I'm sure they are," he said through gritted teeth.

"But I'm glad I missed that killer Easter Bunny up at church," Gertrude said. "Hop, chop, hop—"

"Mrs. Grover!" Glenn was getting red in the face. "*Please.* We're trying to conduct an investigation here." He moved a step closer to Judith, who was seated next to Gertrude. "Could you please make your mother stop talking nonsense?" he requested in a low voice. "I realize she's elderly and delusional, but she's impeding our interrogation."

"She's elderly, but she's not delusional," Judith said softly.

"Then you both must be crackers," Trash asserted. "Is that part of your alleged disease, Mrs. Flynn?"

"No," Judith said, then turned to Gertrude. "Mother, you'd better let me tell these detectives what happened or we'll never get rid of them."

Seeing the wisdom in her daughter's words, Gertrude shut up. Judith began to recount the events that had led to the discovery of the ersatz milkman in the trunk of her car. Sweetums wandered into the parlor just as she was getting to the part she hadn't mentioned the previous day.

"The UPS man told me that the parcel for the Blands was a once-a-year delivery," Judith explained. "Naturally, I was curious. I went on the porch to look at the box. It came from Kopfstein, Austria."

"Why didn't you mention that yesterday?" Glenn demanded as Sweetums wove between his feet.

"I didn't want you to think I was a snoop," Judith replied.

"But your whole story involves snooping," Glenn pointed out, trying to sidestep the cat.

"I know," Judith admitted. "It was stupid of me. But it didn't seem important at the time."

"Are you certain you're telling everything now?" Glenn asked, taking a couple of steps away from Sweetums.

"Yes."

Sweetums was undeterred. He rubbed up against Glenn's neatly pressed trouser leg and purred loudly. The detective jumped, knocked over the fire tools, and stepped on Sweetums's tail. The cat growled and took the offensive, clawing the fine trouser fabric. In an instant, Sweetums had torn four six-inch rents, from midcalf to cuff. Glenn swore out loud as he tried to grab the cat, who eluded him by ducking under Gertrude's wheelchair.

"This is an outrage!" Glenn shouted. "That animal ought to be put to sleep!"

"I could use a nap myself," Trash said, feigning a yawn. "Are we done yet?"

Glenn examined the rips in his slacks. "We are now," he huffed. "I'll send you a bill for this," he added, pointing to Judith.

"If you do, I'll report you to the SPCA," Judith shot back. "You deliberately stepped on Sweetums. No wonder he got upset. And what was the point of all this anyway?"

"To learn those details you conveniently forgot or omitted yesterday," Glenn asserted, trying to ignore the growls and hisses coming from Sweetums.

Judith had gotten to her feet, though Trash still lolled about in the window embrasure. "You have the whole story now," she said, annoyed. "Tell me who I was carrying around in my trunk. I don't like giving rides to strangers."

"You wouldn't know him," Glenn responded. "He's nobody, just some lowlife."

"But he's got a name, and I want to know it," Judith argued, "especially if you think I killed him."

"You killed somebody?" Gertrude asked. "That's a switch."

"You heard what I just told the detectives," Judith retorted. "Somebody put the body in my trunk while I was looking around the house and grounds."

Gertrude grunted. "Is that why you're cruising around in Lunkhead's jalopy?"

"You promised not to call him 'Lunkhead' anymore," Judith admonished.

"Okay, Knucklehead, then. So where's your car? At the mortuary?"

"Later, Mother," Judith said impatiently. "I'll fill you in after these detectives have gone. But," she continued, turning to Glenn, "I insist upon knowing the victim's name. I also insist on knowing whether I'm still a suspect."

"A person of interest," Glenn replied. "How's that?"

"Dumb," Judith declared. "If you really thought I murdered the guy, you'd probably figure out that I knew who he was. Come on, give me the dead man's name."

Glenn sighed. "I'll tell you because the name won't mean a thing. The man was Frank Purvis, address unknown."

Glenn was right. The name meant nothing to Judith.

Well," Gertrude huffed after the detectives had left, "it looks like you got yourself into another big mess." She cocked an eye at her daughter. "You can tell me—did you really bump off the milkman?"

"Of course not, Mother," Judith replied. "And he

wasn't a milkman. I never heard of anyone named Frank Purvis."

"I did," Gertrude asserted, wheeling herself back to the kitchen. "He worked for one of the lumber mills. He was a Freemason and had a glass eye. I went to school with his wife, Charlotte. Carrie, she was called. Homely girl. She got to that gawky stage and never left it."

"Did they have children?" Judith asked.

"I hope not." Gertrude had retrieved her snack and was about to take a bite out of a dill pickle. "The results would have been fearsome." The old lady loudly crunched her pickle and swallowed it before speaking again. "I lost track of Carrie after she got married. I think they moved away during the Depression."

The tiny speck of hope was snuffed out. Gertrude's recognition of the name was a coincidence. But someone must have known the Frank Purvis who had ended up dead in Judith's trunk. The "address unknown" troubled her. The bogus milkman she'd met on Moonfleet Street didn't look homeless. He'd appeared well nourished and well kempt. If the police knew the victim's name, there must have been some kind of identification on his person.

"It could have been a Social Security card," Renie suggested when Judith called her half an hour later. "Or credit cards. They don't list addresses."

"But the credit-card company would know where to send the bill," Judith pointed out.

"Yes," Renie said in a sour voice, "they always know where to find you. I changed our address once to

Buckingham Palace, but it didn't work. The queen said she wouldn't be caught dead in a Notre Dame sweatshirt. She especially hated the Fighting Irish logo."

"But no driver's license, no checkbook, no voter's registration," Judith said, ignoring Renie's flight of fancy. Or possibly, reality. Sometimes it was hard to tell with Renie. "It's as if Frank Purvis didn't want to be traced."

"Then why have any ID at all?" Renie queried.

"That's my point," Judith said, holding the phone between her jaw and shoulder as she sliced cucumbers. "I wonder if Glenn Morris didn't make up a name just to shut me up."

"Why would he do that?" Renie asked.

"Just because," Judith said. "I looked Frank Purvis up in the phone book. Like the Blands, there was no listing. I even called directory assistance to see if someone by that name lived in the suburbs. No luck."

"Did you try the Internet?"

Judith sighed. "Yes. I found three men named Frank Purvis. One in Baton Rouge, another in Sherman Oaks, and the third in Duluth. I've hit the wall."

"Maybe it's an alias," Renie suggested.

"The police must have taken his fingerprints," Judith said. "Glenn referred to Purvis as a 'lowlife,' which indicates some kind of criminal record. Maybe they know more than they're telling us."

"I assume they'll release his name to the media," Renie remarked. "It'll be interesting to see if there's an obituary in the paper in the next couple of days. Maybe we should visit the morgue."

"To do what? Go through Frank Purvis's meager belongings?"

"I meant the newspaper morgue," Renie clarified. "And not for Purvis, but the Blands. You can go back only a few years into the archives on the Internet."

"I suppose it could be helpful," Judith allowed. "Were you thinking of marriage, births—that kind of information?"

"Yes, but I also wonder if they haven't made the news in a less mundane way," Renie said. "I'm thinking feature articles, like an unusual hobby or rescuing a child from a vicious dog."

"They don't strike me as publicity hounds," Judith noted. "I picture them as going out of their way to avoid the limelight."

"Except sometimes people can't escape it," Renie pointed out. "It's up to you. I could go tomorrow morning. After ten, of course."

The cousins agreed on the time. The rest of the day passed swiftly. Besides her guests, Judith had to prepare another meal for Mike and the boys, as well as Uncle Al. The group seemed in high humor, having gone to the zoo after their trip to the lake and visit to Gertrude. Judith was put off by Mike's attitude. It seemed to her that he should be wallowing in misery. She also felt that Mac and Joe-Joe didn't seem to miss their mother very much.

As they were all leaving, Judith cornered Mike, dragging him into the parlor. "I want a progress report," she demanded. "What are you and Kristin doing to solve your problems?"

Mike shrugged. "She's going home to stay with her folks on their wheat ranch for a while. She's leaving Saturday. The boys and I'll go back to the ranger station Sunday."

"That's not progress," Judith noted.

"Yes, it is," Mike replied. "She feels claustrophobic up at the summit. She needs to get back to her roots to think."

Judith didn't comment on Kristin's needs. "I would expect the children to miss her," she said.

Mike grinned. "They're having a ball. This is all one big holiday to them. Tomorrow we're going to the aquarium and then to do the rides at the civic center. Not to mention that Uncle Al spoils them rotten. You know how he is with kids."

"Yes." Not having children of his own, Al Grover doted on his various nieces and nephews. "But," Judith went on, "I'll bet Mac and Joe-Joe will miss their mother when you get back to the ranger station."

Mike's expression turned glum. "Probably. We all will."

"Then," Judith said, putting her hands on her son's shoulders, "you'd better think very hard about what the rest of your life is going to be like. Not to mention the boys'. I've seldom seen the yo-yo effect on children do them much good."

Mike looked puzzled. "Yo-yo?"

Judith nodded. "Pulling them back and forth. A weekend with Dad, a workweek with Mom, summers and other school breaks up for grabs. And by the way, your father and I are too old—and too busy—to be babysitters."

"That's harsh." Mike sounded resentful.

"No, it's not. Oh, I'm not talking about the occasional day or overnight," Judith explained. "I mean having to help raise them. Children are supposed to be brought up by their parents, not their grandparents. It's called *a family.*"

"It's not a family when there's conflict," Mike declared. "It's a war zone."

Judith kissed her son's cheek. "Then make peace."

Mike's mood was still gloomy when he left. Judith felt both sad and frustrated. She understood that it was impossible to read what was in another person's mind and heart, even when that person was her own child. But Mike didn't know everything about Judith. It was strange, she thought, how once having left the nest, children seemed to think that their parents had no life without them. Mike probably never thought much about what running a B&B required or considered the physical pain Judith still suffered. Mothers were always mothers to their children. *One role fits all,* Judith thought as she finished cleaning up from dinner.

She wondered what Mike would think if he knew his mother had been suspected of murdering a milkman who wasn't a milkman.

Not much, Judith realized, as long as a rump roast was on the dinner table.

Joe called that night around nine. Progress was being made on the insurance case, and the company hoped to have the lawsuit dismissed. He expected to be home late Saturday. Judith evaded his questions about what was happening at Hillside Manor. She didn't dare tell him about the police investigation, and there was no need to burden him with her distress over Mike and Kristin. He was already upset about the breakup. Judith wouldn't distract him further. Joe had to focus on the business at hand.

At eleven, she tuned into KINE-TV, watching her old acquaintance, Mavis Lean-Brodie, deliver the news. Neither she nor her new coanchor, John Shinn, mentioned the murder. It seemed to be a slow news night. A lengthy feature on the upcoming first day of summer provided some lovely photography of sunlit beaches, verdant parks, and gurgling mountain streams. The reporter, a handsome young man named Adam Blake, made it sound as if there hadn't been a moment of bad weather since the first of June. Apparently, he'd been spending too much time inside the studio.

At the broadcast's conclusion, Judith switched off the TV and tried to go to sleep. She tossed and turned for almost an hour. When she finally drifted off, she dreamed of tennis balls flying back and forth over a steel net. The balls had faces. They belonged to Mac and Joe-Joe.

A division of labor?" Renie asked in a sleepy voice when Judith suggested they split up the next morning. "Okay, I'll do the newspaper thing. You call on Anna French at Nordquist's. We can rendezvous at one o'-clock for lunch at the Crab House."

"When I woke up," Judith said into the phone, "it dawned on me that if we can't get inside the Blands' house, the next best thing is talking to the other family members. At least we know where Anna works. Let's hope she can lead us to the others."

"Right." Renie yawned. "Ah. The digital clock on

my oven just turned to ten-oh-one. I think my brain's in gear. I suddenly remembered that Garth Doyle called me last night."

"About what? SuperGerm?"

"No," Renie replied. "Garth takes a walk every day, around noon. Yesterday he saw the yellow tape around the Moonfleet house. He called me to ask if I knew about it. I feigned innocence. He asked a couple of neighbors what was going on, but all they could tell him was that the police had been there just a few minutes before he came by."

"Did you still pretend to be ignorant?" Judith inquired.

"I didn't have to try too hard," Renie admitted. "But Garth said when he saw the crime-scene tape, he tried to remember if he'd noticed anything unusual in the neighborhood the previous day. He'd taken a different route, so he hadn't passed by the Blands' house. But around the corner on the west side—the opposite of the end of the alley where you parked your car—he noticed a Dairyland truck pulled in at the curb down the block. Bear in mind that Garth is a very visual person. As far as he could tell, there was no one in the truck and the engine had been turned off."

Judith considered Renie's words. "So what you're saying is that the phony milkman was somewhere else, probably up to no good."

"That's right," Renie agreed.

"Like, for example," Judith said slowly, "being murdered."

NINE

JUDITH REMEMBERED TO fix Gertrude's lunch before leaving. Although Phyliss was on duty, it would never do to have the cleaning woman deliver a meal to Judith's mother. Indeed, Judith kept the two women as far apart as possible, as if there were a Maginot Line between the house and the toolshed. They always ended up in a shouting match over religion, with Phyliss threatening to quit and Gertrude informing her she was already fired.

Arriving at Nordquist's, Judith asked the concierge where she might find Anna French. The smiling, impeccably garbed young woman behind the desk asked if she had an appointment.

"Yes," Judith lied. "For eleven-fifteen. It's about the fall sportswear line. We have a problem."

The concierge looked alarmed. "Nordquist's can't have problems. Go right up."

The corporate offices were on the top floor; the buyers' section took up at least a third of the space. Upon meeting the receptionist, Judith expressed indignation when her name wasn't found in Anna's appointment book.

"New York won't be happy," she declared. "I'm sure Ms. French is as anxious to salvage our account as we are."

The receptionist, who was also chic and attractive, momentarily looked put-upon, but quickly resurrected her smile. "I'll show you in at once," she said, and led Judith to the designer-sportswear buyer's door.

Anna French's office was small and crowded with catalogs, fabric samples, and designer sketches. When Judith came through the door, Anna was on her hands and knees, sorting microfiber swatches. She looked up in surprise.

"Excuse me," Anna said, "who are you?"

"I'm a fraud," Judith replied. "My name's Judith Flynn. I don't want to waste your time or mine. The man who was killed at your parents' home was put in the trunk of my car. I need your help."

Frowning, Anna got up, brushing off her straight black skirt and adjusting the collar of her pale yellow silk blouse. "Is this a joke?"

"No," Judith responded. "Far from it. As you must know, the police think that the man named Frank Purvis was killed on your family's property."

Anna French sat on the edge of her desk, which was piled high with more catalogs and sketches. She didn't offer Judith a seat.

"I don't see how I could possibly help you," she declared. "That man certainly wasn't murdered by my elderly parents or my feeble aunt. How the body managed to get into your trunk seems to be your problem, not ours. In fact, why was your car parked on my parents' grounds in the first place?"

Briefly, Judith studied Anna. She was fortyish, dark, rail thin, and of medium height, with striking features so artfully enhanced that she could have been a mannequin. But unlike a dress dummy, she moved with grace and confidence.

"Wait a minute," Anna said before Judith could speak. "Are you one of the women who came by the house yesterday with some tall tale about writing a magazine article?"

Obviously, Lynette had related the cousins' visit to her sister-in-law. Judith felt trapped. "Yes," she finally confessed just before inspiration struck. "I'm FATSO."

"What?" Anna was taken aback. "You don't look very fat to me. You're tall. You can carry a few extra pounds. I can't. You'd look particularly good in Max Mara or Donna Karan or—" She clamped her lips shut. The fashion maven in Anna had momentarily taken over. "What the hell are you talking about?"

As much as Judith hated referring to her semi-celebrity, she explained about the Web site and her work as an amateur sleuth. "So you can't blame me for wanting to find out as much as I can about the circumstances of this Purvis's death. I'm implicated. I have to try to figure out what happened. And you can't blame my cousin for being intrigued by your parents' house. It's certainly an anomaly."

"Perhaps." Anna was frowning again. "But I don't know what to tell you. My parents have never been social. When Dad came back from the war, he was a wreck. Mom was always shy. They preferred their own company."

"Didn't your father have to work?" Judith asked.

Anna shook her head. "He had a disability pension from the army. We lived frugally." She glanced down at her expensive black pumps. "I guess that's why I went into fashion. I was always the worst-dressed girl in my class."

"My family didn't have any money, either," Judith confided. "I had to wear my cousin Renie's hand-me-downs. They were pretty worn out by the time I got them, because they'd been passed on to her by our cousin Sue. The only nice clothes I owned were sewn by our grandmother. But she used the same pattern for all the granddaughters, so we all dressed alike, except sometimes she'd change the fabric colors."

Anna's expression softened. "I had a weight problem when I was young. I've spent my entire adult life counting calories."

"Who hasn't?" Judith responded. "I weighed over two hundred pounds in high school."

"At least you were tall," Anna noted. "I looked like a basketball."

Relieved that a bond seemed to have been created, Judith steered the conversation back on course. "Growing up can be so difficult. I was an only child. That can be very isolating. Did your family ever have company?" It would have been impossible to feel isolated in the Grover clan. There were always visitors when she was a child—relatives, friends, neighbors. Grandma Grover had laughed about it, saying she felt as if she were running a hotel. It had only seemed natural for Judith to turn the family home into a hostelry.

"Not really," Anna replied. "A knock on the door caused anxiety with my parents. Sometimes it was the Fuller Brush man or the insurance agent making his monthly collection or somebody with a petition."

"You had no other family nearby?"

Anna shook her head. "Only Aunt Sally. She came to live with us before I was born. Dad was from Kansas. He never went back after the war." Sliding gracefully off the desk, she pointed to the piles of fabric on the floor. "Look, I'm sorry I can't help you. I'm under the gun right now. I leave next week on a buying trip to Milan."

"I'd like to explain myself to your sister-in-law," Judith said. "Where does Lynette work?"

"The phone company," Anna replied. "She's just a couple of blocks away in the Qwiver corporate headquarters. She might have gone to lunch by now."

Judith thanked Anna for her time. The words were acknowledged with a brief nod. Anna was again fingering fabrics, completely wrapped up in her work. It struck Judith as odd that Anna seemed undisturbed about a man being murdered on the grounds of her old family home.

It was ten minutes until noon when Judith reached the head offices of Qwiver. Maybe she could catch Lynette Bland before she went to lunch. The building had strict security. Judith went up to the desk in the lobby and asked after Ms. Bland.

"I don't have an appointment," she admitted. "Just tell her I'm here about the milkman."

The buxom uniformed woman behind the desk gave her a curious look, but picked up the phone. Judith's message was relayed. The response at the other end was brief.

"I'm sorry," the woman said as she hung up the phone. "Ms. Bland can't see you. She's tied up in meetings all day."

Judith thanked the woman and walked out of the building. But she lingered by one of the pillars, keeping her eyes on the entrances. Lynette was avoiding her, Judith was sure of that. A steady stream of employees exited the building as Judith's watch registered exactly noon. She found it difficult to keep track of all four double doors. The seconds and then the minutes ticked by. The exodus began to dwindle. Maybe Lynette really was in a meeting that would go past the lunch hour.

But at twelve-oh-six, Judith spotted her prey. Lynette Bland was wearing a different linen suit, white, with a mauve blouse showing at the collar of her jacket.

Lynette walked briskly past her. She was headed for the south corner. Judith forced herself to keep up, though maintaining a six-foot distance. They both made the light; Lynette continued south for another block before turning the corner by a florist's shop. Two doors down, she entered a crowded café. By the time Judith came in the door, Lynette was sitting down at a table for two where a man wearing what looked like expensive designer sunglasses was studying the menu.

"Drat!" Judith breathed. There were no vacant tables and a line had already formed. Lynette and her companion exchanged a few words, but seemed more interested in the menus than in each other.

The hostess inquired after Judith's needs. "I'm waiting for someone," she said in response. "There's no rush."

Judith wondered if the man was Luke Bland, Lynette's husband. He was the right age, late forties, with graying brown hair. Average size, Judith guessed. It was hard to tell, since he was seated. The navy sport coat, white shirt, and tie indicated he was a professional. When he put the menu aside, he picked up a thick binder from under the table and began studying it. Lynette spoke to him, but he merely shrugged. After their order was taken, she stared across the busy room with unseeing eyes. Luke—assuming it was Luke—made notations in the binder.

Judith felt she was wasting her time. She could approach the couple and explain herself, but there was no room for her to sit down. Standing up would make it awkward to apologize for the fabrication of writing a magazine article or for explaining about the body in her trunk. Judith surrendered and left the café.

Inspiration struck as she walked by the florist on the corner. If she couldn't explain, she could still apologize. She couldn't take time to have something made. A striking arrangement of yellow gladioli, bells of Ireland, and baby's breath caught her eye.

"How much?" she asked the curly-haired young woman behind the counter.

"Forty-five dollars, plus tax and delivery."

"I'll deliver it myself," Judith said, trying not to shudder at the price. "I'm taking it just down the street to Qwiver Towers."

Judith reached the phone-company lobby by twelve-thirty. The buxom security guard had been replaced by a dark-skinned youth who couldn't have been more than twenty.

"I want to take this bouquet to Lynette Bland," Judith said, offering the guard her most ingratiating smile. "It's a surprise."

The youth looked uncertain. "We can deliver it for you."

Judith shook her head. "I just saw Lynette at lunch. I want to have it on her desk when she gets back, and I haven't had time yet to write the note."

Apparently, Judith didn't look like a terrorist or an industrial spy. The young man shrugged. "You know where her office is?"

"No," Judith said. "We're social friends, not business associates."

The guard checked his directory. "She's in fiber optics, fifteen twenty-two."

"Thanks," Judith said, and hurried to catch an elevator that was about to go up.

There was no receptionist in the area and the only employee Judith saw was a woman absorbed in eating lunch at her desk in a nearby cubicle. Judith walked past several offices until she found the one with Lynette's nameplate beside the door.

Lynette's office was as spartan as her sister-in-law's was cluttered. A watercolor of the Grand Canyon hung on one wall; her framed MBA from the University was displayed on another. A single file folder sat in the middle of her desk. A couple of pens, an in- and an out-basket, a telephone, a company directory, and a day calendar were the only other items. There was plenty of room for the floral arrangement. Judith hastily scribbled on the notecard provided by the florist:

Lynette—Sorry I missed you. This is my peace offering. I have something very important to tell you. Please call me.

Judith added her name and phone number. Glancing at the day calendar, she saw that Lynette did indeed have a meeting at one, but it was to be held at another of the phone company's buildings, some six blocks away. There was no point in waiting.

She took one last look around the office. Atop a filing cabinet was a thick notebook that almost but not quite obscured the tops of a double picture frame. Carefully, Judith reached around the notebook and picked up the photos. Lynette and her companion from the café were standing on a windswept beach. They were both much younger, perhaps not yet thirty. Judith had guessed correctly. Lynette had lunched with her husband, Luke. They looked much happier in the picture than they had in the café.

The other photo was of a handsome young man in commencement regalia. He was blond and wore an engaging smile. No doubt it was their son, Alan. Judith looked more closely. There was something familiar about that face, especially the smile. She tried to picture him ten years older.

Judith knew him. Not as Alan Bland, but as Adam Blake, KINE-TV reporter.

Excuse me," said a rich masculine voice. "Are you looking for something?"

Startled, Judith almost dropped the picture frames. She turned around to face Luke Bland in the office doorway.

"I was admiring your photos," Judith replied, struggling with her composure. "Your son's on television, isn't he?"

Luke moved closer to the desk. "Yes, but he uses a different name. I'm sorry—do I know you?"

"No," Judith admitted, recovering from her surprise. "But I recognized you from the photo with Lynette."

"I'm afraid you have me at a disadvantage," Luke replied, looking bemused. "Do you work with Lynette?"

"No." Suddenly Judith remembered something Renie had told her about seizing control in a business situation. Abruptly, she sat down in Lynette's chair. Now, according to Renie, Judith was in charge. Or was it the other way around? Did the person who was standing up have the upper hand because he or she was looking down on a presumed inferior? Judith was befuddled.

"I'm the one with the body," she blurted, casting power plays aside. "I brought Lynette some flowers because my cousin and I pestered her yesterday about what had happened at your parents' house."

Putting one foot on a visitor's chair in front of the desk, Luke Bland chuckled. "I heard about that. You pretended to be writers. Well, that's understandable. You must have been shocked when you discovered what was in your trunk. That would be enough to make anyone behave a bit recklessly. No hard feelings, I'm sure."

Up close, Luke was good-looking in a worn, craggy kind of way. His manner was smooth, pleasant, and not quite sincere. Certainly his demeanor was much less austere than it had been with his own wife.

"Yes," Judith said, "I was stunned when I opened my car. I hope this whole situation hasn't been too hard on your parents."

Luke smiled softly. "We've played it down with them. With Aunt Sally, as well. At their age, it wouldn't be right to let them get upset. And really, it has nothing to do with them. It was just one of those freakish accidents."

"But the man was murdered," Judith said.

Luke shrugged. "I gather that may be so. But he was some sort of impostor, probably running from the law. That type of person is often done in by his own kind. The fact that he may have been killed near my parents' house is irrelevant. It's no different than if a pedestrian had been run over out on Moonfleet Street."

Judith didn't argue. "I'm glad your parents haven't been too affected by the tragedy," she remarked.

"A blessing," Luke replied, removing his foot from the chair and moving around the room to straighten the Grand Canyon painting. "Still, it's one more reason why they shouldn't stay in that big old house. In a way, it's a magnet for crime."

Judith figured she might as well stand up. "How is that?"

Luke's smile struck Judith as disingenuous. "Teenagers, mainly. They see a place like that and think maybe it's abandoned. They try to climb over the fence, throw rocks at the windows, party out in the alley. I've been trying to talk Mom and Dad into moving to a retirement home. They're at a point where they need assisted care."

"There must be stairs," Judith remarked, "and quite a distance from one room to another in such a big house. It must be difficult for them to get around." She put aside her own fears for the future, when her hip might not allow her to manage the four stories of Hillside Manor. "I assume they must be rather crippled at their age."

"They have their bad days," Luke allowed. "There are plenty of other problems. The gas furnace is very old and the heating bills are outrageous. They've had problems with animal life, too—raccoons chewing on the exterior and getting into the basement, squirrels entering the attic to set up housekeeping, bees making nests in the walls, even the occasional rat—and mice, of course. The grounds are a sanctuary for small creatures. Still, my parents don't want to leave."

"I take it Aunt Sally doesn't want to, either?"

"Aunt Sally doesn't know what she wants," Luke said with a hint of disparagement. "But she's certainly not fit to stay there." He stopped roaming around the office and approached the desk. "Excuse me, but I have to get Lynette's keys out of the drawer. I'm borrowing her car this afternoon. Mine's in the shop."

"Oh." Judith came around to the other side of the desk. "I mustn't keep you. In fact, I'm late for a luncheon appointment."

Luke had opened the drawer. "It was nice meeting you. By the way, I should give you one of my cards." He reached inside his jacket. "Here. If you're ever in the mood to buy or sell, give me a call. Enjoy your lunch."

As soon as Judith was in the main hallway, she looked at the card. It read:

LUKE BLAND
REAL ESTATE AND PROPERTY INVESTMENT
COMMERCIAL AND RESIDENTIAL
Our Professionals Meet All Your Needs

Judith should have guessed that Luke Bland was some kind of salesman. Knowing that, it was easy to understand why Luke wanted his parents out of the big house on Moonfleet Street. Despite its state of disrepair, the family home with its three legal lots would fetch a bundle on the real-estate market.

I was beginning to worry," Renie said as Judith was shown to their booth at the Crab House. "You're twenty minutes late."

"I've had a few encounters," Judith said, noting that Renie had thoughtfully ordered her a Scotch rocks. "But not necessarily of a beneficial kind."

"Tell me all," Renie urged.

Judith did, although it took a quarter of an hour and several sips of Scotch. When she finished, she leaned back in the booth and, for the first time, looked out at the marina next to the lakeside restaurant. The sun was shining and the water sparkled. Suddenly it looked like the first day of summer. The yachts and catamarans and smaller craft bobbed gently at their moorage while a four-man crew plied the lake. A float-plane landed close by; another took off farther north. From this vantage point, Judith could look straight ahead to the Langford neighborhood some three miles away.

"In other words," Renie said drolly, "you struck out."

Judith took umbrage. "What do you mean? I found out several things, especially about the Bland family."

Renie paused as their server arrived to take their orders. Judith hadn't had time to read the menu, so she asked for the same entrée Renie requested—Dungeness crab and melted cheddar on an English muffin, with coleslaw and fries on the side.

"What I mean," Renie explained, "is that they sound pretty normal. Old folks who don't want to give up their home, a son in real estate who'd like to make a big profit off the house, a grandson in TV news, a daughter-in-law who works for the phone company, and a daughter who's a buyer for Nordquist's. Her husband—Phil, is it?—probably holds down a perfectly normal job, too. They hardly sound like candidates for committing homicide."

Judith eyed Renie over the rim of her glass. "Come on, coz—you know that we've come across plenty of so-called normal people who've turned out to be murderers. I'll admit, on the surface, everything sounds ordinary. Even the house itself, if you accept the fact that some people are reclusive by nature and don't give a hoot about appearances. But you're the one who got me started on all this in the first place. I expect more support."

"True." Renie sighed. "I blame my overactive imagination."

"Your imagination didn't kill Frank Purvis."

"No." Renie was looking somber, the expression that Judith always called her cousin's "boardroom face." "Let's leave the Blands out of this for a minute. They're old, they're feeble, they're eccentric. But that doesn't make them killers. So who would want to murder a phony milkman?"

Judith pondered Renie's question. "What was Frank Purvis doing there in the first place? Why was he pretending to be a milkman?" She wagged a finger at Renie. "Purvis was doing the same thing I was doing. He was watching the house. I was there by chance, but he wasn't. He knew that a parcel was being delivered to the Blands. That's why he was lurking around the grounds."

Renie nodded. "That makes sense. You say Purvis arrived before the package did. He couldn't be sure when the UPS van would show up. Purvis pretends to deliver the Blands' order. Maybe he looks inside the milk box, thinking the delivery might already be there. It's not, so he has to wait. He parks the truck around the corner and down the street, where Garth Doyle spotted it. Then he hangs out around back, maybe in the alley. He must have been killed there, though the police certainly haven't verified that information."

Judith nodded slowly. A cabin cruiser was being untied from its moorage, getting ready to sail. Judith noticed that there were several "For Sale" signs along the piers. That was not uncommon. As someone had once said, the two happiest days in a boat owner's life were the day of the purchase and the day of sale. Boats were expensive to buy and expensive to maintain. Judith was glad that Joe had never had a hankering to ply the local waterways.

But the concept of luxury made her wonder what was so valuable about the package that had been delivered to the house on Moonfleet Street. Yachts weren't the only costly items that people coveted. Jewelry, art, rare coins, even postage stamps were of great value. And drugs, of course. But somehow, Judith still couldn't see the Blands involved in dealing illegal substances.

"No one notices a milkman—or a mailman or a UPS deliveryman—coming and going," Judith finally said. "Not even at the Blands'. Purvis used a good cover for whatever he was up to. Except somebody figured it out. Who?"

"I suppose," Renie ventured, "the police interviewed the other neighbors, especially the people who live in the houses across the alley. Of course they're both cut off from the Bland house by all the trees and shrubs as well as the fence."

Judith finished her drink and took a sip of ice water. "You're suggesting those neighbors might be involved?"

Renie shrugged. "It's not impossible. Maybe we should talk to them."

"The ones on the east side weren't home the other day," Judith noted. "They probably work. I really didn't pay much attention to the house on the other side of the block."

Renie was silent for a moment. "Austria," she said at last. "Why Austria? I looked up Kopfstein on a map last night. It's located in the Bavarian Alps, and it's tiny. In fact, it's not even listed in my *Webster's Geographical Dictionary*."

"Tiny or not, somebody must live there," Judith pointed out as their orders arrived. "Did you turn up anything of interest at the newspaper morgue?"

After her first bite of crab and cheddar, Renie was looking ecstatic. "A few small items," she finally said. "Richard and Jane—her maiden name was Goss—took out their marriage license August third, 1947. They were married two weeks later in the old Langford Lutheran Church, which, I believe, was torn down and is now the site of an East Indian restaurant and a used-book store."

Judith smiled wistfully. "Think how this city has grown in just over fifty years. Back in the forties—and into the sixties—the newspapers ran all the marriage licenses, birth announcements, and even the divorce decrees. Not to mention that almost everybody could get their wedding notice—including photos—into what was called the society section."

"Engagements, too," Renie recalled, "though I didn't find one for the Blands. However, the wedding story was fairly complete. The bride wore silk trimmed with seed pearls, a fingertip veil, and so on. Her maid of honor—Lucille Almstead—had a pink dress with a sweetheart neckline. They both carried roses—white for Jane, pink for Lucille. She was the only attendant."

"That's odd," Judith commented. "What about Sally, Jane's sister? It's unusual when sisters aren't included in the wedding party, especially as attendants. Cousins we may be, but you were mine and I was yours."

"That's true," Renie said. "Jane and Sally were local girls. Maybe Sally had moved away and couldn't make it to the wedding."

"Maybe," Judith allowed, "but I still think it's strange. Who was the best man?"

"Steven Carnofsky." Renie spelled the name out loud. "He was from Wichita, Kansas. That's where Dick Bland grew up, right? Steven was probably a boyhood chum."

"That's it?" Judith inquired.

"Not quite," Renie responded, removing a piece of shredded cabbage from her sleeveless chartreuse sweater. "Remember how they used to list college degrees and current employment of the bride and groom? Jane was a secretary for the Great Northern Railroad. No college, but a secretarial school was mentioned. Dick attended the University of Kansas for a year before he went into the service. He was discharged as a first lieutenant in '46 after serving with the Seventh and Third Armies in Europe. The article said he was self-employed."

Judith frowned. "Or unemployed. According to Anna, her father was a nervous wreck after the war. Maybe he couldn't work. In fact, somebody told us—was it Mrs. Harmon?—that Dick Bland had been wounded."

"He had a disability pension," Renie reminded Judith. "I don't know how much that would've been—or still is—but they had enough money to buy the house on Moonfleet Street, apparently right after they were married."

Judith nodded. "So far, all this fits with what we've heard about the Blands. Did you check birth announcements?"

"For Anna?" Renie speared a couple of french fries. "Yes. Born in April of '58."

"So Dick's wound did, in fact, permit him to conceive a child," Judith mused. "Unless . . ." She gave Renie a meaningful look.

"Always a possibility," Renie said. "Dick doesn't sound like the most exciting man in town. Jane may have strayed."

"Jane doesn't sound too exciting, either," Judith said. Then, after finishing her coleslaw, she asked if Renie had found anything else of interest.

"No. Luke's adoption wouldn't be in the daily papers," Renie said. "But it occurred to me that it might be worthwhile to check out the neighborhood weekly newspaper. It's still around, and even if they don't have microfiche, they probably have bound volumes. Do you think it's worth the trouble?"

Judith considered. "Not really. There's no secret about the adoption."

"I was thinking of other things as well," Renie said. "For instance, don't you remember the police-beat column? It was written in a flippant but factual style. Even when they didn't mention names or addresses, you could still get an inkling of who was doing what to whom."

"I don't remember it, in fact," Judith admitted. "I guess I was too young when we moved to Heraldsgate Hill."

"It was a comprehensive paper, too," Renie said. "They covered everything in the neighborhood. When I was in fourth grade, I was on the front page for getting first prize in the city with my drawing of our chicken, Madame de Pompadour."

"I do remember that," Judith said with a smile. "You were so skinny that some of the readers thought you were a war refugee and sent food."

"I was allergic to most of it," Renie said, "which was why I was so skinny in the first place. The only thing I could eat was the two dozen Hershey bars. I polished them off in three days and got hives."

"But you still didn't gain weight," Judith said with an ironic expression. "I would have turned into a blimp. Of course I had my own set of allergies, but luckily—or not—to food. We were a pair of sickly—" She stopped suddenly, staring out the window. "Coz!" she cried, lowering her voice. "Look discreetly at the three men on the dock by that very large yacht. Do you see who I see?"

Casually, Renie turned in her seat. "Good Lord!" she whispered. "It's Glenn Morris and the Trashman. What are they doing here? And who's the other guy with them?"

Judith didn't answer right away. The trio was going aboard the yacht, which had a "For Sale" sign on its starboard side.

"I'm guessing," Judith finally replied. "The unknown person is in his forties, well dressed, and—this is a stretch—could have a sinister look. Do you suppose that could be Philip French, Anna's husband?"

"It could," Renie said slowly, "but are the three of them here for police business or boating pleasure?"

"A good question," Judith murmured as the men disappeared inside the yacht. "I think I know how to find out."

TEN

JUDITH WAS DIALING a number on her cell phone. Renie was licking mocha residue off of her upper lip.

"Hello?" Judith said with a thumbs-up sign for Renie. "Yes, I'm calling about the"—she paused, grimacing as she tried to calculate the length of the yacht that was for sale—"forty-foot yacht that's moored by the Crab House. How much is it?"

Renie didn't take her eyes off Judith even as she accepted the bill from their server.

"Three-fifty?" Judith said. "You mean . . . Yes, that's what I thought. Three-hundred and fifty thousand dollars." She gave Renie a look of incredulity. "How many previous owners? . . . Oh, just one. Good . . . Is that right? How interesting . . . Yes, I would like to look at it. If possible, I'd prefer that the owner shows me around. Mr. French would know the yacht intimately. When would be a good time? . . . He is? Can you reach him? I could be there in . . . ten minutes . . . Certainly. My cell phone number is . . ."

Renie was holding her head.

"Have another mocha," Judith advised. "We're in for the long haul."

"So Philip French owns that very expensive yacht?" Renie inquired, dumping the contents of her fourth raw sugar packet into what was left of her mocha.

"Philip French of French's Fleet," Judith replied, looking a bit smug. "It's a tugboat company. I've heard of them. Haven't you?"

"Sure," Renie replied. "My dad worked for a big tugboat company after the war."

"That's right," Judith remarked. "But it wouldn't be French's outfit. The person who answered the phone said Philip was the owner and founder."

"He must have found some money in it along the way," Renie said. "He had to come up with a bundle to buy that baby brand new."

Judith was staring out the window. "Here they come. Glenn and Trash don't look very happy. Phil, however, seems unperturbed."

"And sinister, no doubt," said Renie, resolutely not looking toward the window behind her.

"I can't really say that," Judith replied. "He's fairly tall, balding brown hair, goatee, Nordquist's finest men's casual wear. I'd opt for 'urbane.' "

"People who own big yachts have to act urbane." Renie slipped her credit card inside the leatherette folder. "You know, ascots and captain's caps and navy blazers with gold buttons."

"Right," Judith said vaguely as she watched the men move out of sight. "I hope French's Fleet calls back soon. It's almost two-thirty. I have to get home to prepare for my guests."

"Viewing the yacht is your idea," Renie responded. "If we stay here long enough, I can order seconds."

"Glenn and Trash must have been interviewing Phil," Judith surmised. "Cops can't afford yachts. You have my word on that."

The server came to collect the bill. Renie refrained from ordering another mocha. "Are you really going through the charade of being a potential buyer?" she asked. "Surely Phil French must know who you are by now."

Judith considered. "Only to toss out the bait. After I reel him in, I'll be candid," she said as her cell phone rang.

It was Phil himself who was making the call. "Yes," Judith said. "In fact, I'm already here. In the restaurant, that is. Ask for Jones. The reservation is in my cousin's name."

Renie waited for Judith to disconnect. "Is he biting?"

Judith smiled. "He said he could be here in two minutes."

"Did he recognize your name?"

"I don't think so," Judith said as their server returned with Renie's receipts. "I'm not the only Mrs. Flynn in town."

Renie's eyes twinkled with mischief. "At least one Mrs. Flynn is in Florida."

"Thank heavens," Judith murmured. "That's the worst thing about summer. Herself usually comes back to town for a few months."

"Phil should sit on my side of the booth," Renie declared. "You'll want to face him."

"Yes." Judith looked up as the hostess arrived with Philip French.

"Good afternoon," he said with a congenial smile. "Which of you is Mrs. Flynn?"

The hostess moved away. Judith raised her hand. "That would be me. Please call me Judith. This is my cousin, Serena Jones."

"Take a seat," Renie said, patting the place next to her in the booth. "Can we order something for you?"

Phil eased himself onto the upholstered banquette. "A martini would do, but it's on me. What will you two be having?"

"Drambuie, straight up," Renie said without hesitation.

"Galliano on the rocks," Judith responded.

Phil, with a subtle show of long practice, signaled for the server and relayed the drink orders. "So," he said, after the server had gone off to the bar, "you're interested in the *Moonfleet*."

Judith gave a little start. "Ah . . . yes, I am." Confused about whether Phil was referring to the yacht or the family home, she decided that silence was her best ally.

"Great ship," Phil said. "I wouldn't sell it, but we need something a bit larger. I use the *Moonfleet* for company business. Two staterooms aren't enough when you take her out with a group of potential business prospects."

The drinks arrived. Now that she knew which Moonfleet Phil was talking about, Judith decided it was time for candor. "I'm not a buyer," she confessed. "I'm trying to keep out of jail."

Apparently, Phil thought she was joking. "So are a few of my business associates. Do you want to buy the

Moonfleet to sail to some country that doesn't have an extradition treaty with the United States?"

"No," Judith replied, vigorously shaking her head. "I mean it. Those detectives you were with this afternoon think I may have killed the man who apparently died on your family property. He ended up in the trunk of my car."

Phil threw back his head and guffawed. "This," he said when he finished laughing, "is a unique approach to bartering. I'm not coming down in price, Mrs. Flynn. It's firm and it's fair."

Renie was looking irked. She was swinging her feet under the table, and accidentally kicked Judith. "Sorry," Renie apologized before she turned to Phil. "I'm just sitting here listening to an incredible conversation and wondering if I should set my hair on fire to put an end to it. Please take my cousin seriously. Or do you honestly not know about the murder of Frank Purvis?"

Philip French's olive skin turned pale; his hand shook as he put down his martini. "Frank's been murdered? You're kidding!" He reached inside his jacket, then suddenly withdrew his hand. "Damn! There's no smoking here. I could use a cigarette. And another one of these." He tapped his half-empty glass.

"Did you know Frank?" Judith asked, recovering from her surprise at Phil's reaction.

"Yes. Yes, he was interested in the *Moonfleet*." Phil's color had returned, but he was starting to perspire. "We looked at the yacht Monday. He said he'd get back to me by the end of the week."

"It looks like you lost a potential buyer," Renie said. "Didn't the cops tell you his name just now?"

After a gulp of his drink, Phil shook his head. "They didn't mention a name." He stared at Judith. "You *are* serious. Frank's body was found in your trunk?"

"Yes. I've no idea how it got there. I mean," Judith clarified, "I don't know who put it in my car. It certainly wasn't me. The detectives seem to think otherwise, or at least haven't eliminated me from their list of suspects. Did they mention my name by any chance?"

Phil shook his head again. He still seemed dazed. "We didn't talk long. They got kind of interested in seeing the boat."

"How long had you known Frank Purvis?" Judith asked.

"Not long," Phil replied, indicating to their server that he could use another round. "I met him a couple of months ago on the golf course. It turned out he was interested in buying a yacht. I hadn't made up my mind to sell yet, so I told him to call me in a month or so. He did."

"He must have been well-heeled," Judith said, wondering why Glenn Morris had referred to Frank as a "lowlife." "How did he make his money?"

Phil finished his first martini just as the second arrived. "Investments. I guess he was one of the lucky stiffs—excuse the expression—who didn't bomb out in the market."

"Were you playing a private course?" Judith inquired.

Phil nodded. "Broadwood. I'm a member."

Judith knew that Broadwood was one of the most exclusive—and expensive—courses in the area. "Did Frank belong?"

"I don't know," Phil replied, lapping up some of the new martini. "I guess so."

"I don't suppose," Judith said, "you'd have any idea why Frank would impersonate a milkman?"

"I sure don't." Phil devoured half of the olive. "It must have been a prank."

Phil didn't look as if he believed his own words, and Judith certainly didn't. "You have no idea why Frank Purvis would have an interest in your in-laws' house?"

"Well . . ." Phil was beginning to look a trifle bleary-eyed. Maybe, Judith thought, these weren't his first drinks of the day. She guessed that the *Moonfleet* had a well-stocked bar. For three hundred and fifty grand, it should come with a bartender and a case of Hangover Helper.

"Yes?" Judith urged as Phil faltered.

"The only thing I can think of," Phil said slowly, "is that maybe he was interested in buying the house. Luke and Lynette—Anna, too—have been pressuring the old folks to move to a retirement home. Maybe Frank wanted to look around the place without being noticed. I mean, who pays any attention to a milkman?"

"Because they can't afford yachts?" Renie put in.

"No, of course not," Phil said, giving Renie an unpleasant look. "What are you—the semicomic relief?"

"I'm not 'semi' anything," Renie shot back. "And 'comic' doesn't exactly describe my present mood. Besides, only a nutcase would wear a disguise to check out a house. Frank Purvis must have been up to something other than real-estate speculation."

Judith glanced at her watch. It was after three o'-clock. "We have to go, I'm afraid. I'm sorry about the deception, but it was the only way I could think of to meet you."

"Yeah, sure, fine." Phil was more than halfway through his second martini. Grudgingly, he got out of the booth so that Renie could make her exit. "Say," he said to Judith as she stood up and slung her purse over her shoulder, "if you think you could swing it, you'd find yourself in a whole new world if you bought the *Moonfleet*."

"Like a world of debt," Renie muttered.

"We'll keep in touch," Judith said.

The cousins left Phil just as he signaled for a third hit.

What's wrong with that picture?" Judith asked as they walked to their cars. "As in how much coincidence can you accept?"

"You mean Phil knowing Frank Purvis?"

"That's just part of it," Judith declared. "Why did Glenn Morris say that Frank was a lowlife? Granted, there are some wealthy people who are sleazes, but that's usually not the way they're described. And how did Frank meet Phil? Did Frank plan it? Or was it the other way around? And why was Frank so interested in the Blands' house?"

"It *is* possible," Renie said as they reached the Joneses' Camry, "that he may have been checking it out as a potential real-estate project. If the place is as dilapidated inside as it is outside, it could be a teardown and at least three houses could be built on the property.

Didn't Phil say that Frank had made his money in investments?"

"That's what he told us," Judith replied, "but it all sounded vague to me. I think Frank was casing the joint with a plan to steal whatever was being delivered to the Blands. Surely everyone in the family knows they get only one UPS delivery a year. They may not know what it is, but it would be the kind of thing you'd talk and speculate about."

"How could the younger generation know?" Renie asked, digging into her purse for her car keys.

"Think about it, coz," Judith responded. "Luke and Anna wouldn't be any less curious than other kids. A big box arrives. Being children, they hope it's something for them. But it never is. They're disappointed. Not to mention that the family leads a very dull life. Eventually, they realize that the annual delivery is strictly for the grown-ups. But they never forget."

"That's true," Renie agreed. "The box always comes in June. Luke and Anna would be out of school. They played outside—I do remember seeing wagons and tricycles and other toys in the front yard. It was one of the few signs of life I ever noticed around the place. It's likely that they might have seen the deliveryman come to the house."

"Exactly." Judith squinted up into the bright sky. "I gather that Phil and Anna are childless. I wonder how they get along. Judging from what I saw at the café, Luke and Lynette seem to be on rather frosty terms. I couldn't help but think that if Mike and Kristin stayed married for the sake of the children, they'd end up like

Luke and Lynette—couples who are strangers to each other."

"Maybe you just caught the younger Blands on a bad day," Renie said, opening the door to her car. "Remember, there are no easy answers."

"No," Judith agreed. "Not for Mike and Kristin, not for any of us, really."

And, she thought, waving Renie off, certainly not when it came to the house on Moonfleet.

The hors d'oeuvres were prepared; the first four guests had arrived; and Mike had left a message saying that he and Uncle Al and the boys were eating out. With one ear cocked for the doorbell, Judith dialed the Broadwood Golf and Country Club's number. Having once dealt with residents of an exclusive community, she knew that protecting members' privacy was a priority. Thus she was forced to invent a ruse.

"I'm a friend of the late Frank Purvis," she lied to the smooth-voiced woman who'd answered the phone. "I've lost his address, and I want to send a sympathy card to his family. If you can't release that information, then I'll send the card to you and you can forward it. If it isn't too much trouble."

"One moment," said the voice. "I'm sorry," she said after a full minute had passed, "we have no Frank Purvis listed as a member. There must be some mistake."

"Is it possible that he lives in the gated community next to the golf course?" Judith inquired. "I know he has some connection to Broadwood."

"I'm sorry," the voice apologized again. "I checked

the residential listings as well as the membership rolls. We have no one named Purvis connected to Broadwood."

Judith thanked the receptionist and hung up. Frank had somehow finagled an invitation to play at Broadwood. Was it for the sole purpose of meeting Phil French? Was it possible that Phil was an accomplice in whatever scheme Frank had concocted?

It was Friday. Joe would be home the following day, or Sunday at the latest. Judith had to act fast. Anna French was the only Bland family member with whom she'd established any sort of rapport. And Anna was about to leave town. She'd probably be working late. Six more guests—sorority sisters from Missouri—arrived and had to be settled in before Judith was able to dial Anna's office just before six o'clock.

Anna was in. "Yes, I'm stuck here until nine at least," she informed Judith. "Can you make this quick?"

"Actually, no," Judith said. "May I buy you dinner when you get off work?"

"Dinner?" Anna sounded surprised. "I don't know . . . I'll probably just want to go home and crash. I have to be back at the store by nine tomorrow."

"This is important, Anna," Judith said. "I met your husband today. I'm worried about him. Did you know that he knew the man who was killed?"

There was an audible gasp at the other end of the line. "No! I haven't talked to Phil since breakfast. Okay, where shall we meet?"

"Where do you live?" Judith inquired. "I'd like to make this easy for you."

"We live over in Hamilton Park," Anna said, referring to the upscale neighborhood near Broadwood. "We have a condo on the lake. It would be just as easy if you met me downtown. How about Julio's? It's close to the street I take to go directly to Hamilton Park."

"Fine," Judith said. "I'm on the south slope of Heraldsgate Hill. It'll take me less than ten minutes to get there. How about nine-fifteen?"

That worked for Anna. It didn't work quite so well for Judith, since she wouldn't be at Hillside Manor to lock up at ten. But time was of the essence. And if Anna was worn out, her defenses might be down.

"You call this dinner?" Gertrude demanded, looking at the tray Judith had brought to her. "I don't recognize anything but the plate."

"I made a casserole out of the leftover chicken from the other night," Judith replied. "It has noodles and broccoli and peas in it. That's a cheese sauce for the filling."

"Cheese sauce?" Gertrude snorted. "It looks like motor oil. What kind of cheese did you use? Part of the moon? It's green."

"You're looking at the vegetables," Judith said. "You've got peanut-butter cookies, too."

"They're stale," Gertrude asserted. "When did you make them? April?"

"Monday," Judith responded. "There wouldn't be any left if Renie wasn't allergic to peanuts and Joe hadn't left town. As it is, those are the last three. Mike and the boys love them."

Gertrude fingered one of the cookies. "Too bad I can't skate anymore. I could use these for hockey pucks. By the way, do you remember when I was in the Olympics?"

Judith stared at her mother. "As in mountains? Yes, of course. Daddy had his first teaching job in the area."

"Oh. Sure he did." But Gertrude looked bewildered. "Maybe they didn't understand."

"Who?" Judith was feeling as confused as her mother.

"The movie people. I guess they thought I meant I'd been in the Olympic Games, not the Olympic Mountains. Anyways, they've got a part in the script where I won a silver medal in the 1928 Olympics in Amsterdam for the hundred-meter backstroke. I may be great, but I don't remember being that great."

"You weren't. I mean," Judith added hastily, "you didn't swim in the Olympics. You'd better tell them to take that out of the script."

"Yes." Gertrude rubbed at her wrinkled cheek. "I'll them it was the 1936 Olympics. That was in Berlin, right? Then I could say I beat the pants off of Hitler's Nazi amazons."

"Why not?" Judith had given up arguing over the accuracy of the script. Apparently, so had Gertrude. Both the writer and the agent had told them that the character of Gertrude—who might actually be called by another name in the film—was a composite of several women who had been part of the Greatest Generation. For all Judith knew, her mother could end up being Eleanor Roosevelt.

Judith left the house at nine after asking Arlene and Carl Rankers to keep an eye on the place. In their typical good-hearted manner, Arlene and Carl readily agreed to house-sit and to entertain Gertrude. Judith said she owed them—again.

Julio's was an intimate Italian restaurant with valet parking. Arriving first, Judith waited to order. Five, ten, fifteen minutes passed before a waiter came over to her corner table and asked if she was Mrs. Flynn. Judith said she was. The waiter asked if she'd please take a telephone call at the maître d's desk.

"I'll bet my friend's still stuck at work," Judith said to the waiter as he led the way to the front of the restaurant.

The maître d', who was appropriately suave, offered a cordless phone to Judith. "For privacy, *signora,*" he said, pointing to an alcove near the coatroom.

"Grazie," Judith replied, proud of herself for remembering the word from her travels in Italy. "Anna?" she said when she reached the alcove. "It's Judith."

"I can't make it." The words were rushed and barely audible.

Judith frowned at the near wall, which was decorated with a poster of La Scala in Milan. "Did you say you can't make it? Are you still working?"

"No." There was a pause. "I'm being followed."

"What? Where are you?"

There was no reply. The phone went dead in Judith's ear.

ELEVEN

JUDITH WAS FLUMMOXED. There was no Caller ID feature on the phone she'd been given. She hurried back to the maître d', but he was showing a couple to their table. She tried hitting *69 on the cordless phone, but the call had been blocked. Then she looked at the main console on the desk. It did have Caller ID, so she pressed the button. An Eastside number came up. That couldn't be Anna; the area code was outside the city. Judith figured that another customer had phoned the restaurant after Anna called. Going on to the next listing, she saw "Security Screen—000-000-0000." The time of the call was nine thirty-one. It was now nine thirty-six. The screened call must have come from Anna. Judith swore under her breath, then wondered if she should contact the police.

But what could she tell them? That a dark-haired five-foot-six well-dressed woman in her forties was somewhere downtown and thought she was being followed? That wouldn't do.

Judith had her purse with her. She had gotten her

valet parking stub out of her wallet when the maître d' returned.

"I'm so sorry," she apologized. "There's been an emergency and we'll have to cancel."

The maître d' nodded in understanding and was about to say something when Judith bolted through the front door. She handed the parking stub and a ten-dollar bill to the young attendant on duty.

"Hurry, if you can," she said. "It's an emergency."

Judith had no idea where the MG had been parked, but it careened around the corner and to the restaurant entrance in less than a minute. Thanking the attendant, she jumped into the car and headed uptown to the large underground parking garage across the street from Nordquist's.

The garage had four floors, each marked by a different Pacific Northwest symbol—a salmon, a deer, a spotted owl, and a wild rhododendron. It was the logical place for Anna to park, since the four-story shopping plaza aboveground was connected to the store by a sky bridge. Anna had mentioned that she wanted to eat at Julio's because it was on the street that led directly to her Hamilton Park neighborhood. Thus, Judith figured, she'd planned to move her car to the restaurant so she could head straight home.

But had Anna called from the parking garage by Nordquist's or from somewhere along the six-block route to the restaurant? Judith had no idea what kind of car Anna drove. Going on ten o'clock, traffic was light, but Judith still couldn't have spotted Anna's vehicle even if she'd known what it looked like. It might be the longest day of the year, but darkness had almost settled in over the city. Judith's only chance was to ask someone at the garage if they'd seen Ms. French drive out. She must be a regular; somebody ought to have recognized her leaving.

Judith pulled into the valet parking lane. Two attendants were chatting near the curb. The younger one, a Hispanic with a name tag that read TOMAS, hurried over to the MG.

Judith gave the young man Anna's name and a brief description.

"Sure," Tomas replied. "We all know Ms. French on this shift. She works late quite a bit. But no, we haven't seen her drive out."

"Does she valet park?" Judith asked.

Tomas shook his head. "All the Nordquist employees have a special area on the deer level. They pay by the month. But Ms. French uses the east exit," he went on, pointing to his right. "I guess that's quicker for her. She probably comes in that way, too."

Judith thanked the attendant. "She may be having car trouble. Could you notify security? Meanwhile, if you don't mind, I'll drive down to the second level to look for her."

Tomas grimaced. "We'll have to charge you the minimum."

"No problem." With effort, Judith smiled and started down the winding ramp to the deer level.

Since the garage had entrances on both sides of the block, there was some confusion about where one level ended and the other began, not to mention that each level seemed to be split into separate halves. On several occasions, Judith had had problems locating her car, and Renie had once been forced to ride around on the security guard's cart to find Cammy.

With the stores closed and only the building's movie theaters and restaurants open for business, the parking places were sparsely occupied. Judith realized she was already befuddled when she passed the bank of elevators for the spotted-owl level. She had gone too far. Feeling frustrated and panicky, she managed to get back to the second level. So far, she had seen no one—not even a security guard. The gray concrete walls, floors, ceilings, and pillars struck her as vaultlike, evoking the stone crypts under an ancient cathedral. Even the handful of parked vehicles looked as if they'd been abandoned and should have been shrouded in dust and cobwebs.

She returned to the deer level. Except that it wasn't. She saw the salmon on the door to the elevators and realized she'd somehow missed the second level entirely. Reaching the second floor again, she felt as if the entire garage was full of echoes. But it wasn't just an echo. A car was coming down the ramp behind her. In the rearview mirror, she could see a dark blue—or maybe black—sedan. The windows were tinted. She couldn't tell who was driving.

But she was sure it wasn't Anna. There would be no reason for her to be coming back down into the garage. Judith pulled into a vacant parking place. The sedan—an Infiniti, she noticed—passed by. Slowly. Too slowly. Judith tensed and waited for the car to keep going.

To her relief, it did. Judith slumped over the wheel, gathering her composure. Her quest for Anna seemed doomed. Maybe she'd already left, and the attendants hadn't noticed. It was absurd to try to find someone in a parking garage that made searching seem like looking for a needle in a haystack. Judith rubbed at her temples where a headache was incubating, and decided to go home. Assuming, of course, she could find her way out.

The thud on the passenger window wrenched a scream from Judith's throat. Anxiously, she looked up and turned to her right. A disheveled Anna French stood next to the MG.

"Let me in! Please!" she cried.

Judith reached over to unlock the passenger door. Anna virtually fell into the bucket seat. "Get us out of here! Quick!"

Judith reversed into the exit lane, driving at a speed most unsuitable for a parking garage. "What happened?" she asked Anna. "Are you okay?"

Anna, who was breathing hard, nodded. "I am now. Or will be, when we're out on the street. Thank God I saw you pull in! I couldn't believe it was really you!"

"It was. It is," Judith said as they approached the pay box near the exit. Only then did she remember that parking stubs had to be taken to the cashier inside the building. "Damn! We can't get out of here unless we run through the barrier! I don't dare do that in the MG!"

"Here," Anna said, groping in her handbag. "Use my monthly pass."

The pass worked. The automated arm swung up. Three seconds later they had exited the garage.

Anna leaned back in the bucket seat. "Oh, my God! That was horrible!"

Rattled, Judith offered to pull over into a loading zone in the next block. "What happened to you?"

"Don't stop! Keep going!"

Judith pressed down on the accelerator and automatically headed for Heraldsgate Hill. "Can you talk about it?" she inquired of Anna.

The other woman nodded. "I walked out of the store and over the sky bridge, like I always do, since our offices are on the top floor. I took the garage elevators down to the second level."

"Deer, right?" Judith asked, keeping her eye on the rearview mirror. It didn't appear as if anyone was following them, but with normal traffic moving along the same route, she couldn't be sure.

"Yes, deer," Anna said. "I'd seen a bearded man in that kind of headgear they wear in the Middle East by the elevators before I got in." She uttered a lame little laugh. "I know, it's silly, but these days you can't help but notice someone who reminds you of a terrorist. It's sad. Naturally, I didn't want to stare."

To reach the bottom of Heraldsgate Hill, Judith had to change lanes. She noticed that the third car behind her—a sedan—also made the switch. She didn't mention it to Anna. It was probably a coincidence.

"No one else got into the elevator," Anna continued. "We stopped once to let on some people who got off on the main floor where the cashier is located. By the time I got to the deer level, I glimpsed the bearded man exiting the elevator area. He must have taken one of the other cars and it hadn't had to stop. I didn't think much about it, so I started walking to my car, which is always parked at the far end. Before I got there, I heard another car start up. I kept going, but before I could get to my parking place, the car came roaring up behind me, veering into the pedestrian walkway. I ducked behind one of the pillars, thinking that whoever it was must be drunk. I waited for the car to keep going, but it suddenly stopped and reversed. It was slowing down. I ran around the other side of the aisle and headed for the elevators." Anna paused and sat up straight. "I was scared. I hadn't seen a security guard anywhere. There's an emergency phone by the elevators, but when I picked it up and pressed the button, nobody answered. I looked out into the lot and the car had stopped again. I pushed one of the elevator buttons, and luckily, the doors opened right away. I got in and poked the first button I could hit. Unfortunately, it was for the third level. I didn't know what to do. That's when I called the restaurant. Then I tried 911, but the battery had gone out on my phone, probably just as I hung up from talking to you. Oh, God, it was awful!"

Judith had turned onto the street that led up to Heraldsgate Hill. The sedan was still behind her, keeping its distance. But she still didn't mention the possible tail to Anna.

Instead, she interrupted Anna with a question. "There's a fire station at the top of Heraldsgate Hill. Shall we go there to report what happened?"

Anna emphatically shook her head. "No. Not now. I just want to get home. I'll call from there. In fact, I'll call Phil right now. Do you have a cell?"

"It's in my purse," Judith replied. "Dig down as far as you can. It's always at the bottom."

"After that, it was cat and mouse," Anna said, delving into Judith's handbag. "I wasn't thinking properly. I felt dizzy and confused. I should have gone up to the main floor, but all I could think of was reaching my car and getting the hell out of there. I was still ducking and running when I spotted you. I didn't recognize your car, of course, but I could see you in the driver's seat. I couldn't believe you'd come to rescue me. It seemed like a miracle."

"It seemed like the thing to do," Judith replied. "Was the car a dark sedan with tinted windows?"

Anna nodded. "I'm not even sure if the driver was the man with the beard. Whoever it was started to open the car door just as I got into the elevator, but I didn't wait to see who got out. I was too terrified."

"Naturally," said Judith, though her attention was distracted by the sedan that wasn't going away. She couldn't take a chance on whether the driver was an innocent or a villain. The hill was honeycombed with dead ends and winding streets that would eventually lead her in the direction of Anna's Hamilton Park address. Thus she avoided Heraldsgate Avenue, heading instead for the main street on the east side of the hill. Anna seemed too caught up in figuring out how to use Judith's phone to notice the strange route.

"I'm so muddled I can't remember my own phone number," she exclaimed in frustration. "I'll call Phil on his cell. He always leaves it on in case of a business emergency."

Fillmore Street was wide, a good place to pick up speed. Halfway up, Judith shifted down, gunned the engine, and without signaling, turned up a side street that went in two directions at the top. Instead of going straight ahead, she took a sharp turn to the right. If the sedan had followed her, the uphill climb was so short and so steep that the driver couldn't see where she'd gone. On the flat, she took a left, racing up another hill for two blocks, then taking a right. Changing gears on the level ground, she zipped along the residential thoroughfare until she had to stop at an arterial. To her relief, no one was behind her.

Anna had gotten in touch with her husband. "I can't explain right now," she told Phil, "but I'm on my way home. A . . . friend is driving me. And no, I didn't wreck the car. I'll tell you everything when I see you."

Judith had reached the six-way stop that led onto the bridge. "Is he upset?" she asked.

"Worried," Anna replied, returning the cell phone to Judith's purse. "He probably thinks I had a crisis at work." She took a deep breath. "That was some piece of driving! Do you always go so fast in this MG?"

"Never," Judith admitted. "It belongs to my husband. I'm scared to death to drive it at all, but we've been followed since leaving the garage. I lost whoever it was on the side of the hill."

"No!" Anna swiveled around, looking out the rear window. "All I see now is a Jeep. I should have guessed."

Judith took her turn at the arterial. "I know how to get to Hamilton Park. Once we're there, you can tell me how to find your condo. Don't forget to call the police right away. Morris and Trash—the detectives handling the case—probably won't be on duty. But the homicide squad will want to know what happened so they can pass it on to the investigating officers. I'm going to call, too, after I get back to Hillside Manor."

"Hillside Manor?" Anna looked at Judith. "Oh—that's right. You run a B&B. I know that from your FATSO Web site."

"Yes," Judith replied. "It's questionable advertising for an innkeeper."

"Some people say any advertising is good advertising," Anna remarked. She shivered. "But a Nordquist buyer being chased by a lunatic wouldn't be good for the store's image. We're all about *nice.*"

"Have you any idea who it could have been?" Judith asked as they took the turn onto the bridge.

"Of course not." Anna sounded offended at the idea. "The fashion industry's cutthroat, but nobody tries to whack a competitor."

"That's not a very likely theory," Judith replied. "In fact, when you think about it, your bearded man with a elaborate headgear presents other possibilities."

Anna seemed puzzled. "Like what?"

"What else was he wearing?"

"Oh—you know, those baggy pajamalike pants and some sort of loose top. Typical attire for that culture."

"How tall?"

Anna grimaced. "I tried not to stare. Average, I think. Or maybe a little taller than that. What's your point?"

"My point is that your description could be a disguise," Judith replied, exiting at the far end of the bridge to head for Hamilton Park. "Your pursuer could have been an ordinary—if terrifying—American man. Or a woman."

"Good grief!" Anna put both hands over her mouth as she stared out through the windscreen.

"Think about it," Judith said. "Those loose-fitting clothes, the beard, the headgear—they could cover up just about any kind of person. The question is why would anyone try to harm you?"

"I've no idea," Anna said in a breathless voice. "I don't know anything, I haven't done anything—I'm the original innocent bystander."

Judith's expression was ironic. "So am I. But the cops may not agree with me."

"This is all so strange," Anna declared as they passed by the University's medical center. "I can't figure out any of it. What could it possibly have to do with anyone in our family?"

"I have to ask what may be a very important—if prying—question," Judith said, recrossing the canal and turning toward the arboretum. "Have you any idea what's in the UPS box that comes once a year to your parents' house?"

Startled, Anna turned to look at her. "No, I honestly don't. How did you find out about that?"

"I'm FATSO, remember," Judith replied with a quirky little smile. "The delivery was made the same day that Frank Purvis was killed. I know, because I was there. I've already explained that part to you."

"I have to admit," Anna said, "that it seems odd you showed up on that very day."

"Curiosity and coincidence," Judith said, not wanting to discuss the many situations that she'd encountered by chance. "As you should know from my Web site, I have a knack for finding trouble," she added as they wound their way through the verdant arboretum. A half-moon rose high above the tall hemlock, yew, and cedar trees. "Well? What do you know about the annual delivery?"

"I'd almost forgotten about it," Anna murmured, "not having lived at home for so long. It's the third week of June. That's when the box always arrived. The only thing I remember is that my mother said it came from Uncle Franz."

"Uncle Franz in Austria?" Judith inquired.

"Yes." Anna looked surprised. "He lives in a small town near the German border."

"Kopfstein," Judith said, but spoke again before Anna could interrupt. "Have you ever met Uncle Franz?"

"No," Anna replied. "He must be quite old by now."

"An uncle or great-uncle?"

Anna hesitated. "I'm not sure. I've never known a great deal about our relatives. None of them live around here. Except for Aunt Sally, of course."

They had reached the main street that led to Hamilton Park. "Take a left?" Judith inquired.

"Yes, all the way to the lake," Anna replied. "Go right at the boulevard."

Judith glanced to her left. "Broadwood Golf and Country," she noted, "and Broadwood itself. The woman who answered at the country club had never heard of Frank Purvis."

"Why should she?" Anna inquired.

"Because that's where your husband met Frank," Judith said. "That's why I wanted to talk to you tonight. Did Phil ever mention Frank to you?"

"I don't think so," Anna replied. "Phil meets so many people in his business. Frankly, I don't pay much attention. They come, they go."

"Frank went," Judith remarked, "permanently."

"That can't have anything to do with Phil," Anna said, sounding defensive.

"The police might think differently," Judith responded. "They questioned Phil today. I saw them with him at the marina."

"Good Lord," Anna gasped, "you seem to be everywhere."

"Another coincidence," Judith said, turning right onto the boulevard. "My cousin and I like crab. Where to now?"

"Take the next left," Anna directed. "There's a gate to the condo building. Can you poke the keypad buttons to open it?"

"Sure," Judith said, rolling down the window as they stopped by a brick pillar. "Do you trust me to know the code?"

Anna laughed softly. "It seems I've trusted you with my life." She ticked off the numbers to Judith.

"Have the police talked to you yet?" Judith asked, working the keypad.

After a moment's pause, the gate slowly swung open. "No," Anna replied. "Do you think they will?"

"Yes," Judith said, "to cover all the bases. By the way, did you happen to see the license plate on the sedan that was chasing you?"

Anna shook her head. "I was too panicked."

"And I couldn't see it after we got out of the garage because the car was always too far back," Judith said. "When do you leave for Milan?"

"Wednesday," Anna replied, opening the passenger door. "Hey, I can't thank you enough. You may have saved my life. It's only beginning to sink in now. What can I do to repay you?"

"How about a deep discount on Max Mara?"

Anna smiled. "You've got it. We'll be in touch."

You're right about that, Judith thought. But all she said was, "Give my regards to Phil."

Joe had phoned while Judith was out. He'd left a message saying that they'd hit a snag. He wasn't sure when he'd be able to come home. "I hope everything's all right at your end," his recorded voice had said with a touch of anxiety. "It isn't like you to be gone this late when you've got guests. Call me when you get a chance."

Joe had called at a little after eleven, Omaha time. It was now one in the morning in the Midwest. But she didn't want him worrying about her. After several minutes of arguing with herself, she dialed his hotel's number. When she was connected to his room, he answered in a sleep-fogged voice.

"I'm so sorry," she apologized. "I'm fine. I must have turned off the phone by mistake. Go back to sleep."

"Unhh," Joe said, and clicked off.

Judith reasoned the fib was for a very good cause. She was exhausted. Suddenly it occurred to her that

Arlene or Carl should have answered the phone. They'd arrived at the B&B a few minutes before Judith left at nine. She looked out through the kitchen window. The Rankerses' lights were still on. They were early-to-bed, early-to-rise. She'd assumed that once the guests had all returned, the Rankerses would go home. Judith dialed their number, but got their answering machine.

There was another possibility. The lights had been on in the toolshed when Judith had put the MG in the garage and entered the house through the back door. Gertrude always stayed up to watch the eleven o'clock news, so there'd been no cause for concern.

Judith went back outside and knocked once on the toolshed door.

"Come in," Arlene called in her cheerful voice.

Gertrude, Carl, and Arlene were playing three-handed pinochle.

"As usual," Arlene said with a merry laugh, "your mother is taking us to the cleaners. Carl and I've lost two dollars between us."

Gertrude chortled. A green visor sat atop her white hair and she puffed on a cigarette. All that she needed to complete the picture were garters on her housecoat sleeves. "These two are real suckers," the old lady asserted. "I've won four out of five games, and put both of them way down in the hole twice."

"Amazing," Carl murmured. "Mrs. G, you've got one of the best heads for playing cards that I ever ran into. You ought to join my poker club."

"They're all men, Carl," Arlene snapped. "And I

don't think our sweet darling here likes beer that much. She certainly wouldn't enjoy the belching contests."

"I just might," Gertrude put in. "I can belch with the best of 'em. And I can touch my nose with my tongue. When I take out my dentures, that is. Want to see?"

"No!" Judith cried. "Please, Mother, don't be crude."

Arlene patted Gertrude's arm. "This dear lady couldn't be crude if she tried."

"Damned tootin'," Gertrude replied. "Which reminds me—"

"Mother, stop it!" After glaring at Gertrude, Judith looked at Arlene. "Did everything go smoothly at the B&B?"

Arlene nodded. "Beautifully. Everyone was tucked in before ten o'clock. Except for the man with the heart attack, of course."

Judith blanched. "What man? What heart attack?"

Arlene was studying her cards. "His name is . . ." She looked at Carl. "Griffin? Griffith? Gervin?"

Carl shrugged. "Something like that."

"Greenwalt," Judith said, feeling panicky as she recalled the names on the guest registry. "George and Lucy Greenwalt, from Nashville. Is he okay?"

Arlene shrugged. "The doctors will know more by morning, after he has some tests."

"He's in the hospital?"

Carl nodded. "Norway General. Mrs. . . . Greenwalt is spending the night with him there."

"Did he have the heart attack *here*?" Judith asked.

"Yes," Arlene replied. "In the entrance hall. He

and his wife came in just a few minutes after you left." She looked at Carl. "Who dealt?"

"Mrs. G," he replied. "I'm in. The bid's up to you."

"Please," Judith implored, "what happened to Mr. Greenwalt?"

"What?" Arlene turned to glance at Judith. "Oh. We were chatting by the elephant umbrella stand when Sweetums leaped off the banister and landed on Mr. Greenwalt's head. The poor man collapsed. Just like that." Arlene snapped her fingers. "I *think* Mrs. Greenwalt said her husband had a phobia about cats. When he was very young, he was chased by someone wearing a Sylvester the Puttycat costume at a Halloween party."

"Hey," Gertrude interrupted, "are we going to talk or play cards?"

Arlene patted the old lady's arm. "Just give me a teensy minute, sweetheart. Your daughter seems impatient."

Gertrude scowled through her visor. "What else is new? She knows I don't like to mix cards with a lot of blah-blah. She's just trying to get my goat."

"Anyway," Arlene went on, with an apologetic expression for Gertrude, "Carl called 911. Naturally, they came right away."

They would, Judith thought. All the emergency personnel knew the way to Hillside Manor. She sat down on the arm of the sofa. "Good Lord! I hope he recovers quickly." Visions of lawsuits danced through her head.

"The EMTs didn't seem to think it was too serious," Carl said, then nudged his wife. "Are you going to bid or what?"

"Two hundred," Arlene said.

"Two-ten," Gertrude responded.

"Pass," said Carl.

"Hold it," Judith interrupted. "Nothing else happened that I should know about?"

"Nothing important," Arlene replied, concentrating on her cards.

"Oh, go ahead and tell her," Gertrude rasped. "Otherwise, she won't go away and we'll never finish this game."

Arlene turned to Judith. "They arrested Sweetums."

Judith almost fell off the sofa. *"What?"*

Carl made a face at Arlene before he spoke. "They didn't actually arrest him. They took him to a vet to see if he's rabid. If he isn't, you can pick him up in the morning."

"Two-twenty," Arlene said.

"Two-thirty," Gertrude shot back.

Since Carl had already passed, Judith stood up and leaned over to speak into his ear. "Which veterinarian?"

"I don't know the vet's name," Carl said softly, "but it's the Cat Clinique. You know, over in the Langford district."

"Thanks," Judith replied, giving Carl's shoulder a squeeze. "Thanks for everything."

"Sure." He looked up. "Who got the bid?"

"I did," Gertrude retorted. "For two-eighty." She sorted her cards, discarded three, and laid down fifteen-hundred trump in clubs. "I'm out again. Pony up those quarters."

Judith left quietly, following the concrete walk to the house. But the path that loomed in her mind led to Sweetums and the veterinarian in Langford. Fate was pushing her in that direction, and Judith wondered if she'd eventually find a killer at the end of the journey.

TWELVE

WHEN JUDITH FINALLY had time to look at the morning newspaper, she turned first to the obituary section. There still wasn't a death notice for Frank Purvis. But, as had become her habit in recent years, she scanned the rest of the obits. Judith was at an age where occasionally she'd find one of her peers, often an old school chum. More numerous were the parents of the youngsters she'd grown up with or met later in life. Occasionally it was a guest who'd stayed at Hillside Manor, a fellow SOT—as our Lady, Star of the Sea parishioners called themselves—or some other resident of Heraldsgate Hill. It didn't strike Judith as morbid. Rather, it was her interest in people and sense of community that compelled her to find out who had passed on. The city had grown a great deal since she was a child, but making a connection, even to the dead, enforced the idea that she didn't live in a faceless metropolis.

One surname tweaked her memory: Pettibone, Alfred Earl. She had gone to school with an Albert Pettibone, who was listed as a surviving brother.

One of four children, Alfred was several years younger than his brother. Judith vaguely recalled an Alexis Pettibone, one of two sisters mentioned. Alexis had been a couple of years behind her in school. She was only a blurred memory, but Judith did recall Bert, as he was known—a bright, skinny student with curly brown hair and a shy manner. Alfred, a longtime federal government employee, had also left behind a wife, Andrea, and two sons. Remembrances were to be made to the local humane society.

Just as Judith was about to call Renie, Mrs. Greenwalt phoned from Norway Hospital. George was doing well, Lucy Greenwalt reported, but he'd have to stay until Sunday. She, however, would return to Hillside Manor, since they'd booked their room for two nights.

"You will," Lucy said in a soft but firm manner, "have that horrid animal put to sleep. He could have killed my husband."

Judith winced. "I'm taking care of the matter this morning," she said. Maybe the vet could keep Sweetums at the clinic until the Greenwalts were gone. At least Lucy Greenwalt hadn't mentioned a lawsuit. Yet.

Having planned to collect Sweetums as soon as the other guests were out and about, Judith called the Cat Clinique.

"Your pet isn't rabid," the woman at the other end said, "but he should be enrolled in an anger management program. There are three different groupings—Ill-Natured, Bad-Tempered, and Incorrigible. Your pet would be put in the third group. You'd be amazed. He could emerge with a Happy Cat Award."

"I'll think about that," Judith said.

"You really should. Soon. How soon can you collect him?"

"Well—I was wondering if you could keep him overnight," Judith said.

"Are you kidding?" the woman retorted. "He already bit Dr. Pettibone twice."

"Dr. Pettibone?" Judith echoed. "What's his first name?"

"Albert," the woman replied. "He was on emergency call here last night when your animal was brought in. Believe me, he has enough troubles already. His brother's funeral is Monday."

"Oh!" Judith couldn't keep the surprise out of her voice. "I went to school with Bert. I saw his brother's obituary in this morning's paper. I'm so sorry. He was only in his late forties. Was it sudden? The notice didn't mention cause of death."

"Fred Pettibone died very suddenly," the woman replied. "I have two other calls on hold. Please come get your cat as soon as possible."

As soon as the sorority sisters had bounded out the door, Judith called Renie to bring her up to speed on the latest developments.

"A car chase?" Renie cried. "What are you trying to do? Get a part in an action movie? The next thing I know, you'll be hanging by your thumbs from a thirty-story window somewhere."

"It *could* have been a coincidence," Judith said lamely. "It may not have been the same car that tried to run down Anna in the garage."

"Ha! You should be so lucky!" Renie paused. "Well, you *were* lucky—to escape unscathed."

"So," Judith went on after having finished filling Renie in, "would you mind taking Sweetums just until tomorrow?"

"Are you nuts?" Renie shot back. "What would he do to Clarence?"

"Sweetums could stay outside," Judith suggested.

"Outside our immediate neighborhood," Renie retorted. "Really, coz, I couldn't take that chance. If anything happened to our darling bunny . . . well, I can't even think about it. Try Arlene and Carl. They haven't had any pets since their dog Farky met an untimely—and mysterious—end."

"Farky was a bit of a pest," Judith allowed. "But I couldn't ask them. They've already had to bail me out this weekend. And don't suggest the Dooleys. They have such a menagerie of kids and pets of their own that they'd probably let Sweetums out by accident and he'd be right back here. In fact, that could happen with any of the neighbors in the cul-de-sac. Sweetums is very sneaky."

"Hey," Renie said, her voice brightening, "what about Uncle Al? Mike and the kids are going to be there one more night. I'll bet they'd like to have Sweetums around."

"Brilliant," Judith enthused. "I'll call them right now before they take off on their round of playtime pleasure."

It was Mike who answered. After getting Uncle Al's approval, he told his mother she'd better hurry. They were leaving before noon to go to a farm that had pony rides and a petting zoo.

Judith left the B&B a few minutes after eleven. The feline veterinarian clinic was located only a few blocks away from Uncle Al's. The woman behind the desk, whose nameplate identified her as Alma Burke, eyed Judith suspiciously.

"You wouldn't happen to be Mrs. Flynn, would you?" she asked.

"Yes," Judith replied. "I've come to collect my cat."

"Good," Alma said. "I'll go get him."

Judith remained by the desk, discreetly observing the people in the waiting room. An older woman stroked a long-haired calico; a teenage girl had a black kitten in a carrier; a young woman in workout attire held a sleek Siamese. Judith wondered if Bert Pettibone was still on duty.

Alma returned carrying a cardboard box that had holes punched in it. "Here he is," she said, shoving the box at Judith. "That'll be one hundred and forty dollars. Cash, check, or credit card?"

Startled by the large sum, Judith stammered her reply: "C-c-credit c-c-card." She leaned her head closer to the box. "I can't hear Sweetums. Are you sure he's okay?"

"Define 'okay,' " Alma shot back. "Yes, he's just fine."

Judith was skeptical. She put the box down on the floor and began to open it.

"Don't!" Alma shouted. "Wait until you get outside!"

"Hey," Judith said, anger replacing astonishment, "I want to make sure before I fork out a hundred and forty bucks."

The first thing she saw was Sweetums's yellow eyes, glaring like traffic warnings. Then she saw the muzzle on the lower part of his face and the restraints on his legs.

"My God!" she shouted. "My cat looks like Hannibal Lecter! What have you done to him?"

"Precautions," Alma responded. "Let's see that credit card."

Judith fumbled in her wallet, finally producing the card. "I'm paying this under protest," she announced. "Sweetums better be in perfect condition when I get him home."

"Perfectly horrific." Alma sneered as she scanned Judith's card. "Really, even though he's not a young cat, you should train him. Indeed, if there's an elderly person in your family, you ought to let him or her help. It's a fact that dogs and cats and older people bond very quickly, and the animal often takes on the characteristics of its owner."

Judith narrowed her eyes at Alma. "That," she asserted, "is why Sweetums is Sweetums."

Mac and Joe-Joe were delighted to see Sweetums, whose restraints had been removed as soon as Judith arrived at Uncle Al's. She'd hated to keep him fettered, but was afraid he might go on a rampage in the MG and do some serious damage to the leather upholstery.

The boys wanted to take Sweetums with them to the farm, but Mike said no. Judith, however, worried about leaving the animal in Uncle Al's house.

"Stop fussing," Uncle Al said. "We made a litter box. He'll be fine."

"But he might destroy your furniture," Judith protested. "He's not in a good mood after his stay with the vet."

Uncle Al, who was tall, burly, and had a perpetual twinkle in his sea blue eyes, glanced at Sweetums, who was permitting himself to be petted by the boys. "He looks happy to me. Besides, there's nothing here that can't be replaced. I'll bet you ten bucks he doesn't do any damage."

Judith smiled sheepishly at her uncle. "I'd never bet against you. You're too lucky."

Uncle Al shrugged. "I suppose I could ask Tess to come over and stay with him," he said, referring to his longtime lady friend, who had money as well as looks and lived in an elegant condo only a few blocks away.

"I wouldn't want you to bother her," Judith said. "Besides, as I recall, she's not a cat person."

"She doesn't hate cats," Al said. "She just doesn't want to be bothered with pets. You run along now. We'll work it out."

Judith kissed the boys, hugged her son and her uncle, and headed off in the MG. Five blocks away, she reached the intersection where she could turn right for Heraldsgate Hill—or keep going straight to Moonfleet Street. But, she asked herself, waiting for the light to change, what would be the point of driving by the Blands' house? None, really. She put on her turn signal to take the usual route home.

Only then did she realize that vehicles were backing up on the cross street. The light turned green. Judith followed the two cars ahead of her and looked to her left. Six blocks down, at a five-way traffic signal, she saw flashing red and green lights. Apparently, there had been an accident, not uncommon at such a major intersection.

Judith went straight ahead to avoid the tie-up. She turned onto the main artery through Langford, going less than a block before she had to stop at the next traffic light. As she waited, she admired the floral display in front of the grocery store on her left. There was a special on gladioli, nine stems for ten dollars. The glads in Judith's garden wouldn't bloom for another month. She had the perfect vase for them—tall, curving slightly, with a glazed green finish—which she always put in the entry hall near the guest registry. When the light changed, Judith moved up a space and turned into the parking lot.

It took her a few minutes to decide on the colors. Finally, she decided on a combination of yellow, purple, and chartreuse. Upon entering the store, she noticed three cardboard boxes filled with groceries. One box was marked GONZALES; another read JOHNSTON; the third was inscribed with BLAND.

Judith hurried into the express lane. Impatiently, she waited for the man ahead of her to pay for his six-pack of beer and bag of potato chips. As soon as he left, Judith accosted the frizzy-haired blond checker whose name tag identified her as Jaimie.

"Is that box by the door being picked up by the Blands?" Judith inquired.

Jaimie glanced toward the entrance. "It should be. Why? Are you the designated driver this week?"

"Yes," Judith replied glibly. "Anna couldn't make it."

"Anna?" Jaimie's high forehead wrinkled. "Is that the one who looks like she stepped out of *Vogue*?"

"Right," Judith agreed. "Is everything there?"

"Let me find out," Jaimie replied before calling over to the clerk at the next checkout stand. "Is the Bland order ready to go?"

The clerk, a young man with close-cropped hair, studied what appeared to be a list next to the register. "No. They need a pound of hamburger, a cut-up fryer, and a turkey breast."

"I'll take that order to them," Judith volunteered, aware that at least two people were in line behind her. "Go ahead, Jaimie, I'll pay for my flowers now."

"One of the courtesy clerks will bring the meat order," Jaimie said, ringing up the glads. "You're not one of the regulars, are you? Do you have the address?"

"Yes, on Moonfleet, right?"

Jaimie nodded as she accepted Judith's money. "Personally," she said with a puckish grin, "I like it when the young guy comes in. He's on the TV news, you know."

"Yes, that would be Adam Blake, as he calls himself," Judith said.

"His first name is really Alan. He changed his name for television," Jaimie went on. "He's the Bland grandson. But there's nothing bland about his looks." She smiled some more. "He wasn't on last night. Mavis Lean-Brodie mentioned that he'd been sent on a special assignment. Frankly, he's the only reason I watch KINE-TV instead of KINK or one of the other channels. Thanks. Enjoy your flowers."

The courtesy clerk had put the late additions into the carton and picked it up. "Your trunk?" he asked as they went out into the parking lot.

Judith winced. Even though it was the Subaru's trunk that had held Frank Purvis's dead body, she wasn't keen on any semblance of a reenactment. "You can put it in the bucket seat next to me," she said.

"Will do."

It took Judith less than five minutes to reach the Blands' house. The yellow tape was gone. That didn't surprise her. The murder was now four days old. Morris and Trash's crime-scene experts should have finished collecting evidence from the Bland property by now.

Since it was Saturday, on-street parking was hard to find. Judith went around the block twice without spotting an open space. She couldn't carry the heavy box of groceries very far. In addition to the meats, there was a loaf of bread, a head of lettuce, three bottles of wine, and several cans of soup, vegetables, and fruit. Judith had no choice but to pull into the rutted alley and park near the back door.

Her next problem was getting through the overgrown shrubbery while carrying the box. She stumbled over roots and deadwood, got scratched by blackberry vines, and narrowly avoided being poked in the eye by a forsythia branch. Out of breath, she proceeded through the tall grass, weeds, ferns, and rocks.

Still panting, she set the box down on the small moss-covered stone porch that rose only a few inches from the ground. The door was arched and made of solid wood with a tile surround, two wrought-iron hinges, and a handle to match. Judith wound up like a pitcher and pounded the door as hard as she could.

Looking at her watch, she decided to wait at least a

full minute for someone to respond. Sixty-eight seconds later a curious Alan Bland stood in the small entryway.

"Excuse me?" he said.

Judith pointed to the groceries near her feet. "I'm Judith Flynn. I didn't think Anna would be able to collect the order, so I thought I'd drop it off for her."

Alan's handsome face grew puzzled. "It wasn't Anna's turn. It was mine. I was going to the grocery store in just a few minutes. Who are you?"

"It's a long story," Judith said with a sigh. "May I come in for a moment? I had a hard time cutting through from the alley. There was no place to park out front."

"Everybody in this neighborhood seems to have two cars," Alan remarked, still eyeing Judith with curiosity. "Did you say you're a friend of Aunt Anna's?"

Judith avoided a direct answer. "I took her home from work last night. Have you spoken with her today?"

Alan shook his head and stepped aside. "Come in. I'll get the groceries. Is Aunt Anna okay?"

"Yes, she's fine," Judith said, going into the kitchen. One glance made her feel as if she'd moved back in time. Even though the sun was coming through the single window with its colored panes, the room seemed dark. The green gas range looked as if it had been installed in the twenties; so did the matching refrigerator. The tiles on the counter and the walls were faded and chipped. The old-fashioned sink and the tiled floor also showed considerable wear and tear. There was no dishwasher, no microwave, no garbage disposal. Only the wooden table and chairs looked as if they'd come from a later era by about twenty-five years. Even the quartet of metal canisters on a wooden shelf appeared to be at least a half century old. The musty air and the tomblike silence in the rest of the house gave Judith a chill.

Alan noticed. "Are you all right? Your arms are bleeding. Can I get you some Band-Aids or antiseptic?"

"A towel will do," Judith replied. "They're only scratches."

Alan pulled out a drawer that seemed to stick just a bit and handed Judith a dish towel thin enough that she could see through it. She had to be careful walking across the floor. The tiles were so grooved and cracked that they upset her balance. At the sink, she turned on the warm water tap. It sputtered a bit, then released the water in fits and starts.

"I know what you're thinking," Alan said with a wry chuckle as he stashed groceries in the ancient fridge. "You're wondering why my grandparents haven't done some renovating. The truth is, they don't have the money and they don't care."

"Really." Judith dabbed at her scratches. "So even though your folks and your aunt and uncle—and you—are doing quite well, your grandparents don't want to be bothered?"

"You got it," Alan replied. "Too much hassle, they say. Workmen all over the house, lots of noise, confusion, being inconvenienced—the whole gig. But hey—as long as they don't care, it's their home after all."

"It's such a beautiful house," Judith said. "That is, it could be a real showplace if it were fixed up."

"That's what my dad says," Alan responded. "He

keeps trying to talk them into moving to a retirement place. But they refuse to budge."

"Aunt Sally concurs, I assume," said Judith.

Alan looked amused. "Aunt Sally—well, she goes along with whatever my grandparents want."

"Aunt Sally is your grandmother's sister, right?"

Alan nodded. "In her younger years, she was quite the adventurer," he replied, taking the towel from Judith. "For her time, of course. She was a photographer. She even had some of her photos published in *National Geographic.*"

"She must have traveled widely," Judith remarked.

"She did," Alan replied, placing the worn towel on the counter. "Africa, Asia, Europe, South America—somehow she never got to Australia or New Zealand. That's one of the reasons I went into TV. I want to work my way up to reporting from the field. See the world and be where the action is."

"I understand you're on special assignment right now," Judith said. "I assume—since you're here—you don't have to travel for this job."

Alan looked away. "No. But sometimes I do. I've been to L.A. and San Francisco and Vancouver, B.C."

"What are you investigating?" Judith asked.

Alan hesitated, then looked again at Judith. "I'm sorry, I can't talk about it. At this stage, it's confidential."

"Oh." Judith was edging toward the door that led out of the kitchen. "I understand. My husband's been a private detective since he retired from the police force. Once in a while he gets a case he can't discuss. In fact, he's working on one right now. All I know is that it's some insurance scam. At least that's what the carrier is trying to prove."

Alan's keen blue eyes were regarding Judith with apprehension. "Were you thinking of going out the front way?"

She was standing on the threshold, which led to the dining room. The drapes were pulled. All she could glimpse was a table and a couple of chairs.

"No," she replied. "I was wondering if the rest of the house was furnished in Spanish-style furniture."

Alan laughed. "It's furnished with whatever my grandparents could get at secondhand stores. It's just plain old-fashioned furniture. I think some of it came with the house. The previous owner didn't want it, I guess."

"It's so dark," Judith noted. "Why don't they open the drapes on such a nice day?"

"My grandmother has very weak eyes," Alan replied. "So does Aunt Sally. It runs in the family. I hope I don't inherit it when I get older."

Desperately, Judith was trying to figure out an excuse for seeing more of the house and at least one of its inhabitants. "You know," she said in a wistful voice, "I've never met your grandparents. I understand they're very private people. But as long as I'm delivering their groceries, I thought it might be polite to introduce myself."

Alan looked regretful. "They're resting right now. They always take a little siesta after lunch."

"Oh. Aunt Sally is resting, too?"

"Aunt Sally is always resting," Alan replied in an ironic tone. "She's very frail."

"How old are they?" Judith inquired. "My own mother is quite elderly. She doesn't take regular naps, but she does tend to doze off now and then."

Alan tapped his cheek, apparently calculating ages. "Grandpa is in his eighties. Grandma is up in her seventies. Aunt Sally is a few years younger."

Compared to Gertrude, the trio was still fairly young. But, Judith realized, her own mother couldn't be compared to other human beings. "I understand your grandfather never really recovered from his war experiences," she said. "My Uncle Corky never has either. He was in the army, serving in Europe. At least once a week, he still feels a need to shoot at crows and seagulls and an occasional piece of garden statuary. Twice, he's used his pickup to take out a couple of utility poles. He calls his truck 'Tank.' "

Alan nodded. "Grandpa served in Europe, too, under General Patton. The carnage was horrendous."

"Really? That's who Uncle Corky served under. Patton may have had his flaws, but my uncle adored Old Blood and Guts."

"Grandpa didn't feel the same way about Patton," Alan said. "Of course, he doesn't like to talk about his war experiences. I wanted to interview him a while back for a feature on World War Two veterans, but he turned me down. I guess it stirred up too many bad—"

A phone rang somewhere nearby. Judith didn't see one in the kitchen, but before she could peek into the dining room, Alan removed his cell from his back pocket.

"Hi, Aunt Anna," he said in a bright voice. "What? . . . Oh, no, everything's fine. A friend of yours stopped by. Judith Flynn." He glanced at Judith to confirm that he'd gotten her name right. "Yes, she's here with me in the kitchen. She picked up the week's supply of groceries . . . Really?" Alan shot Judith a curious look. "I didn't know that . . . Yes, of course I will. Talk to you later."

Alan clicked off the phone. His expression had grown troubled. "Aunt Anna said to say hello." He hesitated, wincing slightly. "She told me who you really are. You're FATSO. I'm afraid you'll have to go."

THIRTEEN

IT DID NO good to try to explain it was Mavis-Lean Brodie's fault that Judith had gained such notoriety. Alan was polite but firm. The Blands were private people. They didn't want some amateur sleuth—especially someone whose car had held Frank Purvis's corpse—lurking around the family home.

Unencumbered by the heavy groceries she'd delivered, Judith managed to reach the alley without doing any more damage to herself. She settled in behind the MG's steering wheel, then suddenly thought it might be a good idea to take a look in the boot. She didn't want to cart around another body in a Flynn automobile. Judith lurched out of the car and apprehensively raised the boot's lid. Except for some of Joe's belongings, it was empty. She sighed with relief.

Driving home, she grew angry with Anna French. After rescuing the woman, Judith expected a more gracious response. Anna had acted grateful the previous night, but now she seemed to have turned her back on her savior.

And yet . . .

Judith had come away from the house on Moonfleet feeling as if she had missed something. It might have been a remark by Alan, the conversation between him and his aunt, or the house itself. Whatever it had been, she felt an immediate need to talk to Renie.

Carefully parking the MG on the steep hill in front of the Joneses' Dutch Colonial, she spotted her cousin in the front yard. Half-hidden by ornamental evergreens, Renie was wielding a broom and cussing. A fat gray squirrel fled through a patch of St. John's wort.

"Coz!" Judith called from the parking strip. "It's me."

"Yikes!" Renie cried, almost falling over a cherub statue that had been a birthday present from Judith. "You startled me! I'm obsessed with those damned squirrels since they got inside our attic and set up a condo two years ago. They've been lurking around all spring, trying to get back into the house. I don't trust them an inch. What's worse, they're smarter than I am."

"I thought Bill had screened off all the areas where they could come in," Judith said as Renie came out of the garden and down to the sidewalk.

"He did," Renie replied, keeping a wary eye on the squirrel's path of flight. "They removed the duct tape and ate two of the screens."

"They keep digging up my bulbs," Judith complained, before changing the subject. "You got a minute?"

"Sure," Renie replied. "Let's go out on the deck, where I can exercise vigilance if Squeldon the Squirrel tries to attack from the rear. Do you want something to drink?"

"Water will do," Judith said as they went inside and down the hall to the kitchen. "Where's Bill?"

"Running his usual Saturday errands," Renie responded, taking two glasses out of the cupboard. "You know—the Swedish bakery, the German deli, the Japanese market. Bill's very global."

Judith accepted a glass of ice water; Renie removed a can of Pepsi from the fridge. The cousins went out onto the deck, where they had a clear view of the mountains and the northeastern section of the city.

"So what's up?" Renie inquired, putting on her sunglasses.

In detail, Judith explained about the impromptu visit to the Blands' house and her chat with Alan. Then, with equal precision, she related Alan's conversation with his aunt.

Renie, who had listened without interruption, frowned and stared down into the big backyard. Atop the garage, which faced the street in back of the house, stood Squeldon—or one of his cohorts. Renie glared at the squirrel; the squirrel glared back.

"Beat it!" Renie yelled.

But Squeldon—or his henchman—skittered to the near end of the garage and jumped into a mountain ash tree. "Now what?" Renie muttered as the squirrel climbed down the tree and disappeared behind the tall rockery that separated the upper garden from the lower section. "What were you saying? Oh! That darkness—it does seem very strange. I mean, even if you've got weak eyes—and I do—you'd think that as you got older you'd need some natural light to help you move around."

"Blind people get used to their surroundings," Judith pointed out. "After all, the Blands have lived there for over fifty years."

"Fresh air's another matter, though," Renie noted. "Did the place feel stuffy?"

"Very," Judith replied. "As if it hadn't been aired out in fifty years."

"Hunh." Renie became pensive again. "Go over that one part again—about the elder Blands being feeble."

Judith repeated what she'd already told her cousin. "Except for Jane Bland and Aunt Sally's eye conditions, Alan didn't mention any other specific physical problems."

"Inertia," Renie said. "Lack of exercise and fresh air. Can you imagine how you'd atrophy in such a house?"

"Except that it's very big and they must have plenty of stairs," Judith pointed out.

"But that's about it," Renie said. "They obviously aren't gardeners." She sighed. "Talk about dysfunctional families—the senior Blands don't seem to function at all. Luckily, it seems that their two children haven't inherited their parents' reclusive traits."

"That's true," Judith allowed, waving off an inquisitive bee. "But remember, Luke was adopted."

"Yes," Renie agreed. "I'd forgotten." She turned abruptly in her lounge chair to face Judith. "Alan is Luke's son. Why would he worry about having the same eye problems as his grandmother and his aunt? They're not related by blood."

Judith stared at Renie. "He wouldn't. But the only time I saw Luke Bland was in that café, and he was wearing sunglasses."

"Lots of people do that," Renie said, "especially around here, or if they think they look cool."

"Luke was reading," Judith responded. "First the menu, then something from a big binder. He kept the sunglasses on the whole time."

"They might be prescription sunglasses," Renie pointed out.

"Damn!" Judith breathed. "Adoption papers are sealed. How do we find out? And why would someone lie about adopting a child?"

"Because the child belonged to someone near and dear?" Renie suggested.

"Like Aunt Sally?" Judith scowled. "Sally's a widow. Not that we can't rule out an illegitimate baby. Maybe she had an affair."

"Maybe this has nothing to do with Frank Purvis's murder," Renie pointed out. "But often there's a mystery within a mystery."

Squeldon, accompanied by two accomplices, was on the stone stairs that led to the lower part of the garden. They had surrounded a wooden planter next to the steps and were attempting to tip it over.

"You vile wretches!" Renie shrieked, jumping up from her chair and running from the back porch toward the stone stairs just as the planter was upended. The villains fled, furry tails a-flying.

"They're smirking, I swear it!" Renie called up to Judith. "That's the fourth time they've done that this week!" She stooped down, using her bare hands to scoop the plants and the soil. "They've just about ruined this planter. Dad made it for us when Bill and I moved into this house years ago. I'm taking it into the basement."

Renie disappeared under the deck, where the basement door was located. Two minutes later, she reappeared, brushing her hands off on her jeans.

"Land mines," she muttered as she returned to the deck. "That's what we need. They know about traps and such. They can even deactivate them and remove the nuts. They probably think it's just a game on my part." With a sigh, she sat down again. "Have you heard from Morris and Trash?"

Judith shook her head. "For being their original suspect, they've kept me at arm's length. It makes me wonder if they have a line on who really did it. There's been nothing in the paper, not even an obit for Purvis."

"I know," Renie said. "I've been searching the papers, too, and even—gag—watching the local TV news."

"I've caught the late news on KINE," Judith said. "I often do, especially when Joe's home. I figure he's got a thing for Mavis. By the way, I tried to find out what kind of special assignment Alan—or Adam Blake, if you prefer—had been given, but he couldn't talk about it."

"Sounds like city politics," Renie said. "Somebody's got a hand in the till, I'll bet."

Judith glanced at her watch. "Good grief! It's after one! Mother must be starving. I'd better get home."

"Doesn't she have about a six-month supply of microwave foods in the toolshed?" Renie asked. "Why do you have to knock yourself out to wait on her hand and foot?"

Rising from her chair, Judith shot her cousin a challenging look. "How many times have you talked to your mother today?"

"Uh . . ." Renie also stood up. "Twice. I'll drop by her apartment for a bit after Bill gets home with the car." Grinning, she put a hand on Judith's arm. "They spoiled us, we spoil them. I guess it's only fair."

"There's fair," Judith murmured as they entered the kitchen, "and there's unfair. I still can't understand how Anna French could be so uncooperative after what I did for her last night."

"You know perfectly well that life is not fair, and neither are people," Renie declared, walking Judith to the front door.

"It's not just that," Judith said, "it's that she told Alan to say hello to me. I'm getting a mixed message there. I wonder what else she had to say to her nephew."

Renie shrugged. "You'll probably never know."

Reaching the porch, Judith eyed her cousin closely. "If I have anything to do about it, I will."

Uncle Corky and Aunt Theodora lived on an island across the bay. The surroundings were rural; their A-frame house was set among tall firs and other varieties of evergreens. They rarely took the ferry into the city, but far from being reclusive like the Blands, they remained active in community affairs and frequently traveled abroad. Uncle Corky particularly enjoyed going to Europe and visiting the sites where he'd served during World War II. He was smart, outspoken, and profane. In fact, he was not unlike his hero, General Patton.

On a whim, Judith decided to call her uncle. After a greeting of hearty expletives, Uncle Corky asked why Judith was calling.

"We don't usually hear from you unless it's the annual invitation for Christmas, Easter, and Thanksgiving," he said in his rich baritone. "What's up? Don't tell me my freaking sister-in-law bought the Big One?"

"No, Mother's fine," Judith answered. Briefly, she considered telling her uncle about Mike and Kristin's estrangement. But for now, the less said, the better, Judith decided. "I'm doing a little research. I know you were in Innsbruck at the end of the war. Have you ever heard of a town in Austria named Kopfstein?"

"Kopfstein." Uncle Corky was obviously turning the word over in his agile mind. "Yes, as I recall, it's closer to Salzburg than it is to Innsbruck. In fact, it's right on the German border in the Bavarian Alps, near Berchtesgaden."

"That's interesting," Judith said. "I mean, being so close to Hitler's mountain retreat."

"Beautiful country," Corky noted. "Too freaking good for that crazy bastard."

"So Kopfstein is just a dot on the map," Judith said. "That is, there's nothing unusual about it?"

"Not that I know of," Uncle Corky replied. "Along with the freaking French, we overran that whole part of Austria, accepting the surrender of the German freaking soldiers. Then it was balls-up with a lot of our soldiers. They really cut loose. Who the hell could blame those poor SOBs after all they'd gone through? To the victor go the spoils, as they say. They raided the Nazi big shots' liquor cabinets and wine cellars, they snatched up a bunch of souvenirs, they traded loot with each other, and took everything with a swastika on it. One big item was the Hitler freaking Youth daggers. I wouldn't have used one of those freaking things to cut up a seagull. But besides the souvenirs, our men got to sleep indoors, take showers, wear clean uniforms. And when it came to women, well, there were plenty of lonely broads in Europe after the war. Our guys were more than happy to console them."

"They had free time on their hands," Judith remarked. "That must have been a terrific adjustment."

"You bet your butt it was," Corky retorted. "I had an office on the third floor of a seventeenth-century building in Innsbruck. The town had been shot up pretty goddamned well, but that Baroque beauty survived. Anyway, I'd sit on my dead ass and watch the GIs down in the street. Sometimes it seemed as if they were wandering around in a freaking daze, not quite sure how to act without some crazy Kraut bastard shooting from a roof or a window or a doorway. Fear's hard to shake. We didn't just liberate Europe, we liberated ourselves. Sudden freedom is heady freaking stuff. It's no wonder some of our guys got out of control."

"Those of us who've never been through it really can't understand," Judith said, then paused before continuing. "I've got a silly question for you, Uncle Corky. Does the name Dick Bland mean anything to you?"

"In connection with the war? Not offhand," Corky replied. "Who *is* the bastard?"

"Someone I know who served under Patton, maybe in the same places you did," Judith replied.

"He could have," Corky said. "But he wasn't in my

company. Hey—I've got a perfect freaking shot at a seagull. The SOB's about to crap on Tank. Keep your pecker up, as my mom used to say."

Hanging up the phone, Judith smiled. Grandma Grover had been a true lady, but her favorite words of encouragement to her children and grandchildren had been given without regard to gender—or delicacy. It was her only vulgarity, but the phrase had served Judith well.

As she prepared various cheeses and a crab dip for the guests' appetizers, Judith considered how she could approach Lynette and Luke Bland. But what was the point? Nobody in the family seemed willing to surrender any kind of useful information. Still, Judith reasoned as she melted cream cheese for the crab dip, casual conversation often elicited revealing tidbits that the speaker unwittingly let slip.

She was bringing the hors d'oeuvres tray into the living room when the phone rang. Juggling the tray, Judith swore under her breath. Luckily, none of the guests had come downstairs yet for the social hour. Before she could safely set the tray down on the oak buffet, the call switched over to Voice Messaging. Judith fetched the chafing dish with the crab dip before dialing her mailbox's number.

"This is Lynette Bland," said the brisk recorded voice. "I wanted to thank you for the lovely bouquet you brought to my office. I'm sorry I missed you. You don't need to call me back."

Judith, however, immediately dialed the Blands' home number, which had shown up on her Caller ID. Lynette answered on the second ring.

"Really," she said, "you didn't have to return my call. This is probably a busy time for you."

"I have everything under control," Judith assured Lynette. "I'm so glad you liked the flowers. I bought some glads for myself today. In fact, I got them at the grocery store in Langford and ended up delivering your in-laws' weekly order."

"I heard about that," Lynette replied in an ironic tone. "You certainly cover all the bases."

Judith sat down in one of the kitchen chairs. "Do you blame me? If you'd found a dead man in the trunk of your car, wouldn't you want to know why?"

"Maybe." Lynette sounded unsure.

"I can't help it," Judith confessed. "It's my nature. That's how I got to be . . . FATSO."

"I suppose it is," Lynette said without enthusiasm. "Frankly, I've always felt that the less you know about certain things, the better."

"Sometimes that's true," Judith agreed. "Ignorance can protect you. It can save you from worry and heartbreak. Yes, I see what you mean. We've all had the opportunity to seek Truth, but couldn't face it because it was too painful. Don't you wonder, though, if not knowing eats away at your insides?"

"Well . . ." Lynette paused. "Perhaps."

"Or what's worse," Judith went on, forcing herself to sound long-suffering, "it can build barriers between people who should be close. You might think you're protecting someone else, for instance, when, in fact, you're only creating mistrust. Goodness, I ought to know," she continued, now speaking from the heart as she recalled the years she'd let Mike believe that Dan

McMonigle was his biological father. "I've been through that with my own son. Can you imagine what anguish it caused?"

"Really?" The indifference had seeped out of Lynette's voice. "Did he resent you for it?"

"Not in the long run," Judith admitted. "He'd sort of figured it out on his own after he became an adult. But he was almost thirty by that time. In retrospect, it was more painful for me than it was for him."

"Did it cause a rift between you?" Lynette asked.

Judith winced. "Yes," she lied, her mind's eye recalling the chilly scene between Luke and Lynette at the café. "He knew I was keeping something from him, something I was too ashamed to tell him. We grew apart for many years." Not a complete lie; Mike had been posted to Montana as a forest ranger. "I can't tell you how difficult it was to let my wretched secret come between us."

"Yes. I mean," Lynette amended, "I can see how that might happen."

"Before I forget," Judith hurriedly put in when Lynette didn't seem inclined to speak further, "your own son seems like such a nice young man. I've seen him on TV, of course, but he made an even better impression on me when I met him at your in-laws' house this afternoon. You must be very proud of him."

"I am," Lynette asserted. "Luke and I both are."

"I was trying to figure out who he resembles," Judith said as she heard bouncing footsteps and giggles from the front staircase. The sorority sisters had descended for the social hour. "He has your blond hair, of course, but his facial features resemble your husband."

"He looks a little like both of us," Lynette said, "but he mostly takes after my father."

No help there, Judith thought. Lynette's family didn't seem to play any part in the little drama going on at the house on Moonfleet.

"I'm afraid I have to go," Judith said with reluctance. "My guests are gathering in the living room."

Lynette thanked her again for the flowers and hung up. All Judith could hope was that her surmise was right: Luke Bland was keeping a big secret from his wife. Maybe Judith's discourse on the agony of withholding information would spur Lynette to discover the truth. More likely, she'd often tried and always failed. But Frank Purvis's murder may have brought matters to a head. Judith could but hope.

"Good evening," she said to the young women. "There's wine and other beverages in the dining room." Hillside Manor's bar was a converted washstand that had once stood in an upstairs bathroom. "That dip is crab. Just a warning in case anyone has allergies."

The foursome giggled some more and headed straight for the dining room. Mrs. Greenwalt and a middle-aged couple from Dallas named Durning came down the stairs and entered the living room. Mrs. Greenwalt zeroed in on Judith.

"The cat, I trust, is dead," she said, her plump face a mask of disgust.

"The cat's gone," Judith replied, looking forsaken.

"How is Mr. Greenwalt? Are you going back to the hospital tonight?"

"Yes, for an hour or so." Mrs. Greenwalt sighed heavily. "I spent much of the day there. Fortunately, my husband is recovering. We'll be able to leave for home tomorrow. You'll receive the airline and hotel bills directly."

"Airline and hotels?" Judith gulped.

Mrs. Greenwalt nodded stiffly. "Of course. Our original plans were to travel for another week. Now we've had to cancel everything because of your homicidal pet. It's only fair that you should pay for our return fare. Obviously, we couldn't get a decent rate on such short notice. There's no direct flight from here to Nashville, which means we'll have a layover in Chicago and another in St. Louis. Obviously, George can't wait around in airports. We'll have to spend two nights in hotels. It will take us three days to get to Nashville."

Judith was speechless. The Durnings, meanwhile, were plundering the appetizers while the sorority sisters guzzled wine in the dining room. Before Judith could think of something to say, the doorbell rang.

Mike and the boys stood on the front porch. All three of them were carrying bags and boxes from KFC. "Hi, Mom," Mike said with a big grin. "I hope you haven't started dinner. We brought it with us. Is Dad home yet?"

"Uh . . . no," Judith responded. "He's stuck in Omaha for a couple more days. I forgot to tell you."

Mac and Joe-Joe made a beeline for the kitchen, scattering the sorority sisters, who proclaimed the little boys' adorability in high-pitched admiration.

"Chicken! Let's eat now!" Mac cried. "I'm hungry!"

"Cluck-cluck!" Joe-Joe exclaimed. "Cock-a-doodle-doo!"

"Go ahead," Judith said to Mike. "But get Granny out of the toolshed. She loves fried chicken. And she'll love seeing all of you."

"That's what I figured," Mike replied, heading for the kitchen. "Since the boys and I are going back to the ranger station tomorrow, I'm not sure when we'll—"

Mrs. Greenwalt had come into the entry hall. "You keep your mother in a *toolshed*? What kind of a place *is* this?"

"The toolshed's been converted—" Judith was interrupted again by the doorbell. "Excuse me." She turned away from Mrs. Greenwalt.

"Police," Glenn Morris announced, flashing his badge just in case Judith might have forgotten.

"Ah!" exclaimed Mrs. Greenwalt, who had traipsed after Judith. "It's about time! I hope you're going to arrest her."

"Who's this broad?" Jonathan Trashman asked, pointing to Mrs. Greenwalt as he lumbered into the entry hall.

"I beg your pardon!" Lucy Greenwalt huffed. *"You* look like last week's laundry!"

Judith stepped between the pair. "Mrs. Greenwalt is one of my guests," she said through gritted teeth. "Shouldn't we adjourn to the front parlor?"

"No need," Glenn said airily. "We wanted to tell you in person that you're no longer a homicide suspect."

"Not as far as I'm concerned," Lucy Greenwalt put in, moving her plump figure in front of Glenn and Trash. "I knew I should have called the authorities myself, but it seems some other concerned soul did it for me. Mrs. Flynn's culpable of attempted murder at least!"

Glenn eyed Mrs. Greenwalt with interest. "Really? Who is the victim?"

"My poor husband," Mrs. Greenwalt snapped. "As if you didn't know!"

Glenn's gaze turned to Judith. "Is there something you haven't told us?"

"Plenty," Judith retorted. "But it has nothing to do with Frank Purvis. Believe me, this is all a silly—"

"Old fart coming through!" shouted Gertrude, wheeling herself into the entry hall. "What's all this commotion? I want to have my supper in peace!" On the run, Mac and Joe-Joe led the way, crashing into Glenn and Mrs. Greenwalt.

"Cluck-cluck!" Joe-Joe shouted, tugging at Mrs. Greenwalt's too-tight green slacks. "Big fat chicken!"

Lucy Greenwalt yanked Joe-Joe's small hands from her slacks. "Mind your manners, little boy! They should keep *you* in the doghouse!"

"Woof, woof," Joe-Joe barked, scampering away.

The sorority sisters stared and the Durnings gaped. Mike started toward his mother, but she waved him off.

"Later," Judith mouthed.

"What's with these two bozos?" Gertrude asked, gesturing at the detectives.

Judith grasped the handles on Gertrude's wheelchair

and started to turn the old lady around. "Never mind, Mother. You'd better eat your supper while it's hot."

Gertrude, however, set the wheelchair's brake. "I don't like the looks of 'em. Don't let those two get near Grandma Grover's breakfront. They might steal her Royal Doulton gravy boat."

Glenn, whose composure had previously seemed unflappable, began to look slightly dazed. "Yes," he informed Judith, "the parlor. Now."

"Pat 'em down before they go!" Gertrude shouted as Judith moved quickly through the parlor door with Glenn and Trash on her heels. Mrs. Greenwalt attempted to follow, but Trash slammed the hall door in her face while Glenn secured the door to the living room.

"We won't keep you from your . . . whatever they are," Glenn said, assuming his accustomed stance in front of the fireplace. "We merely wanted to advise you that you're no longer a suspect. In fact, you're no longer a person of interest."

"As in"—Trash chuckled—"you're really boring! Ha-ha!"

Judith felt like rolling her eyes, but she already had a throbbing headache. "Does that mean you have an actual suspect?"

Glenn gave Judith a thin smile. "We can't reveal that information. But you may claim your car from the impound lot Monday morning. We're finished with it."

"Good," Judith said. At least she'd have the Subaru back before Joe came home. "Did you find anything helpful?"

Glenn shook his head. "I can't say."

"How was he killed?" Judith persisted.

"The classic blunt instrument to the skull. A garden tool, in this case." Glenn made a dismissive gesture. "I can't go into details."

"Did Frank Purvis leave any survivors?" Judith asked.

"Not that we could find," Glenn replied. "No one has stepped forward to claim the victim."

"What happens to the body?" Judith inquired, vaguely recalling that Joe had once mentioned that the county or the city was responsible for disposing of the remains in such cases.

"We take care of that," Glenn answered with an appropriately grim expression.

Judith wasn't satisfied with the response. "I realize that, but how?"

"We roast 'em and toast 'em," Trash said. "The ashes go in a metal box and get sent to a crypt someplace. Purvis is a done deal. Well-done, I might add. Ha-ha."

"What information goes on the metal box?" Judith asked.

Trash shrugged. "Name, date of death, and, if we know it, date of birth. That's it."

"Does that happen often?"

Glenn gave Judith an impatient look. "Too often these days, with all the homeless."

Judith cringed. "That sounds so . . . awful."

"It's reality," Glenn stated flatly.

"I suppose it is," Judith murmured. Then, in a stronger voice, she posed another question: "Why are you working on a Saturday?"

"We're shorthanded," Glenn replied. "We'll leave

you now. Thanks for your cooperation." The detectives went out of the parlor the way they'd come in.

Judith remained in the room, staring at the fireplace's empty grate. The explanation jibed with what Joe had told her. Except for the part about Purvis having already been cremated. If she remembered correctly, homicide victims were kept in the city morgue for some time if the body had not yet been claimed.

But maybe it had. Maybe somebody out there wanted Frank Purvis's earthly remains destroyed.

Judith wondered who—and why.

FOURTEEN

JUDITH HAD TO choke back tears when Mike and the grandchildren left around seven-thirty Saturday evening for the ranger station. They weren't going more than fifty miles from Hillside Manor, and they were only a phone call away, but she felt as if a new distance had grown between her and Mike. It was an emotional gap, a generational chasm, a disparity in values.

At least Mike had managed to find a sitter for the boys. But Kristin was headed for her family's wheat ranch across the state, presumably to mull over her options. Judith wanted to shake her Valkyrie-like daughter-in-law. But that would be like a willow trying to move an oak. Nor would it be wise to interfere or offer advice to Kristin. Maybe her parents would be able to make her see reason. Unfortunately, Judith wasn't optimistic.

"They're gone," Judith said to Renie over the phone. "And Joe's not here to help me cope with my emotions. I feel miserable."

"How do you think I feel with all three of our

kids in far-flung places?" Renie shot back. "Bill and I waited forever for them to get married and leave home. Then, when they all did it at the same time, I was bereft. I still am."

"But none of them are breaking up," Judith pointed out, sounding bitter.

"Not so far," Renie replied. "Heck, they've only been married for a little over a year. Cheer up. Get your mind back on murder."

"That's hard to do," Judith declared, but promptly regaled her cousin with the latest homicide-related news.

"What are you saying?" Renie asked after Judith had finished. "That someone did in fact claim Frank Purvis's body, but it's a big secret? Isn't there a record of who the body was released to?"

"Maybe. Maybe not."

"In other words, money passed hands," Renie speculated.

"It's not impossible," Judith said, "though bribes were almost nonexistent in the homicide squad when Joe was there. Or so he insisted."

"No city is immune to police corruption," Renie remarked. "I wouldn't trust Glenn and Trash an inch."

"Neither would my mother," Judith said, "but she doesn't trust most people. As she puts it, if you can't trust the weather around here, who can you trust?"

"Maybe that's why so many of us natives are skeptics."

"Maybe," Judith conceded. "But it wouldn't have to be Glenn or Trash who were coerced into releasing the body. It could have been a higher-up or maybe even somebody in the morgue. The question is, who would want to dispose of Purvis's corpse and why? And who *was* Frank Purvis in the first place?"

"What about checking with the people at Dairyland?"

"The police must have done that already," Judith said. "Dairyland keeps its trucks in a lot a couple of blocks from Emerald Lake. That neighborhood adjoins the Langford district. How hard would it be to steal a truck and a uniform? It'd take some daring, unless Purvis arrived earlier than the other drivers and employees."

"Who's awake at four in the morning?" Renie remarked. "I'd be a zombie. I wouldn't notice a woolly mammoth in the bathtub."

"People who work those shifts are used to getting up early. On the other hand, they probably do things by routine, each employee in his or her own little world."

"Purvis had to know Vern Benson's route," Renie noted. "Maybe the drivers keep their route and schedule in their trucks. All Purvis would have to do is scout the Moonfleet area and take down the truck number when Vern made his deliveries."

Judith sighed. "The one thing we know is that Frank definitely stole Vern's truck and jacket. I saw him with my own eyes, both alive and dead."

"I suppose we can dismiss any complicity on the part of the real Vern Benson," Renie said.

"I think so," Judith replied. "He seemed like a nice, hardworking young man. Still . . ."

"Still what?"

"You never know—as we've discovered before," Judith asserted. "The real question is how and why did Frank Purvis show up on the day of the UPS delivery? Where does he fit into the picture with regard to the Blands? Was he really going to steal the package on the porch?"

"Teamsters?" Renie suggested.

"Huh?"

"I was thinking—I assume UPS and the Dairyland drivers belong to the Teamsters," Renie explained. "If Frank Purvis was an actual truck driver, maybe he heard about the peculiar annual delivery to the spooky house. It's the kind of oddity that people would talk about."

"That's true," Judith responded slowly. "If not at union meetings, then with other UPS drivers." She paused, testing her memory. "Kevin, that was the driver's name." She paused again. "Drat—the office wouldn't be open on a Saturday night except to take pickup orders or trace deliveries. I'll have to wait until Monday to find out Kevin's last name. Why didn't I think of this before?"

"You've been kind of busy," Renie said dryly. "As for me, I'm out of work at the moment now that SuperGerm's been delivered and I finished the Bucky Beaver art for Mom. All I did today was work in the yard, chase squirrels, and run some errands. Which reminds me, I should put the sympathy card I bought for Alyssa Barnes in the mail tomorrow on the way to Mass."

"Who's Alyssa Barnes?" Judith inquired.

"She works for the gas company in marketing. I've

done some projects for her and we have lunch together a couple of times a year. Her brother, Fred, died this week. I'm not going to the funeral Monday, so I figured the least I could do is send her a card. Good PR on my part."

"You might have mentioned kindness," Judith said as something clicked in her brain. "Is Barnes her maiden name?"

"No, it was Pettibone. In fact," Renie went on, "Lyssa's—that's what she goes by—other brother is the vet at the Cat Clinique where you collected Sweetums. When are you bringing him home from Uncle Al's?"

"Tomorrow," Judith said tersely, her mind veering in a different direction. "This Pettibone thing is curious, but I'm not sure why. I saw Fred's obituary in the paper. In fact, I sent my condolences to Bert through his receptionist or whatever she is at the clinic. I went to school with Bert. I also remember an Alexis Pettibone."

"They're an old Langford family," Renie noted. "Lexis teaches nursing at the University. I don't recall her married name. Why are you so intrigued?"

"I'm not sure," Judith said. "Maybe I'm just obsessed with Langford these days. Or maybe I'm losing my mind."

"We've got roots in Langford," Renie pointed out. "Uncle Al still lives there. Heck, Morty the Mailman's still on a Langford route. You've said it yourself, this city may be big in some ways, but for those of us who go back a few generations, it's still a small town. You ought to know—how many times have you met somebody, gotten them to open up a little, and discovered that their first cousin is somehow related to you on your mother's side of the family?"

"Twice, actually," Judith admitted.

"And what about our Anne? We go back to visit Bill's relatives in Wisconsin, she takes one look at a graduation photo on his sister's endtable, screams, and runs out of the house because she'd made out with the guy at a high-school party. By coincidence—or what you will—he's our brother-in-law's nephew whose family moved here years ago."

"I remember that," Judith said. "Yes, it's true. If we've lived here for any length of time, we all seem to be interconnected."

"Ask my mother," Renie responded. "She's like you, she knows everybody."

"Maybe I should ask her," Judith said in a musing tone. "She probably remembers the Pettibones. Uncle Al might, for that matter."

"Sorry, coz," Renie said with a sigh, "I'm not following your train of thought. I mean, why do you care about the Pettibones?"

"Because," Judith replied, "we've got a body that's disappeared. Or has it? Would you care to change your mind and attend Fred Pettibone's funeral with me Monday?"

Renie had hemmed and hawed, but finally said she'd go, even if she thought Judith was crazy. "Bert Pettibone may not remember me," Judith had argued. "At least you've been in recent contact with the deceased's sister. You have a reason to be there. I don't."

Judith attended eight o'clock Mass Sunday morning, after setting up brunch for her guests. Mrs. Greenwalt hadn't appeared when Judith returned a few minutes after nine. She still hadn't shown up by a quarter to eleven. The other guests had finished and were in the process of checking out. While eleven was the deadline for departure six days a week, Judith allowed an extra hour on Sundays.

Waving off the sorority sisters at eleven-fifteen, Judith decided to go upstairs and see if Mrs. Greenwalt was all right. A single knock on the door evoked a sharp response.

"What is it?"

"I was making sure you're awake," Judith said through the door. "Did you want to eat before you check out at noon?"

Yanking open the door, Lucy Greenwalt stood before Judith in a zebra-striped bathrobe and matching zebra slippers. "I'll leave when I leave," she declared. "George can't be released from the hospital until one. We'll go straight from there to the airport. Our flight's at three-fifteen. Our *first* flight, that is. I'd like a tray in my room. Three scrambled eggs, ham, hot biscuits with gravy, fried cornmeal mush, grits, and strong, hot coffee with sugar and cream. Frankly, I've been very disappointed with your breakfasts. Omelettes with fish? Crab on a muffin? And those bagels with very thin sliced . . . what is it, salmon? What kind of breakfast food is that?"

"Salmon omelettes and Dungeness crab and Nova Scotia lox are considered delicacies around here," Judith retorted. "I can do the scrambled eggs and ham, maybe even whip up some biscuits, but the grits and gravy are out. Sorry." She stalked off down the hall to the back stairs.

She reached the kitchen just as the phone rang. It was Uncle Al. "Your gang left here around ten," he said. "We went out to breakfast first. Tess came along, too. We had a swell time."

"Good," Judith said. "Thanks so much for letting them stay with you. I really appreciate it. I'll be over to get Sweetums in an hour or so. Is that okay?"

"It would be," Al said, his voice no longer so chipper. "The only problem is, Sweetums isn't here."

"What do you mean?"

"He took off right after Mike and the boys left," Al explained. "You'd better wait until he shows up again."

"But he might not," Judith said, sounding agitated. "He doesn't know the neighborhood."

"Hey, kiddo, he'll be fine," Uncle Al soothed. "He's probably exploring the alley out back. I'll give you ten-to-one odds that when he gets hungry he'll wander up to the door. I'll call you when he gets here. How's that?"

"That" had to be sufficient. But Judith was unsettled. Sweetums had never been let loose anywhere except in his familiar Hillside Manor surroundings. It was four miles from the B&B to Uncle Al's house. No matter how Sweetums might try to head home, he'd have to cross a bridge. To Judith's knowledge, the cat had never been on a bridge. Indeed, he'd never strayed far enough to confront a stream of traffic.

She wouldn't tell Gertrude about Sweetums's defection. There was no point in upsetting the old girl. Not yet, anyway. For the next twenty minutes she busied herself with baking biscuits, making more scrambled eggs, and reheating the ham that was left on the sideboard.

Lucy Greenwalt accepted the food with ill grace. "It took you long enough," she declared. "Will you please order a taxi for twelve-thirty?"

"There's a phone for guests by the wicker sofa in the hall," Judith retorted.

Mrs. Greenwalt glared at her hostess. "Will you please order a taxi for twelve-thirty?" she repeated. "I don't know the cab company's number. You do."

Rather than exacerbate the situation, Judith ordered the taxi from the downstairs phone. She felt like telling the dispatcher to send the company's most reckless driver, especially one who didn't speak English.

The last straw came when Mrs. Greenwalt asked Judith to carry her luggage downstairs. Lucy and George had two large suitcases, two carry-on bags, and a garment bag. There were also two shopping bags from local stores where the Greenwalts had made purchases.

"I simply can't pick up anything that weighs over ten pounds," Judith stated. "I have an artificial hip."

"As in 'phony'?" Mrs. Greenwalt snapped. "This whole place is phony, if you ask me. Well? If you can't, who will?"

"Ask the taxi driver," Judith shot back. "I'll take those shopping bags and I'm sure you can manage the carry-ons. The driver can get the suitcases and the garment bag."

"What about my purse?" Mrs. Greenwalt demanded, wielding a huge handbag decorated with sequined roses.

"Isn't that a shoulder bag?" Judith asked wearily.

"I don't like to carry it over my shoulder. That makes it too easy for purse snatchers."

"Inside the house?"

"You never know," Mrs. Greenwalt snapped. "Especially *this* house."

The doorbell rang. Judith hurried out of the guest room and down the hall to the stairs, taking the shopping bags with her. Opening the door, she faced the taxi driver, a huskily built platinum blonde with long dangling earrings.

"Hiya, hon," the woman said, chewing gum. "Are you Greenwalt?"

"No," Judith replied. "She'll be right down. Would you mind helping with her luggage?"

"Is this an airport run?" the driver inquired with an eager expression.

"I don't think so," Judith replied as Lucy Greenwalt came huffing down the stairs with the two smaller bags and her big purse.

Disappointment crossed the driver's florid face. "Rats. Oh, well." She shrugged. An airport trip cost at least thirty dollars. "Is the stuff upstairs?"

"Yes," said Mrs. Greenwalt. "Room Five. And be *very* careful with the garment bag. I have some extremely fragile items in it."

"Gotcha," the driver said, and took the stairs two at a time.

Mrs. Greenwalt turned to Judith. "I'm not paying our bill. You owe us, as I'm sure you're aware. Good-bye." She flounced out of the house, all three bags swinging this way and that.

Bag is right, Judith thought, watching her guest place her belongings into the taxi's backseat. Mrs. Greenwalt, however, waited at the curb.

"Piece of work, huh?" the driver said, coming down the stairs and easily managing the suitcases and the garment bag.

"Just awful," Judith replied, moving onto the porch.

"From around here?" the driver inquired.

"No," Judith said softly. "An out-of-towner."

The driver chortled. "Then I think I'll take her for a little ride."

"Good," Judith said, noting that Mrs. Greenwalt was watching them with a wary eye.

"Mind that garment bag!" she shouted.

"Gotcha," the driver called back, then spoke under her breath to Judith. "In more ways than one."

After the morning haze had lifted, the sun came out and the temperature rose. High sixties, Judith calculated. It was a lovely day. But somehow, it didn't feel like it.

It was after two before Judith had the rooms cleaned and ready for the next batch of visitors. Phyliss never worked on the Sabbath; she rarely worked on the day before the Sabbath, either, insisting that she had to get herself into the proper mood for worship. Over the past few months, Judith had considered hiring someone part-time to help with the weekend tasks. Now might be a good time. Students would be looking for summer jobs. She decided to put an ad in the paper.

Wanting to stay near the phone, she took it with her while she worked in the yard. But after two hours, there was no call from Uncle Al. It was likely that he'd gone out to the track for the afternoon. The ponies took precedence over all other animals, including Sweetums.

"Where's that wretched cat?" Gertrude asked, wheeling her way to the small patio. "I heard about his latest shenanigans from Arlene. Too bad he didn't claw that pain in the butt into shreds. I've no time for people like that. They think they're big shots, just because they can afford to travel. Phooey."

Judith looked up from the flower bed next to the fence that separated Hillside Manor from the Dooleys' property. Maybe it was best to be candid. "Sweetums decided to go exploring at Uncle Al's. I think Uncle Al went to the horse races. I'll call around seven. He should be back by then. The last race goes off at six."

Gertrude's face crinkled with worry. "You think so?" She gave herself a little shake. "Sure he will. He's too ornery to miss supper."

Like owner, like pet, Judith thought. Gertrude probably envied Sweetums's ability to take off and savor liberty. Maybe the old girl was vicariously enjoying the cat's escapade.

But when Judith got hold of Uncle Al at seven-thirty, Sweet-ums still hadn't shown up.

"I stuck around until almost four," he said, concern edging into his voice. "Then I drove out to the track to catch the last three races. When I got home a little before seven, he still wasn't here. I put some chow out for him on the back porch before I left, but it hasn't been touched."

"Maybe he'll come back after dark," Judith said hopefully. "The trouble is, it stays light so long this time of year."

"Let's bet on it," Uncle Al replied. "Seven-to-two odds. I'll call you as soon as your cat crosses the finish line at the door."

Judith had barely clicked off when the phone rang in her hand. It was Joe.

"I had the day off, being Sunday," he announced, sounding cheerful. "I called your Aunt Ellen and Uncle Win last night in Beatrice, and they offered to meet me halfway in Lincoln. I didn't realize they were long-time Cornhusker ticket holders. I guess the Nebraska supporters wear red even in the off-season. We had a good time touring the campus, and then we ate some excellent steak at a restaurant I'd found in the tourist guide."

"Not one recommended by Aunt Ellen?" Judith inquired.

"I knew better than that," Joe replied. "Your aunt's the only person I know who can still find a four-dollar buffet this side of Nevada. The part I don't get is that she insists on paying for seconds, even the coffee refills."

"Aunt Ellen is not only thrifty, but incredibly honest," Judith replied. "She once stood on a downtown street corner for twenty minutes with a nickel she'd found in the gutter and waited for someone to claim it. But she's also very moral. She wouldn't give it to a wino, and ended up putting it into an expired parking meter to save somebody a ticket."

"So how are things at home?" Joe asked.

Judith informed him about Mike's departure, but tried to keep her sorrow to herself.

She was unsuccessful. Joe knew his wife too well. "You can't let this thing eat away at you. Frankly, I'm glad I had to go out of town," he said. "It keeps my mind off of Mike's marital troubles. You should focus on something else. It's too bad you couldn't find a dead body someplace. Ha-ha. Only kidding," he added hastily.

"Right," Judith murmured. "So you think you'll be home Tuesday night?"

"I'll know for sure by tomorrow afternoon," Joe said. "I'll call you around seven your time, okay?"

Judith said that would be fine. Feeling desolate, she hung up. No husband, no cat, no reconciliation, no killer. It had not been a good day.

Here's my plan," Judith said to Renie over the phone the next morning. "The Pettibone funeral's at noon, Langford United Methodist Church. I can get out of here right after eleven. If you could pick me up, I can collect the Subaru from the impound and then we could drive separately to the service."

"Nuttier and nuttier," Renie muttered. "Okay, why not?"

"I take it Bill doesn't need the car today?"

"Not until this afternoon," Renie replied. "Right now he's in the basement, playing with his dirk."

Bill Jones had a limited but choice collection of swords, daggers, and other antique blades. At one point, Renie had urged him to buy a fifteenth-century pikestaff that she wanted to use as a hat rack. Bill demurred.

Renie picked Judith up at eleven-fifteen. Phyliss, who proclaimed that Sweetums wasn't really missing but had finally turned back into the Archfiend, was knee-deep in the weekend's accumulated laundry. The parish's senior-citizen bus had picked up Gertrude, who had gone off to bridge club with Aunt Deb.

To Judith's surprise, there was no problem retrieving her car. The officers on duty were courteous and efficient. Judith didn't mention Joe's name. She felt it was best to be discreet, lest the saga get back to Joe. The thought of him blowing a gasket wasn't pleasant.

Renie led the way to the church, which was located about a mile from Uncle Al's and a half mile from the Blands' house. The day was warm and the small church was packed. Dying young always attracted a crowd, Judith thought as she and Renie allowed an usher to find them places on the aisle in the next to the last row of pews. Unlike the elderly, those who were taken too soon left behind many friends and relatives.

Renie twisted this way and that in her seat, trying to look over and around the people in front of her. "Alyssa," she whispered to Judith. "Second row on the right, short dark hair, black suit with white trim on the collar."

Being almost a half-foot taller than Renie and on the aisle, Judith spotted Alyssa Pettibone Barnes with comparative ease. "I don't see Bert," she said under her breath. "He must be a pallbearer."

"He is," Renie replied, checking the memorial program the usher had given them. "There's a Barnes, too. That must be Lyssa's husband."

The soloist had concluded singing "The Old Rugged Cross." There was a pause before the minister appeared on the altar and the organ played the notes to begin the service. The mourners all stood as the casket was moved slowly into the church proper.

The six pallbearers seemed to come from two generations—young and middle-aged. Judith recognized Bert Pettibone, despite the forty years that had passed since she'd seen him last in grade school. He wasn't as thin, he now wore glasses, and his graying brown hair had receded, but the features were basically the same.

The casket, adorned with a spray of lilies and roses, rolled past the cousins. Judith bowed her head and said a prayer for Alfred Pettibone's soul and for his survivors.

The funeral was conducted with dignity and simplicity: hymns, prayers, and a eulogy by the pastor. Alfred—or Fred, as he was better known—had been a hardworking individual, a man of faith, and devoted to his family. Fred and his wife had a daughter and a son, now grown. The deceased had spent most of his life working for the government and earning high praise from his superiors. He had been taken before his time, but that was God's will.

"Bull," Renie muttered. "That's not how it works. God gets too much blame for humankind's flaws."

Judith nodded, but remained silent as the pastor concluded by announcing that the casket would be opened for viewing and that a reception would follow in the church hall.

"The only dead bodies I look at are the ones you find," Renie whispered to Judith. "I'm going to track down Lyssa and give her my condolences. Gawk, if you want to."

Doubts about her reason for attending the services began to assail Judith. Was there any point in viewing the deceased? The hunch had come from out of left field. Often, her intuition had been proved right. But she had also been wrong on numerous occasions.

Approximately two thirds of the mourners were queued up to pay their last respects to Fred Pettibone. Judith moved into her place near the end of the line. It was a slow process. The closer she got to the coffin, the more she heard sniffles and weeping. Fred must have been well loved. Certainly the minister had made him sound like a fine man. Maybe Renie was right. Judith was going crazy.

At last she approached the casket. Taking a deep breath, she looked at the dead man.

She was right.

He might be Fred Pettibone to the rest of the world, but he was Frank Purvis to Judith.

FIFTEEN

YOU'RE KIDDING!" RENIE exclaimed when she and Judith rendezvoused outside the church. "How in the hell did you figure that one out before you saw the body?"

A couple of older women apparently coming from the church overheard Renie and briefly stopped in their tracks on the stone walkway. Judith looked away from them and shielded her eyes from the midday sun. "It was the way the body was handled by the police," Judith said, keeping her voice down as other mourners trickled out of the church. "It didn't sound right, not according to what Joe has told me about unclaimed victims. Then it dawned on me that Alfred Pettibone was about the same age as Frank Purvis. There was no mention of how he died in the obituary, nor did the minister refer to it just now. Also, remembrances were to be made to the humane society. That's a good cause, but usually when someone passes away in their forties, it's heart or cancer, and the memorials are sent to related research associations or to a hospice."

"A lucky guess," Renie remarked drolly, but her expression became thoughtful. "Yes, not to mention that if it's cancer, there's often a brief account of the deceased's courage or the family's appreciation for caregivers. If it's an accident of some sort, there's a reference to the 'senseless tragedy.' But I still don't quite get it."

Judith and Renie had moved under the shade of a dogwood tree. "It was the initials, too," Judith said. "All of the Pettibones had names that began with *A*, but they were known by their nicknames—Bert for Albert, Fred for Alfred, Lyssa for Alyssa, and, as I recall, Lexi, for Alexis."

"So?"

"Fred Pettibone—the names start with the same initials as Frank Purvis," Judith pointed out. "And, by the way, what did Frank—I mean, Fred—do for the federal government? His résumé was far from complete."

"That's true," Renie said. "There weren't any memories from the congregation, either. Not that I mind—those things can go on until I want to jump in the casket and get wheeled away along with the corpse."

"You've got to introduce me to Lyssa," Judith declared. "Then maybe I can meet Fred's widow. Andrea, I think her name is."

"I assume they don't call her 'Drea,' " Renie murmured, then narrowed her eyes at her cousin. "Surely you don't mean meeting them now?"

"Why not?" Judith responded. "I'm not going to drill either one of them, but I'd like an entrée into the family."

Renie looked grim. "Okay, let's go back inside." Suddenly she brightened. "Maybe they have some decent food at the reception."

"You graze, I talk," Judith said as they returned to the church and headed down a flight of stairs.

"But you don't conduct an interrogation," Renie warned. "May I remind you, this isn't the place for it."

"I know, I know," Judith replied. "I'll be discreet."

The reception line had dwindled to a half-dozen people. The other guests were sitting at round tables, eating finger food from the buffet that was set up under a large painting of Jesus feeding the multitudes with loaves and fishes.

Renie started for the buffet, but Judith grabbed her arm. "Hold it. Introductions first, food second."

Renie frowned at the selection of fruit, raw vegetables, crackers, and cheese. She turned to a gray-haired woman wearing an apron and pointed to the picture of Jesus.

"Could I have what He's serving?" Renie asked.

Staring with disapproval at Renie, the woman stomped away in her sturdy shoes.

"And you criticize me," Judith muttered, hauling Renie over to the Pettibone family, where they were receiving condolences from the last of the funeral attendees.

"Lyssa," Renie said with a sympathetic expression that probably fooled everybody except Judith, "I couldn't leave without introducing you to my cousin Judith Flynn. We had a car problem, so she came with me. I'm sure you've heard me speak of her."

Lyssa Barnes's smile was about as convincing as Renie's sympathy. "Oh, yes. You run a motel, don't you?"

"A bed-and-breakfast," Judith replied. "I understand you work for the gas company."

Lyssa, a plump woman with auburn hair and deep green eyes, nodded. "That's how I met Serena."

"I went to grade school with Bert," Judith said.

"Really?" Lyssa gazed across the room to where her brother was now standing by the buffet table. "I was a few years behind Bert."

"I'm sorry about your other brother," Judith said, noticing that the Widow Pettibone was about to move on. "I must convey my condolences to your sister-in-law. And Bert, of course."

Lyssa called after Andrea, who had taken a few steps away from where the receiving line had formed. Andrea turned. She was a pretty woman, though pale and drawn. Lyssa made the introductions.

"I was widowed quite young, too," Judith said, putting out her hand. "Believe me, I know what you're going through."

"Thank you," Andrea said, her handshake limp. "You went to school with Bert?"

Judith nodded. "Grade school. I lived in Langford for a few years before my family moved to Heraldsgate Hill. How are your children coping?"

Andrea looked in the direction of the two young adults who were talking to Bert and a woman who might have been his wife. "They're still in a state of shock. When someone passes so suddenly, it's terribly hard. Excuse me, I should be with them."

Judith was left alone in the middle of the room. More people were leaving. Renie, in fact, had deserted Judith and was edging her way into the kitchen. Lyssa had also moved off, speaking with an older couple who were seated at a table toward the end of the church hall.

Having no idea of what Alexis Pettibone looked like, Judith figured Bert was her last hope. He was still with his presumed wife, niece, nephew, and Andrea. It would be gauche to breach the family circle.

But a moment later, Bert left the others and headed for the exit. Judith moved swiftly, catching her prey just before he left the hall.

"Bert," she said, putting a hand on his arm. "Do you remember me? I was Judith Grover in grade school."

Bert peered through his glasses, studying Judith's face. "I'm sorry, I don't, offhand."

"We lived on Hyde Park Place, that triangle block," Judith said as she heard loud noises coming from the kitchen area.

Bert peered some more. "Oh—yes, you look quite different. You used to be . . ."

"Fat," Judith put in, ignoring a couple of shouts that also emanated from the kitchen. "And my hair was jet-black, not silver. It started to turn gray when I was in my early twenties, just like my mother's did."

"You're looking well," Bert said in his studious manner. If no longer shy, he had retained a certain diffidence. "Did you know my brother?"

"No," Judith said, then explained about the connection between Renie and Lyssa. "I have a question for you," she continued. "It won't take a minute. My cat, Sweetums, was at your clinic the other night. He wasn't hurt, but he'd done some damage to one of my guests. I left him with my uncle in Langford until the guests checked out, but now the cat's run off. He doesn't know the neighborhood. What's the best way to find him?"

A hostile glint appeared in Bert's brown eyes. "Sweetums, did you say?"

Judith grimaced. "Yes."

"I heard about Sweetums," Bert replied, his forehead wrinkling. "From what I was told, it might be best not to find him."

If Judith had dared, she would've stamped her foot. But possible hip dislocation was always at the back of her mind. "Sweetums is our beloved family pet. We've had him for years. Of course he can be contrary, even ornery. He's a *cat*, for heaven's sake!"

"Unlike any other," Bert murmured. But he gave Judith a half smile. "Advertise. Put signs on utility poles near your uncle's house. A photo would help. If someone finds your cat, they won't want to keep him. That is," he amended, "they'd want to return him to his human."

"Thanks," Judith said, sounding sarcastic, but quickly remembering her hidden agenda. "Assuming Sweetums is found, I'd like to bring him in for a checkup. It's been a while. There may be a medical reason why he sometimes behaves so . . . aggressively."

Bert's expression was dubious, but his response was polite. "Call the clinic this afternoon. We can make the appointment for later in the week. If your pet doesn't show up by then, it's probably hopeless."

"Don't say that," Judith retorted. "I mean, he has to show up. Is it possible I could see you this afternoon? For grief counseling? I assume you provide such a service for bereaved pet owners."

Bert looked askance. "We don't. We give referrals, however. In any event, I won't be in the office today. I have some personal grief to deal with."

Judith was embarrassed. "Oh, please—I'm really sorry! It's just that I'm so upset. Not just about Sweetums, but the funeral service brought back so many sad memories. You see, I lost my husband when he was still in his forties. It was terrible." She managed to force tears into her eyes, not so much for Dan's loss, but for the waste of his life.

"I didn't realize that," Bert said, sounding genuinely touched. "Was it sudden?"

Judith shook her head, trying to ignore the ongoing commotion in the kitchen. "No. He'd been ill for some time." Drinking and eating for even longer. "But it was still a shock." Especially for the two slim undertakers who had practically had to bring in a crane to move Dan's four hundred pounds out of the house. "As I told your sister-in-law, I realize it's even worse when death comes so unexpectedly. That is, I assume Fred didn't have a long illness."

"No. He did not." Bert's thin lips clamped shut in a grim line. "His health was excellent."

"An accident?" Judith asked in her most compassionate tone.

"If you want to call it that." Bert remained grim.

"That's so sad. I hope it didn't involve a vehicle. That usually means a drunken driver or a reckless teen."

Bert made no comment.

"It's good that he worked for the government," Judith continued quickly, lest Bert start to move on.

"They have excellent benefits, I understand. I suppose, though, that it depends on what branch your brother worked for."

"I suppose it does," Bert said. "Excuse me, I have to find out when the funeral director will be ready to go to the cemetery. Nice to see you again after all these years."

Nice, Judith thought, *but not very helpful.* Her brooding was interrupted by the sight of Renie, holding a chicken leg, and being propelled out of the kitchen by two stout women.

"And stay out!" one of them ordered, letting go of Renie and swiping one hand against the other. "This food is for the poor!"

"Do I look rich to you?" Renie demanded, despite the fact that she was wearing a black bouclé summer suit from Neiman Marcus.

The women didn't bother to answer, but disappeared into the kitchen.

Taking a savage bite out of the chicken leg, Renie approached her cousin. "Sowadidufnow?" she asked with her mouth full.

Judith translated quickly. "Not much. Dr. Bert was very vague about how Fred died or what he did for a living."

"But we know how he died," Renie said after she'd swallowed her food.

It was pointless to chastise Renie for invading the kitchen. Judith surveyed the hall. "Yes." Only a couple of dozen people were left, and most of them seemed to be family members. "Let's go."

"How about some real lunch?" Renie said as they climbed the stairs to the main floor.

"I can't," Judith replied. "I've got to try to sort out this latest development."

"We can do it over menus," Renie suggested. "I can help."

"Let's do it at your house," Judith said. "You have to get your car back for Bill, right?"

Renie looked at her watch. "I've got almost an hour. He won't need it until after two when he finishes his leisurely lunch."

"Okay, then we can stop at Carlo's on the canal," Judith said as they walked out to the sidewalk. "I'll meet you there in five minutes. Unless the bridge is up."

Since it was after one o'clock, the restaurant customers were beginning to leave. The cousins had no trouble getting a window table where they could look out at the various craft that plied the city's only east-west waterway. Because of time constraints, they ordered their food along with their drinks. Judith and Renie requested the same items: screwdrivers, clam chowder, and small Caesar salads with smoked prawns.

"Working for the government can be a euphemism for other things," Judith pointed out.

Renie was buttering a large chunk of warm bread. "Such as serving five to ten in a federal penitentiary?"

"That's one thing," Judith agreed. "Sometimes spies use that expression, especially those employed by the CIA. It can also be a nice way of saying that someone is on the dole, maybe a disability pension or some other form of welfare."

"Did Fred looked disabled to you?" Renie asked as their drinks were served.

"He looked dead," Judith said, raising her glass. "To Fred, whoever he may have been." She took a sip, then shook her head. "No, the Fred I met appeared hale and hearty. But that can be deceptive. Some handicaps are hard to detect. I'm convinced the answer to all this is in the UPS parcel."

"How do you plan to find out what it contained?" Renie inquired.

Judith sighed and gazed at the eight-woman crew rowing a sleek shell under the bridge. "Heaven knows I've already tried. If only we could get inside the house and talk to the elder Blands. We've blown our cover, so that's out. I've run out of ideas."

"How about sending someone else?" Renie suggested. "Like . . ." She paused. "Like Bill?"

Judith made a face. "What does Bill do? Disguise himself as a termite inspector?"

"Squirrel man," Renie responded promptly. "With the problems we've had, he knows all about squirrels. The Blands have them, right? Bill could say that one of the neighbors—like Elsie Bruce across the street—complained."

"It's a wonder she hasn't," Judith murmured. "So what does Bill do when he gets inside? Psychoanalyze the Blands?"

"He's tried psychoanalyzing the squirrels, but it hasn't done much good," Renie replied, tugging at her short chestnut hair. "I don't know. But he'd do something. At least he'd meet the Blands and see more than the entry hall or the kitchen."

"Maybe," Judith allowed. "That place is harder to get into than a bank vault." She paused to smile at the waiter, who was placing steaming bowls of chowder in front of the cousins. "It's worth a shot. Will Bill do it?"

"I can but beg," Renie said. "I have to admit, he's never been very curious about the house, even though I've babbled about it for years."

"Does he know anything about what's been going on?" Judith asked as the salads arrived.

Renie speared a smoked prawn. "Well . . . kind of. I mean, I've told him some of it, but he doesn't always listen."

"A peculiar quality in husbands," Judith murmured. "Joe's the same way. What *does* Bill know?"

"I think the part about finding the body in your trunk registered," Renie said after devouring the huge prawn in one mouthful. "But you've found bodies before, so he didn't react very much. I backtracked then and told him how we'd been scouting the Moonfleet house, which is how you happened to be there when Frank—Fred—was killed. I don't think he heard all of that. But he realizes the situation has caused you concern."

Concentrating on the problem, Judith didn't speak until she'd consumed most of her chowder. "So you'll ask him? When?"

"When I get home," Renie said. "Of course, knowing Bill, he'll have to think it through. You know how he approaches dilemmas—from east, west, north, south, and several compass points in between. Anyway, I'll phone you as soon as I get an answer."

Judith didn't respond. She was watching a tugboat tow a barge out toward the sound. THE LADY JANE was painted on the tug's stern with smaller letters underneath reading *French's Fleet*.

"Doesn't Phil French have his headquarters a mile or so from here on the canal?" she asked Renie.

Renie also looked at the tug. "Yes. Turn right from the restaurant, and go about ten blocks. Which you will do, I assume."

"I shouldn't take the time," Judith said.

Renie smirked. "But you will."

Philip French was in his office, an airy space that overlooked the canal that connected the sound to the large lake that separated the city from the eastside suburbs. Several tugs were tied up along the bank, all named for women. Judith could make out *The Lady Anna* and *The Lady Charlotte*.

Phil tried to look pleased at seeing Judith. "What brings you this way?" he asked, inviting her to sit in a captain's chair on the other side of his teak desk.

Briefly, Judith admired the oil paintings of various French's Fleet tugs as well as the framed maps of regional waters. There were a couple of other handsome ship prints as well, including a Vermeer and a Monet that she recognized from art catalogs. A perfectly scaled model of a vintage tugboat sat on Phil's desk.

"What a wonderful view," Judith remarked, gazing across the canal at the tall poplars that lined the north bank. "I wouldn't mind coming to work in a setting like this."

"I enjoy myself," Phil replied, tapping a finger on the edge of his desk. "Don't tell me you want to lease a tug, Mrs. Flynn."

"No," Judith said with a little laugh. "I was wondering how Anna is getting along after her scare the other night. Is she still leaving for Milan this week?"

"Yes, Wednesday," Phil said, still tapping. "She's feeling fine now. In fact, she thinks it was all a trick of her imagination. You know how everyone is these days—edgy, wary, not trusting anybody who looks . . . strange."

"Yet she's not nervous about traveling to Europe?" Judith asked.

"Not to Italy," Phil replied, abruptly stopping himself from tapping. "That is, she knows Milan fairly well. Rome, too. But she *is* cutting her trip short. She'll be back Sunday instead of next Tuesday."

"Instead of going on to Rome?" Judith asked in an innocent voice.

"Ah . . . no, she'd planned to do a little sightseeing," Phil replied, starting to tap his fingers again. "The Italian hill country or Lake Como or somewhere around there." He cleared his throat, stopped tapping, and turned to look at the pictures on the wall.

"Do give her my bon voyage wishes," Judith said. "I haven't been to Italy for years."

"I will." Phil stood up. "I've got to see a man about a boat. If you'll excuse me—or is there something else you wanted to discuss? A nice little cabin cruiser, perhaps?"

"Ah . . . no, I'm afraid not." Judith was stymied. But she did have one last question for Phil. "Are the tugs named for women in your family?"

"Yes," Phil said, coming around from behind his desk. "Maybe you saw the *Anna* tied up outside. That's for my wife, of course."

"And *Lady Charlotte* would be who?"

"One of my aunts," Phil replied, walking Judith out of his office and down the hall to the reception area. "By the way," he said. "I sold the *Moonfleet*."

It took a moment for his meaning to sink in. "Oh—the yacht," Judith said. "That's wonderful. I'm glad to hear that the downturn in the economy hasn't affected everybody."

Phil shrugged. "There are still people who have money and want to spend it. Anyway, I'm glad to have the yacht off my hands."

"But you're getting another, bigger one, aren't you?" Judith inquired as they reached the company's entrance.

"What?" Phil seemed taken aback. "Oh, yes, when I find exactly what I want. That takes time." He gave Judith one of his urbane smiles. "Thanks for stopping by. I'll send along your good wishes to Anna."

Walking back to her Subaru, Judith had a foreboding that Anna would need them.

An hour after Judith got home, Renie called. "Bill agreed to play Squirrel Man," Renie announced, "if he has a semilegal document to show the Blands."

"Oh, dear," Judith replied, making way for Phyliss, who was wielding a dust mop around the kitchen ceiling. "How do we do that?"

"We already did it. We used Uncle Al," Renie replied. "Good grief, he's got an in with half the city."

It was true. Al Grover had been an outstanding athlete in his day, a well-known sportsman around town, and was a former saloon owner to the Influential, especially labor leaders and city officials. While many of his cronies had passed on to that great arena in the sky, there were still a lot of people who remembered, liked, and admired Al Grover, including at least three county sheriffs.

"I don't know," Judith hemmed and hawed. "It wouldn't be exactly ethical, would it?"

"Oh, put a sock in it," Renie retorted. "Uncle Al has had Bill designated 'Squirrel Man for a Day.' "

"Bill doesn't mind?"

"Bill will do anything to avenge himself on those squirrels," Renie said. "He might even catch one. He's bringing traps."

"He's going today?" Judith asked in surprise.

"Right after his nap. He's taking it early. Right now he's on his way downtown to pick up the license. The trip fits in with his other errands."

"I can't believe you talked him into it," Judith declared. "And so quickly."

"Bill has his routine," Renie said, "but he knows that it's wise to break out of it now and then. Besides, he hates squirrels and he loves nuts. As in the Blands, who must be. Nuts, that is. Reclusive behavior intrigues him. Frankly, it's a type of neurosis he's never dealt with much over the years."

"Are you going with him?" Judith asked in an envious tone.

"Of course not. Like you, I've blown my cover. Besides, this is a job for Squirrel Man. He doesn't need a sidekick."

"I can't wait to hear what he has to say," Judith said. "Why don't you two come for dinner? I'll barbecue some ribs," she added, knowing Bill's fondness for babybacks. "I've got some in the freezer."

"I'll let you know," Renie said, and rang off.

Judith was antsy for the rest of the afternoon. By five-twenty, she still hadn't heard back from Renie. The grill was heating out on the patio; the ribs had been defrosted. Finally, at five-forty, she phoned her cousin.

"Oh!" Renie sounded dismayed. "I'm sorry, I forgot. That is, I got on the phone with Anne and we talked for over half an hour. Then I decided to call Tom and Tony. It's really hard to figure out when to get hold of Tony because Guam is like a day ahead of us."

Judith didn't chastise her cousin. All three of the Jones children and their spouses had moved far away after their marriages. Renie—and even Bill, who otherwise wasn't fond of using the telephone—racked up big long-distance bills every month.

"Are they all okay?" Judith inquired.

"Yes, they're fine, but they're homesick. One of these days . . ." Renie's voice trailed off for a moment. "Yes, we're coming for dinner. Bill's at the Moonfleet house right now. He's been gone almost an hour. I'm really sorry I didn't let you know. I imagine we'll get there around six-thirty. Is that okay?"

"It's fine," Judith said. "I'll feed Mother earlier or she'll have a fit. And the guests should be heading out by then after the social hour. We may actually be able to eat and talk in peace."

Gertrude swore the ribs were underdone and that she'd get trichinosis. Judith assured her mother that pork was supposed to be slightly pink or else it would be like eating cardboard. Which, she added, would be difficult with her mother's dentures.

Gertrude wasn't convinced. "If I croak, I'll sue you," she muttered, using her fork to pick at the meat. "The least you could do is cut it off the bone for me."

Judith did, though she was clumsy.

"What's wrong with you?" the old lady demanded. "You act like Nervous Nelly. You going through the Change? Again?"

"No, Mother," Judith assured her, "I'm really just fine. Except for worrying about Mike and Kristin and the boys."

"Who isn't?" Gertrude retorted. "I've said the rosary so often in the last few days that I've run out of Holy Mysteries. Glorious, Sorrowful, Joyous, Miserable, Hilarious—how many Mysteries are there? I forget. And where's that darned cat?"

"Actually," Judith said, "I believe there is a fourth—real—Mystery of the Rosary. The pope decreed it recently, but I don't remember what it's called. As for Sweetums, I'm afraid I still haven't heard anything about him. He may be exploring new territory. I guess I should put up some signs around here and over by Uncle Al's."

"You'd better do something," Gertrude said in an ominous tone. "Do you want that cat carried off by ravaging wolves?"

Briefly, Judith pitied any wolf that might attempt such a feat. "Cats have instincts," she asserted. "He'll find his way back. I'm sure of it."

But of course Judith feared the worst.

Renie and Bill arrived just after six-thirty. Judith had considered eating outside, but clouds were beginning to gather in the east. She offered cocktails; the Joneses declined. They were both hungry, and Bill, who had suffered from an ulcer, preferred eating between six and seven.

With Renie's help, it took only a couple of minutes to serve the food. Judith could hardly wait to hear Bill's account of his visit to Moonfleet Street.

Bill, however, took his customary deliberate time. "Good ribs," he remarked. "Red cabbage, too. Excellent."

"Tell us," Renie urged. "I practically exploded with curiosity in the car."

Judith looked at her cousin. "You haven't heard what happened?"

Renie shook her head, dislodging a couple of wilted flower petals from her hair. Bill leaned over and plucked a dead leaf from his wife's bangs. "I was waiting in front of the house for him to pick me up," Renie said. "I passed the time working in the garden. When I got in the car, he told me he'd save it until he got here so he wouldn't have to repeat himself."

"You're here now, Bill," Judith said sweetly.

Bill cleared his throat. "I was able to park on the street not far from that dirt alley off Moonfleet. I went to the back door. After a minute or two, the young TV guy responded to my knock. Alan, Adam, Aaron . . . ?"

"Alan's his real name," Judith put in.

"Alan. Say," he said, using up most of the paper napkin to wipe off his greasy fingers, "I could use a warm damp towel." He shot his wife a critical glance. "I don't enjoy feeling as if I'm wallowing around in a pigpen when I eat."

With a sneer for her husband, Renie got up to fetch

the towel. Bill took another bite of ribs and chewed for a few seconds. "I introduced myself—using my real name since it's so common—and showed him my temporary license. He seemed upset, and said he couldn't let me in." Bill forked up a chunk of baked potato.

"So what did you do?" Renie asked.

Bill chewed again, then finally answered the question. "I told Alan that if I didn't check out the complaint, a team of inspectors could be sent to go over every inch of the house. It's not a lie—that's what happens when homeowners refuse admission." He began eating more ribs.

"So what did Alan do?" Judith queried, neglecting her own plate in her anxiety over Bill's visit to the Blands.

Another digestive pause. "He contended that the squirrels were all outside, that several years ago a squirrel remover had trapped a couple of them in the attic and sealed up the whole house. The squirrels had never come back inside." More ribs for Bill.

Renie twitched in her chair before leaning toward her husband. "So?"

"So," Bill replied a moment later after another wipe-down with the towel, "I asked to see where the work had been done. Alan started to stonewall again. That's when the alarm went off."

Judith stared at Bill. "What alarm?"

"They have an alarm system," Bill explained. "The control panel is inside one of the kitchen cupboards. Alan shut it off, but he had to make sure no one was trying to get in the front door or somewhere else in the house."

"He left you alone in the kitchen?" Judith asked.

Bill nodded. He was eating more cabbage.

"What did you do?" Judith urged.

"The rest of the house seemed very dark," Bill replied after another pause. "I went into the next room, the dining room, and saw that all the drapes were pulled and seemed stiff with age. Musty, too. I assumed they hadn't been opened in years. I could make out the table and chairs—good, solid stuff—along with a buffet, a breakfront, and a couple of floral paintings on one wall."

"What was in the breakfront?" Judith asked. "I didn't notice it when I was there."

Bill shook his head. "Dishes, I think. It was hard to tell. I was trying to focus on the house itself, the ambience, the atmosphere. Understand a house, and you understand the people who live there. My initial reaction was that the residents live in fear. But fear of what? Of other people in general? No, that's not necessarily the case." He paused to chew on another rib.

"Towel," Renie murmured, handing the soiled linen to her husband.

Bill shook his head again. "I need a clean one. That's a mess."

With a heavy sigh, Renie returned to Judith's kitchen drawer.

Judith was growing impatient. "They have eye problems," she pointed out. "Or so I heard. Light bothers Jane and Sally."

Bill took the fresh towel from Renie. "I'm not talking about physical ailments. I'm trying to get inside their heads. They're in hiding. They don't want intruders. Are they hiding themselves—or hiding something else?" He stared into space. "That's what I'm trying to work through now. It'll take some time."

"Oh, don't stop now," Renie said with a sneer. "Why don't you dissect your analytical process? We're hanging on every word."

"You have cabbage hanging on your lower lip," Bill noted. "Want to borrow the towel?"

Renie declined and used the back of her hand.

"Isn't there more to the story itself?" Judith urged.

"Let me think," Bill said, then ate some more potato. "Yes," he finally continued, "I heard Alan moving around, so I went back into the kitchen. He didn't sound as if he were coming any closer, but I decided to play it safe and waited. That was when I noticed the mail sitting on the counter."

"What sort of mail?" Judith asked eagerly.

"Three pieces," Bill replied. "A bill, a circular, and"—he paused, presumably for dramatic effect—"a letter from Kopfstein, Austria."

The cousins both gasped. "Who was it to? Was there a name on the return address?" Judith asked.

Bill nodded again. "Very shaky handwriting. The return was from a Franz Steiner. The letter was sent to Frau Franz Steiner. Do you know who that is?"

SIXTEEN

FRAU STEINER HAS to be Sally," Judith declared, "Jane's sister. The so-called Uncle Franz could be her husband. That's her married name, Sally Steiner."

"Then she's not a widow," Renie noted. "But why have she and her husband lived apart for so long?"

Judith turned back to Bill. "We're getting side-tracked. What happened after you looked at the mail?"

Bill wiped his hands on the towel. "Alan returned to the kitchen. He apologized for the interruption, adding that somehow the alarm had been tripped by accident. 'A squirrel, perhaps?' I said. He assured me it wasn't a squirrel, but that they did have an occasional mouse in the basement. 'A squirrel,' I repeated. I know squirrels, dammit. Nobody knows squirrels like I know squirrels."

Bill was getting very red in the face and looking grim. But he collected himself and continued. "Definitely a mouse, Alan insisted, and looked at me as if I were weird. In any event, he went on, the alarm had frightened his grandparents and his great-aunt. They were very upset. This wasn't a good time to check out the house. Perhaps I could come back later? Or better yet, he suddenly added, he'd call the city and make the proper arrangements."

"Eyewash," declared Renie.

Bill shrugged. "Probably. In any event, I had no choice but to leave. But," he added with an intense glint in his blue eyes, "by God, I still say it was a squirrel."

Frowning, Judith picked at her food. Except for the Steiner letter, she was disappointed in Bill's adventure. "Could you see what was beyond the dining room?"

"Just barely," Bill said. "It appeared to be the living room. Leather chairs, a fireplace, more closed drapes. I only got a glimpse." He stopped speaking to finish his last rib, but waved a finger as he chewed. "Wait," he said after he'd swallowed and wiped his chin. "There was one other thing about the dining room. A statue of the Blessed Virgin. It caught what little light there was coming from the kitchen. I didn't think about it until now because you expect to see religious artwork in a Spanish-style house like that."

Judith looked puzzled. "The Blands aren't Catholic as far as I know. Dick and Jane were married in a Protestant church. Lutheran, as I recall, in Langford."

"But Steiner could be a Catholic name," Renie pointed out. "Maybe Franz is Catholic. Sally could be a convert. That might explain why Sally wasn't an attendant at Jane's wedding. In those days, it was frowned upon for Catholics to participate in Protestant ceremonies."

"But it wasn't always enforced," Bill said. "It depended a lot on the parish priest. Some of them winked at those outmoded ideas."

"Maybe Sally was living in Austria at the time," Renie suggested.

"That makes the most sense," Judith agreed. "But when she came back to the States, why didn't she bring Franz with her? Were they estranged by then? If so, why didn't they get a divorce?"

"Because," Bill put in, "Franz is a Catholic? Maybe Sally converted. Hence the Blessed Mother statue."

"But they stayed in contact," Judith murmured. "Morty the Mailman told me that over the years, there'd been letters for someone not named Bland. Sally's lived there forever, according to Elsie Bruce."

"That's a long estrangement," Renie remarked, handing Bill another towel.

Judith stood up, starting to clear the table. Renie joined her cousin in the cleanup process. "I shouldn't have—excuse the expression—ribbed Bill when he started to drone on," Renie said after her husband went out to stretch his legs on the front porch. "He's right. What are the Blands hiding or hiding from?"

"You don't hide when you live in a house for over fifty years," Judith pointed out. "You can be found, even if you're not listed in the phone book. So if it's about hiding, and not just being crazy, then what have they got in the house that they don't want anybody to see? Glenn and Trash must have gotten a search warrant. They must know what's in there."

"They won't tell you," Renie said. "You seem to be completely out of their loop."

"What's for dessert?" Bill asked as he strolled back into the kitchen. "By the way, it's starting to drizzle."

"I made Grandma Grover's cream puffs," Judith replied. "Your favorite."

"Sounds good," Bill said.

To Judith, the cream puffs might sound as well as taste good, but they also brought back memories of the first time she'd encountered murder. Some of her guests had invited a fortune-teller who was subsequently poisoned. The cream puffs had undergone their share of suspicion.

During dessert, the topic changed from murder to marriage, specifically the unions of Mike and the three Jones offspring. The cousins did most of the talking, while Bill consumed every last crumb of his cream puff. He was thinking, of course, and as he pulled away from the table, he made his pronouncement.

"I'd suggest therapy for Mike and Kristin," he said, "but I don't believe in it. What they need is a good kick in the butt."

"Amen," said Judith.

Joe didn't call that night. Judith assumed he was working long hours and was probably worn out. She was tempted to phone his hotel but resisted the urge. With any luck, he'd be home in twenty-four hours. Judith wasn't worried about his return now that she was no longer a murder suspect and had the Subaru back from the police impound.

But the phone rang around eleven-thirty, just as Judith was undressing. It wouldn't be Joe; it was one-thirty in Omaha. Maybe it was Mike. Judith grabbed the receiver with one hand and her bathrobe with the other.

"Arthur," Renie said. "What about Arthur?"

"Arthur?" Judith echoed, sitting down on the bed. "Oh! Anna's first husband. What about him?"

"That's what I'm asking," Renie replied doggedly. "Did I wake you?"

"No, of course not," Judith said. "You know I usually don't go to bed until around this time."

"Neither do I," Renie said, "which makes it very hard for me to understand how you can get up so early in the morning and actually function. But back to Arthur. I know it's off-the-wall, but did you really believe Elsie Bruce when she told us that Arthur drowned in the Blands' fishpond?"

"No, I didn't," Judith answered after a pause to recollect the conversation with the Blands' neighbor. It had been less than a week since the cousins had called on Elsie. It seemed more like a month. "That is, I realized she was confused about some things, or making them up out of sheer spite. Luke, for example, being an inventor, rather than a developer. It also occurred to me that Arthur didn't drown in the fishpond. From the way you described it, the pond had been empty for ages."

"It wouldn't have been deep enough to drown a grown man," Renie pointed out. "I don't think it was more than a foot, if that. Someone would have had to hold Arthur down. Unless, of course, he was drunk and fell in. But you're right—Arthur's been dead for what? Fifteen, twenty years? I'd say that pond's been dried up for a good thirty. I don't remember seeing it more than a couple of times when I was a kid."

Judith grimaced. "You're evil. You're trying to make sure I can't get a good night's rest. Frankly, I hadn't thought much about Arthur. But now that you mention it . . ." She paused, trying to recall something else Mrs. Bruce had said. "His last name was Craig. I remember asking if he'd drowned in a boating accident. Elsie Bruce sneered at that, and said something about 'Where would Arthur get a boat?' I wonder if he got one from Philip French?"

"Ah." Renie laughed quietly. "Phil, in love with Anna, maybe having an affair with her, takes Arthur out on his yacht—and pushes him overboard."

"Assuming Phil had a yacht in those days," Judith said as the rain began to come down hard enough to make splattering noises on the tree near the bedroom window. "He would've just been getting started in the tug business." She turned to look outside at the rain. "Maybe we're going out on a limb."

"We can check the records on Arthur Craig tomorrow," Renie said. "That is, Bill can. He has to go to the courthouse to turn in his temporary license to make everything legal. It was good only for today."

"If we find the date of death," Judith put in, "we can look his obit up in the newspaper archives."

"Unfortunately," Renie pointed out, "the Internet archives don't go back that far. We'll have to go there in person. Unless, of course, I can con Bill into stopping on the way home from the courthouse."

After Judith had hung up, she wondered why they were going to such trouble to find out about the demise of Arthur Craig. He'd been dead for over fifteen years. It'd be much simpler to merely ask Anna or some other family member what had happened to him.

Judith finished getting ready for bed, and went to sleep with dreams about big orange koi swimming in an Olympic-size pool with Mark Spitz.

Tuesday was Allergy Morning for Judith. She was accustomed to allergies. Both cousins suffered from them. But on this particular gloomy day in June, four of her guests had submitted their lists of what they couldn't eat, including eggs, pork, wheat, and milk. Breakfast would have to provide alternatives. Rye toast, artificial eggs, hamburger patties, and fruit would fill the bill and, Judith hoped, the tummies.

"I need a vacation," Judith complained to Phyliss Rackley. "Unfortunately, that's impossible until fall. I can't leave Hillside Manor in the summer."

"Idle hands are the devil's workshop," Phyliss retorted. "Speaking of which, I don't see your wicked cat anywhere."

"I know," Judith said with a sigh. "As soon as I clear up from breakfast, I'm going to make some signs."

"Signs," murmured Phyliss. "There are many signs in the Bible and one of the bad ones is your furry familiar." She flipped a dustrag for emphasis and headed upstairs.

Renie called around eleven. Bill, who was an early-to-bed, early-to-rise type, had just gotten back from the courthouse. He'd found Arthur Andrew Craig's death certificate. He had died June 3, 1985, at the age of thirty-one. Cause of death was listed as accidental drowning.

"But not necessarily in a fishpond?" Judith remarked.

"Not necessarily," Renie replied. "I think we can save a trip to the newspaper if I coax my buddy Melissa to check the archives."

Melissa Bargroom was the newspaper's music critic. Judith had met her a few times, and considered her anything but the stodgy classical critic she had originally envisioned. If Melissa had to stand on her head, twirl like a dervish, and sing Lucia di Lammermoor's Mad Scene, she'd be up to the task.

"I'll let you know what she finds out," Renie said, "wild-goose chase, or not. Come to think of it, there's an opera about a goose girl, but it's kind of obscure."

"I should think so," Judith said, and rang off.

She got six feet from the phone when it rang again.

"Late lunch break," Joe said in a weary voice. "We've got a slight hitch. I won't be home until tomorrow."

"Is the hitch a serious problem?" Judith asked.

"No," he replied, "we're waiting for some expert to show up from New York and his flight was canceled. He won't get in until this evening."

"You've never mentioned what kind of case you're working on," Judith said. "Is it hush-hush?"

"Yes. That's why I never mentioned it." Joe sighed. "I'll be able to tell you when it's finally wrapped up and I get home. No big deal. It's not exactly dangerous. What's going on at your end?"

Judith kept her recital brief, though she did relay the worrisome news about Sweetums.

"You know," Joe said softly, "he's an old cat. He may have just crawled off somewhere and—"

"No!" Judith broke in. "Sweetums isn't *that* old! We got him after I moved back home. Some cats live to be in their twenties, especially the really pampered ones. And you can't say that Sweetums isn't that."

"No," Joe said in a musing tone, "I certainly can't. And he's tough. I'll give the little beast that much."

The phone call galvanized Judith into making up some signs on the computer. She had a half-dozen photos of Sweetums, but two showed him asleep; two more showed only his rear end and plumelike tail. In the pair of remaining pictures, he looked so ornery that she was afraid he might scare off would-be finders. Indeed, she thought as she printed out the signs, if there had been a "Ten Most Wanted" cat gallery at the post office, Sweetums would be Human Enemy Number One.

After making Gertrude's lunch, Judith spent the next half hour posting the signs in the immediate neighborhood and along Heraldsgate Avenue all the way to the turnoffs for the two nearest bridges. She had another dozen left, so she headed to Langford and Uncle Al's.

Her uncle was home, watching a baseball game on TV. Or four baseball games, since Al Grover had two TV sets, both of which had picture-in-picture inset features.

"You've struck out, haven't you?" Al said, not looking away from the games in progress. "I feel terrible about it. I'm not used to having pets."

"It's not your fault," Judith assured him. "Sweetums has never been out of our neighborhood until this. The person to blame is that Mrs. Greenwalt, who insisted on his absence from Hillside Manor. I didn't know what to do."

"He may still show up," Uncle Al said, grimacing as one of the four second basemen made a fielding error. "Did you know I've got an autographed ball from Jackie Robinson?"

"No," Judith said. "How'd you manage that?"

"I asked him for it," Uncle Al replied. "It's worth a bundle now, but I wouldn't part with it at any price. I keep it in a safe with my souvenirs from the war."

"I saw some of those when I was a kid," Judith said. "I think it was right after you got out of the navy."

"Probably," Al replied, pausing as one of the four batters smacked a line drive home run just over the right field wall. "I don't know how much that stuff is worth. Somehow, it seems as if the collectors' items from the Pacific don't gain as much in value as Corky's stash from Europe. I think I'll sell the stuff anyway. I could use the money to buy another TV. You know, one of those big jobs with the flat screen."

Judith laughed, as much in astonishment as amusement. "What on earth would you watch with so many sets?"

"Plenty of good stuff," her uncle replied, picking up a TV schedule. "I've got that special sports package that shows games and other events all over the world. It'd be a moneymaker in the long run. I'd be able to see more, and thus, bet more wisely."

"What does your bookie say about that?" Judith asked.

Uncle Al finally looked at his niece. "Not *bookie*. You

know they're illegal around here. I have a sports *broker.* In fact, he's also my stockbroker. A very versatile guy."

That figured, Judith thought. Uncle Al was also pretty versatile, at least when it came to making a buck.

She ran out of signs about a mile from Uncle Al's house. By that time, the rain had begun to soak through her clothes. But she was only a few blocks from Moonfleet Street. She couldn't resist driving by the Bland property.

The worn stucco and tiles looked even more dilapidated through the rain. Slowing down near the walkway to the front door, she saw Luke Bland leaving the house. Fortunately, there was a parking place behind what looked like a brand-new Toyota SUV. By the time Judith had turned off the engine, Luke had opened the SUV and was reaching into the back.

Judith got out of her car. "Hi," she called to Luke, whose upper torso was still inside the vehicle. "Are you delivering the groceries this week?"

Startled, Luke stopped whatever he was doing and stared at her. Despite the rain and gloomy clouds, he was wearing his sunglasses. "Ah!" he exclaimed, forcing a smile. "Mrs. Flynn. What can I do for you?"

"Nothing, really," Judith said, approaching him. "I just happened to be driving by on the way home from my uncle's place. I saw you coming out of your parents' and thought I'd say hello. How is everybody?"

"Fine, fine," Luke replied in a jovial voice that, to Judith's surprise, struck her as genuine. "Say, you shouldn't be standing out in this rain. It's coming down pretty hard."

Judith declined to take the hint. "I'm a native. I don't mind."

"I'm not," he replied, "and I want to get back under cover. Hold on." He rummaged around inside the SUV, finally pulling out a tool kit and what looked like a wooden sign with matching posts. Setting his burden down on the parking strip, he grinned at Judith. "As long as you're here," he said, picking up the sign and turning it around, "are you interested in buying a house? This one's for sale."

SEVENTEEN

JUDITH COULDN'T HIDE her astonishment. "For sale? What about your parents? And your aunt?"

Luke was still smiling. "We finally convinced them they'd be far better off in a retirement home. The police intrusion last week, and the possibility that a man was killed near the house, made them realize that it was time to move on. Lynette and I—along with Anna and Phil—are making the arrangements. We've found a very nice place for them not too far away."

Judith was still flabbergasted. She studied the sign, which read:

FOR SALE
By appointment only—contact
LUKE BLAND
REAL ESTATE AND PROPERTY INVESTMENT

"I'd love to see the inside of the house," Judith said. "When is it possible to do that?"

"Not until after the first of the month," Luke

replied. "I'll start setting up appointments as soon as I hear from prospective buyers. We have to get the old folks settled, move the belongings they want to keep, and do some cleanup."

"What about an estate sale?" Judith inquired, moving closer to the shelter of a tall cedar tree. "They must have some valuable pieces. Or at least items that would qualify as antiques after fifty years."

Luke shrugged. "My parents couldn't afford expensive furnishings. Oh, I know that with so much restoration of older homes these days, people will pay exorbitant prices for anything that fits their period decor. Anna keeps up with that kind of thing. She says the best way to handle it is to sell the whole lot to an estate auction house."

"That makes sense," Judith said, flinching as a large drop of rain dripped from a cedar branch onto her nose. "What's the asking price?"

"Four ninety-five," Luke replied, no longer smiling. "I'm afraid the house needs quite a bit of work."

"Yes," Judith murmured, moving another step or two to avoid the *drip-drip-drip* of the big cedar. "It'll have to be brought up to code."

Luke bent down to open the tool kit. "I'd better get this sign up before I catch pneumonia. If you're really interested in seeing the house, give me a call along about Friday."

"I will," Judith said as Lynette Bland came out of the house.

"What's taking you so long?" she called to her husband as she came down the walk.

Luke looked up from the post he'd started to pound

into the damp ground. "What? Oh, I was talking to Mrs. Flynn here."

Just before reaching the sidewalk, Lynette spotted Judith. "Oh." She didn't look too happy to see their visitor. "Are you in the market for a house?"

"Not really," Judith said, "but one of my cousins is. They're moving here from Nebraska. This might be just the right kind of property for them," she went on, elaborating on her fib. "Spanish style is unusual in Beatrice, where they live now. Not to mention that they're very handy at repair work."

Lynette's pale face brightened slightly. "Really? If they're still in Nebraska, they can take a virtual tour of the house once Luke has it ready to show on the Internet. Excuse me," she said, noting that Luke had almost finished his task. "I have to go back inside to get my purse. I took the afternoon off from work, so we're heading home."

"I'll get your purse," Luke said, adjusting the sign, which hung from two short chains. "I want to say good-bye to the oldsters." He headed for the house. The rain had almost stopped.

"Would you mind showing me something?" Judith asked Lynette.

"What?"

"My cousins have always wanted a water feature," Judith lied. "They're great gardeners, too, especially with wildflowers and native plants. Did someone say there'd been a fishpond here?"

Lynette frowned. "Yes, years ago."

"Does it still exist?"

"Sort of." Lynette had started walking down the

street toward the far corner. "You can see what's left of it from the side of the house."

Through the fence and next to the collapsed greenhouse covered with blackberry vines was the outline of a concrete pond. Two thirds of it was overgrown with scilla now past its prime, ferns, vetch, and weeds. All but the rim of the formation was covered with moss. Renie was right. It was no more than a foot deep, though it was five feet wide and about eight feet long.

"It could be salvaged," Judith remarked. "I assume the pipes are still underground."

"I wouldn't know," Lynette replied. "It was before my time."

"Just as well to leave it drained," Judith said, and then lied some more. "I once heard of a child who wandered into someone's yard and drowned in a pond that was unattended."

Lynette nodded once. "Like those refrigerators people leave in their yards. Kids can't resist exploring."

"Speaking of drowning," Judith said as they walked back down to the corner, "I understand Anna's first husband, Arthur, drowned. How awful. Was he swimming?"

"Fishing," Lynette said. "Alcohol and trout don't mix."

"Oh, dear," Judith said softly, "that's so sad. Was he alone?"

"No. He was with some shirttail relation visiting from out of town. They'd both been drinking. They were on a lake someplace up near Blue Mountain. The boat tipped over, I guess. The other fellow managed to save himself, but he couldn't rescue Art. It was very hard on Anna. They'd been married seven years."

"No children, though?"

Lynette shook her head. "Anna can't have children. I'm not sure she really wanted them. She's very career-minded, and neither Art nor Phil seemed to care."

"She was lucky to find Phil," Judith noted. "That is, another man who didn't insist on raising a family. Was the problem hereditary?"

Lynette looked blankly at Judith. "How do you mean?"

"Well," Judith said, feeling awkward, "her mother, Jane, apparently didn't think she could have children or they wouldn't have adopted Luke. But after several years, she got pregnant with Anna."

"Yes." Lynette glanced across the street toward Elsie Bruce's house. "But I don't think the medical conditions were similar. Anyway, she'd known Phil for years. I think they met in high school. They didn't date, in fact, they didn't run into each—" Lynette stopped just short of Judith's car. "Why am I telling you this?"

"People tend to do that with me," Judith said with a wry smile, though she knew the thaw between them was partially caused by her relations' alleged interest in buying the house. "I'm told I invite confidences."

Lynette shrugged. "Well, none of this is confidential. But I'm usually not a babbler. Ah," she went on, espying her husband coming across the sidewalk, "Luke's ready to go. Check the Internet in a couple of weeks. You can tell your relatives to watch for it, too."

Judith said she would. But of course the only relative she was going to tell was Renie.

* * *

They can't do that," Renie declared, insisting that Judith stand by the heat vent in the Joneses' living room. "Don't move. You're very dampish and likely to grow mold."

"What do you mean?" Judith asked. "If Mr. and Mrs. Bland have agreed to sell the house, why shouldn't they?"

"Because," Renie stated in a stubborn voice, "it's bad business to put a house up for sale shortly after a crime has been committed there. It's much better to wait six months. There's such a thing as 'disclosure,' you know."

"I thought it was one of those 'don't ask, don't tell' situations," Judith responded, shaking out her cotton slacks.

"That happens sometimes," Renie admitted, "but it's unethical and dishonest."

Judith slowly shook her head. "The problem is that no one except those of us directly involved know that a murder occurred on the Bland property. What little media coverage there was mentioned that the victim was found in the trunk of a car on Heraldsgate Hill. As far as the public is concerned, there's no connection with Moonfleet Street."

"Luckily," Renie noted with some asperity, "there's no public connection with you, either. But I still don't think it's right for Luke Bland to sell the house so soon after the tragedy. The neighbors know *something* happened there, or the cops wouldn't have shown up. You can bet Elsie Bruce would give prospective buyers an earful."

"That's true," Judith allowed. "Elsie's probably already jabbering her head off to Teresa about the 'For Sale' sign." She snapped her fingers. "Teresa! Why haven't I talked to her? She warned us to keep away from the house. Why?"

Renie looked thoughtful. "Superstitious? If I had to look at that house every day, I'd get the willies, too. As it was, I used to see it maybe once every couple of weeks during the school year. I merely became obsessed."

"We should ask her," Judith said. "Where did you last toss your phone?"

Renie tended to be careless with her cordless phone, leaving it outside in flower beds, on top of the garbage can, and inside the clothes dryer. Judith felt it was fortunate that her cousin had a lease agreement allowing her to have the phones replaced after they'd been on the spin cycle too long.

"Ah . . ." Renie glanced around the living and dining rooms. "The kitchen, I think. Yes, it's in the silverware drawer. Hold on, I'll get it."

"The directory, too," Judith shouted after her cousin.

Renie returned with both items and handed them to Judith. "Remember, Elsie's still listed under her late husband's name."

"I know," Judith said, moving from the heat vent to an armchair. Finding Elsie's number, she pressed the buttons. The "3" seemed to stick, but the call went through. "What did you spill on this?" Judith murmured.

"Pepsi," Renie replied, unconcerned.

Teresa answered on the fourth ring. *"Hola,"* she said.

Judith identified herself. "My cousin and I called on Mrs. Bruce last week."

"Oh, sure," Teresa said with a little laugh. "You were grilling her about the Blands."

"Yes," Judith responded, "and when we were leaving, you warned us to stay away from the Blands' house. How come?"

There was a pause at the other end. "Sorry," Teresa said, "I had to move into another room on the off chance Mrs. Bruce could catch a word or two." She cleared her throat. "I was probably being silly. But when I first came to work for Mrs. Bruce a couple of years ago, she told me—while I pretended not to understand, of course—that the house was haunted. She said there'd been strange doings there at night a long time ago, and she insisted she'd seen a ghost walking in the grounds after that." Teresa paused again. "Mrs. Bruce forgets some things, she gets them mixed up, she rambles. In any event, she never mentioned the house being haunted after that. But about three weeks before you stopped by, I had to get up in the middle of the night to go to the bathroom. Hold on."

Teresa apparently turned away from the receiver. *"Sí, señora!"* she called. *"Las esmeraldas, sí, sí. Ahora, pronto, sí."*

"More emeralds," Teresa said into the phone. "Gimme a break. Where was I?"

"Going to the bathroom," Judith said, anxiously waiting for Teresa to finish her tale.

"Right. The moon was out that night, and from the upstairs bathroom window, you can look out on the Bland place. I swear to God, I saw what looked like a ghost."

"You saw a ghost?" Judith said for Renie's benefit.

"You may think I'm nuts," Teresa said, "but I do believe in ghosts. Our neighbors in Medford had one when I was growing up. I never saw it—actually, it was a her—but it was all pretty convincing. Rumpled quilts, lights turned on by themselves, furniture moved—the whole bit."

"What exactly did you see from the bathroom window?" Judith asked.

"A white figure, moving slowly in front of the house and then disappearing around the other side. I'll admit," Teresa went on, "it was hard to see with all the trees and shrubs over there. But I caught several glimpses between the greenery until the figure went out of sight."

"The white figure was moving west or east?" Judith inquired as Renie stood rooted to a spot in front of the sofa.

"Is that important?"

"Just curious," Judith said.

"Umm . . . it would be to the west," Teresa replied. "Toward the back of the house where the garage is located, if you know where I mean."

"Yes," said Judith, "I know where the garage is. Did you see anything else?"

"No. I waited for several minutes," Teresa said. "Finally, the moon went behind a cloud and I couldn't see much of anything. Look, I'm probably being silly. I shouldn't have scared you. But that place is really creepy, ghost or no ghost. I couldn't get back to sleep the rest of the night."

"It's creepy all right," Judith agreed.

"I'll be relieved when they sell it and move out,"

Teresa declared. "On top of everything else, now their blasted alarm system keeps going off. You can hear it everywhere. Fortunately, Mrs. Bruce is immune as long as she doesn't have her hearing aids turned on. Oh—by the way, did you know the house is for sale?"

"I did, actually," Judith said. "I'm afraid I didn't heed your warning."

"Well, as long as you haven't seen any—*sí, señora! Oro, muy bonito!*" Teresa lowered her voice. "Now she's on the gold wagon. Gotta go."

"Ghosts, huh?" Renie said when Judith rang off.

"Ghostlike figure," Judith replied. "I suppose it could be one of the Blands in a nightshirt, getting some fresh air. They certainly don't go outside very often during the day."

"Chasing squirrels, maybe," Renie remarked. "Hey, you're pretty well dried out."

Judith didn't respond immediately. She'd stood up and put the phone down in the armchair. Pacing around the living room, she didn't hear Renie. "Prepare yourself, coz," she said suddenly. "We're going in."

Renie's brown eyes widened. "In where?"

Judith smiled grimly. "Into the Blands' house. Tonight, after dark. Wear camouflage."

Good grief!" Renie cried, collapsing on the sofa. "You're kidding!"

"I am not."

"Camouflage? What kind? Squirrel suits?"

Judith shook her head. "Just something dark."

"What about the alarm system?"

"Teresa says it's going off every so often," Judith

replied. "They'll think it's another false alarm. Squirrels, no doubt. Or," she added on an optimistic note, "they may have had to disconnect it. The alarm-system companies—and the cops—don't like it when those things get tripped by accident. The owners can get penalized."

"You're taking a big risk," Renie pointed out. "I mean, *we're* taking a big risk. Oh, hell," she fretted, "we aren't really going to do this, are we?"

But Renie saw the answer in the obstinate set of Judith's face.

Judith had her own qualms about breaking into the Blands' house. It was illegal, dangerous, and foolhardy. It was also the only way she could ever discover the truth about the mystery on Moonfleet. There were other things that disturbed her, too, or at least raised some important questions. Sitting in front of the computer, she began to type a list:

What are Blands hiding—or hiding from?

Uncle Franz Steiner—annual parcel; Kopfstein, Austria

Arthur Craig—accidental drowning or not?

Car chasing Anna in and from parking garage

Frank Purvis a.k.a. Fred Pettibone

Cops & media downplay FP's murder

There were other, smaller unanswered queries, but these were the ones that plagued her most. For at least five minutes, she stared at the notations on the screen.

Woody Price was still out of town. No help there from the police grapevine. She'd talked to all of the younger Blands, the neighbors, and the Pettibone family. What if—the thought made Judith groan aloud—Frank Purvis had been killed by someone who had no connection to the Blands? He might have been prowling around the house while his stolen milk truck was parked on the other side of the street. Or was he sneaking a peek at the houses lining the other side of the dirt track?

Judith didn't believe that. For one thing, contact had been established between Phil and Frank. To her, he'd always be Frank rather than Fred, since it was in his guise as Frank that she'd carted his corpse around Heraldsgate Hill. It had to be Frank who'd sought out Phil on the golf course. Frank Purvis wasn't a member; he would've had to get someone to sponsor him. There might be a record of the sponsorship at the country club, but their privacy policy wouldn't allow her to find out the member's name.

Interlocking her hands behind her head, Judith sighed. Getting inside the house might help her solve the mystery. It was a desperate measure, but she had to try it. Otherwise, she seemed to have tapped every resource, followed every lead.

But one.

A name jumped out at her from the past: Addison Kirby, city-hall reporter, and widower of the actress Joan Fremont, who had been murdered while staying at Good Cheer Hospital. Addison had regular contact with the police. Judith had found him to be a decent man and they had parted on good terms. She dialed the number for the newspaper's city desk and asked for Addison Kirby.

By luck, he was at his desk. "How could I ever forget you, Judith?" he asked. "You exposed the villain who killed my wife. Among others," he added grimly. "How's your hip?"

"Fairly good," Judith replied. "How's your leg?"

"Almost as good as new," Addison said, referring to the broken bones he'd suffered when the killer ran him down in the hospital parking lot. "Last night, I danced the tango. Joan taught me how years ago, but I never really got into it until I met Amalia."

"Is she a special friend?"

"Yes," Addison replied, his voice softening. "I'll never stop missing Joan, but Amalia has given me a reason to keep going."

"Good for you," Judith declared.

"You know how it is—you lost your first husband, right?"

"Lost" always seemed a peculiar way to describe Dan McMonigle's demise. Dan had been so huge that Judith couldn't have "lost" him unless he'd been fired off into outer space.

"Yes, Dan died young, too," Judith said. "You met Joe, of course. He's wonderful. Which," she went on, "is part of the reason I'm calling. Joe's not only retired from the force, but he's out of town, and so is his former partner, Woody Price. I have no real in with the police, and somehow I got involved with . . ."

Judith hit the high points of her story, not wanting to get off the track with details that would be out of Addison's purview. "So you see," she concluded, "I don't understand why Frank Purvis's murder has been played down in the media. Have you heard anything about it?"

"I did, in fact," Addison answered. "One of the new reporters on the police beat picked it up off the log. I can't believe you were the one with the body in your car."

"I can," Judith murmured. "That is, it was a terrible shock, of course. Do you know why your reporter didn't follow up on the story?"

Addison's laugh was bleak. "If you read the paper, you can see that there's almost a murder a day in this region. As for the city, maybe one a week. Most of them are fueled by alcohol or drugs. Who wants to read about a wife who wallops her husband with a cast-iron skillet while they're both drunk as skunks? Or a couple of guys in a bar shoot-out? It's horrible, it's sordid, and it's—unfortunately—too common to make big headlines. I'd seen the article, but figured a couple of bozos got into it during a midday drinking bout and one of them whacked the other one."

"So you don't find it odd that there wasn't a second story with more details?" Judith asked, disappointed.

"Well—no." Addison sounded apologetic. "For one thing, the police don't release names until they notify next of kin."

"But don't the original articles state cause of death?"

"If it's obvious—like a stabbing or a shooting—they do," Addison replied. "But I gather that in this case, the cops wanted to wait for an autopsy. Anyway, a day or so later, Chico—that's the new guy on the police beat—got assigned to a gang shooting in the south end. It involved two innocent victims, including a pregnant woman—a random act of violence. Chico, you see, is writing a book on the subject. Or trying to. There's only so many hours in a day and so much space in the paper."

Judith recalled seeing a couple of articles about the drive-by shootings, but hadn't paid much attention. Like the drug-related killings and the drunken domestic homicides, the gang murders hadn't piqued her interest. As Addison said, they were too common.

"But," Judith pointed out, "the rest of the media seemed to ignore Frank Purvis, too."

"Same thing," Addison said. "Thirty minutes less commercial breaks, weather, sports, and features—the broadcasters can't cover everything."

Judith was silent for a moment. "I still think it's odd. Would you mind asking Chico if he *tried* to do a follow-up on the original story?"

"I'll ask him right now," Addison replied. "He just walked into the newsroom."

Judith waited impatiently while she heard the murmur of masculine voices at the other end of the line. Finally, Addison again spoke into the receiver.

"Chico says he did try to find out if the guy was officially ID'd, but he was told that the victim was using an alias. That's when he gave up," Addison recounted before lowering his voice. "That's also about the time they had the gang shoot-out."

"Frank Purvis was using an alias," Judith stated. "He was really Alfred Pettibone, a solid citizen and a civil servant."

"No kidding!" Addison sounded intrigued. "How do you know?"

Judith told him about attending Fred Pettibone's funeral. "It was just a hunch until I saw the body," she added.

"You really are something," Addison said in an awed tone. "Maybe you should sell your B&B and take up detective work along with your husband."

"I'd rather not," Judith replied, "but thanks for the compliment."

"You know," Addison said, still speaking softly, "I owe you one. A big one, in fact. Chico won't mind. He's writhing his way through Chapter Three on why bad guys go badder. I think I'll do a little digging of my own."

"Would you?" Judith was excited at the prospect.

"Sure. I'll start now. City hall's budget crisis is beginning to bore me. And the readers, too. I'll let you know what I find out."

Judith expressed her gratitude and hung up. Turning back to her list on the monitor, she had another brainstorm. If Uncle Franz could call for a UPS pickup from Kopfstein, then he might have a telephone. Tiny Alpine village or not, no place on earth was too remote these days. According to the phone book, there was a nine-hour time difference, making it shortly after eleven at night in Austria. No matter. Maybe Uncle Franz kept late hours. She dialed international information, and after a couple of transfers, reached Salzburg and an operator who spoke almost flawless English.

Judith, however, didn't speak any German, flawed or unflawed. The gruff voice that answered after several rings was unintelligible to her.

"Is this Franz Steiner?" she asked, slowly and loudly.

"*Ja, ja,* so vot?"

"I'm Judith . . . Hoffman," she said, using Gertrude's maiden name in the hope of creating an Austro-Germanic bond.

"Are you a Chew?"

"What?"

"A Chew," Franz repeated loudly. "Of the Chewish race."

"No, I'm a Catholic," Judith replied, realizing that Franz meant "Jew." "Why does it matter?"

"Never mind. Vot about Sally? Is she dead?"

"No, she's fine," Judith asserted. "She doesn't see too well. She can't dial the phone. I'm calling for her."

"Vy not Lukas? Or Anna? Vere is Lukas?"

Judith assumed the old man meant Luke. "He's home, with Lynette."

"Oh." Franz sounded relieved, but resumed his gruff tone. "Vy so late? I vas abed."

"I'm sorry, but this is important." Judith swallowed hard before she spoke again. "Your last package was . . . lost."

"Vot?" Franz sounded as if he were going to explode.

"Was it insured?"

"Nein, nein . . . no, no. I never insure. You ring off phone. I call Sally. *Mein Gott,* I haven't heard her—" The call ended abruptly.

Judith frowned at the mute receiver. She wasn't sure she'd taken the right approach. Maybe she shouldn't have mentioned the parcel at all. But at least she'd found out that Franz Steiner was alive and grumpy in Kopfstein, Austria.

But maybe the expensive prime-time international call hadn't been wasted. Judith dialed Renie's number.

"What's up?" Renie asked, panting.

"Are you okay?" Judith inquired.

"Yes, yes, I'm okay, if you call 'okay' trying to replant the primroses the squirrels dug up last night. I'm under an azalea bush, retrieving a purple one that the little wretches tossed there. Fortunately, I brought the phone outside."

"Don't turn the hose on the receiver like you did a month or so ago," Judith cautioned.

"I didn't mean to," Renie replied, catching her breath. "I was aiming for the squirrels."

"Guess what," Judith said. "I just had a chat with Uncle Franz."

"You did?" Renie sounded aghast.

"It was brief, but more interesting than I thought at first." Succinctly, she recounted the conversation.

"Lord, you're a pathological liar," Renie said with a sigh. "You're getting out of hand. What was so interesting other than that you're probably going to hell?"

"Funny coz," Judith murmured. "I'll tell you what I realized after he hung up on me. He referred to Lukas, not Luke. Thus I don't think Luke Bland was adopted. I think he's Franz and Sally Steiner's son."

EIGHTEEN

OKAY," RENIE SAID with only a hint of skepticism, "tell me how you came to the conclusion that Luke is Sally and Franz's kid."

"Never mind that right now," Judith said. "Luke's eye problem has always bothered me."

"Not as much as it bothers him."

"Hush." Judith didn't need interruptions. She was running behind on her daily schedule and still had to prepare the appetizers for the incoming guests. "If it's hereditary, it may have come down from his mother's side. It'd be too much of a coincidence for Dick and Jane Bland to adopt a kid who had a similar eye condition. But Sally has it, too. Thus Sally is Luke's mother. When Luke and I were talking about the rain, he mentioned that he's not a native. I didn't think much of it at the time, assuming the Blands had gotten him from another state, or even from east of the mountains, where the weather is very different. Then Uncle Franz called him 'Lukas' and seemed more interested in him than in Anna. It finally all came together. Sally may have had her baby in Austria, and for reasons I still don't know, sent him to live with the Blands and they adopted him."

"Why couldn't Sally have come at the same time with the kid?" Renie asked as Judith paused for breath.

"Maybe she did," Judith replied. "She's been here for many years. But why stay married to Franz? Why didn't Franz come with her? Why is he still in Austria?"

"He likes it there?" Renie suggested.

"That's possible," Judith allowed. "The other possibility is that he couldn't join Sally and Luke because he wasn't able to get into the country."

"Hmm." Renie was silent for a moment. "Are you thinking 'Nazi'?"

"Nazi sympathizer, maybe," Judith said. "That came to mind when he asked if I was Jewish. Let's face it, some of those old folks in Europe still have anti-Semitic feelings, not to mention Nazi sympathies. Remember, Austria had its own National Socialist party before the war."

"I know that, I've seen *The Sound of Music* six times," Renie said. "So what you're saying is that Uncle Franz may not have *dared* to enter the U.S."

"Right," Judith responded, trying to ignore Phyliss, who had just come up from the basement and was groaning loudly while she massaged her left knee. "Sally, being an American, didn't have that problem. But because she wanted to be with Franz, she may have sent the baby here, using the ruse of adoption by the Blands."

"I hate to admit it," Renie said, "but you're making

sense." She paused. "How about your own son? Any word from Mike?"

"No," Judith replied as Phyliss hopped into the kitchen on one leg. Obviously, another attack of hypochondria had beset the cleaning woman.

"How about Sweetums?" Renie inquired.

"No." Judith couldn't ignore Phyliss, who was now sprawled on the floor. "I'm trying to keep distracted." She glanced at the twitching figure just a few feet away. "It's not as hard as you might think."

As Judith said good-bye to Renie, Phyliss raised her head. "I'm paralyzed," she declared.

"From what?" Judith asked, long accustomed to such complaints.

"Arthritis. Rheumatism. Lumbago." Phyliss groaned some more. "The Lord loves those He punishes."

"That's never made much sense to me," Judith said. "Do you want me to help you get up or would you like to just lie there for a day or two?"

"You could call an ambulance," Phyliss said between moans.

"I could," Judith agreed, "but over the years, we've had our share of emergency vehicles here in the cul-de-sac. What I can do is go out to the car and get the tire jack and lift you up with that."

"What? Are you crazy?" Phyliss shrieked.

"Not at all," Judith replied calmly. "I'm not sure I can manage to raise you without damaging my artificial hip."

"You could be real careful. I'm not heavy, I'm your hired help." Phyliss went limp.

Sighing, Judith pulled a chair away from the kitchen

table and sat down in an effort to spare her hip. "Did you twist your knee?"

"It twists itself," Phyliss replied, facedown again on the faux pine flooring.

Judith bent over just far enough to grasp the ties on Phyliss's apron. "Guess what," she said, unable to budge the cleaning woman without cooperation. "If you lie there like a rag doll, I can't help you. I suggest prayer."

Phyliss didn't react for several moments. Then she began to wail and shout hymns of praise. Or something. Judith couldn't be sure, but it seemed to work. Suddenly Phyliss bolted onto her knees, let out a few more worshipful paeans, and finally struggled to her feet.

"It's a miracle!" she cried, embracing Judith with fervor. "Hallelujah! I'm cured!" Phyliss hesitated. "For now."

"Good," Judith said, patting Phyliss's back before wriggling free. "I assume you mopped the kitchen floor earlier."

" 'Course I did," Phyliss said, a scowl replacing exultation. "Do you think I'd wallow around on a floor with ungodly germs? I'm almost done except for the living and dining rooms and the front parlor. I'd like to go home a little early so I can put together my miraculous witness for our Bible study group tonight."

"Fine, Phyliss," Judith said, opening the fridge and considering the possibilities for the guests' hors d'oeuvres.

After the morning and early afternoon's hustle and bustle, the rest of the day seemed to drag. Judith kept busy, but she was anxious to head for Moonfleet Street. Luckily, the weather had remained overcast, which meant that it should get completely dark around ten o'clock, instead of closer to ten-thirty.

Just before eight, she called Renie again. "I'll pick you up at ten," she told her cousin. "What are you telling Bill?"

"Not much," Renie replied, speaking in a low voice. "And don't come until after ten-fifteen. Bill should be heading for bed by then. If he misses me, I'll leave a note, saying I had to go over to the B&B to help you with some unruly guests."

"Let's make it ten-thirty," Judith said. "I can lock up the house at ten, and we want to make sure the Blands are in bed."

"How do we do that?" Renie asked.

"When all the lights are out," Judith said.

"*The* light, you mean," Renie noted. "I've never seen more than one on at a time in that house."

"Correct." Judith took a deep breath. "Are you nervous?"

"No. I'm drunk."

"Coz!"

"Just kidding," Renie said. "I'm not as much nervous as I am curious after all these years of wondering what went on inside that house. I can barely sit still. While Bill's watching De Niro and Pacino in *Heat* for the forty-third time, I told him I was going to organize my closet. I've been all over the house like a damned grasshopper."

"We'll be okay," Judith asserted. "What's the worst thing that can happen?"

"Getting arrested? Getting killed?"

"Either. Both. See you at ten-thirty."

Fortunately, all the guests except a thirtysomething couple from Little Rock, Arkansas, had returned to Hillside Manor by ten o'clock. The latecomers had their key and their instructions. After making sure Gertrude was all right, Judith put her domestic responsibilities behind her and drove off to collect Renie.

Misgivings began to overcome Judith by the time she reached the top of the hill. As she descended the north slope, the misgivings became qualms. By the time she reached the Joneses' house, doubts loomed large before her.

Renie, clad in black slacks, a black long-sleeved sweater, and a black watch cap covering her hair, slipped out through the front door and locked it behind her. She could have passed for a cat burglar if she hadn't tripped over the edge of the doormat and bounced off the porch railing.

"Don't try that at the Blands'," Judith warned when her cousin got into the Subaru.

"Shut up and drive," Renie snapped.

"I like the watch cap," Judith remarked as they took the turn to the bridge. "I settled for a head scarf to complete my all-black ensemble."

"You always did look good in black," Renie said. "Are you nervous?"

Judith decided to keep her fears to herself. "No. Why?"

"Because you just ran the arterial at the six-way

stop," Renie said. "It's a good thing there's not much traffic this time of night."

Judith grimaced. "Okay, so I'm a little on edge. Aren't you?"

"Anxious is more like it," Renie replied. "You don't think Teresa really saw a ghost, do you?"

"No," Judith answered. "I think it was a real person."

"Bill believes in ghosts," Renie said. "I allow for the possibility."

Judith didn't respond. They were turning off the bridge, heading for Langford.

"Do we have a plan?" Renie asked after another minute of silence.

"Yes," Judith replied in a solemn tone. "I pick the lock on the front door."

"Okay."

Renie didn't question her cousin's expertise. During Judith's marriage to Dan McMonigle, she'd been forced to learn how to pick various locks and even open a safe to find where Dan had hidden his gambling money. Though they might be stony-broke and unable to buy groceries, Dan had considered his betting stash untouchable. Judith hadn't agreed.

"What happens next?" Renie inquired, twitching anxiously in her seat.

"We'll have to wait and see." Judith didn't speak again until they were a block away from Moonfleet Street. "I'm going to chance it and pull into the alley."

"Okay," Renie said in a faint voice.

The Subaru crept across the intersection. On her left, Judith could see the outline of the tile roof and chimney through the big trees and dense foliage. All lay in darkness. No rain, no moon, no breeze, only a charcoal sky above them. She reversed slowly onto the dirt track, stopping the car just out of sight of any late-night passersby.

"I think I'll wait here," Renie said, folding her arms.

Judith looked stern. "Come on, before I lose my nerve, too."

Reluctantly, Renie got out of the car. Judith opened the back door on the driver's side and handed her cousin one of two police-issue flashlights. "These are Joe's," she said in a quiet voice before pointing to the shrubbery next to the alley. "Come on, we're going through here, but we don't dare turn on the flashlights until we're inside."

"Great. I should have worn armor." But Renie followed Judith, who was trying to keep to the same route she'd taken when delivering the Blands' groceries.

The rain had stopped early enough that the ground was now solid and the greenery was dry. But the cousins both stumbled a couple of times and felt the clawing of branches and berry vines on their arms and legs. Reaching the overgrown backyard, they stopped to collect themselves.

Neither spoke, but both gave a start when they heard a rustling noise nearby.

"Squirrel?" Renie breathed.

"Mouse?" Judith whispered back.

Slowly and quietly, they moved around the side of the house and under the arched wing wall. Reaching the front, they passed the jutting single-story section that could have been a den or a parlor. Creeping by the tower, they finally reached the arched mahogany door.

Unzipping the fanny pack she wore under her black sweatshirt, Judith removed a thin, flexible wire and inserted it in the lock.

"Damn!" she cursed under her breath. "It's a dead bolt. That's a bit trickier."

Renie leaned against the tower and kept her mouth shut. Judith let out a big sigh. "I'm going to have to turn on the penlight. Shield me."

Renie moved so that the small dot of light couldn't be seen from the front window on their left. Judith kept working, twisting and turning the wire. Finally, she shook her head.

"You're going to have to hold the penlight," she whispered. "See if you can crouch down in front of me."

Renie managed to squeeze in between her cousin and the door. Judith was beginning to pant with exertion; Renie's knees started to wobble.

Suddenly there was a click as the locks retracted.

"Ah!" Judith exclaimed softly. "Get in and lie flat."

The second the cousins crossed the threshold, the alarm went off. Quickly, but carefully, Judith dropped down onto the cold tiles and rolled to one side of the entry hall. Renie did the same, in the opposite direction. The alarm kept ringing. The cousins scarcely breathed.

The loud, jangling sound continued. Judith closed her eyes, as if that would deaden the cacophony. A minute, two minutes passed. Surely the noise would waken the dead. Unless, Judith thought . . .

But someone was alive in the house. After another

minute had passed, the alarm stopped. Judith figured that whoever had hit the switch must have done it in the kitchen. Listening intently, she heard faint, slow footsteps. She braced herself, but the sound faded. Whichever member of the household had disconnected the alarm was apparently going away. Upstairs, Judith decided. She couldn't hear a door being closed, and there didn't appear to be any space for bedrooms on the main floor.

Clumsily, she sat up. Her eyes had grown accustomed to the dark and she could see Renie moving on the other side of the entry hall.

"Living room," Judith murmured, realizing that her legs had been blocking the open doorway.

The cousins got to their feet. "Thank God whoever that was didn't use the tower stairs," Renie whispered. "There must be a spiral staircase in there because it's two stories high. If they'd come down that way, I'd have gotten stepped on."

Judith didn't respond. The floor seemed to moan under her footsteps. She turned on her regular flashlight and slowly aimed it around the room. Bill had been right: the furniture was covered in leather, a Spanish style appearing so old that Ferdinand and Isabella might have sat on it. There was wrought iron, too, in the chandelier with its candle-shaped bulbs and the heavy fire screen that reminded Judith of gates to a country mansion. The odor of mold and age hung on the air; the flashlight caught clouds of dust particles. The house felt like a museum that had been closed for years. Or maybe, Judith thought with a shiver, more like a mausoleum.

Renie was examining a pair of lamps on a pecan demilune chest. "Look," she said under her breath. "Real peacock feathers around the top, amber beads on the bottom—but the silk shades are rotting away. It's a wonder they don't catch fire."

"I'm beginning to doubt Alan's word when he told me his grandparents furnished this house on the cheap," Judith murmured. "Originally, this stuff must have been costly, even if some of it was left here by the previous owners." She aimed her flashlight onto the stucco walls. "See these urns on the mantel? The blue is beautiful on the plain one and the flowers on the other are so delicate."

Renie used her own flashlight to look at the urns. "The gold scrollwork on both of them looks real. These didn't come out of a factory. The craftsmanship is too good." She moved the beam of light to a pair of pastoral miniatures above the mantel. "These little guys are lovely, too. They almost look real."

The phone rang close by. Judith stifled a cry and Renie jumped. The phone rang again. Pointing her flashlight in the direction of the sound, Judith spotted the old-fashioned black dial phone on a small end table next to the sofa. Gingerly, she picked the receiver up in the middle of the third ring.

"Speak up," said a hoarse female voice on what Judith figured was an upstairs extension. "I can't hear you."

"It's me, *Liebchen*, your Franz."

Judith mouthed the caller's name to Renie, who hissed "Sally?" in response. Judith nodded.

"Why are you calling so late?" Sally demanded. "I was asleep."

"Ven are you not?" Franz retorted in an ironic tone. "Anyvays, it's morning here."

"You never remember the time difference," Sally scolded. "After all these years . . . Oh, what's the use? You never listen."

Renie had moved to stand next to Judith, trying to catch at least part of the conversation.

"You listen to me," Franz ordered in his gruff voice. "Vy didn't you telephone me about the package? Who is this voman who told me yesterday it vas lost?"

"I don't know what you're talking about," Sally declared. "I think you've finally gone crazy, Franz. And by the way, yesterday to you is still today to me."

"Vot?"

Sally emitted a deep sigh. "Never mind."

"I vaited to call until now so it vould be morning," Franz said doggedly. "I didn't vant to vake you."

"Fine, fine. What about the package? It arrived last week, safe and sound. And who is this woman you're jabbering about?"

"I don't know," Franz replied. "She didn't say her name."

"Tell me more about the woman," Sally demanded.

"I don't know more," Franz snapped. "She said she was a friend, and you were not able to speak. It vouldn't be the first time you couldn't talk on the telephone. But the package is there?"

"You're mean," Sally retorted. "Yes, the package arrived safely and on time, thank you," she went on, her tone growing more affable. "Porcelain candlesticks fetch a good price. The silverware needs polishing, but at least the settings are almost complete. I'm not sure about the wall plaque. Are you certain it came from an Italian palazzo?"

"I am alvays certain," Franz huffed. "It vas part of a ceiling. There are more panels, but I save them for later."

"All right." Sally cleared her throat. "But I still don't like this business about some woman calling you. Was she an American?"

"*Ja,*" Franz replied.

"That's very interesting," Sally said in a musing tone. "But perhaps it doesn't matter."

"It mattered to me," Franz asserted. "She knew Lukas. And you and Anna, too. How is Lukas?"

"Very well," Sally assured him. "His eyes, of course, trouble him. You received my letter?"

"Letter? Not yet. Is one coming?"

"Yes. It should be there tomorrow or the next day. We have big news," Sally said in a smug tone. "I won't say more now, but I'll be seeing you very soon."

"*Vot?*" Franz's shout was so loud that both cousins gave a start.

"I'm hanging up now." Sally's voice had begun to slur. "I'm very tired."

Judith heard the dial tone. "Well." She set the receiver down in its cradle. "Do we know now what this is all about?"

"Black-market goods? Smuggling?" Renie suggested.

"There may be more to it than that," Judith murmured. "Let's check that other room across the hall."

The door was locked. Once again, Judith got out her wire tool. Unlike the first time, the lock to the single-story room clicked open after less than a minute.

Judith felt as if she had stepped outside. The air was fresh; the sense of decay had evaporated. And the room itself seemed empty. Judith pointed her flashlight toward the arched front window. There were no rotting drapes. Instead, a taut shade blotted out the light.

She began to scan the stucco walls. There were two paintings directly in front of her. "Golly," Judith said, "these are beautiful prints. They've even installed lights over them."

One was a Rubens nude, the other a Fragonard landscape. Moving closer, Renie reached up to touch the Rubens. Then she ran her fingers over the Fragonard. For what seemed like a long time to Judith, her cousin stared at the paintings. Finally, she turned around.

"Prints?" Renie said softly. "These are the real thing."

"What do you mean, 'real'?" Judith inquired in a low, puzzled voice.

"I'm not an art expert," Renie averred, "but I can tell a print from a painting. If these aren't originals, they're outstanding copies. Put your light up close, feel the texture. The canvas has small cracks. It's paint."

Judith followed Renie's instructions. Sure enough, she could feel the brushstrokes. Shaking her head in disbelief, she turned around to see what Renie was doing.

"Holy cats!" Renie breathed. "A Holbein, a Joos van Cleve, a Titian, a Van Eyck, a couple of small Monets—this is incredible!"

Her voice had risen with excitement. Judith waved

at Renie to tone it down. "Surely," Judith whispered, "these can't all be authentic."

Renie was hopping with excitement. "Then why go to such trouble to have a controlled atmosphere? Why, when the rest of the place is practically falling down, keep these in a special room?" She turned back to gaze at the Titian. "Stolen artwork? Stolen twice, that is? *By* the Nazis and *from* the Nazis?"

"It makes sense," Judith said, speaking in an awed whisper, "especially after what Uncle Corky told me about how the soldiers looted the area around Kopfstein, which happens to be very close to Berchtesgaden, where Hitler and his henchmen had their mountain retreats."

Renie seemed mesmerized. "I can't believe we're looking at genuine art treasures. It's like being in the Louvre or the Prado."

"How long have the Blands been selling this stuff?" Judith murmured.

"And keeping what they couldn't part with?" Renie gestured at the closed drapes. "No wonder they never let in any light. It wasn't just sensitivity of their eyes, but an effort to preserve their treasures."

"And keep them from being seen by other people," Judith pointed out. "That's something I don't understand. Great art should be shared with the world, but some collectors hide their masterpieces. It's so selfish and such a waste."

"But profitable, if you're able to sell some of it," Renie noted, still gawking at the paintings. "Now what do we do? Besides swipe the small Monets, of course."

Judith adjusted her head scarf, which had started to

slip off her hair. "We'll go out the back way so we can check out the dining room."

"We're tempting fate," Renie noted, "but it's worth it."

Going into the hall, Judith carefully closed the door behind her. "Sally sounded as if she were half-asleep when she hung up, so we may be safe for a bit. I'd like to see that statue of the Madonna that Bill noticed."

Renie was already at the door to the dining room. The pecan and wrought iron furnishings matched the living room, though the chairs around the long table had canvaslike leather backs and seats. They looked uncomfortable to Judith, but she had a feeling they hadn't been used in years. There were a half-dozen iron wall sconces, also with candle-shaped bulbs.

There were no more paintings, but the breakfront held some exquisite china and glassware, along with what appeared to be a quartet of Dresden figurines.

Judith gazed at the Madonna, a two-foot-high statue that might have come out of a seventeenth-century church. The stars in her halo sparkled like genuine diamonds; the gold trim on her blue mantle seemed real; the serpent beneath her feet had flashing emerald eyes. The work was very old, very lifelike, and very beautiful. Judith was compelled to say a prayer for safe passage out of the house.

Apparently, the Ave Maria worked. Or maybe, Judith thought as she quietly closed the back door, they just got lucky.

"Whew!" Renie exclaimed under her breath. "I can't believe we did it!"

"Neither can I," Judith admitted.

"We're middle-aged, soon-to-be-dowagers," Renie

said as they moved off the small porch. "We should be at home knitting or some damned thing."

"You can't knit," Judith pointed out.

"Neither can you," Renie retorted. "I'll never forget the dishrag you knitted for me when you were in high school. It was wool. When it got wet, the kitchen smelled like a dead sheep until I threw the blasted thing out. And speaking of kitchens," she added, pointing back to the house, "that furniture in there *is* old and crappy."

"Yes," Judith agreed, walking to her left. "I wonder—"

"Hold it," Renie interrupted. "Why are we going this way?" She gestured over her shoulder. "The car's over there. Aren't we done here?"

"I want to look at that fishpond up close," Judith said, almost tripping over a moss-covered rock.

"I guarantee there aren't any fish," Renie declared. "Let's make this quick. I'm getting nervous. *More* nervous, I should say."

But Judith kept going. A moment later, they'd reached the pond by the collapsed greenhouse. Playing the flashlight around the broken glass, shattered wood, and remnants of plant stands, she saw nothing of interest. Ivy and berry vines crisscrossed what was left of the roof. The small structure seemed to have caved in with age and disuse.

Judith turned the light onto the outline of the pond. "This will be completely overgrown in another year. In fact, the plant and lichen growth look even thicker than they did this afternoon. That's weird."

"The rain," Renie said. "This time of year, you can practically watch stuff grow."

"Not this fast," Judith responded. "I can't bend so well. Would you mind?"

Renie complied, dropping down to the pond's edge. "You're right. There's a whole patch of Irish moss and another of creeping thyme that looks as if it's just been planted. In fact," she continued, reaching down to pat the plants, "they're still wet, even though everything else has dried out from the rain."

Judith leaned over as far as she dared. "The thyme is blooming. It certainly wasn't there when I came by with Lynette."

A skittering sound from the side of the house startled the cousins. They both turned, but saw nothing. The noise stopped. Judith took a deep breath.

"More rodents," she murmured.

"Not rats, I hope," Renie remarked, her attention once more focused on the pond. "This is odd, too. Can you see how the cement at the bottom of the pond doesn't match the sides?"

Judith studied the seam near her feet. "You're right. And," she added on a sad note, "so am I."

"Huh?" Renie stood up, brushing leaves and other debris from her black slacks.

Judith's expression was bleak. "This pond was once much deeper. It had to be, for fish to survive." As a sudden breeze blew through the tall trees, she shuddered. "I hate to say it, but I think this is a grave."

Renie grimaced. "Any idea who's in there?"

"I can guess," Judith replied grimly.

"After all this time," Renie said softly, "the more I know of this house, the creepier it gets. But oh, those paintings!"

"They'd be worth killing for," Judith said, still gazing down into the pond. "There's definitely a sinister aura around here."

Renie, who was facing Judith, looked toward the house with a shocked expression. "There sure is," she said in a barely audible voice. "Don't look now, but I swear to God I see a ghost."

NINETEEN

BOTH COUSINS IMMEDIATELY switched off their flashlights. Despite Renie's caution not to look at the apparition, Judith turned her head. A white-clad figure stood on the end of the second-floor balcony at the front of the house. A halolike aura glowed around the head.

"Holy Mother," Renie breathed, "if that's a real ghost, I'm one up on Bill. Let's get a closer look."

The wraithlike figure might have convinced most skeptics. But Judith, who relied on logic, shook her head. "Wait a minute. Let's see what your so-called ghost does next."

Even as Judith spoke, the figure moved farther down the balcony and out of sight.

"I don't believe in ghosts," Judith declared. "I wonder if whoever that was noticed us."

"It better be a ghost," Renie said stubbornly. "Then I can tell Bill. He'll be jealous."

"You're about to find out," Judith whispered. "Here comes your spectral buddy now."

The apparition was coming through the back

door. Clad all in white, with the luminous shimmer around the long white hair, the figure seemed to drift rather than walk toward the cousins.

Renie made a whooping sound. "Watch! I bet I can put my hand right through this ghost! Boo!" she shouted.

But Renie's waving fingers met with all-too-real resistance. Not only did she make contact, but a gun suddenly appeared from the folds of the diaphanous white fabric.

"Who are you?" the figure demanded in the hoarse, slightly slurred voice Judith recognized from the overheard telephone call with Franz.

Judith gulped before she spoke. "Mrs. Steiner? It's me, Judith Flynn."

"Flynn?" Sally Steiner stopped about ten feet from the cousins. "I know that name." While she kept looking at Judith and Renie, her expression became confused. "Flynn," she repeated to herself before speaking louder and moving a few steps closer. "You're trespassers. I can shoot you. Why are you here?"

"To see you," Judith replied, trying to focus not on the gun, but on Sally. She wasn't wearing a bathrobe as Judith had first assumed, but a long-sleeved chiffon evening gown. Or, judging from the seed pearls that decorated the bodice, a wedding dress—a very old wedding dress, dating from a half century earlier. The shimmer in her hair was a small tiara attached to a long veil. Both dress and veil were slightly tattered and yellowed with age.

"I can't visit with you right now," Sally said in the slurred voice that had become dreamy. "I'm going to meet my groom."

"How nice," Judith said. "Where is he?"

"Far away," Sally said. "But I can get there in time. The church is very pretty, with an onion-shaped dome. You have to leave now."

Judith noticed that although Sally looked glassy-eyed, the hand that held the gun didn't waver.

"Are Dick and Jane going with you?" Judith inquired in a voice that wasn't quite steady.

Sally slowly shook her head. "They're already gone."

"You mean they're dead," Judith said quietly, surprised at the calm in her voice. She waved an arm behind her. "They're buried in that fishpond, aren't they? Is Arthur there, too?"

"Arthur!" Sally's voice was tinged with contempt. "Arthur couldn't hold his liquor like I can. He fell out of a boat. A happy accident, I figured. Arthur had ethics. Anna has no sense when it comes to men."

"But you must have been shrewd at choosing a husband," Judith noted. "Why haven't you lived with Franz all these years?"

"Franz loves his homeland more than he loves me," Sally said in a sad voice. " I didn't like the village where he lived. I felt isolated." She frowned. "Like here. But it's different. I can do as I please. Now."

Judith glanced at Renie, who was looking more annoyed than frightened. Sally was coming closer. Judith wondered how well she could see. Was her sight better in the dark than in daylight? The woman's skin was relatively unlined. She wasn't that old—late sixties, early seventies. She looked wiry and perhaps strong.

"Luke is your son, isn't he?" Judith asked. "Yours and Franz's."

"He's *my* son," Sally replied, her voice growing a trifle stronger. "I was only eighteen and naive, seeing the world right out of high school. I wanted to find a prince and a fairy-tale castle. It wasn't long after the war. There was plenty of royalty in those days. I thought that princes and dukes and counts must be everywhere. But alas, I met a cruel wolf—like Little Red Riding Hood instead of Cinderella—and I was violated and conceived a babe. Then I met Franz. His first wife had died young and left him childless. He wasn't royal, and he didn't own a castle, but he offered to marry me. Franz grew fond of Luke. But I couldn't let my boy be raised in a remote Austrian village. It wasn't like a fairy tale. For several years, after Dick and Jane had adopted him, I stayed with Franz out of loyalty and gratitude." She waved the gun, which Judith recognized as a Luger. "Now you must leave or I'll have to shoot you."

"This house," Renie said, speaking to Sally for the first time. "I grew up around here. I was fascinated by the place."

The sound of a car caught all three women's attention. It had stopped close by, perhaps at the opposite end of the alley from where Judith had parked.

Lunging across the five feet that separated the cousins from Sally, Renie dove at their adversary. Caught off guard, the other woman crumpled to the ground with Renie on top of her. But Sally managed to hold on to the gun.

"Wicked witch!" Sally shrieked as Judith hurried to help her cousin.

Going for the hand that grasped the Luger, Judith

tried to loosen Sally's grip. But her adversary was tenacious. Sally managed to wrench free, aiming the gun at Judith.

"Hold it!" a male voice called out. "Police!"

The cousins both froze. Sally went limp, though the gun was still in her hand. Judith turned in the direction of the approaching footsteps. Glenn Morris was striding purposefully across the grounds. There was no sign of his partner, Trash.

"I'll take the weapon," Glenn said, lowering his voice to its normal, cool level.

The Luger slipped out of Sally's grasp, but she didn't try to get up, even after the cousins were on their feet.

"Thank God you came by," Judith breathed. "She was going to shoot us."

Glenn nodded curtly. He quickly walked over to Sally and retrieved the Luger. "Can you stand? I can help you."

"I'll sit," she replied, allowing Glenn to give her a boost.

Judith let out a sigh of relief; Renie gave herself a good shake.

Sally was sitting up, her arms clasping her knees. She took several deep breaths before speaking again to Glenn. "You're late," she said in a sulky tone.

"Sorry," Glenn apologized. "The patrol car was responding to your alarm. The shift change is at eleven, so they were coming from the local precinct station. I sent them away." He turned to the cousins. "You look like burglars to me. I assume you got inside the house?"

Judith couldn't think of a fib that would cover their illegal activities. Despite her relief, she felt helpless—and confused. Which, she realized, was better than being dead. Still, something wasn't right. A shiver of fear crept up her spine.

"It's my fault," Renie declared to Glenn. "You know about my obsession with this house. I couldn't resist the opportunity of having a look inside before the place was sold."

"You could have looked when it went on the market," Glenn pointed out, still holding the Luger.

"No," Renie replied. "That would have been too late. I wanted to see it while the Blands still lived here."

Judith found her voice. "I don't think they do," she asserted. "Live, that is. Check out the fishpond. If you remove the concrete, you'll find Dick and Sally Bland's remains."

Glenn smirked. "You *are* inventive, Mrs. Flynn. But you can't talk your way out of this one. You two broke into the house, setting off the alarm system summoning the police. You may have stolen some of the family's prize possessions. The patrol officers didn't get here in time because of the shift change, not to mention the recent false alarms. Mrs. Steiner chased you out of the house, but you turned on her. She'll have the bruises to show for it. Thus she has every right to shoot you."

"Oh, do hush, Glenn," Sally broke in. "Now we must kill them. I'm taking a chill."

The realization struck Judith like a flash of summer lightning. "You're wrong!" she gasped at Glenn, who was now aiming the Luger straight at her. "I should have known!"

"You do now," Glenn said in his cool, calm voice.

"How did you get on the force?" Judith asked, still reeling from the shock. "How did you get assigned to this case?"

"Simple. I quit the LAPD and got on up here. As for this investigation, I happened to be in the area." He laughed low in his throat. "Cause and effect, you might say. Come, come, Mrs. Flynn, surely you don't think all of the local cops are lily-white? You're married to an ex-cop. You've heard stories."

"Yes." Judith was barely able to mouth the word.

Renie was wearing her most perverse expression. "You killed the man known as Frank Purvis," she said to Glenn. "You stonewalled the whole case. That's why we could never find out anything. But we discovered that Purvis was really Fred Pettibone. Why did you kill him?"

"Purvis was an alias," Glenn replied. "Frank Pettibone was an undercover agent, assigned to international smuggling operations. He was about to nail Sally. I couldn't let that happen. But more agents would come—we had to vacate the house. You see, I've bought a yacht, and tomorrow I'm sailing away with some very nice paintings. Asia, I think. The market in Japan and Hong Kong is good, despite the economy. There are always buyers for a true masterpiece."

"You bought the yacht from Phil," Judith said, recovering her voice along with some of her composure.

Glenn sneered. " 'Bought'? Phil French had no choice but to give me the *Moonfleet*. Like the rest of the family, he doesn't want to be charged with conspiracy to defraud or as accessories to murder."

"They're all in on it?" Renie asked in amazement.

"Of course not," Sally snapped, her vaporous mood hardening. "They're too stupid to handle such arrangements. They had to keep their mouths shut, though, or else they'd—" She clamped her lips shut.

"End up in the fishpond," Renie finished for her.

Sally shrugged. "They hadn't had fish in there for fifty years. Dick and Jane have only been there for two. They don't have to sleep with the fishes. Fish smell bad."

"What about Trash?" Judith asked, stalling for time. Maybe the regular patrol car would come by. Maybe Teresa was in the bathroom across the street. Maybe pigs would fly.

"Trash?" Glenn snickered. "That clod? He doesn't know anything. Last Wednesday, he was hungry, so I dropped him off at Doc's Drive-in before I caught up with the milk truck. The only one who might have worried me was Alan—word leaked out that there was a sting operation to uncover a smuggling ring in the area. Someone was being sent to confiscate a delivery."

"Fred Pettibone," Judith murmured, "disguised as a milkman."

Glenn ignored the comment. "Alan was given the assignment, but he was afraid it would lead him to his family. The poor twit's been putting the station off for days while he struggles with his conscience. By the time he makes up his mind, I'll be gone and so will the artworks."

Sally was on her feet and taking a couple of steps toward Glenn. "If you're not going to shoot these two, I will. It'd be better that way. I'm the one who should fire the gun. They'll test it, won't they?"

"Yes, they will." Without taking his eyes off the cousins, Glenn moved through the tall grass toward Sally's outstretched hand. He was about to hand over the Luger when he suddenly stumbled, let out a yelp, and fell to the ground. The gun flew from his hand, settling only two feet away from Judith.

Glenn was writhing around in the overgrowth, batting at his legs. Something small but fierce clung to his calf. Judith snatched up the gun and backed away. "Quick!" she called to Renie. "Get my cell phone in the car! Call 911!"

Renie ran toward the alley. Judith kept the gun on Glenn's thrashing form, but also watched Sally, who seemed paralyzed. A hissing noise and several growls emanated from the vicinity of Glenn's shredded pants. At last, the vicious creature desisted and leaped onto Glenn's face, where it sat in triumphant splendor.

"Sweetums!" Judith cried.

Yellow eyes glowing in the dark, Sweetums merely looked smug.

Sally toppled over in a dead faint.

Glenn used his scratched and bleeding hands to try to dislodge the cat. But Sweetums seemed intent on smothering his prey. Indeed, the animal was preening a bit, licking his paws and scratching behind one ear.

Renie had rejoined Judith. "They're on their way." A wicked glint shone in her eyes. "I told them, 'Officer down.' "

Judith couldn't help but smile. "Get his gun. It's probably in a shoulder holster."

Renie walked over to the still-struggling Glenn Morris. "Hi, Sweetums," she said. "Nice work." For good measure, she put a foot on Glenn's midsection. "Stop wiggling and stay put or I'll jump up and down on you until you look like a busted balloon."

"By the way," Judith called to Glenn Morris, "I *will* fire this gun if I have to. And I won't hit my cousin."

A strangled cry emerged from Glenn's throat as he finally heaved Sweetums off of his head. The cat landed on his feet, arched his back, hissed, and went right for Glenn's throat. Renie, meanwhile, had managed to dislodge Glenn's 9mm Glock from its holster.

"Check his legs," Judith said. "He may have another one."

"He doesn't," Renie replied. "Frankly, he doesn't have much left in the way of legs—or pants, for that matter. They're all chewed up from Sweetums's fangs."

The sweet sound of sirens was drawing closer. Glenn, whose face was bleeding, tried to subdue Sweetums. But the cat was persistent, his big plume of a tail swinging like a pendulum as he raked the man's throat with his sharp claws. Sally still lay on the ground, motionless. Judith began to wonder if the woman was alive.

Renie looked down at the pistol in her hand. "Should we disarm ourselves? Don't you think the patrol officers might get the wrong idea?"

"Let them," Judith said grimly. "We need to see them in the flesh before we make ourselves vulnerable." Then, as she heard car doors slamming nearby, she raised her voice as loud as she could: "Backyard! By the back door!"

The officers—a man and a woman—approached cautiously from around the side of the house, their weapons drawn.

Judith set the Luger down behind her. "*Now* drop the gun," she said to Renie under her breath.

Sweetums seemed to understand the cease-fire. With one last swipe at Glenn, he jumped off of his victim and padded over to stand by Judith.

The officers held flashlights along with their weapons. The light blinded Judith. She couldn't see anything but an outline of the two figures. "The perps are on the ground," she shouted. "Don't be fooled, you may know one of them as Detective Glenn Morris."

"Who are *you*?" the male officer demanded. "Identify yourselves, please. Don't move. Put your hands over your heads."

The cousins obeyed, although Renie winced a bit. She'd never quite regained full motion after her shoulder surgery.

"Wait!" The word seemed torn out of Glenn's wounded throat. "These women are burglars! Look at them!" He started to get to his knees, crawling painfully toward Sally.

The male officer swung his light onto Glenn. "I can see that," the officer said. "Did they attack you?"

Not only was the patrolman's voice familiar, but now that Judith could see more clearly, she recognized Darnell Hicks and Mercedes Berger. Their former beat had been Heraldsgate Hill.

"It's me!" she screamed as Glenn neared the unconscious woman. "Darnell, Mercedes—it's Judith Flynn!"

Darnell kept his high beam on Glenn, but Mercedes focused on the cousins. "Mrs. Flynn! Mrs. Jones! What's happening?"

"Come on, people," Glenn urged, trying to sound nonchalant, but hampered by the cut on his lower lip. "Don't let these two fool you . . ."

"We know them," Mercedes shot back.

"You know me, too, don't you?" Glenn said. "I work homicide, I've been on the force for almost a year."

"We've known Mrs. Flynn and her husband much longer," Mercedes declared. "Stay where you are," she ordered Glenn. "I'm calling for backup."

"What's with the woman on the ground?" Darnell asked, catching Sally's inert form in the circle of his flashlight.

Sweetums had wandered over to Sally. He sniffed several times, then wrinkled his nose and went back to Judith.

"She passed out," Judith said. "Maybe you should send for an ambulance, too."

"She's drunk," Renie declared. "When I was wrestling with her, I smelled alcohol."

"We have an ambulance and other emergency personnel on the way," Mercedes said.

"We could use a regiment," Renie asserted. "I don't trust this so-called cop an inch."

But Glenn Morris no longer looked intimidating. His bleeding legs, face, and neck were taking their toll. So were the guns that were aimed at him. But most of all, he seemed defeated. Renie hadn't had to jump on him to make the man deflate.

Glenn's bleary gaze turned to Sally. "For God's sake, at least let me see if she's alive."

"I'll check," Judith said, moving cautiously in the direction of Sally's prone form. "Yes, she has a pulse, though it's quite slow." Her glance at Glenn was curious. "Why are you suddenly so concerned about anybody but yourself?"

"Because," Glenn said in a faint voice, "she's my mother."

TWENTY

After a half century of inertia, the house on Moonfleet Street was suddenly transformed into a frenzy of activity by police, firefighters, medics, and other emergency personnel. No official arrests had been made, but both suspects had been taken to the hospital, with squad cars providing escort. Sally had come to just before the medics arrived, and had babbled like a spring torrent. Judith had been able to catch some of her words, but wasn't sure how to sort fact from fairy tale.

The homicide detectives requested that the cousins come into the house and answer questions. Judith and Renie were exhausted, but glad to comply. To their great relief, they knew the team: Edwina Jefferson and Danny Wong had investigated a murder in the gated community of Sunset Cliffs where the cousins had been asked to watch over a wealthy old woman whose life had been threatened.

Edwina, a plump black woman of fifty, beamed at Judith and shook her head. "I can't believe we're meeting up again, girlfriend. Though I've heard about some of your escapades since Junior here and I transferred to the city force after they incorporated the area around Sunset Hills."

Judith sighed. "If only I'd known you two were at headquarters, I would've called to find out what was really going on with this case. Did you have any idea?"

Edwina shook her head. "Junior and I had our own problems with a nasty triple murder in the south end of town." She patted Danny on the arm. He was close to thirty now, a slim, good-looking man of Chinese descent, but to Edwina, he'd always be "Junior." "I didn't know Morris very well," Edwina continued, "but I didn't much like him. Standoffish, cold—and of course, a fairly recent hire. The only good thing was that he took Trash on. Or so I thought at the time. Nobody else wanted to work with Trash after his longtime partner retired. Now I understand why Morris chose him. Trash was too dumb or too indifferent to figure out that Morris was a wrong'un."

Judith frowned. She knew that Glenn Morris would give the police department a black eye. "Wasn't it considered suspicious when the body of Frank—I mean, Fred Pettibone—was secretly released and the story was hushed up?"

"Oh, no," Edwina replied. "That part was legit. The feds stepped in to cover the death of one of their own. Glenn wouldn't have been allowed to talk about it."

"The Pettibones were notified right away," Danny put in. "As far as the government is concerned, Fred died a hero. But any official acknowledgment of his death in the line of duty can't go public."

"It's a shame, really," Edwina said with a shake of

her head. "Fred Pettibone doesn't get recognized for what he did, and the police are going to have to suffer some ugly headlines." She leaned back on the worn leather sofa. "Okay, hit the high spots on your part in all this. We'll take a formal, detailed statement at headquarters tomorrow or the next day."

It was nearing midnight when Judith finished. "Remember," she concluded, petting Sweetums, who was asleep on her lap, "some of my conclusions are speculation, especially the part about Glenn trying to scare Anna in the parking garage. I'm guessing that it was an attempt to make sure her husband gave the *Moonfleet* away. You'll want to ask Phil about that part."

Danny, who had been characteristically silent during Judith's recital, finally asked a question. "I don't quite get it. Just after we arrived—before Mrs. Steiner was put in the ambulance—she mentioned that her other son, Luke, was the one who actually sold the artworks. Did the rest of the family share in the profits, too?"

"Early on, when the children were young, I imagine Sally had someone else as the middleman," Judith replied. "I suspect Sally was sending art objects to them while she was still in Austria and the Blands were given living expenses. Dick Bland apparently didn't ever hold down a job—a neighbor told us he'd come back from the war a shattered man. That would explain why the house seemed so moribund. Jane may have been stuck inside, taking care of Dick and ensuring that he lived in a quiet atmosphere. Luke became involved in investments, which might have included money laundering for Sally's art sales. I figure she couldn't have left Anna out of the loop. Maybe Sally set Phil up in the tugboat business. But in later years, Dick and Jane may have gotten greedy—or scared. Perhaps they were ill and in misery. I'd like to think that, because then it would be more like a mercy killing. Luke and Anna didn't dare go to the police if Sally was their source of big income. And, of course, Sally was Luke's mother."

"Not to mention Glenn's," Renie put in. "That shocked me."

"I heard Sally rambling on about that while they were getting her ready to put in the ambulance," Judith said. "She hadn't been raped—she'd been promiscuous. In fact, she bragged about her escapades after she moved in with the Blands. She'd sneak out at night and meet some man for a romp. In Austria, she'd borne two children out of wedlock before she married Franz. Glenn was the elder, and she let an American couple from California adopt him. Apparently, it took years for him to track down his birth mother, but when he did, he came up here to meet her. She couldn't resist seeing him, which meant he realized right away that something odd was going on and wanted in on it. That's why he transferred from L.A."

"How," Edwina inquired, "did you figure out that no one but Sally lived here?"

"It was the groceries," Judith said. "One box, once a week. There wasn't enough to feed three people. And while wine was included, I'll bet somebody in the family made frequent trips to the liquor store. Maybe somewhere, down deep, Sally felt guilty. Or maybe she was just a souse. She'd once left a delivery from Franz on the porch for a couple of days. What else could account for that but a drunken binge?"

"She was a silly souse," Edwina said in disapproval. "What good did the money do her? Did she enjoy the art?"

"I think she was a miser," Judith said, "but she must have loved the paintings or she would've sold more of them. Only about eight were in the parlor. There were other art treasures, too. I assume Franz sent one annual delivery because of the risk factor—not only possible discovery, but damage. Still Sally must have made millions. But as her sight deteriorated, she couldn't enjoy the remaining paintings, which is why I think she agreed to let Glenn sell them abroad."

"While she settled in with Franz and the goats," Renie put in. "Maybe she thought she'd be safe from the cops in a remote place like Kopfstein. Or she was fantasizing. Alcohol does strange things to people's brains."

"It'd be nice to think those paintings may be returned to their rightful owners," Edwina said. "Assuming they're still alive and could be tracked down. Thank goodness that's not a job for us."

Danny was looking somewhat embarrassed. "Let me get this straight—the paintings and the other art stuff was stolen from thieves after World War Two?"

Edwina offered her partner an amused, if slightly patronizing, look. "Ah, yes, Junior, I keep forgetting you don't even remember the Vietnam War, let alone Korea or the two world wars. You children are woefully ignorant when it comes to history. By the way, did you ever hear of slavery and the Civil War? Does the name Abe Lincoln ring any gongs?"

Danny made a face. "At least I don't think he's a rock band."

"Admittedly," Edwina said, her pleasant face growing serious, "I was born after the war. But my daddy served in it—even though the military wasn't desegregated until after the war was over."

"Gosh!" Danny exclaimed in amazement.

"Anyway," Edwina went on, "a bunch of those Nazi leaders stole all kinds of things including artworks from museums and galleries and individuals. They didn't just kill the poor Jews, they robbed them of everything they owned. Some were rich, and had fabulous possessions." She turned to Judith. "Weren't a lot of those art treasures in Berchtesgaden, where Hitler and his cronies had their vacation hideaways?"

Judith nodded. "Berchtesgaden was in Germany but right on the Austrian border, near Kopfstein. According to my Uncle Corky, who served in that area, some of the allied soldiers ran amok after the war. Not only were they chasing Nazi holdouts and sympathizers, they were enjoying a victor's spoils. Of course there were the pro-Nazi Germans and Austrians who were never arrested and managed to end up with plenty of loot. I assume Sally's husband, Franz, was one of that ilk. His peers may have had some loot, too. Franz may have bartered with them or even outlived them."

Danny was looking thoughtful. "You know, they don't make history very interesting in school."

"That," Renie asserted, "is because texts and teachers don't realize that history is really old gossip. They don't give it any personality. History is about people, as far as I'm concerned, which is far more interesting than politics and ideas."

"I never thought of that," Danny admitted.

"You're not alone," Renie remarked before turning to Edwina. "What will happen to the rest of the family?"

Edwina shrugged. "I leave that stuff up to the prosecutors. Luke and Anna and the others may plea-bargain their way out of it. For all we know, Sally threatened them, told them they'd end up buried in the backyard, too. We'll start excavating tomorrow. Say," she said, pointing to the sleeping Sweetums, "is that your cat?"

Judith grinned. "Yes. I'm not sure how he ended up here, but I figure he was trying to get home from my uncle's and came this way. The poor little guy was probably hungry. He found a feast of mice and maybe even rats, and settled right in. This house may be a den of iniquity, but it's also a feline paradise. I assume that Sweetums was the one who kept tripping the alarm while he was prowling around in and out of the house. There must be at least one or two places where raccoons or squirrels have chewed their way inside."

Edwina stood up, straightening the navy blue linen skirt that wrapped around her ample hips. "It's Junior's bedtime. We've got personnel watching the house. And you two must be worn out." She enfolded Judith and Renie in a big hug. "We'll be in touch. You take care, you hear?"

Judith gave Edwina a baleful look. "We usually try."

"But not tonight," Edwina said. "And by the way, try to avoid the breaking-and-entering act. Next time, we might actually have to arrest you."

Judith smiled fondly at the other woman. "There *is* one more thing."

Edwina looked curious. "Oh? What's that?"

"I want my shoes back."

Judith didn't hear the alarm go off the next morning. When she finally woke up, it was almost ten o'clock. With a shriek, she sat up and took several deep breaths. Her guests must be furious. Gertrude would be wild. In a whirl of activity, she showered, dressed, and scurried downstairs.

But as she was halfway down the second flight that led into the kitchen, she smelled coffee, bacon, and other breakfast aromas. Going along the narrow hallway, she saw Joe hanging up the phone.

"Hi, sleepyhead," he said in greeting. "Feeling rested?"

"Joe!" She flew into his arms, covering his face with kisses. "When did you get home?"

"Just before six," he replied, squeezing her waist. "I took the red-eye."

Judith glanced at the phone on the counter. "Was that for me?"

"Nothing that can't wait," Joe said, ruffling her salt-and-pepper hair.

Slipping out of his grasp, Judith peeked into the dining room. Only two guests remained, enjoying coffee and chatting amiably.

"You got everyone fed? Even Mother?"

Joe nodded. "Not to mention Sweetums. I understand he's been missing."

"Um . . . yes, he has." Judith watched as her husband poured her a mug of coffee. She didn't know where to start. Joe would have to know. The arrest of two murderers and the discovery of a smuggling operation might not have made the morning paper, but he was bound to find out. Judith sat down at the kitchen table with her coffee while Joe finished loading the dishwasher.

As the remaining guests left the dining room and went upstairs, Joe sat down across the table from his wife. Gold flecks danced in his green eyes—magic eyes, Judith called them. "Did you get the trunk lid fixed on the Subaru?"

"Ah . . . not yet," Judith replied, avoiding those magic eyes. "I've been really busy. We had some problems with a guest who ended up in the hospital. Sweetums took a dislike to him. There was something of a fracas."

Joe nodded once. "So that's why he looks so scruffy. Your mother seems pleased to have him home."

"Yes," Judith said, still not meeting her husband's gaze. "I had to take him to the vet, and the wife of the man who was . . . um . . . scratched didn't want him at the B&B while she was still here. After I picked Sweetums up from the vet, I took him to Uncle Al's. But after Mike and the boys went home, Sweetums ran off. Luckily, I found him."

"Very lucky." The gold flecks gleamed again. "Maybe it's a good thing that despite being old, the beast is so tough and ornery."

"Sweetums is fairly typical of his species."

"I wasn't talking about Sweetums."

"Oh." Judith scowled at Joe. "Don't be mean about Mother."

Joe's expression was ingenuous. "I only meant that

she and Sweetums have some sort of bond. It's natural between pets and their humans, I'm told."

Judith heard footsteps on the front stairs. "Departing guests," she said as the phone rang. "Can you get that? I have to play innkeeper."

"Four of them already left," Joe called after her as he picked up the receiver.

Judith put on her gracious face to send off the couple from Sydney, Australia. They were fairly young, enthusiastic, and ready to head for Canada on their North American tour. "G'day!" they called in unison as they left Hillside Manor.

"G'day," she called back. "And come again!" In Judith's opinion, Australians always made good guests.

Unlike the Greenwalts, Judith thought as she closed the door. She was certain she hadn't heard the end of that sorry episode. In fact, it was back to grim reality—worrying about repercussions from the Greenwalts, agonizing over Mike and Kristin, anxiety building over Joe's reaction when he learned what had really happened in his absence.

Judith was frowning as she cleared off the last items from the dining room table and returned to the kitchen, where Joe was hanging up the phone.

"A reservation request for the Labor Day weekend," he explained. "I told them you'd check to see if there was a vacancy and call back."

"There isn't," Judith said, "but I can put them on standby. Oh!" she exclaimed. "What about that other call?"

"Later," Joe said enigmatically. "You need some downtime."

Judith said nothing, but felt a seed of suspicion being sowed in her brain. She was distracted when Phyliss appeared, carrying a load of laundry from upstairs.

"Say, Mr. Flynn," she called from the bottom of the stairs, "how about a hand? I'm having one of my bad days. My back's gone out."

"Sure, Mrs. R, my pleasure." He met Phyliss halfway down the narrow hall. "How's the Lord these days? You seen Him lately?"

"Not for a couple of weeks," Phyliss replied. "He was in the produce section at the grocery store, picking out avocados."

"No kidding," Joe responded. "I would have thought He'd be at the hardware store, being a carpenter and all . . ."

Their voices trailed off as they headed down the back stairs. The last of the guests came down the front stairs. A taxi was just pulling into the cul-de-sac. Judith performed her duties, waving them good-bye from the front porch.

Maybe, she thought, Joe wouldn't come back upstairs right away. There might be time to call Renie and tell her about the morning's events. She was reaching for the phone when it rang.

"Hi, Mom," Mike said, sounding cheerful. "I meant to call you yesterday, but I was real busy catching up on work. How are you?"

"Fine," Judith answered tersely. "More importantly, how are *you*?"

"Good," he replied. "The clouds are lifting up here. It's going to be a beautiful day. What's it like in town?"

Judith hadn't really noticed. She glanced out the

kitchen window. "The sun's out. But I don't want a weather report, I want—"

"Hang on," Mike interrupted, and apparently turned away from the receiver. "Hey, Kris, see if you can find Joe-Joe's farm animals. He can't find them and he's about to shred one of Mac's books."

"Kris?" Judith echoed. "As in *Kristin*?"

"What?" Mike was speaking into the receiver again. "Oh—right. That's what I was going to call you about. We made up. She just needed a break. And to make some kind of change in her life."

"Which is what?" Judith asked, flabbergasted.

"She's getting her hair highlighted," Mike replied as a child's angry screams could be heard in the background. "You know, one of those foil jobs. Hey, got to run. Joe-Joe's having a tantrum. I think maybe Mac hid the farm animals. By the way, if you want to send Mac some more books, that'd be great. He's reading up a storm these days. Talk to you soon."

Feeling limp, Judith held the dead phone in her hand for almost a full minute. Joe reappeared just as she was setting the receiver on the counter.

"You look pale," Joe said, frowning. "What's wrong?"

"Nothing," Judith said in a hollow voice. "I mean—something's right for a change."

Joe put a hand on Judith's shoulder. "Like what?"

"Mike and Kristin made up."

"Well, hooray!" Joe embraced Judith and kissed her soundly on the lips. But she still looked shaken. "So what's the problem?"

Judith shook her head. "Young people these days

seem to do the right things for all the wrong reasons. Or do the wrong things for . . ." A faint smile brightened her face. "I don't know. It's just that they're . . . different. Maybe they like drama. Maybe they're too self-centered. Maybe they're . . . just not us."

Releasing Judith, Joe took her hand. "Come on, let's have another cup of coffee. Frankly, you look beat. Didn't that sleep-in help?"

"It should have," Judith allowed as they sat down. "Maybe I . . . oh, never mind. What about your trip?"

Joe shrugged. "No big deal, just a lot of sitting around and waiting for other people to make up their minds. Insurance companies take their time."

"Was it fraud?" Judith asked, beginning to gather her composure.

"No," Joe replied. "It was more complicated than that. The company's branch office hired me to check out a local bigwig who'd bought a painting a while back. He wanted it insured but was suspicious about where it came from. It was a real Van Dyck that had been missing for years. He didn't want to go to the cops for fear of getting in trouble and inviting some bad publicity, so he asked the insurance outfit to look into it. I was hired to make sure the bigwig was on the up-and-up, which he was. Anyway, it turned out the painting had been stolen by the Nazis and somehow ended up in this country. A New York art expert was brought in, but the original owners haven't been traced. No insurance until a search is completed."

Judith had made an enormous effort to retain an interested, rather than stunned, expression. It was the perfect opening for her confession. But somehow she couldn't bring herself to unload on Joe. Not yet, anyway.

"Fascinating," she said in a voice that wasn't quite her own, and promptly changed the subject. "By the way, Mike wants us to get more books for Mac. He's very advanced in his reading, you know."

"That's your field," Joe said. "You know what books to send him."

"I've been out of the library business for a long time," Judith noted. "Except for Harry Potter, I don't know what's new. Of course, there are the classics. I should make a list."

Joe didn't respond right away. He sipped his coffee and rubbed his chin. "I remember one book I really liked when I was a kid. Mac might not be ready for it yet. But jot it down."

Judith had gotten up to get a pen and a notepad. "Which one?" she inquired, sitting down again.

"It was about a little boy in England who gets involved with smugglers. I'm sure it's still around. The name of the book is *Moonfleet*." Joe's smile was ironic.

Judith looked her husband right in the magic eyes. "Yes, I remember that. In fact, I could never forget."

"I didn't think you could," said Joe.

The magic eyes danced on.

For more of Mary Daheim's Bed-and-Breakfast mystery series, perfectly capturing her signature tone of screwball comedy and off-kilter menace, join the cousins on a high-seas adventure . . .

Judith and Renie's dreams of R&R on a deluxe cruise ship are dry-docked when murder occurs at a pre-launch party. But the stabbing death of the cruise line owner is only the first in a trio of homicides. They're in good—and bad—company, however. Fellow travelers Rick and Rhoda St. George may be pleasantly plastered, but their eyes aren't blurred to motive, method and mayhem. Along with the ships' Art Deco decor, the St. Georges' breezy 1930s presence (accompanied by their wheezing dog, Asthma) makes Judith and Renie feel as if they're living in a time warp.

Of course the cousins will be lucky to be living at all by the time they sort through the suspects . . .

DEAD MAN DOCKING

Available Summer 2005
in hardcover
from William Morrow

Art Deco ruled the ship's design, from furniture to paneling to floors. Teak and mahogany flowed in clean curves and sleek symmetry. Glass was everywhere—tabletops, doors, wall inserts, and around the saloon where the party was being held.

"Remember," Renie said as they hesitated in the doorway, "we should get into a thirties mood. Snappy patter, wisecracks, screwball antics."

"For us, that sounds contemporary," Judith murmured as an elegant woman in a Grecian gown of flowing white pleats and three-inch gold sandals approached the cousins. Consuela Cruz definitely evoked the gilded edge of the Depression era. She was as lean as her husband, with jet-black hair combed away from a heart-shaped face.

"We're so glad you're here," she said to Renie. "There must have been a misunderstanding regarding your consulting fees. Mags would never dream of cutting you loose so abruptly." Consuela pointed at a young man at the bar. "You know Paul Tanaka, of course?"

Renie nodded. "He often sat in for Mags at our design meetings." She nudged Judith's arm. "My cousin hasn't met him, though."

"We'll attend to that at once," Consuela said. "He's standing by the bar with Mrs. Giddon and Mr. Brooks. And do call me Connie."

Connie Cruz made a graceful gesture with her right hand. "I'll take you both around the room. Almost everyone is here, I think, except the St. Georges and Émile. Of course, Émile is the ship's purser, and may have business to take care of."

The tall, stout woman with the steel-gray hair swept up on top of her head was indeed imposing, Judith thought. It wasn't just her Amazonian size, but her piercing blue eyes and tight, red lips.

"Serena Jones, Judith Flynn," Connie said, "meet Mrs. George Elwood Giddon."

Mrs. Giddon studied the cousins through a jewel-studded lorgnette. She was wearing a long, straight gown of black lace over white taffeta. A parure of diamonds and emeralds adorned her ears, neck, and wrists. The grande dame's imposing presence practically overwhelmed Judith. "A pleasure, I'm sure," Mrs. Giddon proclaimed in a lofty voice. "Who are you?"

"Who—or what?" Renie shot back with a deceptive smile. "The way you're looking through that lorgnette makes me feel like a microbe."

"I said *who*—not *what*," Erma Giddon snapped. "Are you anybody I should know?"

Renie gave a languid shrug. "My forebears came over on the *Mayflower*—first class. They were fleeing their bridge debts. Judith's ancestors were the first white settlers in our city, arriving circa 1850. Before that, they founded Philadelphia."

Mrs. Giddon didn't seem amused. Connie swiftly intervened. "For many years, Serena has been doing the graphic-design work for Mags. Mrs. Flynn is her cousin. Unfortunately, Mr. Jones couldn't get away from his work."

If Mrs. Giddon gave a damn, she didn't say so. Instead, she turned her back on the cousins and asked a server to fetch her evening wrap.

"It's chilly in here," Erma declared. "The captain must adjust the temperature before we sail. You know I'm inclined to chest colds, Consuela."

"Those cold germs must be really tough to get around her chest," Renie said, lowering her voice a mere notch.

"Coz," Judith said in a warning tone.

But Erma had moved her chest and the rest of her away, commanding the youthful blond bartender to mix her a Manhattan.

"Make that Bud in a bottle for me," Renie called out from behind Mrs. Giddon. "Or mead, if you've got it. My family *really* goes way back."

Judith winced. She had a feeling that Renie was going to be difficult, at least as far as Mrs. Giddon was concerned.

"Please don't mind Erma," Connie begged from behind her hand. "She adheres to a very strict social code. Her own family dates back to one of the original San Francisco railroad magnates."

"Which one?" Renie shot back. "The guy who threw the fusies from the back of the crummy?"

Connie looked pained. "No, a Stanford or a Crocker or a Hopkins or a Huntington. You know—the Big Four."

"I thought they met at Yalta, not Nob Hill," Renie muttered. "Or was that just the Big Three?"

Connie's smile was feeble. "Here's Paul Tanaka. I must find Dixie Beales. She's providing a brief entertainment later on."

Paul greeted Renie with a hug. He was a squarely built young man, part Japanese and part African-American. The handshake he offered Judith was firm and the big smile seemed genuine.

"You're Bill's stand-in, I hear," he said. Like the other men, except for the captain, he was wearing a tuxedo with thirties styling. And like several of the other guests, he was smoking. "What happened to him?"

Renie explained, stopping when the other young man who'd been at the bar came forward with a bottle of Budweiser. "I'm Jim Brooks," he said by way of introduction. "I'm attending medical school at Stanford."

"Congratulations," Judith said, releasing Jim's clammy hand. "I gather it's difficult to get accepted there."

Jim flushed slightly. "Yes . . . but sometimes knowing the right people helps." He gave Judith a sheepish look and nodded at a lithe blonde who was talking to Captain Swafford. "I'm engaged to Anemone Giddon. Isn't she beautiful?"

Even from a distance, Judith could see that Mrs. Giddon's daughter was a winsome, lovely creature. In a lavender floral gown made of organza, she looked like a breath of spring.

"Is her father still living?" Judith inquired.

Jim shook his head. "He passed away from a heart attack almost ten years ago."

"Then," Judith asked, "who's the older bald man that just joined Mrs. Giddon?"

Jim Brooks snickered, a reaction befitting his boyish manner. "The great Horace Pankhurst," he replied. "Like Mrs. Giddon, he owns shares in the cruise line. He's also Erma's financial and legal adviser. Excuse me, I must see how Anemone's doing. The bartender asked me to deliver the beer to you, Mrs. Jones."

"Thanks," Renie said without enthusiasm.

Another member of the party had entered, surveying the gathering over a tall vase filled with calla lilies. He was small and spare, with a goatee and a slight limp.

"Émile Grenier," Paul informed the cousins as he followed their gaze to the newcomer. "He's the purser, and he's French. Ergo, he's the biggest snob of all."

"Quite a mixed background for these people," Judith remarked as Renie drifted toward the buffet, with its ice sculpture of a pheasant with a gold ring around its neck and a spray of frozen tail feathers. "Was Mr. Cruz born in Mexico?"

Paul nodded. "But his parents moved—or should I say swam—to the United States when he was a baby."

"A self-made man," Judith observed. "I have the greatest admiration for that type of person. Bloodlines don't impress me."

Paul smirked. "It also helps to marry the granddaughter of a wealthy ranchero from Argentina."

Judith's gaze shifted to the direction that Connie Cruz

had taken upon leaving the little group. But their hostess was nowhere in sight. At that moment, the double doors opened to frame a striking couple with a large white dog. The trio stood very still for just a moment or two, giving the impression that they were striking a pose.

Judith gaped. "The St. Georges?"

Paul nodded. He, too, was looking at the handsome pair. Indeed, everyone was staring with the exception of Erma Giddon, who was fidgeting with an earring. Richard St. George wore a double-breasted midnight-blue tuxedo with silk piping and a gardenia in the left lapel. Slowly, deliberately, he removed his homburg hat, which matched his suit. His manner was casual, his mustache impeccable, and his expression was one of perpetual amusement.

By contrast, Rhoda St. George seemed indifferent to the stares. She was the epitome of thirties chic in a theater suit featuring a black velvet jacket lavishly embroidered with gold thread and the occasional small ruby, topaz, and seed pearl. The long skirt was dark green, gathered around the hips. But it was the hat that drew all eyes: black satin fitted to the head like a skullcap with two long, wide matching streamers, black veiling from hairline to neckline, and a golden rose nestled on top. Rhoda looked wonderfully self-confident. Judith couldn't blame her—any woman who could carry off such an ensemble deserved a medal that matched the gold and jewels on her jacket.

Yet in the end, it was the dog that evoked Renie's comment. "Sugliesmutievasa," she declared, returning from the buffet with her mouth full of shrimp.

Judith had grown accustomed to translating Renie's

food-marred speech. "He's certainly an unusual dog, though not necessarily ugly. I don't think I've seen that breed before."

"It's not a breed," Renie asserted after swallowing the shrimp, "it's a conglomeration. It's got dreadlocks and no feet. It's a dog on wheels."

"The feet must be under all that curling fur," Judith said as the dog glided across the floor.

The St. Georges proceeded into the saloon, where they were effusively greeted by Émile Grenier, Paul Tanaka, Horace Pankhurst, and a platinum-haired beauty in a silver satin evening gown that clung to her curvaceous body like melted cheese on hot toast.

Renie leaned closer to Judith. "Where'd *she* come from?"

Judith shrugged. "The powder room, maybe. She's certainly a Jean Harlow look-alike. I'm beginning to feel like somebody's dowdy maid in Mother's old wedding dress."

"You look fine," Renie assured her. "Come on, get something to eat. You need to put on some pounds."

The cousins made their way to the buffet. Judith paused to admire the pheasant ice sculpture, which was holding up remarkably well.

"The caviar's great," Renie said, swiftly refilling her plate. "So are the wontons with crab and the oysters and the gravlax and—"

"I get the picture," Judith broke in. "It's a good thing you're wearing black. Your spillage doesn't show up very much."

"Huh?" Renie stared down at her bosom. "Oh. Right—it blends."

Connie Cruz had returned, looking a trifle worried. "Everyone, please enjoy the food and make sure you visit the bar in the next few minutes. Our cruise director, Dixie Beales, is going to play some of the great old songs from the thirties in the next room at seven o'clock."

"I never did get a cocktail," Judith noted, carefully choosing a selection of vegetables cut into exotic shapes. "Where's your beer?"

"In that potted palm by the model of the ship," Renie replied. "You know I hate beer. I just wanted to be annoying. Oh, for heaven's sake!" she cried, looking at her cousin's plate. "You're grazing, not eating. Here, have some smoked sockeye salmon *en croûte* and crab dumplings and anything else that might be considered real food. Get the servers to slice off a piece of rare Kobe beef from Japan. I intend to fatten you up."

"Well . . ." Watching a bearded young man wield a gleaming carving knife through a juicy roast tempted Judith. Somehow, she resisted. The cousins had, after all, eaten a late lunch. "Okay, I'll try a couple of dumplings," she said, allowing a waiter with a shaved head and a graying goatee to serve her. "Then we'd better get our drinks before the piano recital starts."

"I'm drinking Pepsi," Renie declared. "I can't bear the thought of alcohol after this morning."

"I don't blame you," Judith said dryly. "Uh-oh," she whispered, "here come the St. Georges with Fido."

Richard St. George nodded at the cousins; Rhoda had lifted her veil and was smoking a cigarette through a silver holder. He ordered two double martinis; so did she. The big white dog with the long curls of fur stopped by the cousins and wheezed at Renie's hem.

"Nice doggie," Renie murmured, trying to disguise her antipathy for canines.

But the large animal moved closer, shedding white fur on Renie's black gown. "Beat it," Renie muttered, holding her hors d'oeuvres plate out of reach.

Wheezing and panting, the dog sat down on Renie's feet. "Excuse me," she said to Rhoda St. George, "would you please make your dog move? I'm immobilized by his very large—yet unusual—body."

Rhoda had just accepted two martini glasses. "Oh, don't mind Asthma," she said with a little laugh. "He's absolutely harmless. In fact, he has respiratory problems. I think he likes you. Or else he's collapsed." His mistress didn't seem particularly distressed by the idea.

Richard St. George, who also had both hands full of martinis, nudged Rhoda with his elbow. "Who's the blond dame with Pankhurst?"

"His latest trollop, darling," his wife replied. "Carole or Cecile or maybe both. I believe she's called CeeCee. Judging from her bust, DeeDee would be more . . . fitting." Rhoda turned back to the cousins. "I'm sorry, we haven't met. I'm Rhoda St. George and this is my slightly inebriated husband, Rick."

Rick had almost finished his first martini. "Swell," he said sarcastically. "You're giving me a poor send-off."

"Don't worry, darling," Rhoda replied. "These ladies have eyes."

"And feet," Renie put in. "I'm Serena Jones and I'd like to move mine. Feet, that is."

"Oh." Rhoda looked down at Asthma, who appeared to have fallen asleep, though it was hard to tell with all the long curls covering not only his body but his face. "Do move him, Ricky," she implored. "Otherwise, Ms. Jones is going to charge him rent."

Setting his now-empty glass on the bar, Rick searched through the fur around the dog's neck, presumably for a collar. "He's a Komondor," Rick said, "a guardian breed, and sometimes considered a working dog. Except I'm afraid he doesn't work very well anymore, poor fellow. Come on, Asthma, strut what's left of your stuff."

"He's . . . big," Renie said. "He must weigh over a hundred pounds."

Rick St. George finally managed to get the dog to move off of Renie's feet. "Yes," he agreed. "Asthma weighs in at a hundred and twenty, or, according to my darling wife, ten pounds more than she does. Good boy!" he said, patting the animal.

Feeling left out, Judith introduced herself. "I'm Serena's cousin."

Both St. Georges expressed their delight, and sounded almost sincere. They were immediately pounced upon by Captain Swafford.

Finally able to put in her drink request, Judith ordered a scotch rocks from Ray the bartender, whose smile was that of a young man eager to please. "Will Glenfiddich do?"

"Definitely," Judith responded.

But there was no Pepsi for Renie, Ray informed her in an apologetic tone. Would a Coke be acceptable? It would, Renie said, between mouthfuls of marinated chicken.

A gong sounded and a sliding door opened at the far end of the room. A golden-haired middle-aged woman wearing a black and red gown that evoked the Orient, held out both arms.

Renie spoke softly in Judith's ear. "May Belle Beales, cruise director—better known as Dixie," Renie said to Judith. "I recognize her from the brochure photos."

"Good evenin', honored guests," Dixie said in a soft Southern drawl. "It's mah pleasure to welcome y'all to an interlude of piano music from that long-ago era of the 1930s. Durin' the cruise itself, we'll have a big band—a verra big band—to play for your listenin' and dancin' enjoyment. Tonight is just a li'l ol' sample, courtesy of mah meager talents. Please join me in the other half of the saloon." With a gracious gesture, Dixie signaled for everyone to join her.

The cousins fell in behind Jim Brooks and Anemone Giddon. The ethereal-looking young woman glanced over her shoulder. "Hi," she said in a breathy voice. "I'm Anemone. Jim says you're the Cousins."

Renie grimaced. "You make us sound like a rock band."

Anemone giggled. "It's how I remember people. I can't ever recall anybody's name, so I give them a description." She pointed up ahead to the St. Georges. "They're the Dipsos, the captain is the Captain, Émile Whoozits is the Purser, my mother's lawyer is—"

"We get it," Renie broke in. "The Cousins get it."

The other half of the saloon was lighted only by mica-shaded wall sconces. Comfortable armchairs had been placed at small round tables. As her eyes adjusted to the demilight, Judith could make out a black grand piano on a cabaret-type stage.

"Sorry about this," Renie whispered in apology. "I didn't know there'd be entertainment that we'll have to pretend to enjoy even if we'd rather be hung from the yardarm."

"That's okay," Judith said, scanning the short program that had been left at each table. "She's going to play just six pieces. Piano arrangements inspired by Duke Ellington, Tommy Dorsey, Glenn Miller, Benny Goodman, and Artie Shaw."

Dixie Beales had arranged herself on the bench. She gazed at the sheet music, flexed her fingers, and scowled. Getting up, she moved to the edge of the stage and spoke to Émile Grenier. He stood up and limped to the rear of the piano.

"A moment only," Dixie announced. "The piano lid hasn't been fully raised."

Anemone and Jim were sitting at the table next to Judith and Renie. "The Fun Lady," Anemone remarked from behind her hand. "I bet she's wearing a wig."

Judith smiled politely. Renie remained immobile.

Dixie had moved to assist Émile. Their efforts were obscured from the audience by the piano itself.

"The lid must be stuck," Jim Brooks said. "Maybe I should help. Émile doesn't look like the strongest guy in the world."

"The purser's small but wiry," Anemone asserted, looking pleased with herself for making the observation. "Though he has a bad leg."

"I'd like to hear some Cole Porter," said Horace Pankhurst at the table adjoining the engaged couple. The big man used a cocktail napkin to pat at perspiration on his thick neck.

"Cold what?" his blond companion asked. "You mean Coldplay? They're a great band. They're Brits, you know."

Horace looked as if he didn't know. "Oh? Well, whatever the music, it's taking long enough to get that piano open. Somebody ought to take a crowbar to it."

"You wouldn't want to use a crowbar on an expensive piano," Renie noted. "My good friend Melissa Bargroom, who just happens to be our newspaper's music critic, says that an instrument like that costs—"

A loud, piercing shriek from Dixie Beales cut through Renie's words. Both cousins stared at the stage. Dixie had disappeared, apparently having fallen to the floor. Émile suddenly went out of sight, too, presumably coming to the cruise director's aid.

Captain Swafford was on his feet. So was Rick St. George. A sense of apprehension engulfed the saloon.

"Stay put, everybody," Rick said in a loud if somewhat slurred voice. "I'll see what's going on."

The other guests seemed to defer to Rick, who bounded onstage, martini glass still in hand. Rick also disappeared behind the piano, but almost immediately resurfaced along with Émile Grenier.

"Is there a doctor in the house?" Rick asked, his speech no longer slurred.

Rhoda St. George burst into derisive laughter. "Oh, Ricky, can't you find a better line than that old cliché?"

But her husband looked serious and ignored the remark, casting his eyes around the room.

Jim stiffened in his chair before looking every which way. "Ah . . ." he began, awkwardly shifting his lanky frame into a standing position. "Um . . . I'm a medical student at Stanford."

"Then you'd better get up here, kiddo," Rick said. "Dixie Beales has passed out." He paused while Jim came forward. "Unfortunately, there's nothing you can do for the corpse in the piano."

Get to know

SHARON SHORT's

sensational Laundromat owner and stain-busting sleuth

JOSIE TOADFERN

DEATH IN THE CARDS

0-06-053798-1/$6.99 US/$9.99 Can

Josie knows her tiny town's dirty clothes and its dirty little secrets. But an upcoming "Psychic Fair" has brought all manner of mystics and soothsayers to Paradise, Ohio, and their arrival has raised the ire of a local evangelist and his minion. It doesn't take a crystal ball to predict that murder will ultimately foul the fair but Josie couldn't foresee that she'd be the one to stumble upon the body.

Death by Deep Dish Pie

0-06-053797-3/$6.50 US/$8.99 Can

Josie eagerly awaits the town's annual Founders Day celebration and its Breitenstrater Pie Company pie-eating contest, sponsored by the town's upper crust enterprise. But when a pie-making bigwig suspiciously drops dead after sampling the company's latest wares, Josie leaps into action.

DEATH OF A DOMESTIC DIVA

0-06-053795-7/$6.50 US/$8.99 Can

When world famous domestic doyenne Tyra Grimes shows up in Paradise to tape a segment for her TV show, Josie is shocked. But rapidly spreading rumors of the insufferable icon's immoral— and quite possibly illegal—carryings-on have sparked Josie's curiosity.

Available wherever books are sold
or please call 1-800-331-3761 to order.

AuthorTracker

SRT 0305